MANGA BIBLE

Names, Games, and the Long Road Trip

D0833154

ZONDERVAN®

Names, Games, and the Long Road Trip
Copyright © 2007 by Lamp Post, Inc.

Library of Congress Cataloging-in-Publication Data
Burner, Brett A., 1969-
Names, games, and the long road trip / adapted by Brett Burner ; original story and art by Young
Shin Lee and Jung Sun Hwang.
     p. cm. -- (The manga Bible ; bk. 1)
    ISBN-13: 978-0-310-71287-9 (softcover)
    ISBN-10: 0-310-71287-4 (softcover)
    1. Bible stories, English--O.T. Genesis. 2. Bible stories, English--O.T. Exodus. I. Lee, Young
Shin. II. Hwang, Jung Sun. III. Title.
    BS551.3.B86 2007
    222'.1109505--dc22

                                                  2007011135

Requests for information should be addressed to: Grand Rapids, Michigan 49530

This book published in conjunction with Lamp Post, Inc.; 8367 Lemon Avenue, La Mesa, CA 91941

Series Editor: Bud Rogers
Editor: Brett Burner
Managing Editor: Bruce Nuffer
Managing Art Director: Sarah Molegraaf

Printed in United States
07 08 09 10 • 7 6 5 4 3 2 1

Names, Games, and the Long Road Trip

Genesis–Exodus

Series Editor: Bud Rogers
Story by Young Shin Lee
Art by Jung Sun Hwang

ZONDERVAN.com/
AUTHORTRACKER
follow your favorite authors

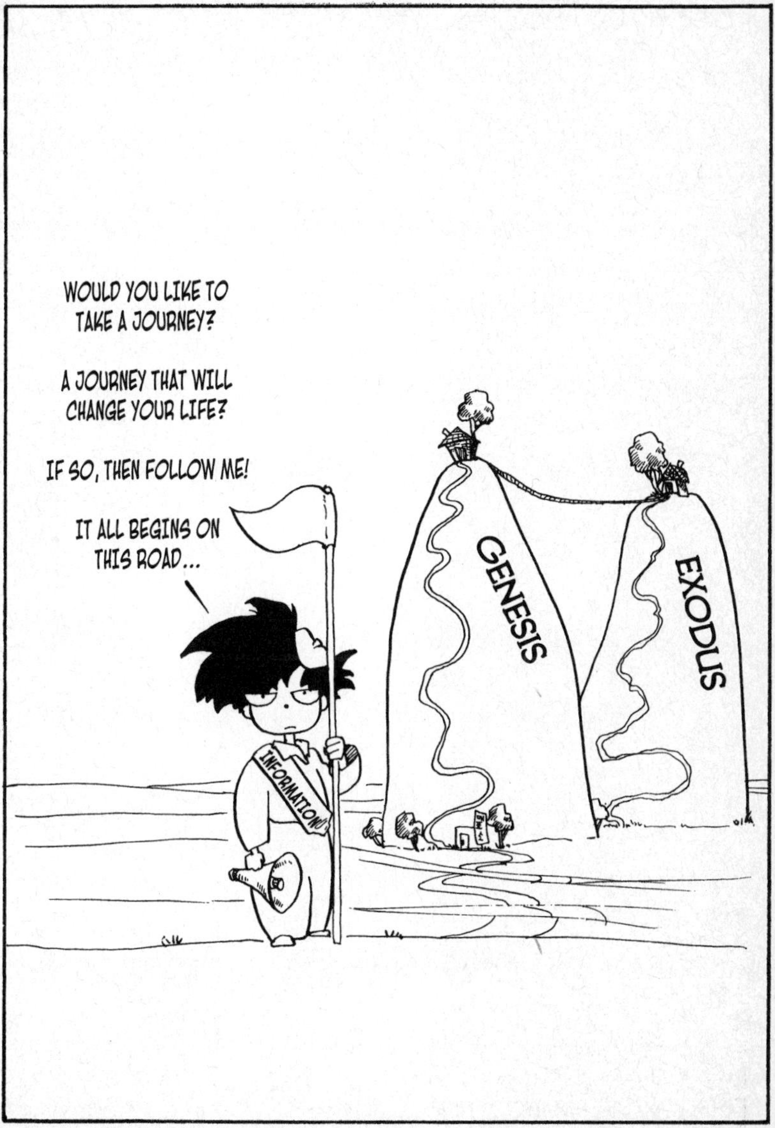
WOULD YOU LIKE TO TAKE A JOURNEY?
A JOURNEY THAT WILL CHANGE YOUR LIFE?
IF SO, THEN FOLLOW ME!
IT ALL BEGINS ON THIS ROAD...
INFORMATION
GENESIS
EXODUS

GENESIS

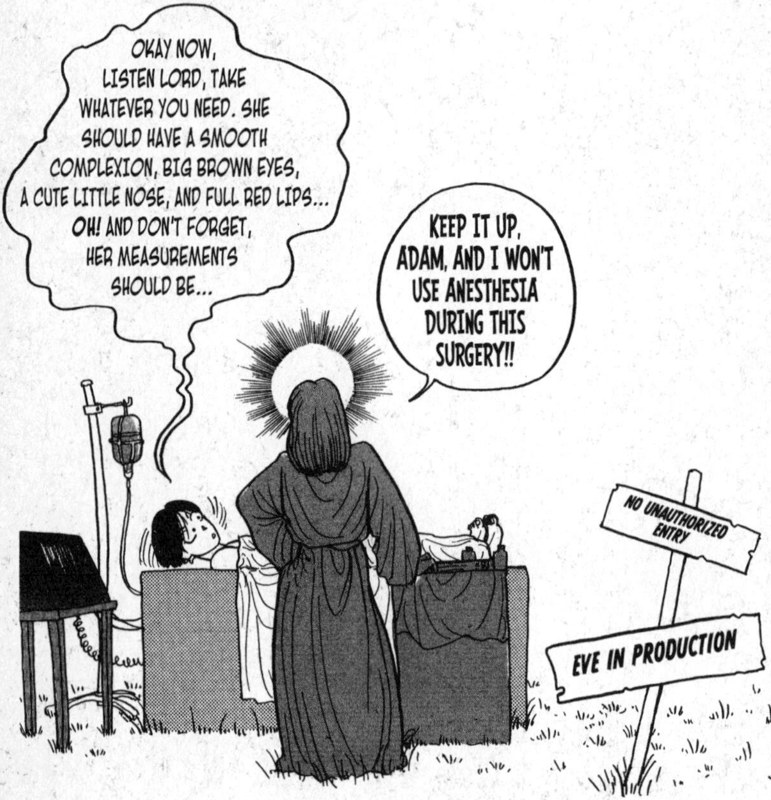
OKAY NOW, LISTEN LORD, TAKE WHATEVER YOU NEED. SHE SHOULD HAVE A SMOOTH COMPLEXION, BIG BROWN EYES, A CUTE LITTLE NOSE, AND FULL RED LIPS... OH! AND DON'T FORGET, HER MEASUREMENTS SHOULD BE...
KEEP IT UP, ADAM, AND I WON'T USE ANESTHESIA DURING THIS SURGERY!!
NO UNAUTHORIZED ENTRY
EVE IN PRODUCTION

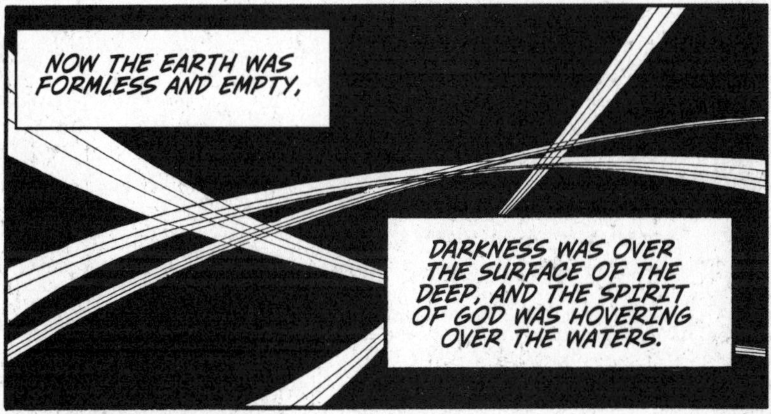
NOW THE EARTH WAS FORMLESS AND EMPTY,
DARKNESS WAS OVER THE SURFACE OF THE DEEP, AND THE SPIRIT OF GOD WAS HOVERING OVER THE WATERS.

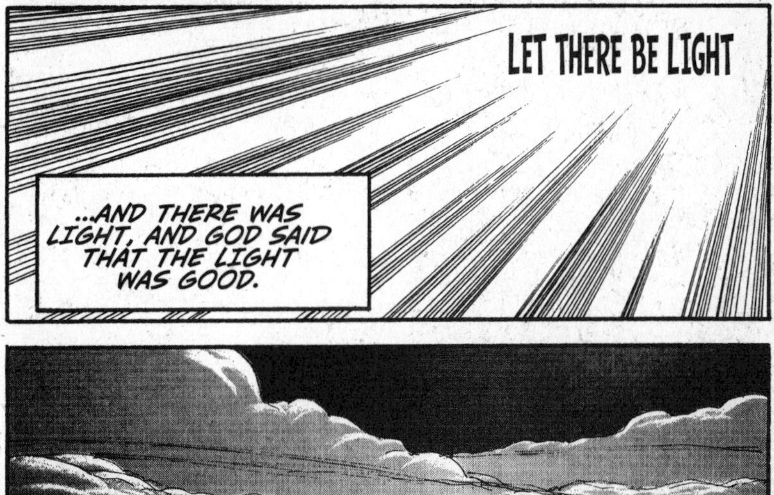
LET THERE BE LIGHT
...AND THERE WAS LIGHT, AND GOD SAID THAT THE LIGHT WAS GOOD.

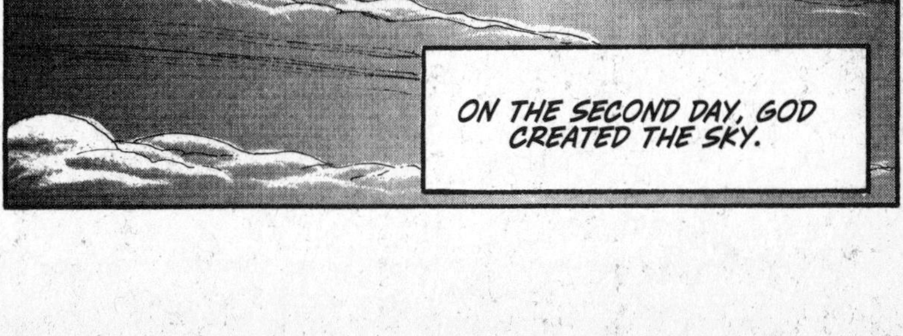
ON THE SECOND DAY, GOD CREATED THE SKY.

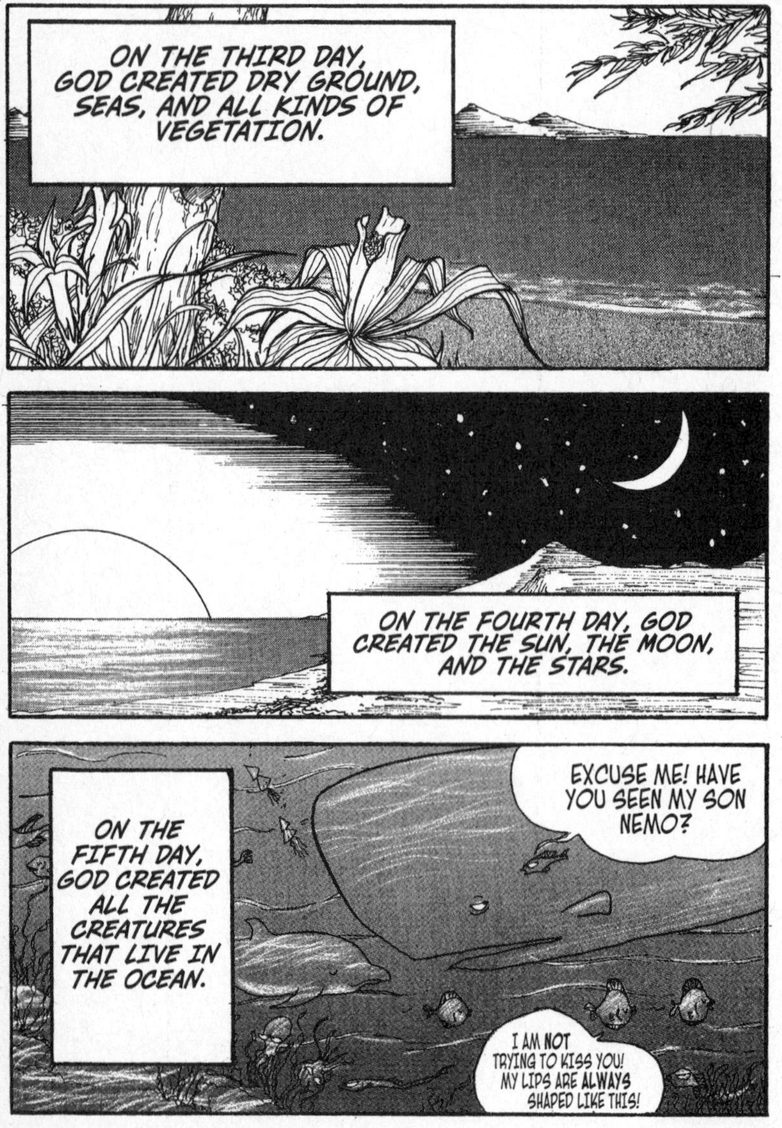
ON THE THIRD DAY, GOD CREATED DRY GROUND, SEAS, AND ALL KINDS OF VEGETATION.
ON THE FOURTH DAY, GOD CREATED THE SUN, THE MOON, AND THE STARS.
ON THE FIFTH DAY, GOD CREATED ALL THE CREATURES THAT LIVE IN THE OCEAN.
EXCUSE ME! HAVE YOU SEEN MY SON NEMO?
I AM NOT TRYING TO KISS YOU! MY LIPS ARE ALWAYS SHAPED LIKE THIS!

AND GOD ALSO CREATED EVERY WINGED BIRD ACCORDING TO ITS KIND.
I'M BALD! CAN YOU BELIEVE IT? HERE, HELP ME COVER THIS UP!
IS IT TRUE THAT A BIG HEAD MEANS A HIGH I.Q?
I HEARD IT WAS BIG FEET!
ON THE SIXTH DAY, GOD CREATED LIVING CREATURES ACCORDING TO THEIR KINDS: LIVESTOCK AND WILD ANIMALS.
ARE YOU A FROG OR A TOAD?
ACTUALLY, I'M A PRINCE!
AND HE ALSO CREATED ALL CREATURES THAT MOVE ALONG THE GROUND.

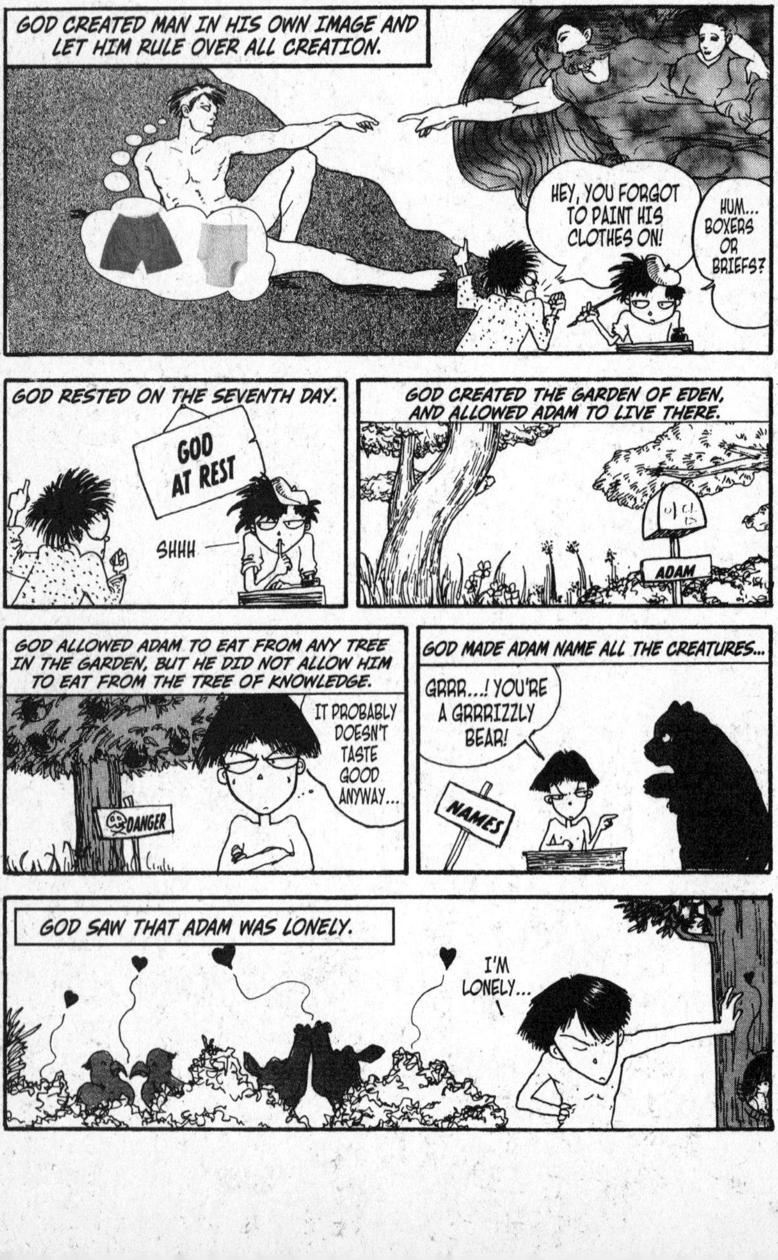
GOD CREATED MAN IN HIS OWN IMAGE AND LET HIM RULE OVER ALL CREATION.
HEY, YOU FORGOT TO PAINT HIS CLOTHES ON!
HUM... BOXERS OR BRIEFS?
GOD RESTED ON THE SEVENTH DAY.
GOD AT REST
SHHH
GOD CREATED THE GARDEN OF EDEN, AND ALLOWED ADAM TO LIVE THERE.
ADAM
GOD ALLOWED ADAM TO EAT FROM ANY TREE IN THE GARDEN, BUT HE DID NOT ALLOW HIM TO EAT FROM THE TREE OF KNOWLEDGE.
IT PROBABLY DOESN'T TASTE GOOD ANYWAY...
DANGER
GOD MADE ADAM NAME ALL THE CREATURES...
GRRR...! YOU'RE A GRRRIZZLY BEAR!
NAMES
GOD SAW THAT ADAM WAS LONELY.
I'M LONELY...

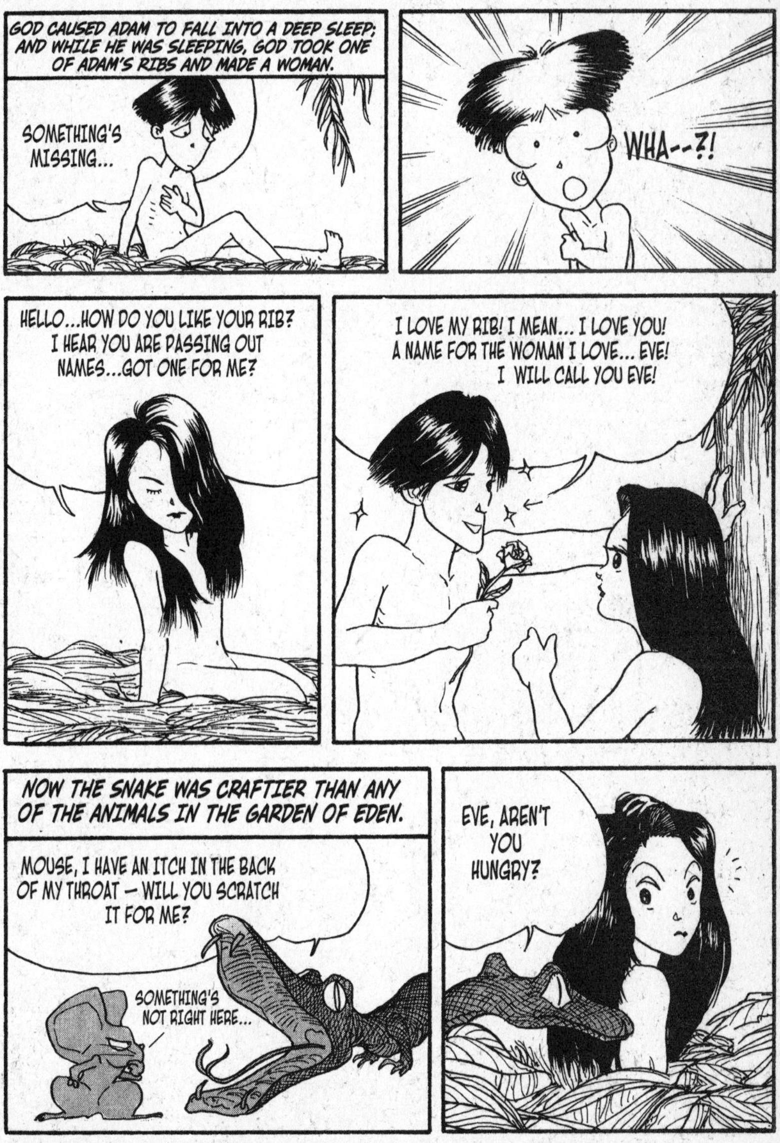
GOD CAUSED ADAM TO FALL INTO A DEEP SLEEP; AND WHILE HE WAS SLEEPING, GOD TOOK ONE OF ADAM'S RIBS AND MADE A WOMAN.
SOMETHING'S MISSING...
WHA--?!
HELLO...HOW DO YOU LIKE YOUR RIB? I HEAR YOU ARE PASSING OUT NAMES...GOT ONE FOR ME?
I LOVE MY RIB! I MEAN... I LOVE YOU! A NAME FOR THE WOMAN I LOVE... EVE! I WILL CALL YOU EVE!
NOW THE SNAKE WAS CRAFTIER THAN ANY OF THE ANIMALS IN THE GARDEN OF EDEN.
MOUSE, I HAVE AN ITCH IN THE BACK OF MY THROAT — WILL YOU SCRATCH IT FOR ME?
SOMETHING'S NOT RIGHT HERE...
EVE, AREN'T YOU HUNGRY?

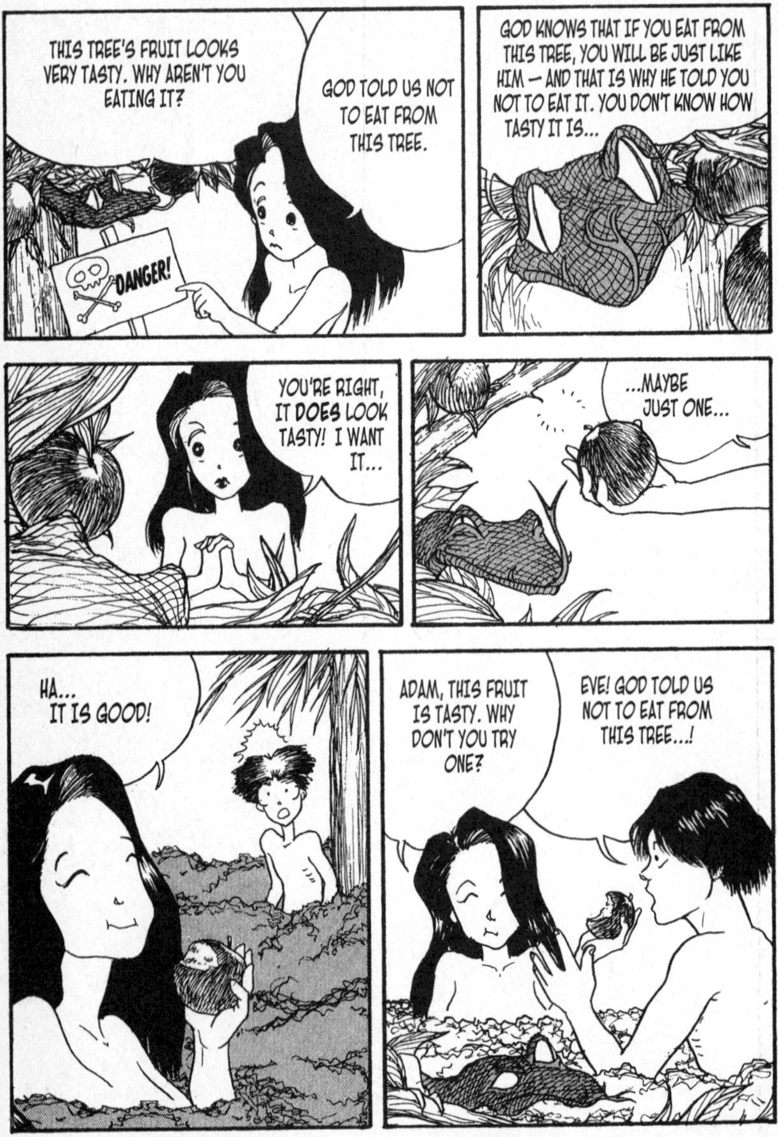
THIS TREE'S FRUIT LOOKS VERY TASTY. WHY AREN'T YOU EATING IT?
GOD TOLD US NOT TO EAT FROM THIS TREE.
DANGER!
GOD KNOWS THAT IF YOU EAT FROM THIS TREE, YOU WILL BE JUST LIKE HIM — AND THAT IS WHY HE TOLD YOU NOT TO EAT IT. YOU DON'T KNOW HOW TASTY IT IS...
YOU'RE RIGHT, IT DOES LOOK TASTY! I WANT IT...
...MAYBE JUST ONE...
HA... IT IS GOOD!
ADAM, THIS FRUIT IS TASTY. WHY DON'T YOU TRY ONE?
EVE! GOD TOLD US NOT TO EAT FROM THIS TREE...!

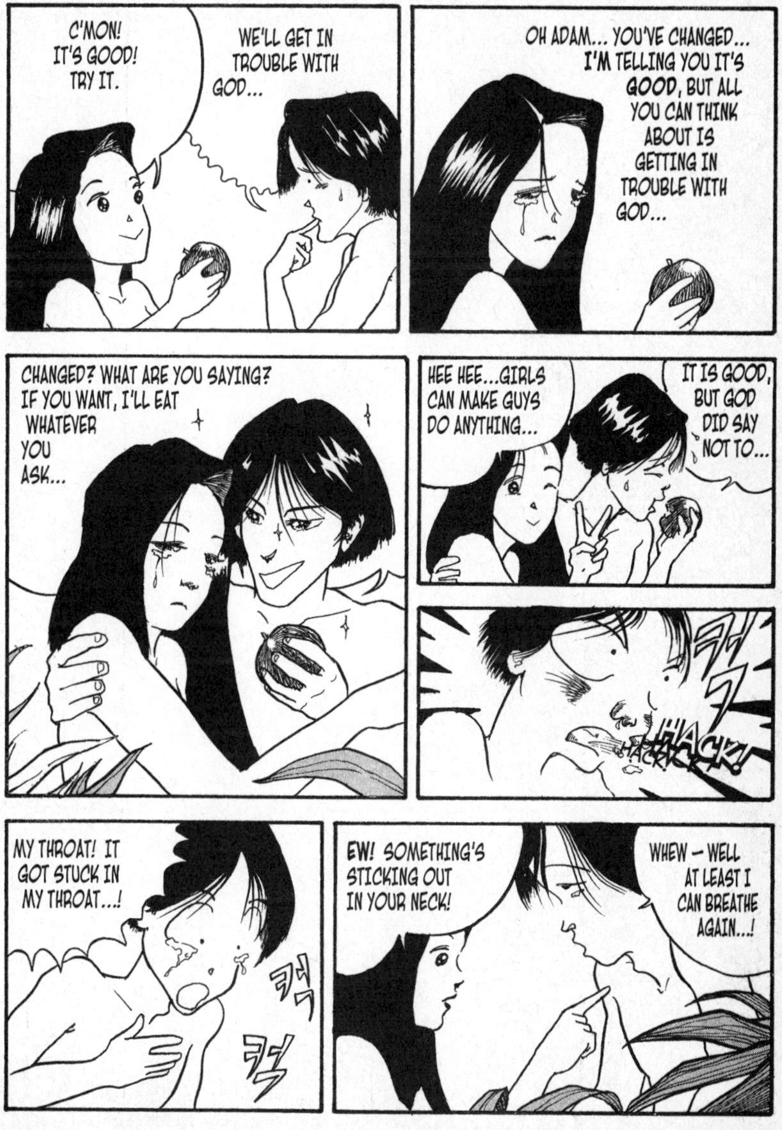
C'MON! IT'S GOOD! TRY IT.
WE'LL GET IN TROUBLE WITH GOD...
OH ADAM... YOU'VE CHANGED... I'M TELLING YOU IT'S GOOD, BUT ALL YOU CAN THINK ABOUT IS GETTING IN TROUBLE WITH GOD...
CHANGED? WHAT ARE YOU SAYING? IF YOU WANT, I'LL EAT WHATEVER YOU ASK...
HEE HEE...GIRLS CAN MAKE GUYS DO ANYTHING...
IT IS GOOD, BUT GOD DID SAY NOT TO...
HACK! HACK!
MY THROAT! IT GOT STUCK IN MY THROAT...!
EW! SOMETHING'S STICKING OUT IN YOUR NECK!
WHEW — WELL AT LEAST I CAN BREATHE AGAIN...!

...DID YOU KNOW... UM... THAT YOU'RE NAKED...?!

AHEM! YOU'RE NAKED TOO...HUM...EMBARRASSING.

ADAM! ADAM! WHERE ARE YOU?

ADAM! COME HERE.

DON'T ANSWER HIM. IF WE KEEP HIDING, WE'LL BE SAFE.

I DON'T KNOW...DON'T YOU THINK HE CAN SEE US?

ADAM! COME OUT HERE!

GOD? I'M EMBARRASSED BECAUSE I'M NAKED. THAT IS WHY I WAS HIDING.

WHO TOLD YOU THAT YOU WERE NAKED? DID YOU EAT FROM THE TREE OF KNOWLEDGE?

I ATE IT BECAUSE THE WOMAN YOU MADE GAVE IT TO ME...!

IT'S TRUE!

IT WAS THE SNAKE! THE SNAKE TRICKED ME INTO EATING IT!

ADAM'S A TATTLE-TALE

IT WAS... UH-OH.

YOU WILL CRAWL ON YOUR BELLY AND YOU WILL EAT DUST ALL THE DAYS OF YOUR LIFE. I WILL PUT ENMITY BETWEEN YOU AND THE WOMAN AND HER OFFSPRING: HE WILL CRUSH YOUR HEAD, AND YOU WILL STRIKE HIS HEEL.

BAM

YOUR PAIN IN CHILDBEARING WILL BE GREATLY INCREASED.

BY THE SWEAT OF YOUR BROW, YOU WILL GET YOUR FOOD UNTIL YOU RETURN TO THE GROUND, SINCE FROM IT YOU WERE TAKEN; FOR YOU ARE DUST, AND TO DUST YOU SHALL RETURN.

GOD BANISHED THEM FROM THE GARDEN OF EDEN. HE PLACED A FLAMING SWORD FLASHING BACK AND FORTH TO GUARD THE WAY TO THE TREE OF LIFE.

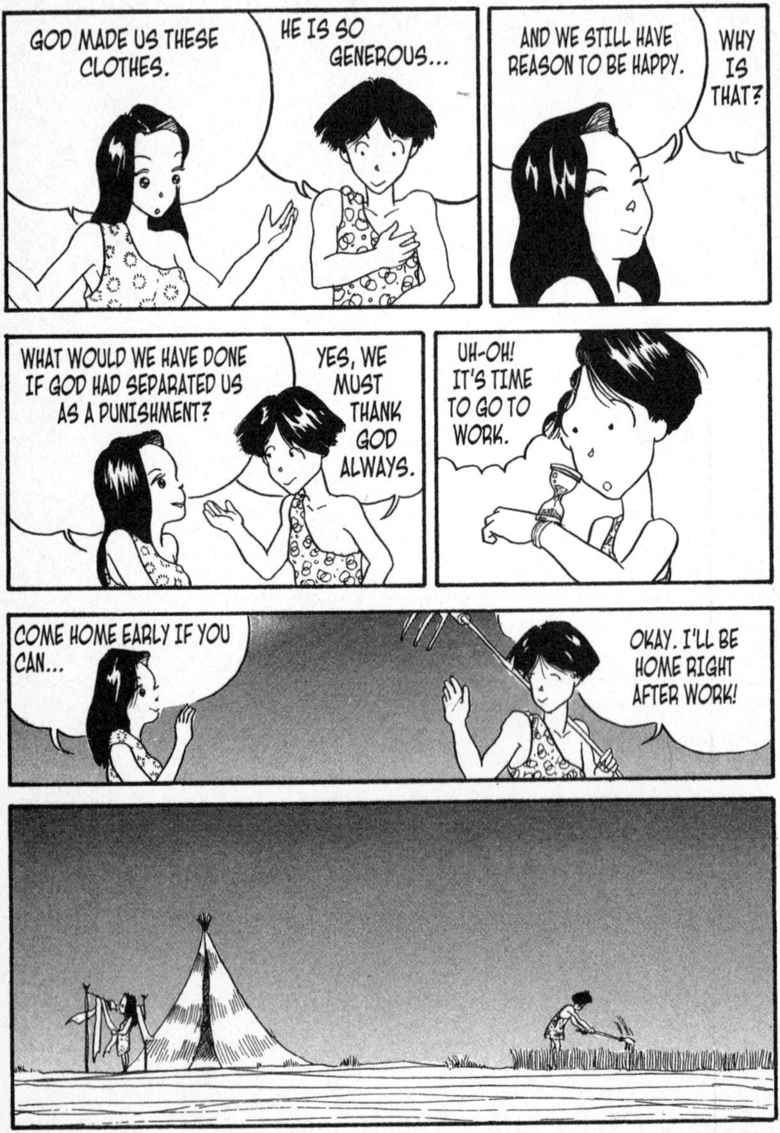
GOD MADE US THESE CLOTHES.
HE IS SO GENEROUS...
AND WE STILL HAVE REASON TO BE HAPPY.
WHY IS THAT?
WHAT WOULD WE HAVE DONE IF GOD HAD SEPARATED US AS A PUNISHMENT?
YES, WE MUST THANK GOD ALWAYS.
UH-OH! IT'S TIME TO GO TO WORK.
COME HOME EARLY IF YOU CAN...
OKAY. I'LL BE HOME RIGHT AFTER WORK!

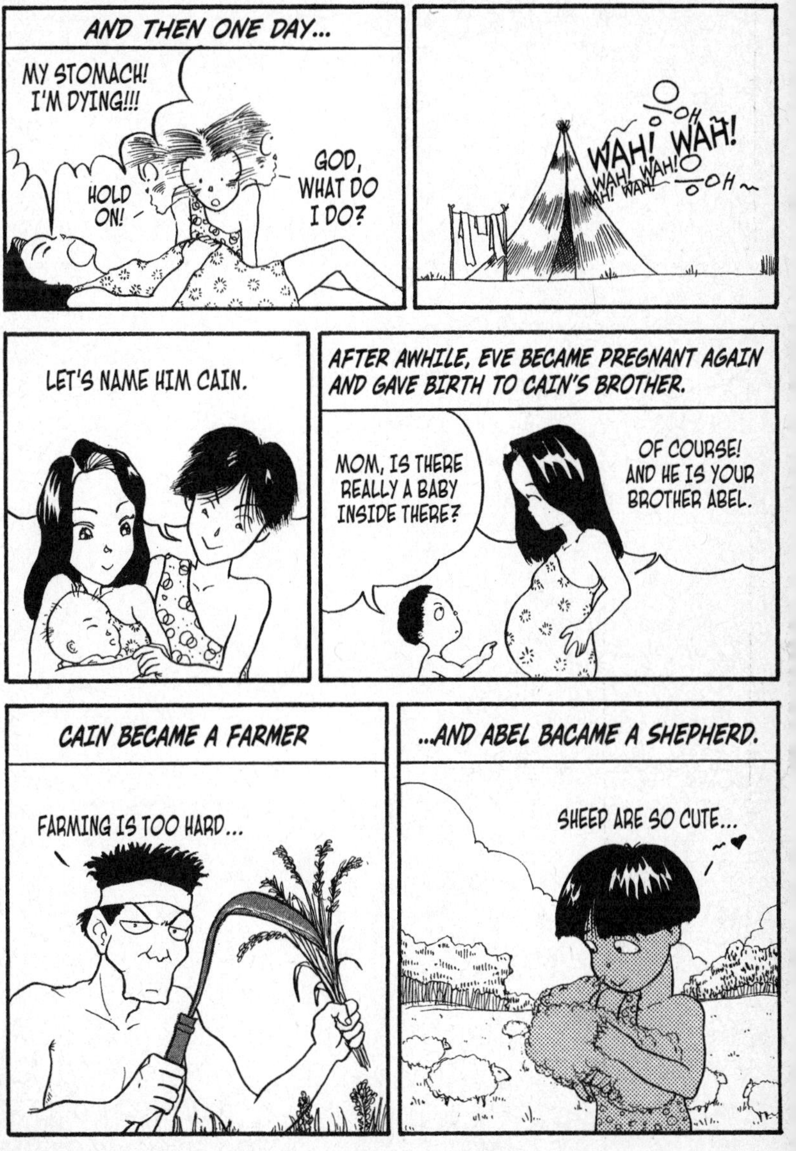
AND THEN ONE DAY...
MY STOMACH! I'M DYING!!!
HOLD ON!
GOD, WHAT DO I DO?
OOOH
WAH! WAH!
WAH! WAH! WAH! WAH!
OOOH~
LET'S NAME HIM CAIN.
AFTER AWHILE, EVE BECAME PREGNANT AGAIN AND GAVE BIRTH TO CAIN'S BROTHER.
MOM, IS THERE REALLY A BABY INSIDE THERE?
OF COURSE! AND HE IS YOUR BROTHER ABEL.
CAIN BECAME A FARMER
FARMING IS TOO HARD...
...AND ABEL BACAME A SHEPHERD.
SHEEP ARE SO CUTE...

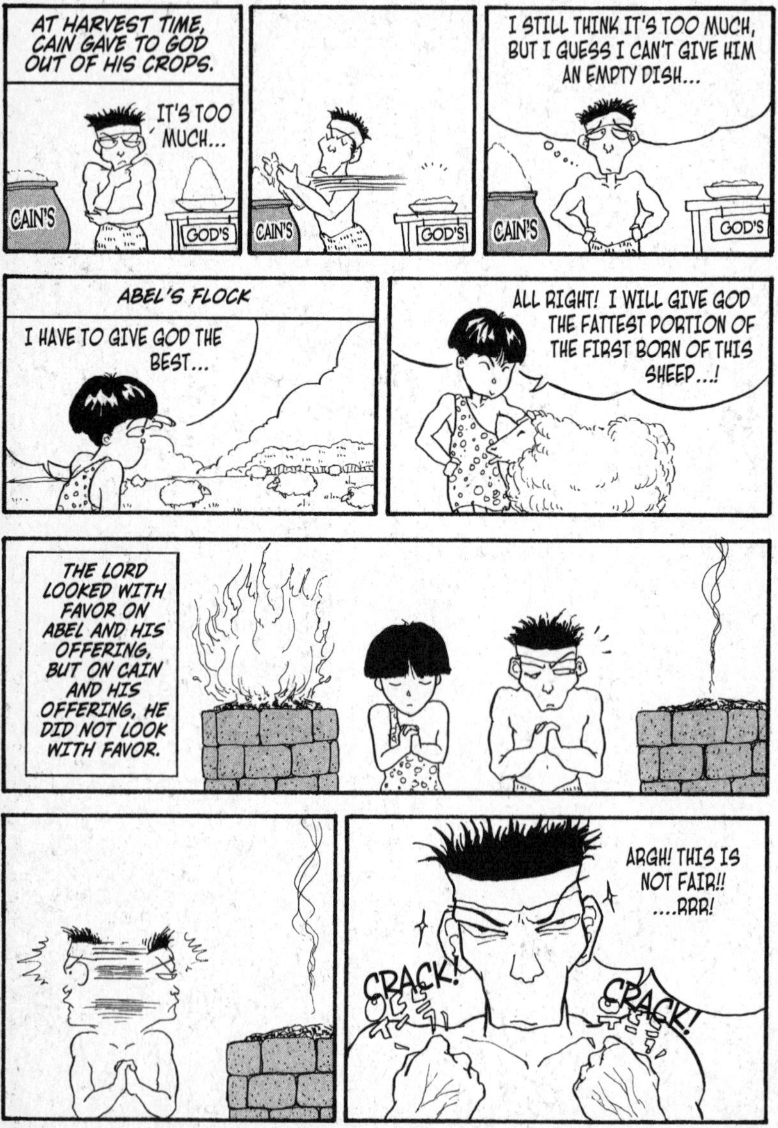
AT HARVEST TIME, CAIN GAVE TO GOD OUT OF HIS CROPS.
IT'S TOO MUCH...
CAIN'S
GOD'S
CAIN'S
GOD'S
I STILL THINK IT'S TOO MUCH, BUT I GUESS I CAN'T GIVE HIM AN EMPTY DISH...
CAIN'S
GOD'S
ABEL'S FLOCK
I HAVE TO GIVE GOD THE BEST...
ALL RIGHT! I WILL GIVE GOD THE FATTEST PORTION OF THE FIRST BORN OF THIS SHEEP...!
THE LORD LOOKED WITH FAVOR ON ABEL AND HIS OFFERING, BUT ON CAIN AND HIS OFFERING, HE DID NOT LOOK WITH FAVOR.
ARGH! THIS IS NOT FAIR!! ....RRR!
CRACK!
CRACK!

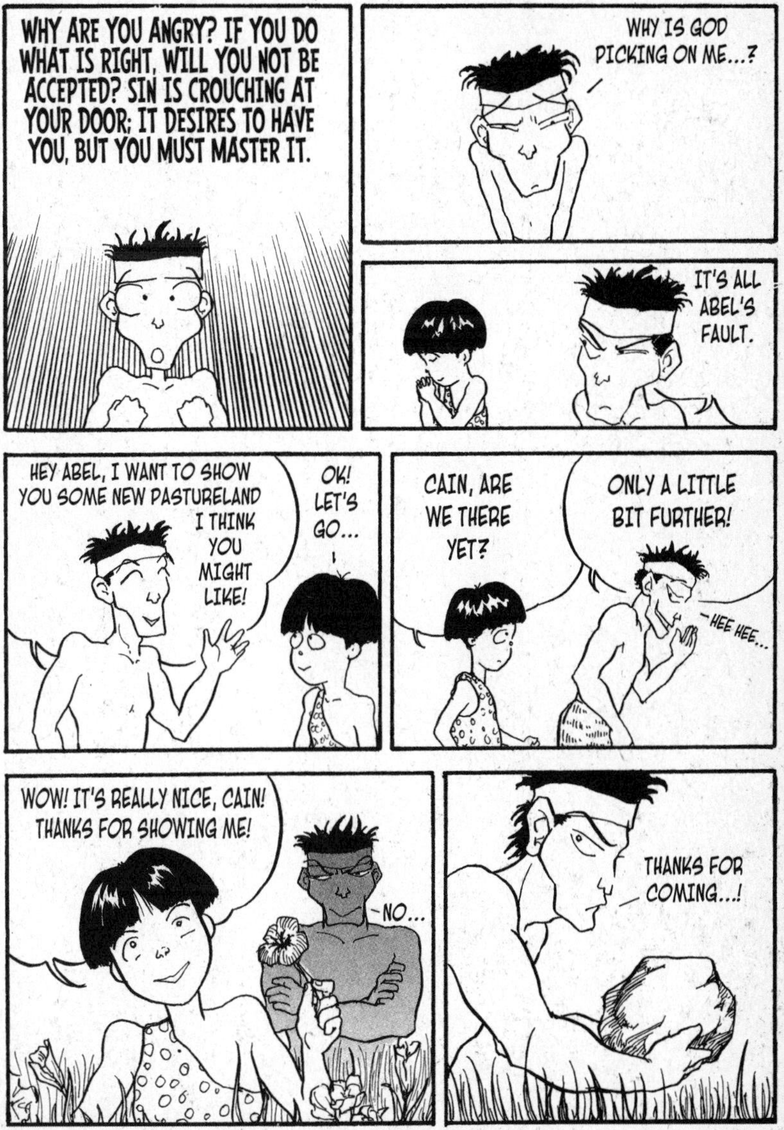
WHY ARE YOU ANGRY? IF YOU DO WHAT IS RIGHT, WILL YOU NOT BE ACCEPTED? SIN IS CROUCHING AT YOUR DOOR; IT DESIRES TO HAVE YOU, BUT YOU MUST MASTER IT.
WHY IS GOD PICKING ON ME...?
IT'S ALL ABEL'S FAULT.
HEY ABEL, I WANT TO SHOW YOU SOME NEW PASTURELAND I THINK YOU MIGHT LIKE!
OK! LET'S GO...
CAIN, ARE WE THERE YET?
ONLY A LITTLE BIT FURTHER!
HEE HEE...
WOW! IT'S REALLY NICE, CAIN! THANKS FOR SHOWING ME!
NO...
THANKS FOR COMING...!

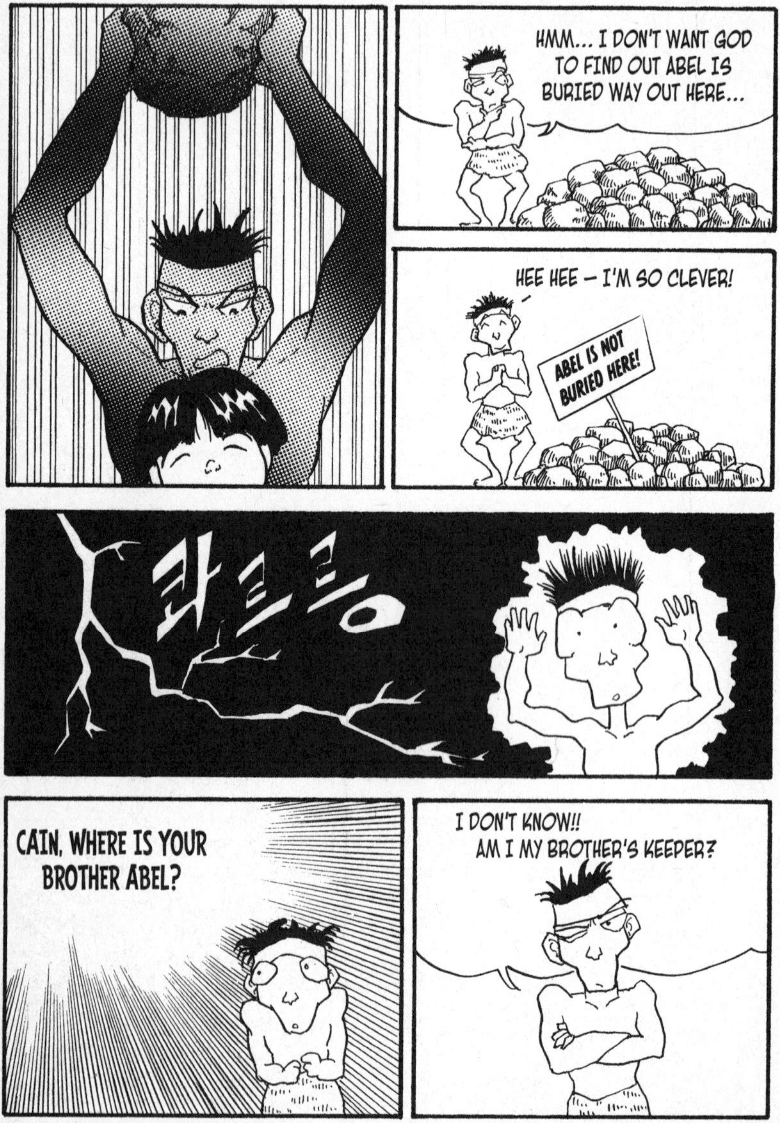
HMM... I DON'T WANT GOD TO FIND OUT ABEL IS BURIED WAY OUT HERE...
HEE HEE – I'M SO CLEVER!
ABEL IS NOT BURIED HERE!
콰르릉
CAIN, WHERE IS YOUR BROTHER ABEL?
I DON'T KNOW!! AM I MY BROTHER'S KEEPER?

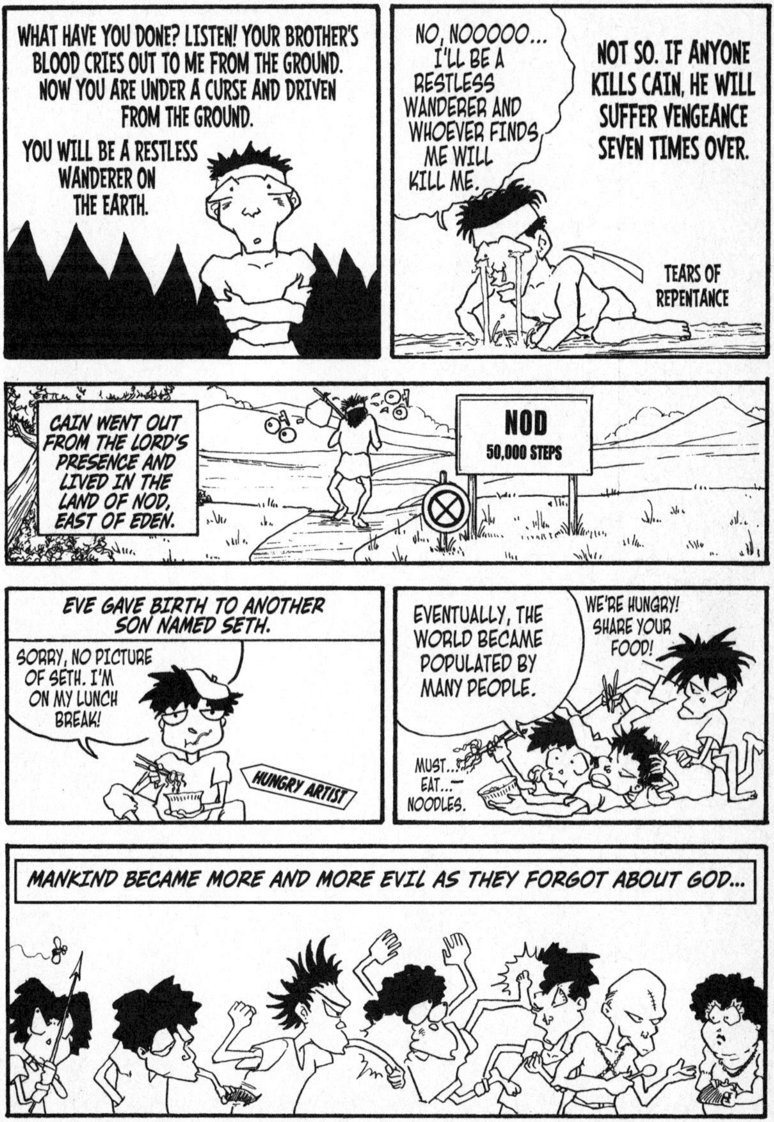
WHAT HAVE YOU DONE? LISTEN! YOUR BROTHER'S BLOOD CRIES OUT TO ME FROM THE GROUND. NOW YOU ARE UNDER A CURSE AND DRIVEN FROM THE GROUND.
YOU WILL BE A RESTLESS WANDERER ON THE EARTH.
NO, NOOOOO... I'LL BE A RESTLESS WANDERER AND WHOEVER FINDS ME WILL KILL ME.
NOT SO. IF ANYONE KILLS CAIN, HE WILL SUFFER VENGEANCE SEVEN TIMES OVER.
TEARS OF REPENTANCE
CAIN WENT OUT FROM THE LORD'S PRESENCE AND LIVED IN THE LAND OF NOD, EAST OF EDEN.
NOD
50,000 STEPS
EVE GAVE BIRTH TO ANOTHER SON NAMED SETH.
SORRY, NO PICTURE OF SETH. I'M ON MY LUNCH BREAK!
HUNGRY ARTIST
EVENTUALLY, THE WORLD BECAME POPULATED BY MANY PEOPLE.
WE'RE HUNGRY! SHARE YOUR FOOD!
MUST... EAT... NOODLES.
MANKIND BECAME MORE AND MORE EVIL AS THEY FORGOT ABOUT GOD...

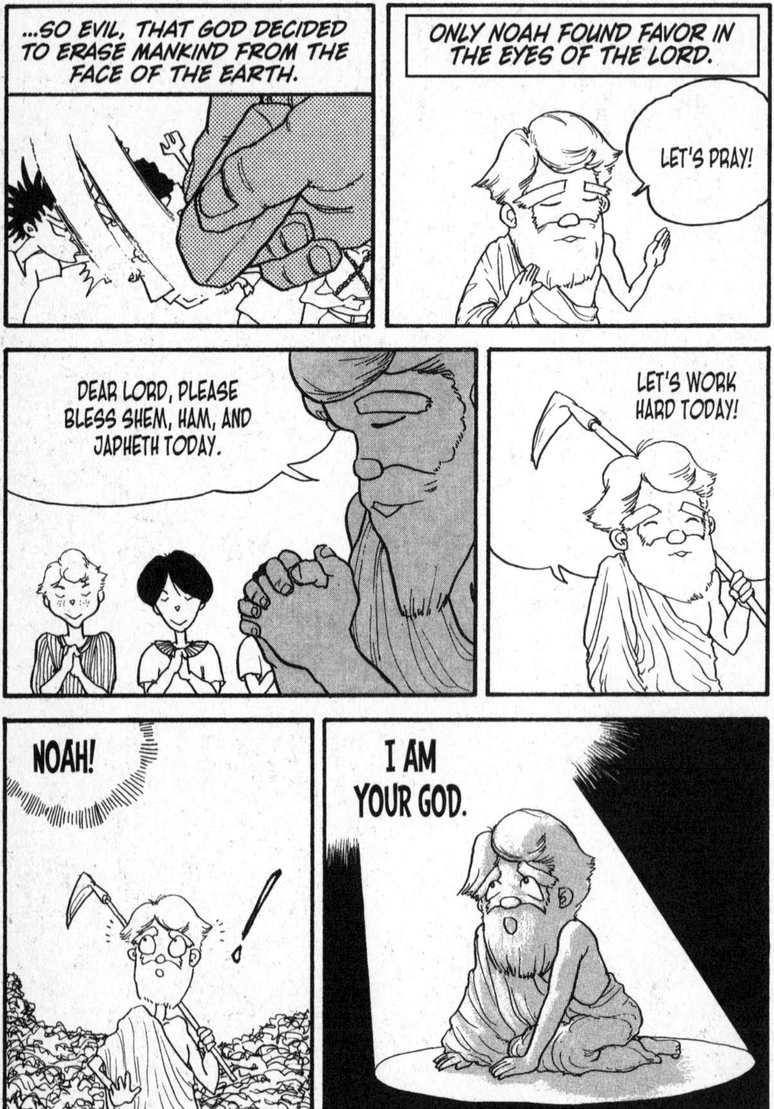
...SO EVIL, THAT GOD DECIDED TO ERASE MANKIND FROM THE FACE OF THE EARTH.
ONLY NOAH FOUND FAVOR IN THE EYES OF THE LORD.
LET'S PRAY!
DEAR LORD, PLEASE BLESS SHEM, HAM, AND JAPHETH TODAY.
LET'S WORK HARD TODAY!
NOAH!
I AM YOUR GOD.

I AM GOING TO DESTROY ALL LIVING CREATURES ON EARTH, FOR THE EARTH IS FILLED WITH VIOLENCE BECAUSE OF THEM. EVERYTHING ON THE EARTH WILL DIE!

Ooo-kay... SO WHY IS HE TELLING ME THIS?

SAFE!

MAKE YOURSELF A BIG SHIP. I PROMISE TO KEEP YOU AND YOUR FAMILY SAFE!

NOAH STARTED TO BUILD A BIG SHIP ON THE MOUNTAIN.

WHAT ARE YOU DOING, DUDE?

OLD MAN, ARE YOU CRAZY? YOU'RE BUILDING A SHIP ON A MOUNTAIN!

ALL THE PEOPLE MADE FUN OF NOAH FOR BUILDING A SHIP ON THE TOP OF THE MOUNTAIN.

HA,HA,HA...

HEE..HEE..

HA,HA,HA...

NOAH STARTED BUILDING THE ARK WHEN HE WAS 480 YEARS OLD. WHEN THE ARK WAS FINISHED HE WAS 600 YEARS OLD! SO, THE ARK TOOK 120 YEARS TO BUILD.

MAN! CALCULATING IS HARDER THAN DRAWING...

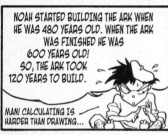

NOAH STORED LOTS OF FOOD IN THE ARK.

NOAH GATHERED SEVEN PAIRS OF EVERY KIND OF CLEAN ANIMAL AND BIRD, AND TWO OF EACH KIND OF UNCLEAN ANIMAL.

PLEASE GET IN LINE!

SIGN IN

MARRIED?

JUST PACKED OUR TRUNKS FOR THE HONEYMOON!

PASS!

MARRIED?

MARRIAGE IS BULL!

FAIL!

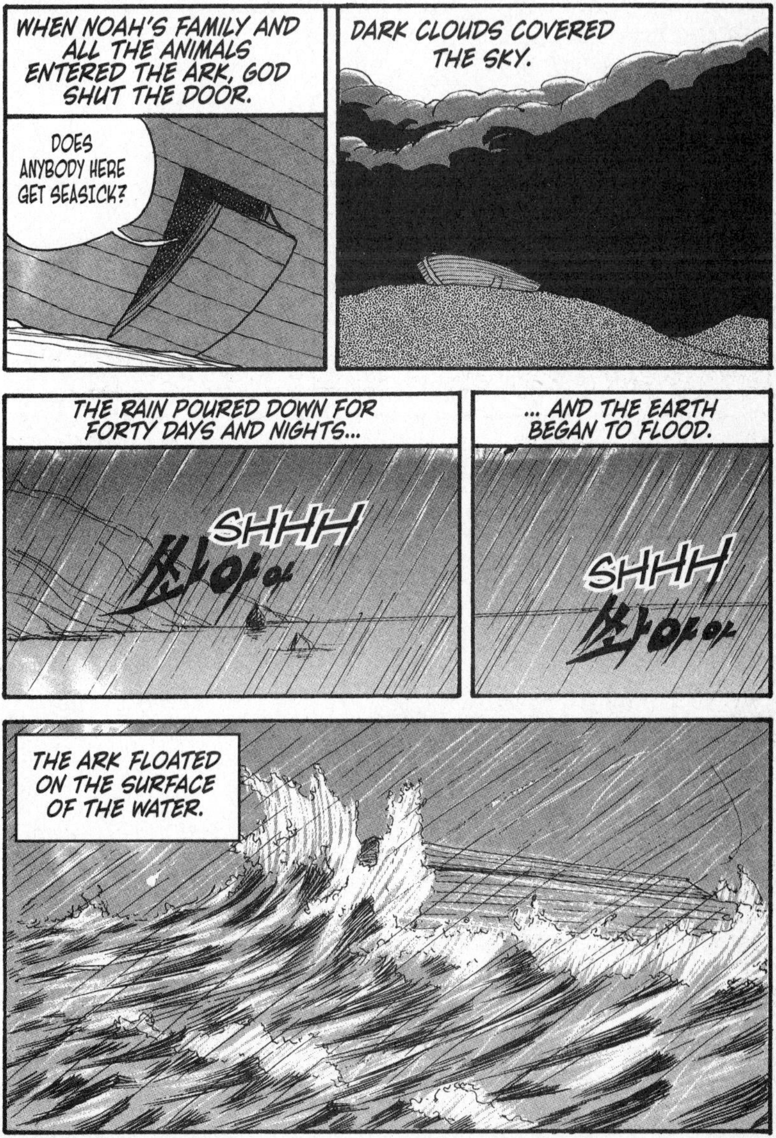

WHEN NOAH'S FAMILY AND ALL THE ANIMALS ENTERED THE ARK, GOD SHUT THE DOOR.
DOES ANYBODY HERE GET SEASICK?
DARK CLOUDS COVERED THE SKY.
THE RAIN POURED DOWN FOR FORTY DAYS AND NIGHTS...
SHHH
쏴아아아
... AND THE EARTH BEGAN TO FLOOD.
SHHH
쏴아아아
THE ARK FLOATED ON THE SURFACE OF THE WATER.

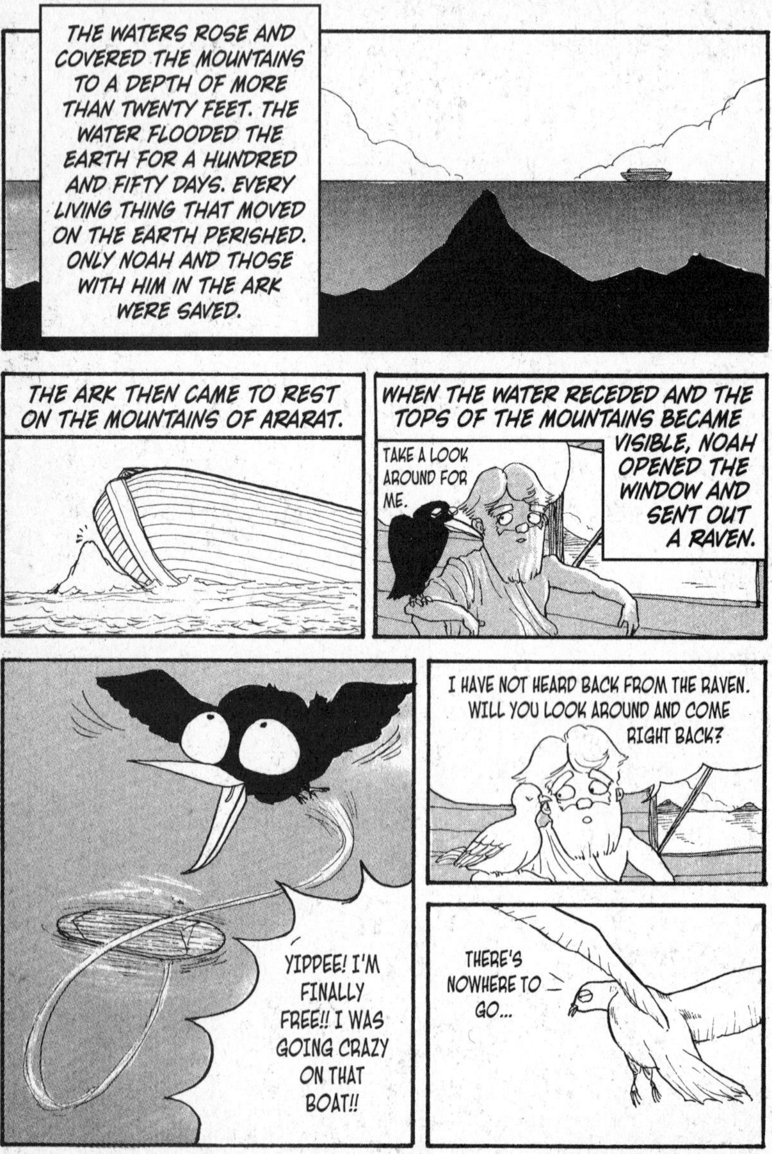
THE WATERS ROSE AND COVERED THE MOUNTAINS TO A DEPTH OF MORE THAN TWENTY FEET. THE WATER FLOODED THE EARTH FOR A HUNDRED AND FIFTY DAYS. EVERY LIVING THING THAT MOVED ON THE EARTH PERISHED. ONLY NOAH AND THOSE WITH HIM IN THE ARK WERE SAVED.
THE ARK THEN CAME TO REST ON THE MOUNTAINS OF ARARAT.
WHEN THE WATER RECEDED AND THE TOPS OF THE MOUNTAINS BECAME VISIBLE, NOAH OPENED THE WINDOW AND SENT OUT A RAVEN.
TAKE A LOOK AROUND FOR ME.
YIPPEE! I'M FINALLY FREE!! I WAS GOING CRAZY ON THAT BOAT!!
I HAVE NOT HEARD BACK FROM THE RAVEN. WILL YOU LOOK AROUND AND COME RIGHT BACK?
THERE'S NOWHERE TO GO...

SEVEN DAYS LATER HE SENT OUT ANOTHER DOVE. WHEN IT RETURNED, IT HAD A FRESHLY PLUCKED OLIVE LEAF IN ITS BEAK!
AFTER ANOTHER SEVEN DAYS HE SENT THE DOVE OUT AGAIN. THIS TIME IT DID NOT RETURN.
THE YEAR NOAH TURNED 601 YEARS OLD, THE WATER DRIED UP FROM THE EARTH
IT'S DRY!
말랐다!
IT'S DRY!
IT'S DRY!
말랐다!
GOD OPENED THE ARK AND ALLOWED NOAH'S FAMILY AND ALL THE ANIMALS TO COME OUT
GOD BLESSED THEM AND PROMISED THAT HE WOULD NEVER AGAIN DESTROY THE EARTH WITH A FLOOD. AS A SIGN OF HIS PROMISE GOD PLACED THE RAINBOW IN THE CLOUDS.

LET'S WORK THE LAND GOD HAS GIVEN TO US.

WE'RE IN TROUBLE! NOAH PLANTED GRAPES!

WE ONLY EAT CABBAGE... SOB!... WHAT ARE WE GOING TO EAT?

NOAH'S VINEYARD PRODUCED MANY GRAPES.

HA-HA... LOOK HOW MANY GRAPES WE HAVE.

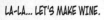

LA-LA... LET'S MAKE WINE.

SHOULD I TRY SOME?

IT'S GOOD.

IT'S VERY GOOD.

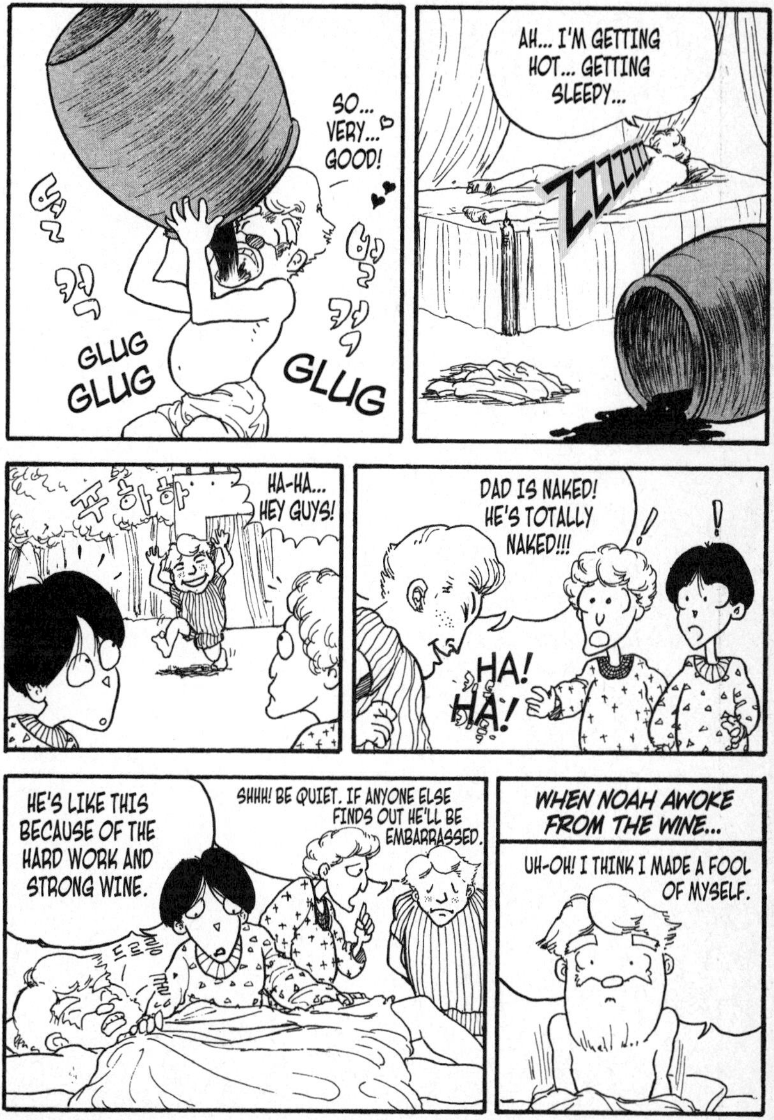
SO... VERY... GOOD!
GLUG GLUG
GLUG
AH... I'M GETTING HOT... GETTING SLEEPY...
ZZZZZZZ
푸하하
HA-HA... HEY GUYS!
DAD IS NAKED! HE'S TOTALLY NAKED!!!
HA! HA!
!
!
HE'S LIKE THIS BECAUSE OF THE HARD WORK AND STRONG WINE.
SHHH! BE QUIET. IF ANYONE ELSE FINDS OUT HE'LL BE EMBARRASSED.
드르렁
WHEN NOAH AWOKE FROM THE WINE...
UH-OH! I THINK I MADE A FOOL OF MYSELF.

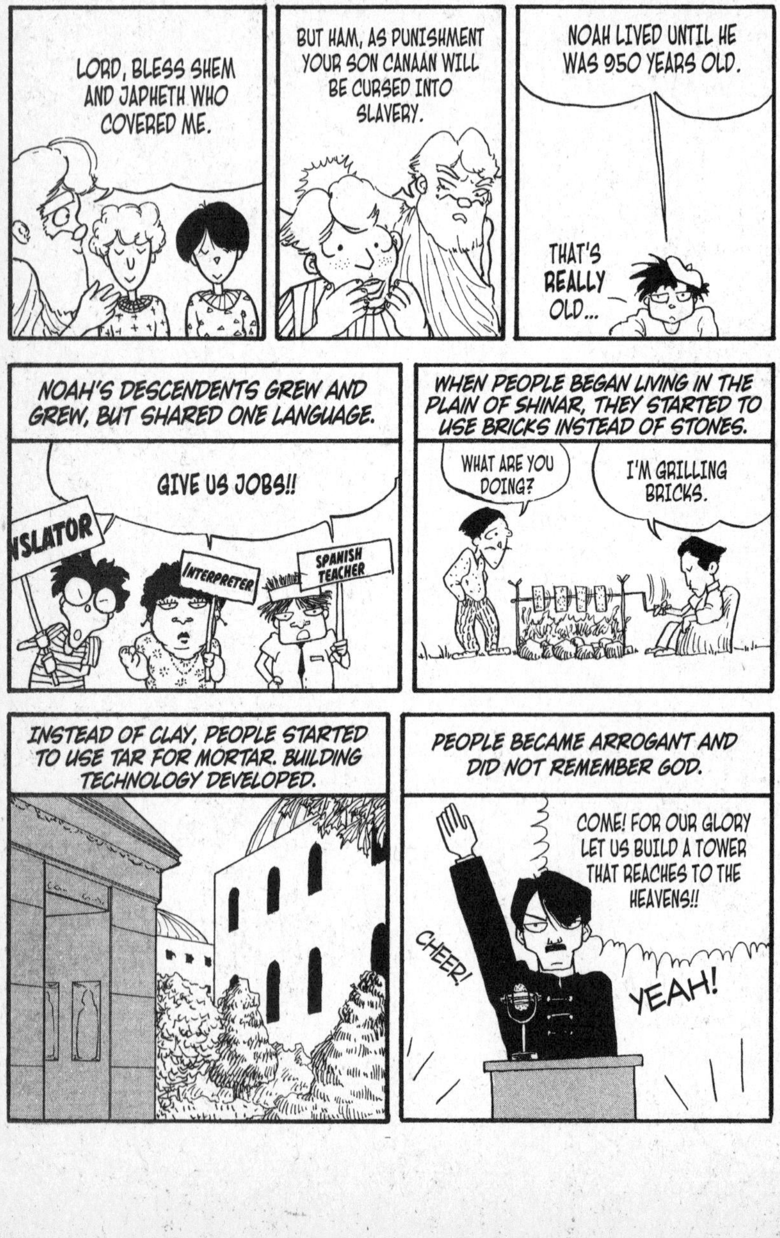
LORD, BLESS SHEM AND JAPHETH WHO COVERED ME.
BUT HAM, AS PUNISHMENT YOUR SON CANAAN WILL BE CURSED INTO SLAVERY.
NOAH LIVED UNTIL HE WAS 950 YEARS OLD.
THAT'S REALLY OLD...
NOAH'S DESCENDENTS GREW AND GREW, BUT SHARED ONE LANGUAGE.
GIVE US JOBS!!
NSLATOR
INTERPRETER
SPANISH TEACHER
WHEN PEOPLE BEGAN LIVING IN THE PLAIN OF SHINAR, THEY STARTED TO USE BRICKS INSTEAD OF STONES.
WHAT ARE YOU DOING?
I'M GRILLING BRICKS.
INSTEAD OF CLAY, PEOPLE STARTED TO USE TAR FOR MORTAR. BUILDING TECHNOLOGY DEVELOPED.
PEOPLE BECAME ARROGANT AND DID NOT REMEMBER GOD.
COME! FOR OUR GLORY LET US BUILD A TOWER THAT REACHES TO THE HEAVENS!!
CHEER!
YEAH!

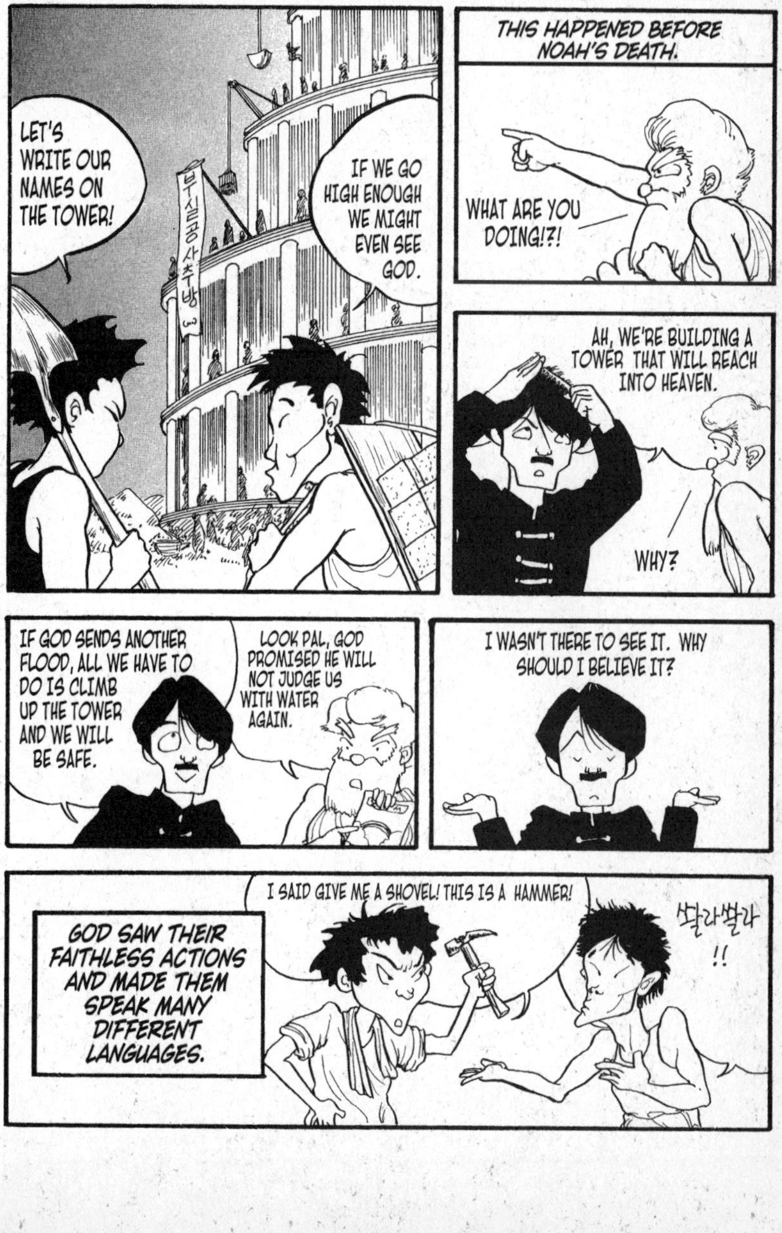
LET'S WRITE OUR NAMES ON THE TOWER!
부실공사추방
IF WE GO HIGH ENOUGH WE MIGHT EVEN SEE GOD.
THIS HAPPENED BEFORE NOAH'S DEATH.
WHAT ARE YOU DOING!?!
AH, WE'RE BUILDING A TOWER THAT WILL REACH INTO HEAVEN.
WHY?
IF GOD SENDS ANOTHER FLOOD, ALL WE HAVE TO DO IS CLIMB UP THE TOWER AND WE WILL BE SAFE.
LOOK PAL, GOD PROMISED HE WILL NOT JUDGE US WITH WATER AGAIN.
I WASN'T THERE TO SEE IT. WHY SHOULD I BELIEVE IT?
GOD SAW THEIR FAITHLESS ACTIONS AND MADE THEM SPEAK MANY DIFFERENT LANGUAGES.
I SAID GIVE ME A SHOVEL! THIS IS A HAMMER!
쏼라쏼라
!!

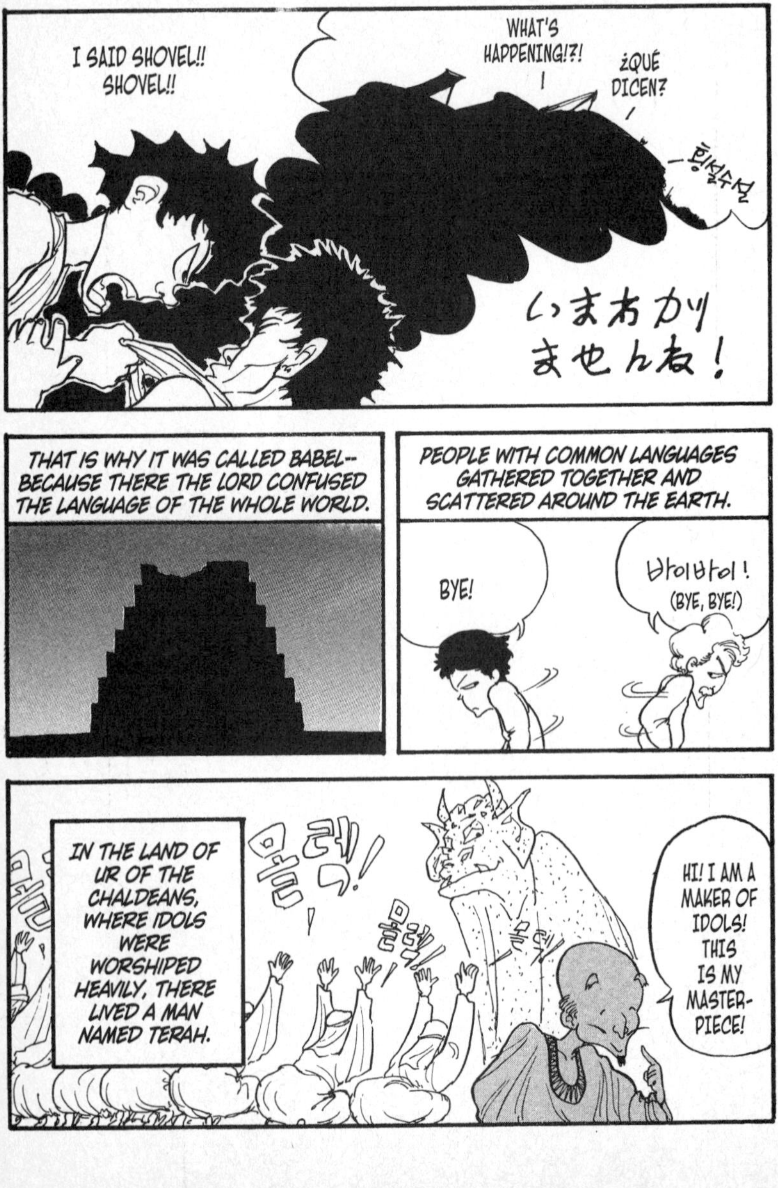
I SAID SHOVEL!! SHOVEL!!
WHAT'S HAPPENING!?!
¿QUÉ DICEN?
횡설수설
いまおかりませんね！
THAT IS WHY IT WAS CALLED BABEL--BECAUSE THERE THE LORD CONFUSED THE LANGUAGE OF THE WHOLE WORLD.
PEOPLE WITH COMMON LANGUAGES GATHERED TOGETHER AND SCATTERED AROUND THE EARTH.
BYE!
바이바이!
(BYE, BYE!)
IN THE LAND OF UR OF THE CHALDEANS, WHERE IDOLS WERE WORSHIPED HEAVILY, THERE LIVED A MAN NAMED TERAH.
몰렉!
몰렉!
몰렉
HI! I AM A MAKER OF IDOLS! THIS IS MY MASTER-PIECE!

NOAH WAS MY GREAT, GREAT, GREAT, GREAT, GREAT, GREAT, GREAT GRANDFATHER!

MY PROFESSION? I AM A MAKER OF IDOLS!

DON'T PUSH!

I NEED AN IDOL!

IDOL! IDOL! IDOL!

I'LL GIVE YOU THE MONEY, JUST MAKE IT FAST!

I MAKE A LOT OF MONEY DOING THIS! I LOVE PEOPLE'S IDOL WORSHIP!

TERAH HAD THREE SONS: ABRAM, NAHOR, AND HARAN. HARAN DIED WHILE THEY LIVED IN UR.

DAD...?

MY SON IS DEAD!!!

— GOD CREATED THE WORLD, ABRAM, AND YOUR GRANDFATHER NOAH BUILT AN ARK...

I LOVE MY MOTHER'S STORIES ABOUT GOD...

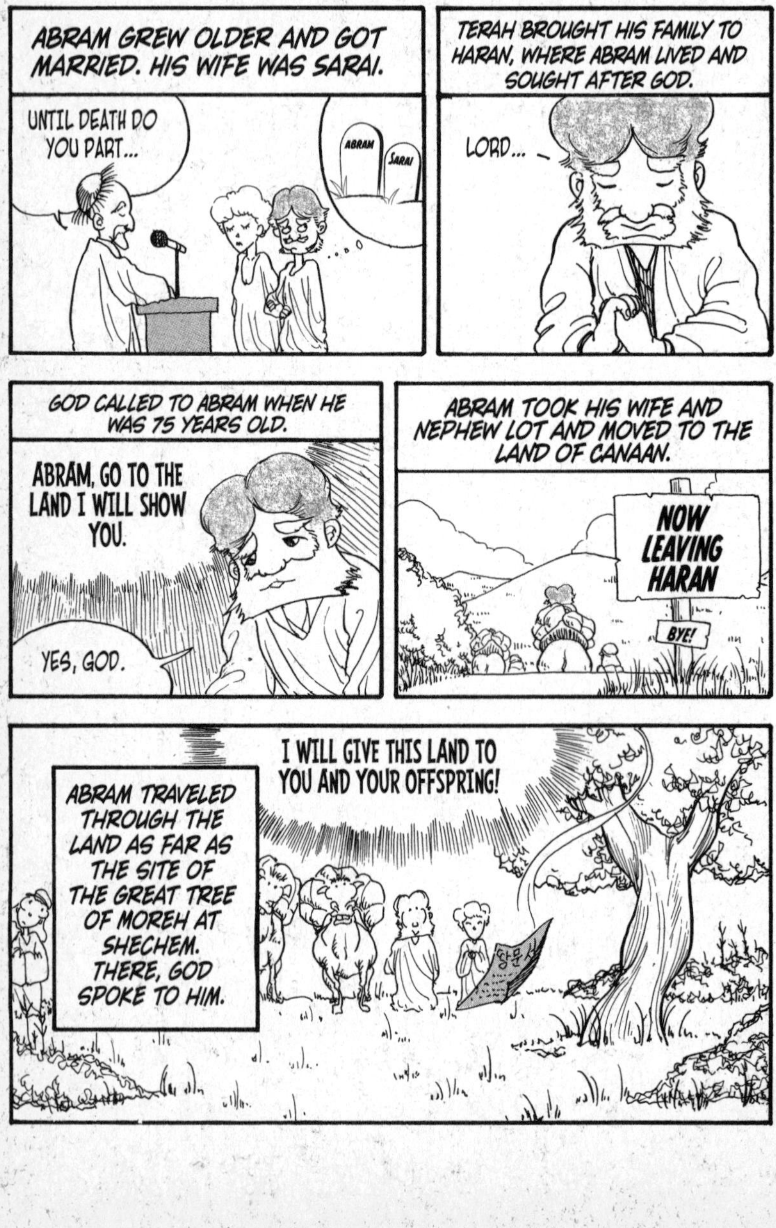
ABRAM GREW OLDER AND GOT MARRIED. HIS WIFE WAS SARAI.
UNTIL DEATH DO YOU PART...
ABRAM
SARAI
TERAH BROUGHT HIS FAMILY TO HARAN, WHERE ABRAM LIVED AND SOUGHT AFTER GOD.
LORD...
GOD CALLED TO ABRAM WHEN HE WAS 75 YEARS OLD.
ABRAM, GO TO THE LAND I WILL SHOW YOU.
YES, GOD.
ABRAM TOOK HIS WIFE AND NEPHEW LOT AND MOVED TO THE LAND OF CANAAN.
NOW LEAVING HARAN
BYE!
ABRAM TRAVELED THROUGH THE LAND AS FAR AS THE SITE OF THE GREAT TREE OF MOREH AT SHECHEM. THERE, GOD SPOKE TO HIM.
I WILL GIVE THIS LAND TO YOU AND YOUR OFFSPRING!

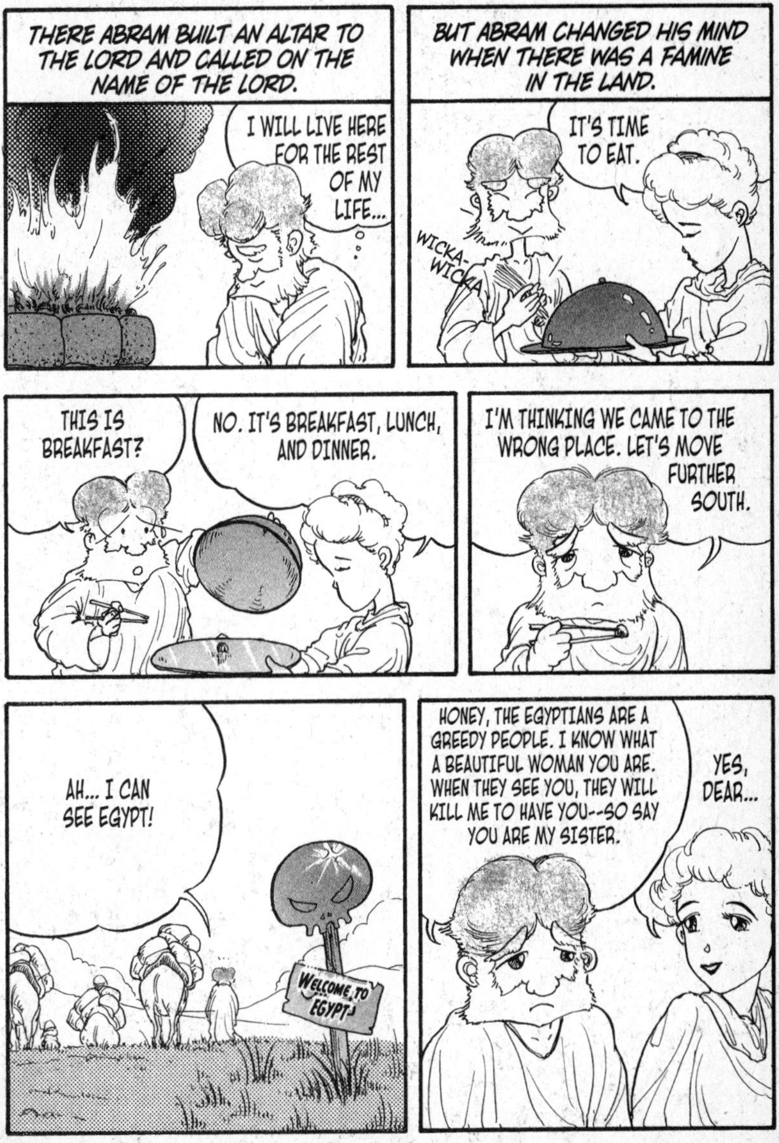
THERE ABRAM BUILT AN ALTAR TO THE LORD AND CALLED ON THE NAME OF THE LORD.
I WILL LIVE HERE FOR THE REST OF MY LIFE...
BUT ABRAM CHANGED HIS MIND WHEN THERE WAS A FAMINE IN THE LAND.
IT'S TIME TO EAT.
WICKA-WICKA
THIS IS BREAKFAST?
NO. IT'S BREAKFAST, LUNCH, AND DINNER.
I'M THINKING WE CAME TO THE WRONG PLACE. LET'S MOVE FURTHER SOUTH.
AH... I CAN SEE EGYPT!
WELCOME TO EGYPT
HONEY, THE EGYPTIANS ARE A GREEDY PEOPLE. I KNOW WHAT A BEAUTIFUL WOMAN YOU ARE. WHEN THEY SEE YOU, THEY WILL KILL ME TO HAVE YOU--SO SAY YOU ARE MY SISTER.
YES, DEAR...

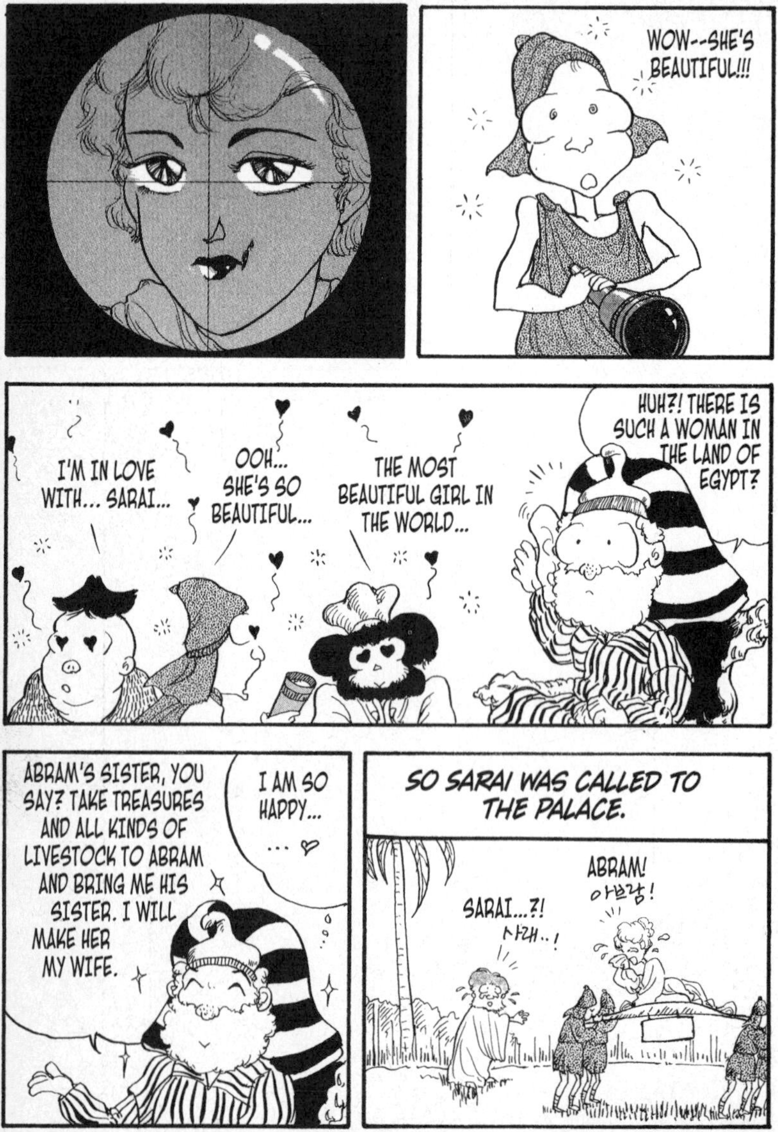
WOW--SHE'S BEAUTIFUL!!!
I'M IN LOVE WITH... SARAI...
OOH... SHE'S SO BEAUTIFUL...
THE MOST BEAUTIFUL GIRL IN THE WORLD...
HUH?! THERE IS SUCH A WOMAN IN THE LAND OF EGYPT?
ABRAM'S SISTER, YOU SAY? TAKE TREASURES AND ALL KINDS OF LIVESTOCK TO ABRAM AND BRING ME HIS SISTER. I WILL MAKE HER MY WIFE.
I AM SO HAPPY...
... ♡
SO SARAI WAS CALLED TO THE PALACE.
SARAI...?!
사래..!
ABRAM!
아브람!

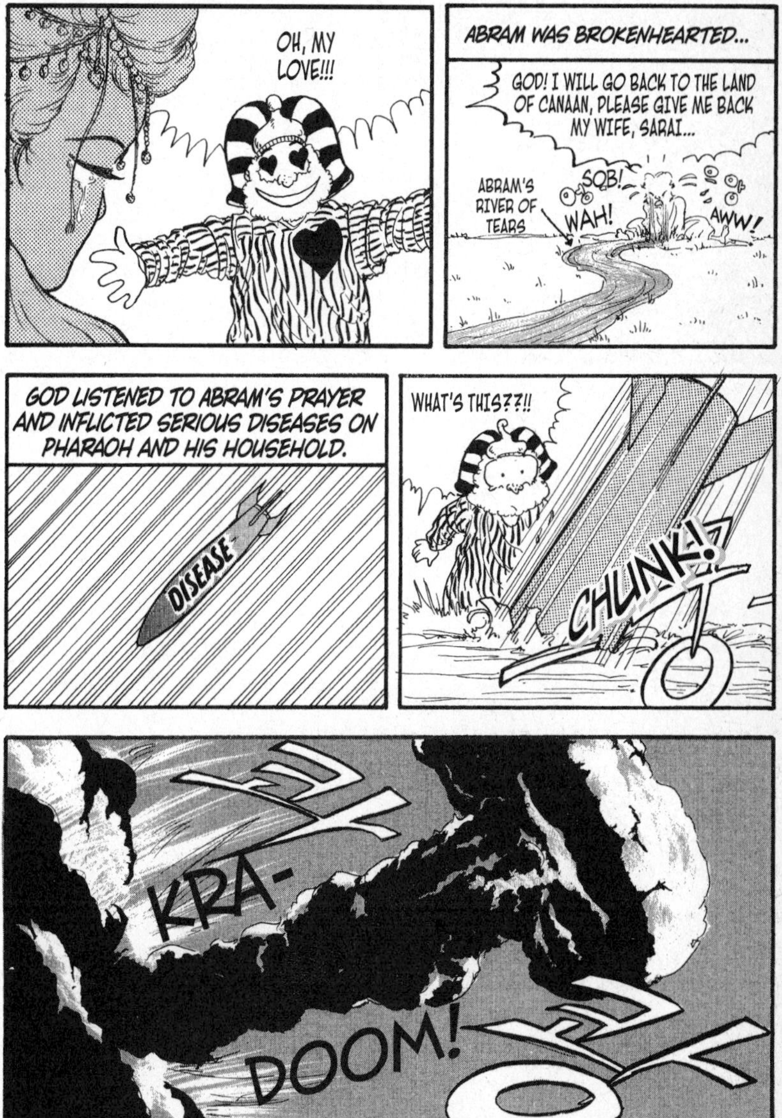
OH, MY LOVE!!!
ABRAM WAS BROKENHEARTED...
GOD! I WILL GO BACK TO THE LAND OF CANAAN, PLEASE GIVE ME BACK MY WIFE, SARAI...
ABRAM'S RIVER OF TEARS
SOB!
WAH!
AWW!
GOD LISTENED TO ABRAM'S PRAYER AND INFLICTED SERIOUS DISEASES ON PHARAOH AND HIS HOUSEHOLD.
DISEASE
WHAT'S THIS??!!
CHUNK!
KRA-
DOOM!

UGH! WHY IS THIS HAPPENING TO ME?
BECAUSE YOU TOOK ABRAM'S WIFE SARAI! GOD IS ANGRY WITH YOU!
COUGH! COUGH! COUGH!
HEY ABRAM! YOU LIED ABOUT SARAI!! GET OUT OF THIS COUNTRY--AND TAKE YOUR "SISTER" WITH YOU!!
UNDER CONSTRUCTION -PHARAOH-
AUTHORIZED PERSONNEL ONLY
ABRAM LEFT EGYPT AND RETURNED TO CANAAN.
GOOD-BYE! -EGYPT-
THANKS FOR LEAVING! -PHARAOH-
CHUGGA-CHUGGA
MANY YEARS PASSED SINCE ABRAM ARRIVED IN CANAAN.
STRANGE... WHY DON'T I HAVE ANY CHILDREN?
ABRAM! ABRAM! LOOK UP! COUNT THE STARS IN THE SKY!
YOUR DESCENDANTS WILL BE THAT MANY!
THERE ARE SO MANY IT WOULD TAKE ME YEARS, GOD!

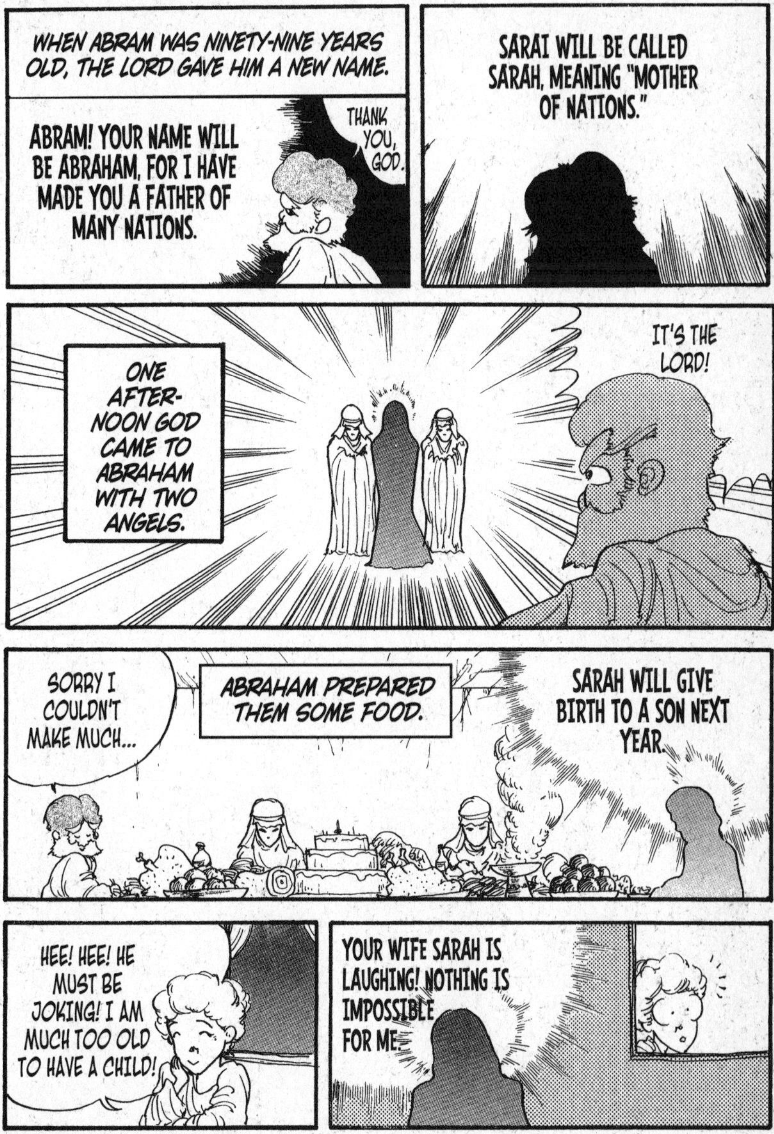
WHEN ABRAM WAS NINETY-NINE YEARS OLD, THE LORD GAVE HIM A NEW NAME.
ABRAM! YOUR NAME WILL BE ABRAHAM, FOR I HAVE MADE YOU A FATHER OF MANY NATIONS.
THANK YOU, GOD.
SARAI WILL BE CALLED SARAH, MEANING "MOTHER OF NATIONS."
ONE AFTER-NOON GOD CAME TO ABRAHAM WITH TWO ANGELS.
IT'S THE LORD!
ABRAHAM PREPARED THEM SOME FOOD.
SORRY I COULDN'T MAKE MUCH...
SARAH WILL GIVE BIRTH TO A SON NEXT YEAR.
HEE! HEE! HE MUST BE JOKING! I AM MUCH TOO OLD TO HAVE A CHILD!
YOUR WIFE SARAH IS LAUGHING! NOTHING IS IMPOSSIBLE FOR ME.

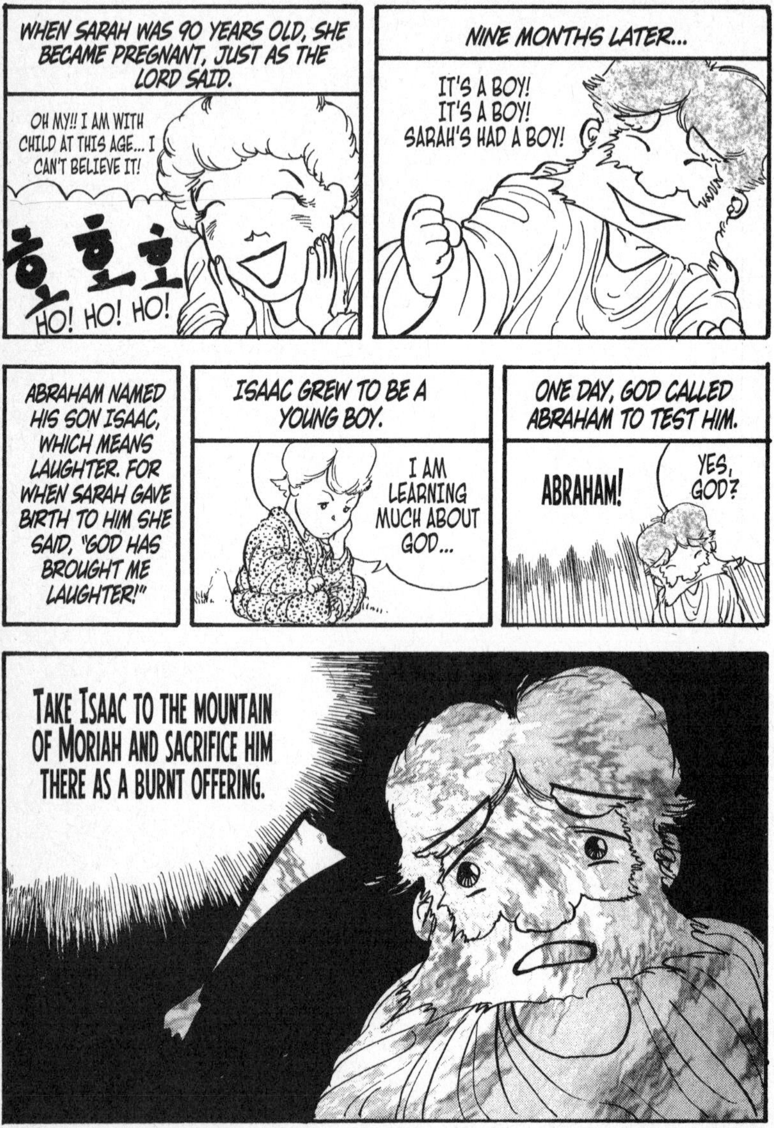
WHEN SARAH WAS 90 YEARS OLD, SHE BECAME PREGNANT, JUST AS THE LORD SAID.
OH MY!! I AM WITH CHILD AT THIS AGE... I CAN'T BELIEVE IT!
호호호
HO! HO! HO!
NINE MONTHS LATER...
IT'S A BOY! IT'S A BOY! SARAH'S HAD A BOY!
ABRAHAM NAMED HIS SON ISAAC, WHICH MEANS LAUGHTER. FOR WHEN SARAH GAVE BIRTH TO HIM SHE SAID, "GOD HAS BROUGHT ME LAUGHTER!"
ISAAC GREW TO BE A YOUNG BOY.
I AM LEARNING MUCH ABOUT GOD...
ONE DAY, GOD CALLED ABRAHAM TO TEST HIM.
ABRAHAM!
YES, GOD?
TAKE ISAAC TO THE MOUNTAIN OF MORIAH AND SACRIFICE HIM THERE AS A BURNT OFFERING.

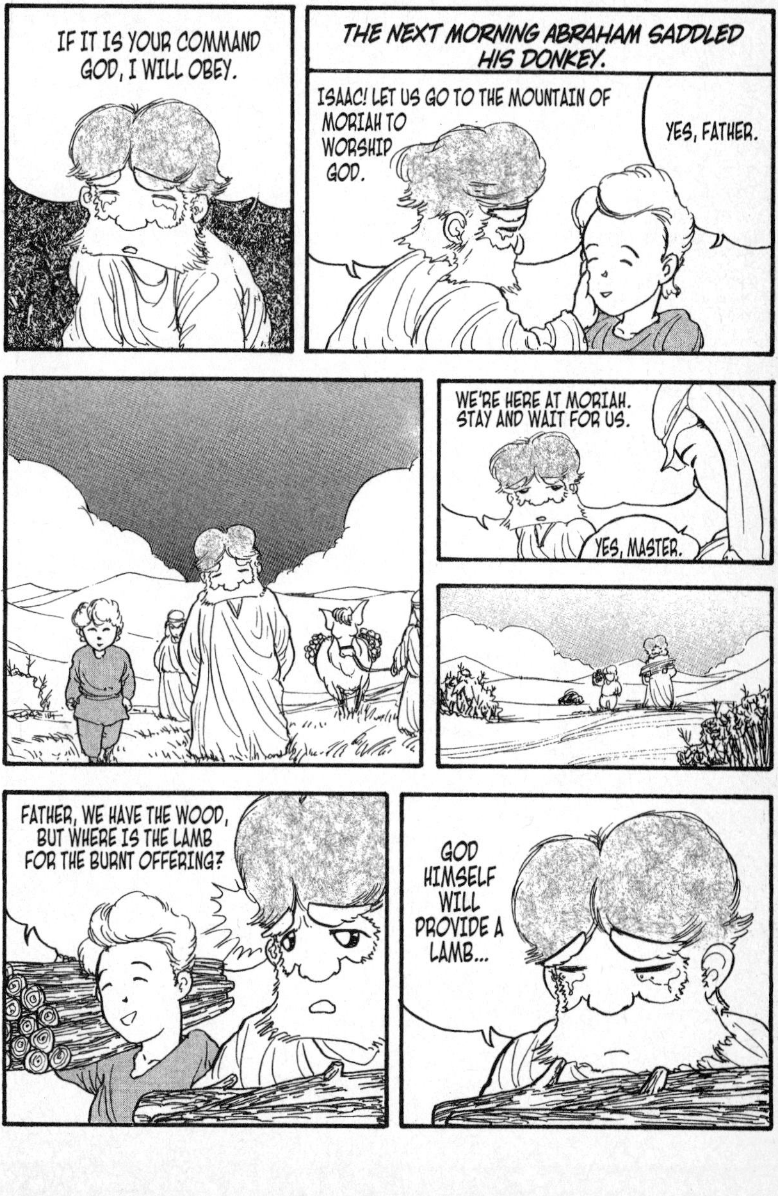
IF IT IS YOUR COMMAND GOD, I WILL OBEY.
THE NEXT MORNING ABRAHAM SADDLED HIS DONKEY.
ISAAC! LET US GO TO THE MOUNTAIN OF MORIAH TO WORSHIP GOD.
YES, FATHER.
WE'RE HERE AT MORIAH. STAY AND WAIT FOR US.
YES, MASTER.
FATHER, WE HAVE THE WOOD, BUT WHERE IS THE LAMB FOR THE BURNT OFFERING?
GOD HIMSELF WILL PROVIDE A LAMB...

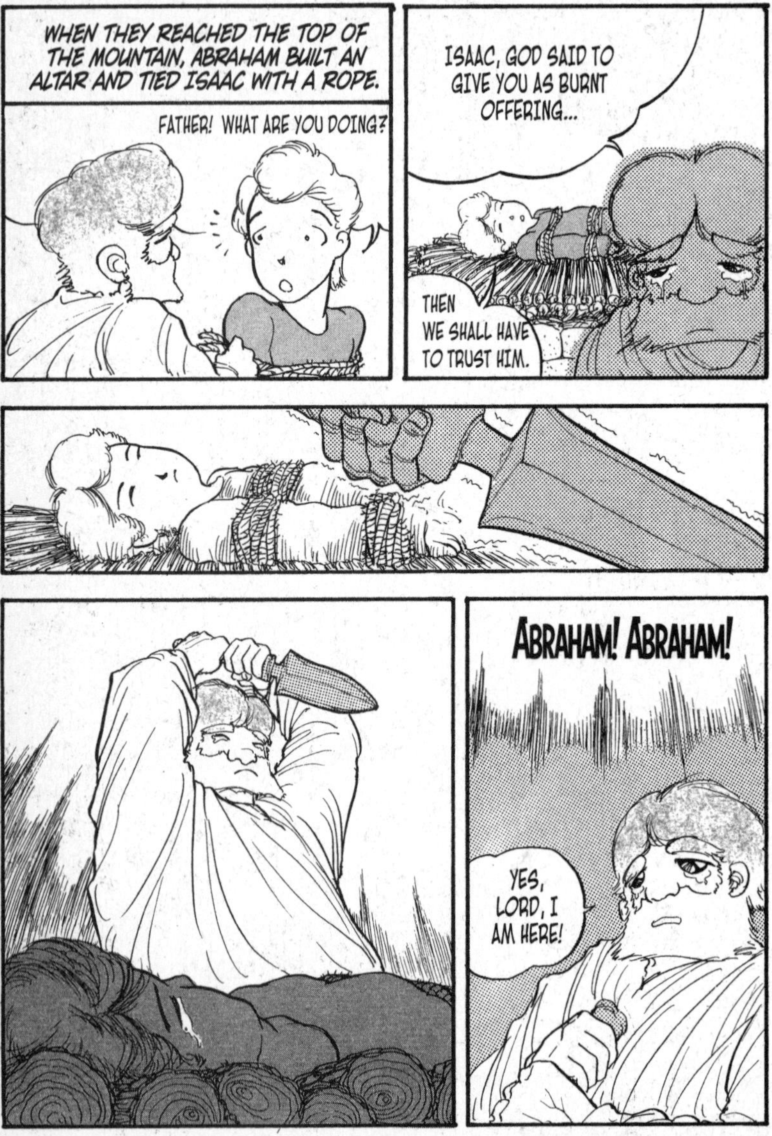
WHEN THEY REACHED THE TOP OF THE MOUNTAIN, ABRAHAM BUILT AN ALTAR AND TIED ISAAC WITH A ROPE.
FATHER! WHAT ARE YOU DOING?
ISAAC, GOD SAID TO GIVE YOU AS BURNT OFFERING...
THEN WE SHALL HAVE TO TRUST HIM.
ABRAHAM! ABRAHAM!
YES, LORD, I AM HERE!

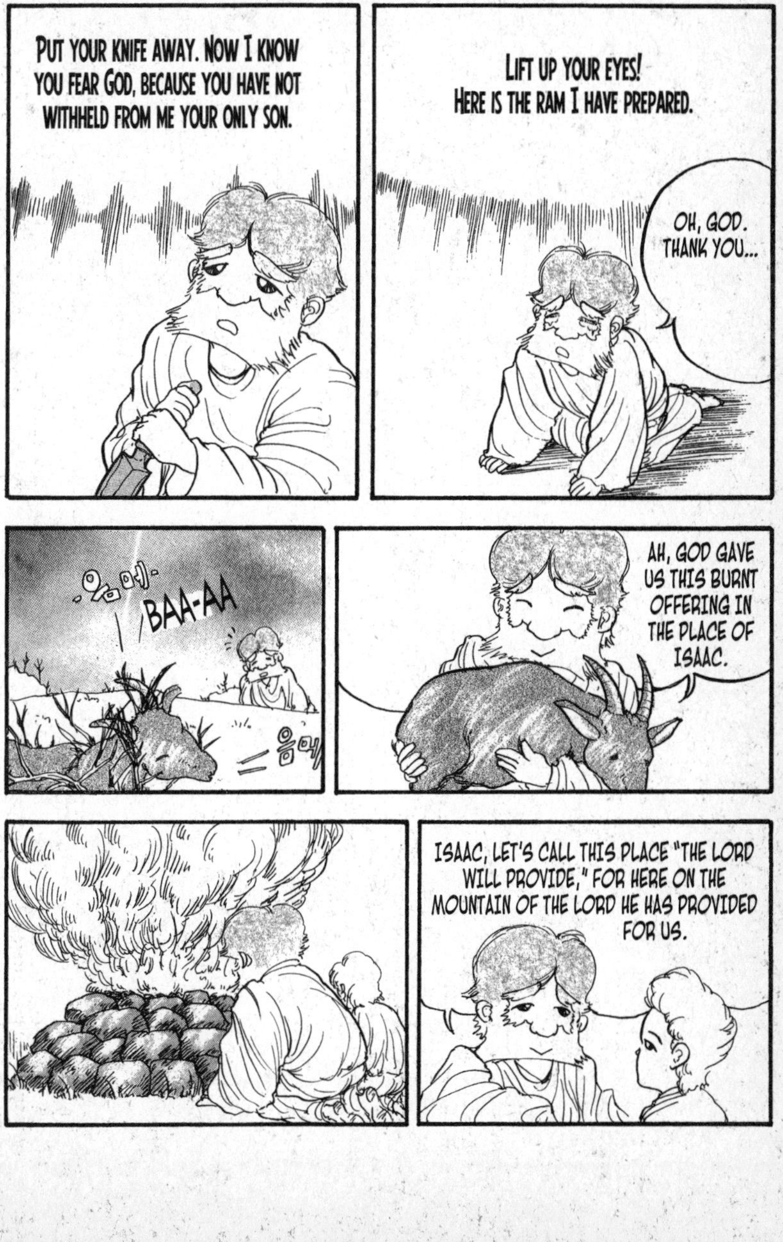
PUT YOUR KNIFE AWAY. NOW I KNOW YOU FEAR GOD, BECAUSE YOU HAVE NOT WITHHELD FROM ME YOUR ONLY SON.
LIFT UP YOUR EYES! HERE IS THE RAM I HAVE PREPARED.
OH, GOD. THANK YOU...
음메
BAA-AA
음메
AH, GOD GAVE US THIS BURNT OFFERING IN THE PLACE OF ISAAC.
ISAAC, LET'S CALL THIS PLACE "THE LORD WILL PROVIDE," FOR HERE ON THE MOUNTAIN OF THE LORD HE HAS PROVIDED FOR US.

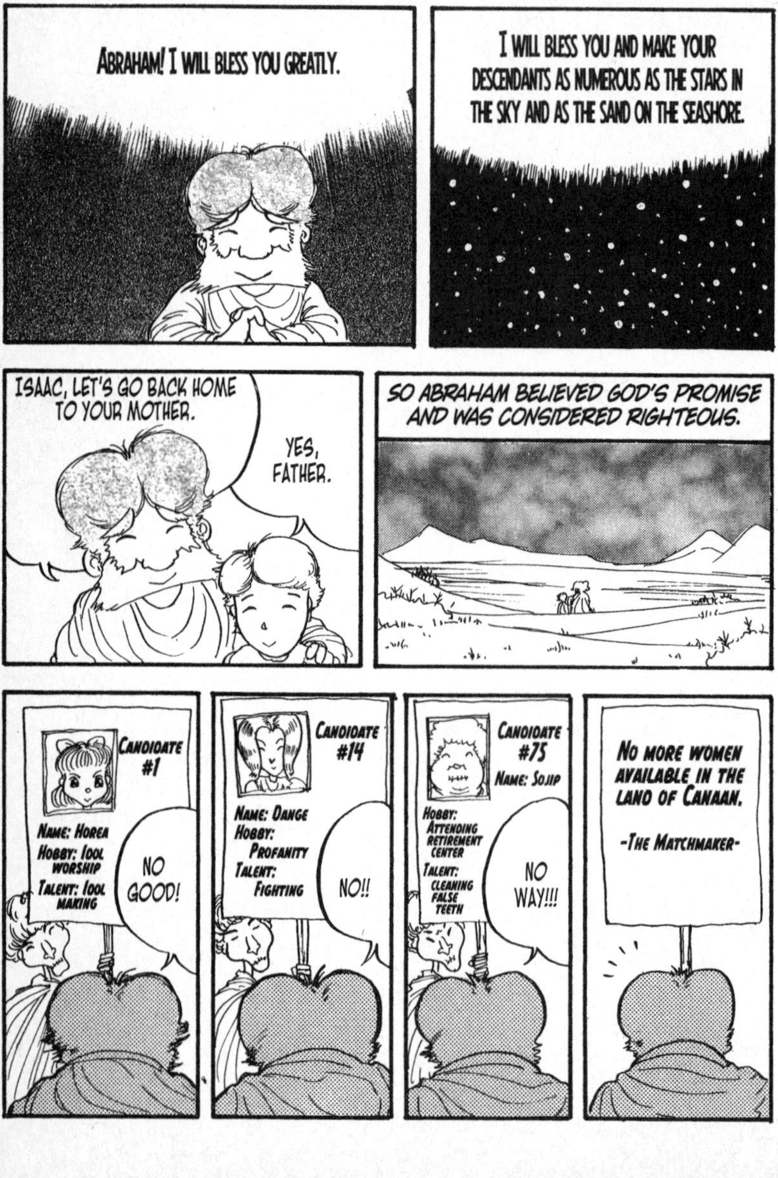
ABRAHAM! I WILL BLESS YOU GREATLY.
I WILL BLESS YOU AND MAKE YOUR DESCENDANTS AS NUMEROUS AS THE STARS IN THE SKY AND AS THE SAND ON THE SEASHORE.
ISAAC, LET'S GO BACK HOME TO YOUR MOTHER.
YES, FATHER.
SO ABRAHAM BELIEVED GOD'S PROMISE AND WAS CONSIDERED RIGHTEOUS.
CANDIDATE #1
NAME: HOREA
HOBBY: IDOL WORSHIP
TALENT: IDOL MAKING
NO GOOD!
CANDIDATE #14
NAME: DANGE
HOBBY: PROFANITY
TALENT: FIGHTING
NO!!
CANDIDATE #75
NAME: SOJIP
HOBBY: ATTENDING RETIREMENT CENTER
TALENT: CLEANING FALSE TEETH
NO WAY!!!
NO MORE WOMEN AVAILABLE IN THE LAND OF CANAAN.
-THE MATCHMAKER-

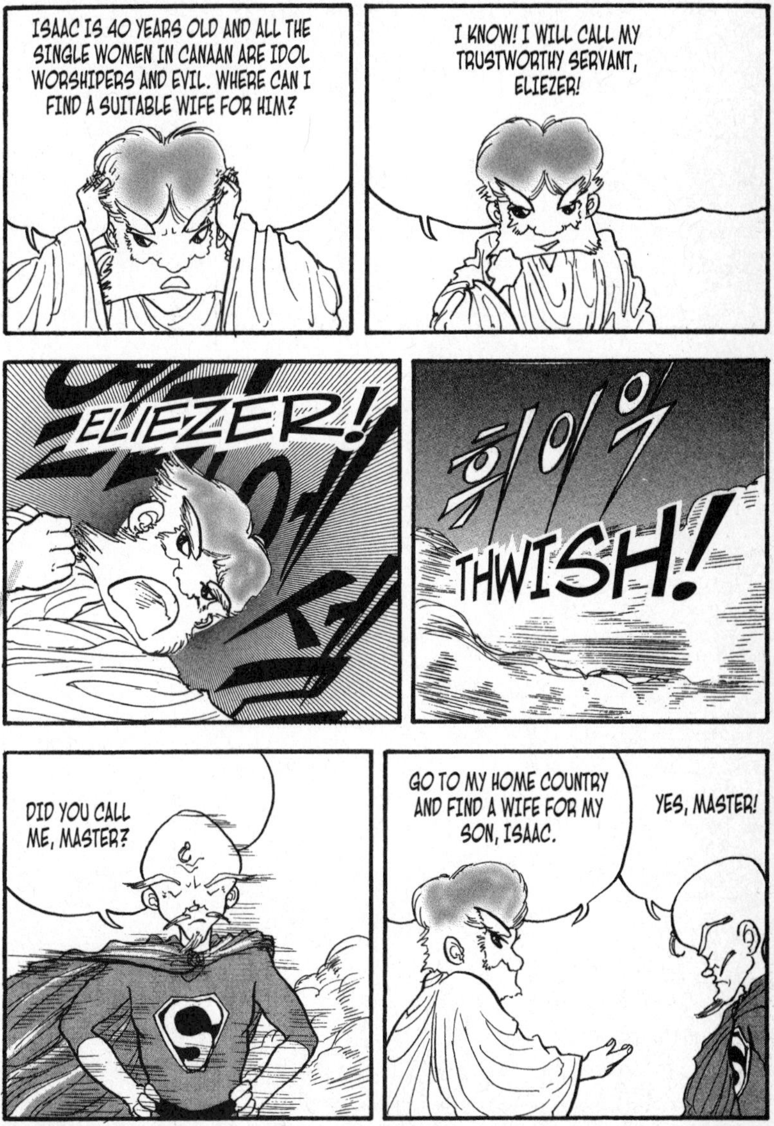
ISAAC IS 40 YEARS OLD AND ALL THE SINGLE WOMEN IN CANAAN ARE IDOL WORSHIPERS AND EVIL. WHERE CAN I FIND A SUITABLE WIFE FOR HIM?
I KNOW! I WILL CALL MY TRUSTWORTHY SERVANT, ELIEZER!
ELIEZER!
THWISH!
DID YOU CALL ME, MASTER?
GO TO MY HOME COUNTRY AND FIND A WIFE FOR MY SON, ISAAC.
YES, MASTER!

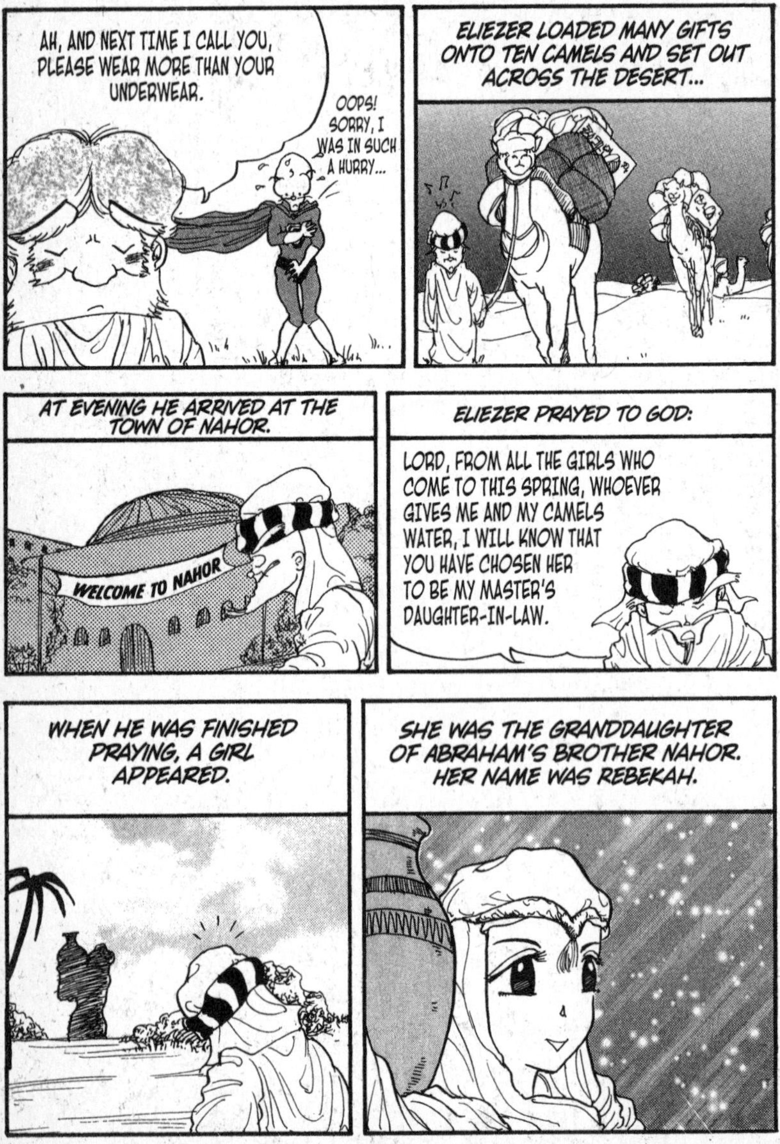
AH, AND NEXT TIME I CALL YOU, PLEASE WEAR MORE THAN YOUR UNDERWEAR.
OOPS! SORRY, I WAS IN SUCH A HURRY...
ELIEZER LOADED MANY GIFTS ONTO TEN CAMELS AND SET OUT ACROSS THE DESERT...
AT EVENING HE ARRIVED AT THE TOWN OF NAHOR.
WELCOME TO NAHOR
ELIEZER PRAYED TO GOD:
LORD, FROM ALL THE GIRLS WHO COME TO THIS SPRING, WHOEVER GIVES ME AND MY CAMELS WATER, I WILL KNOW THAT YOU HAVE CHOSEN HER TO BE MY MASTER'S DAUGHTER-IN-LAW.
WHEN HE WAS FINISHED PRAYING, A GIRL APPEARED.
SHE WAS THE GRANDDAUGHTER OF ABRAHAM'S BROTHER NAHOR. HER NAME WAS REBEKAH.

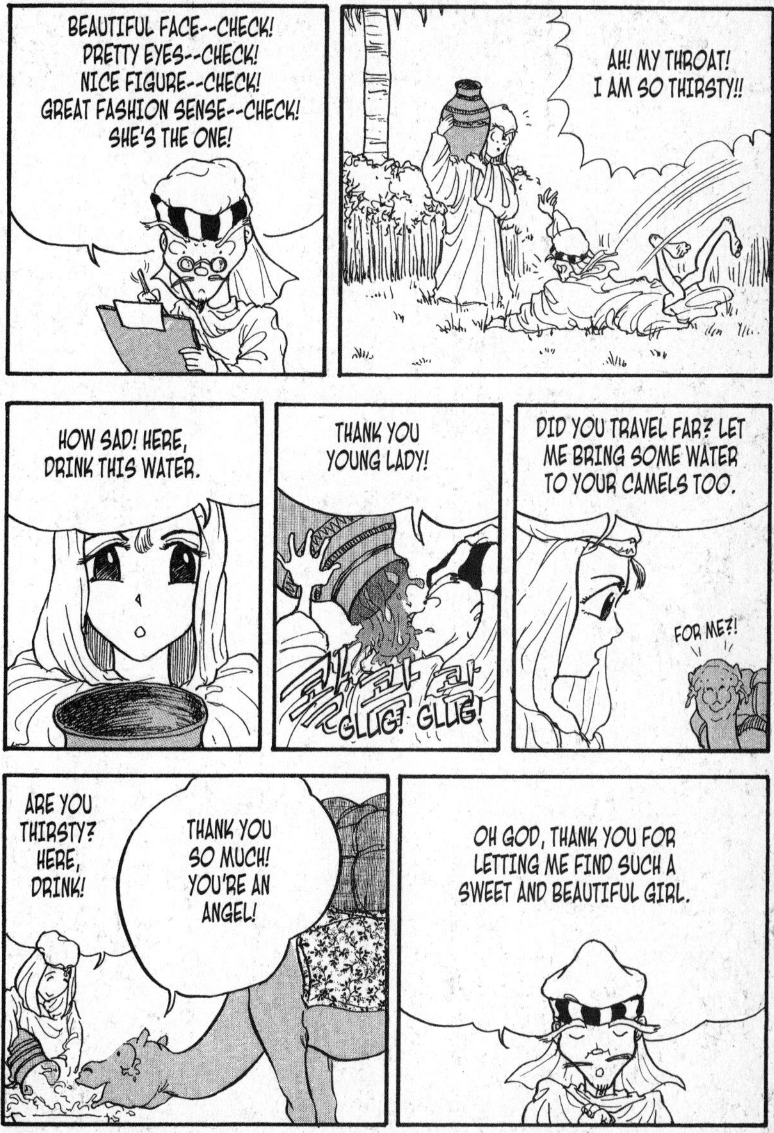
BEAUTIFUL FACE--CHECK! PRETTY EYES--CHECK! NICE FIGURE--CHECK! GREAT FASHION SENSE--CHECK! SHE'S THE ONE!
AH! MY THROAT! I AM SO THIRSTY!!
HOW SAD! HERE, DRINK THIS WATER.
THANK YOU YOUNG LADY!
GLUG! GLUG!
DID YOU TRAVEL FAR? LET ME BRING SOME WATER TO YOUR CAMELS TOO.
FOR ME?!
ARE YOU THIRSTY? HERE, DRINK!
THANK YOU SO MUCH! YOU'RE AN ANGEL!
OH GOD, THANK YOU FOR LETTING ME FIND SUCH A SWEET AND BEAUTIFUL GIRL.

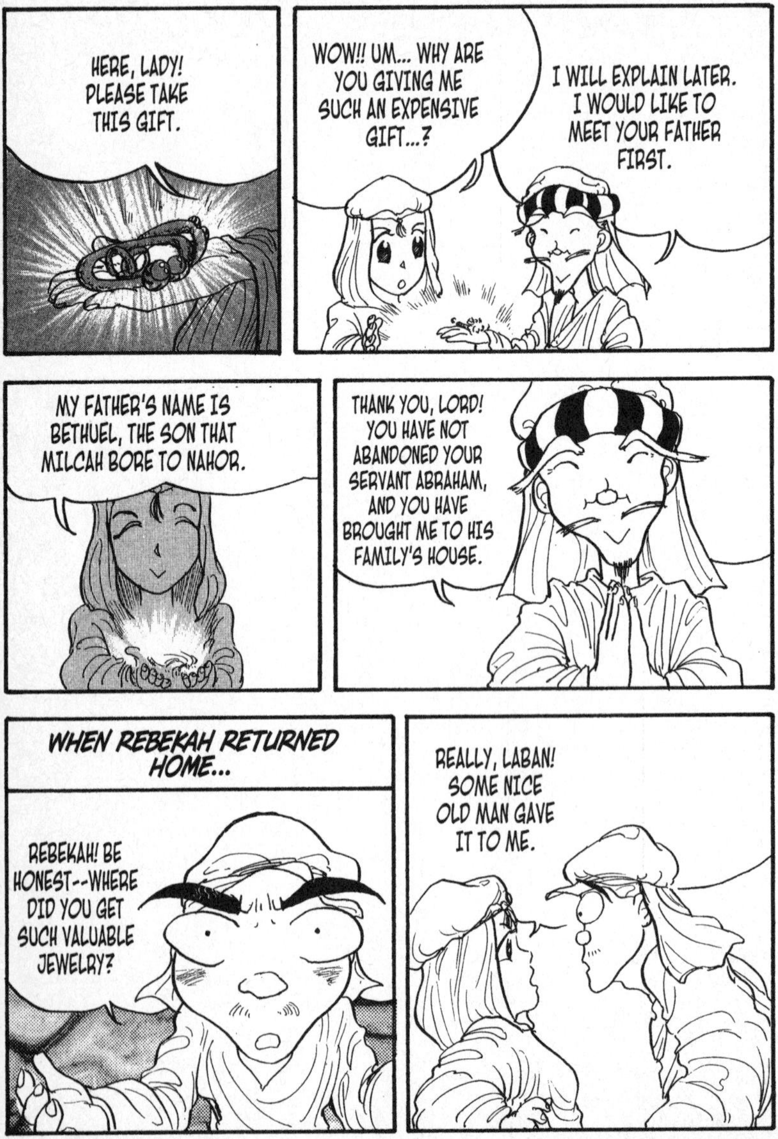
HERE, LADY! PLEASE TAKE THIS GIFT.
WOW!! UM... WHY ARE YOU GIVING ME SUCH AN EXPENSIVE GIFT...?
I WILL EXPLAIN LATER. I WOULD LIKE TO MEET YOUR FATHER FIRST.
MY FATHER'S NAME IS BETHUEL, THE SON THAT MILCAH BORE TO NAHOR.
THANK YOU, LORD! YOU HAVE NOT ABANDONED YOUR SERVANT ABRAHAM, AND YOU HAVE BROUGHT ME TO HIS FAMILY'S HOUSE.
WHEN REBEKAH RETURNED HOME...
REBEKAH! BE HONEST--WHERE DID YOU GET SUCH VALUABLE JEWELRY?
REALLY, LABAN! SOME NICE OLD MAN GAVE IT TO ME.

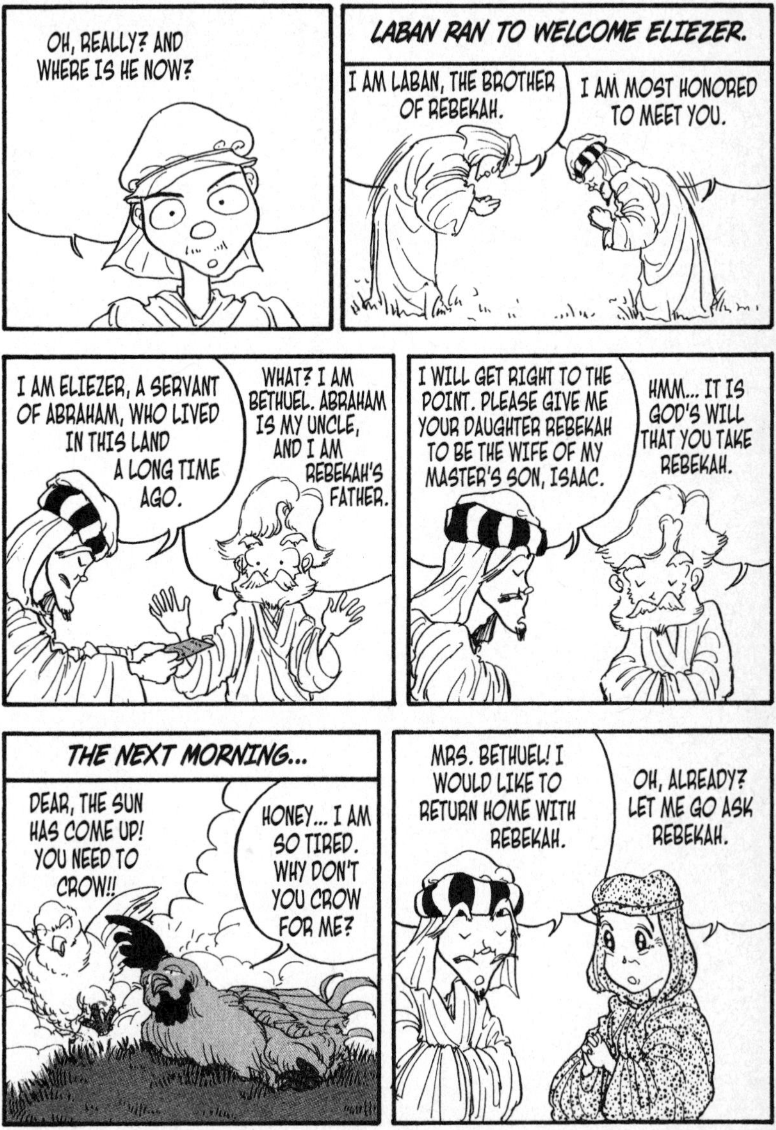
OH, REALLY? AND WHERE IS HE NOW?
LABAN RAN TO WELCOME ELIEZER.
I AM LABAN, THE BROTHER OF REBEKAH.
I AM MOST HONORED TO MEET YOU.
I AM ELIEZER, A SERVANT OF ABRAHAM, WHO LIVED IN THIS LAND A LONG TIME AGO.
WHAT? I AM BETHUEL. ABRAHAM IS MY UNCLE, AND I AM REBEKAH'S FATHER.
I WILL GET RIGHT TO THE POINT. PLEASE GIVE ME YOUR DAUGHTER REBEKAH TO BE THE WIFE OF MY MASTER'S SON, ISAAC.
HMM... IT IS GOD'S WILL THAT YOU TAKE REBEKAH.
THE NEXT MORNING...
DEAR, THE SUN HAS COME UP! YOU NEED TO CROW!!
HONEY... I AM SO TIRED. WHY DON'T YOU CROW FOR ME?
MRS. BETHUEL! I WOULD LIKE TO RETURN HOME WITH REBEKAH.
OH, ALREADY? LET ME GO ASK REBEKAH.

REBEKAH, WILL YOU LEAVE WITH HIM TODAY?

YES, MOTHER, I WILL.

LABAN BLESSED HIS SISTER REBEKAH.

REBEKAH, GO AND BE HAPPY... SOB!!

BLESS, BLESS, BLESS

ELIEZER LEFT WITH REBEKAH TO GO TO ABRAHAM.

OOPS! IT'S MY BOSS!

HEY YOU! DO YOU HAVE TO BE IN THIS SCENE?? YOU CAN BE DRAWING ANYTHING YOU WANT!! CHANGE IT RIGHT AWAY!!

AW! IT'S ALREADY DRAWN! CAN'T I JUST LEAVE IT THE WAY IT IS?

ISAAC WAS PRAYING OUT IN THE FIELD.

DEAR LORD, MAY THE WIFE ELIEZER BRINGS BE BEAUTIFUL, BUT MAY SHE ALSO BELIEVE IN YOU LIKE I DO!

I AM AFRAID OF HAVING A WOMAN WHO DOES NOT LOVE YOU. I DO NOT WANT A WOMAN WITH AN UGLY HEART (AND PREFERABLY NOT AN UGLY **FACE** EITHER!!).

AHH!

ELIEZER IS COMING HOME!

ISAAC FELL IN LOVE WITH REBEKAH, AND THEY MARRIED.

ISAAC AND REBEKAH WERE HAPPY, BUT ISAAC WAS SIXTY YEARS OLD, AND REBEKAH HAD NOT BORNE HIM ANY CHILDREN.

MY DEAR, LET US ASK GOD FOR CHILDREN.

YES, LET'S PRAY TO GOD FOR A SON.

GOD, PLEASE GIVE US A SON.

LORD, PLEASE GIVE US A SON.

GOD ANSWERED REBEKAH'S PRAYER.

WHAM! BIFF! POW!

MY HUSBAND! I THINK THE BABIES ARE FIGHTING IN MY STOMACH.

WHAT! DO YOU MEAN YOU ARE HAVING TWINS?!! THAT'S WONDERFUL!

ARE YOU KIDDING ME? I CAN'T EVEN SLEEP AT NIGHT BECAUSE OF THE FIGHTING.

WHAM!

POW!

BAM!

WHY DON'T YOU ASK GOD WHAT'S HAPPENING?

GOD, MY CHILDREN ARE FIGHTING IN MY STOMACH! WHAT CAN I DO?

GOD ANSWERED:

TWO NATIONS ARE FIGHTING IN YOUR WOMB--AND THE OLDER WILL SERVE THE YOUNGER.

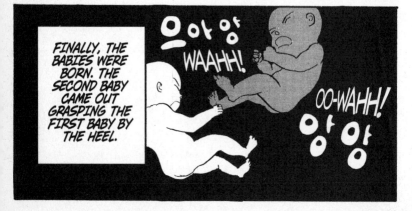

FINALLY, THE BABIES WERE BORN. THE SECOND BABY CAME OUT GRASPING THE FIRST BABY BY THE HEEL.

WAAHH!

OO-WAHH!

THE FIRST TO COME OUT WAS RED, AND HIS WHOLE BODY WAS LIKE A HAIRY GARMENT; SO THEY NAMED HIM ESAU.

IT WAS SO SCARY; THEN I SAW THIS BRIGHT LIGHT ALL AROUND ME...

THE SECOND BABY CAME OUT HOLDING HIS BROTHER'S HEEL; SO HE WAS NAMED JACOB.

HE WAS TRYING TO GET OUT IN FRONT OF ME, SO I GRABBED THE FIRST THING I COULD...

FATHER ISAAC LOVED ESAU BECAUSE HE GREW UP BIG AND STRONG, AND HAD A HEARTY APPETITE.

I'M HUNGRY...

ESAU WAS ALSO A SKILLFUL HUNTER.

FATHER, I'M GOING HUNTING.

YES, GO HAVE FUN!

A SHORT WHILE LATER...

I'M BACK, FATHER.

OH! OH! OH!!

WHAT KIND OF MEAT WOULD YOU LIKE? I CAN COOK ANYTHING!

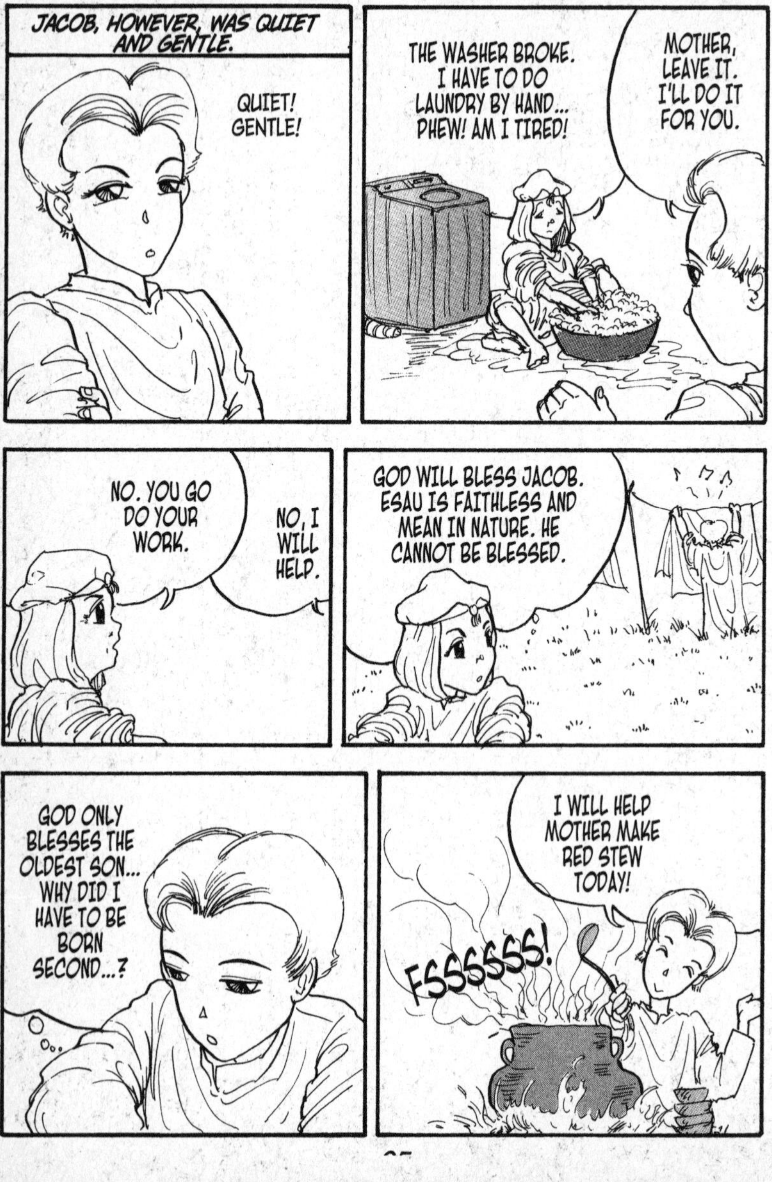
JACOB, HOWEVER, WAS QUIET AND GENTLE.
QUIET! GENTLE!
THE WASHER BROKE. I HAVE TO DO LAUNDRY BY HAND... PHEW! AM I TIRED!
MOTHER, LEAVE IT. I'LL DO IT FOR YOU.
NO. YOU GO DO YOUR WORK.
NO, I WILL HELP.
GOD WILL BLESS JACOB. ESAU IS FAITHLESS AND MEAN IN NATURE. HE CANNOT BE BLESSED.
GOD ONLY BLESSES THE OLDEST SON... WHY DID I HAVE TO BE BORN SECOND...?
I WILL HELP MOTHER MAKE RED STEW TODAY!
FSSSSSS!

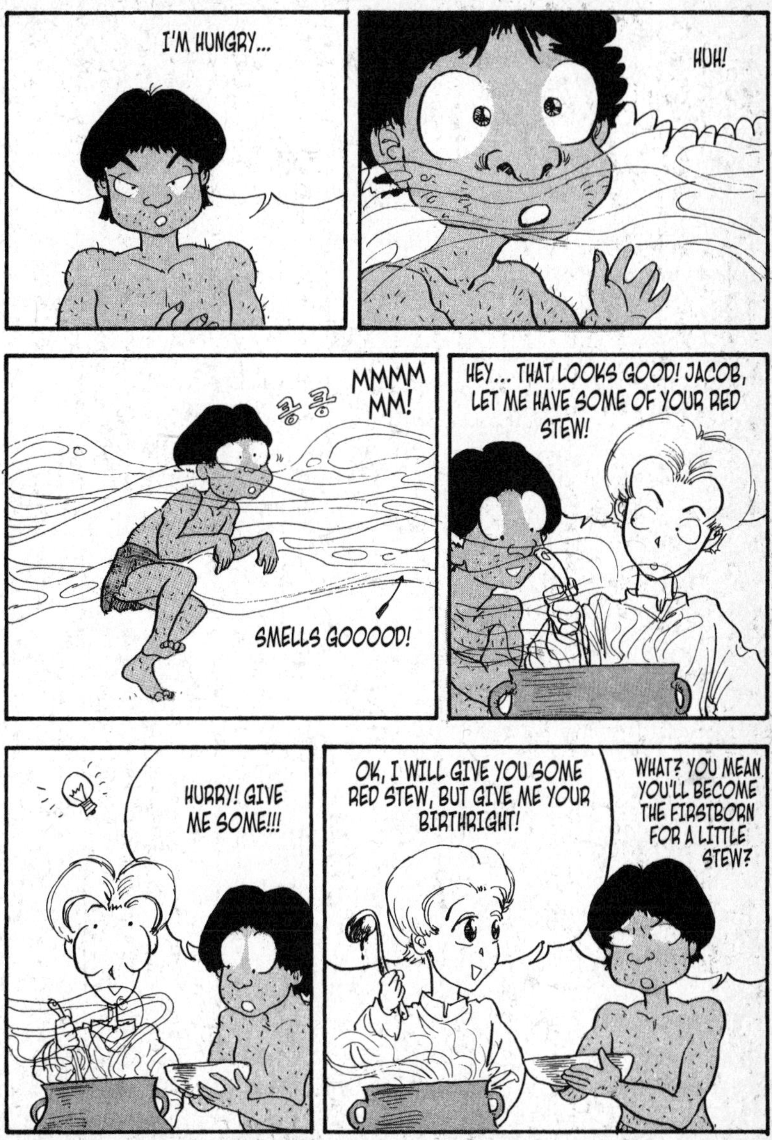
I'M HUNGRY...
HUH!
킁킁
MMMM MM!
SMELLS GOOOOD!
HEY... THAT LOOKS GOOD! JACOB, LET ME HAVE SOME OF YOUR RED STEW!
HURRY! GIVE ME SOME!!!
OK, I WILL GIVE YOU SOME RED STEW, BUT GIVE ME YOUR BIRTHRIGHT!
WHAT? YOU MEAN YOU'LL BECOME THE FIRSTBORN FOR A LITTLE STEW?

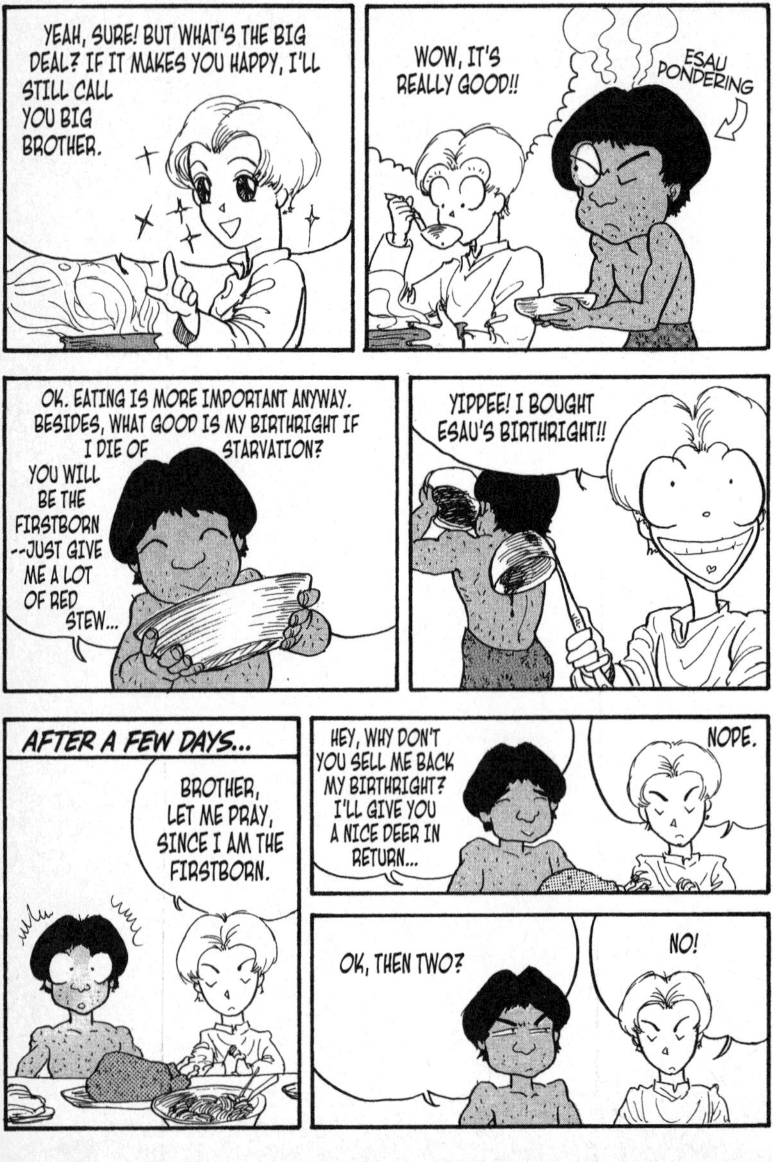
YEAH, SURE! BUT WHAT'S THE BIG DEAL? IF IT MAKES YOU HAPPY, I'LL STILL CALL YOU BIG BROTHER.
WOW, IT'S REALLY GOOD!!
ESAU PONDERING
OK. EATING IS MORE IMPORTANT ANYWAY. BESIDES, WHAT GOOD IS MY BIRTHRIGHT IF I DIE OF STARVATION? YOU WILL BE THE FIRSTBORN --JUST GIVE ME A LOT OF RED STEW...
YIPPEE! I BOUGHT ESAU'S BIRTHRIGHT!!
AFTER A FEW DAYS...
BROTHER, LET ME PRAY, SINCE I AM THE FIRSTBORN.
HEY, WHY DON'T YOU SELL ME BACK MY BIRTHRIGHT? I'LL GIVE YOU A NICE DEER IN RETURN...
NOPE.
OK, THEN TWO?
NO!

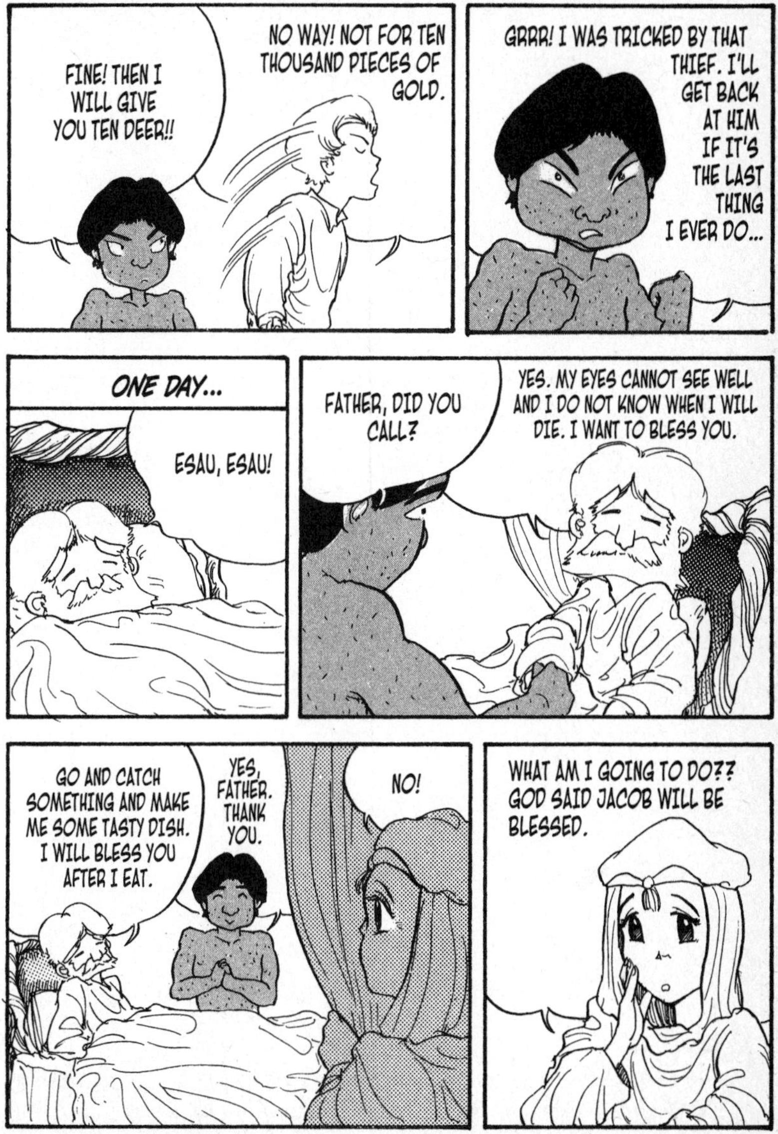
FINE! THEN I WILL GIVE YOU TEN DEER!!
NO WAY! NOT FOR TEN THOUSAND PIECES OF GOLD.
GRRR! I WAS TRICKED BY THAT THIEF. I'LL GET BACK AT HIM IF IT'S THE LAST THING I EVER DO...
ONE DAY...
ESAU, ESAU!
FATHER, DID YOU CALL?
YES. MY EYES CANNOT SEE WELL AND I DO NOT KNOW WHEN I WILL DIE. I WANT TO BLESS YOU.
GO AND CATCH SOMETHING AND MAKE ME SOME TASTY DISH. I WILL BLESS YOU AFTER I EAT.
YES, FATHER. THANK YOU.
NO!
WHAT AM I GOING TO DO?? GOD SAID JACOB WILL BE BLESSED.

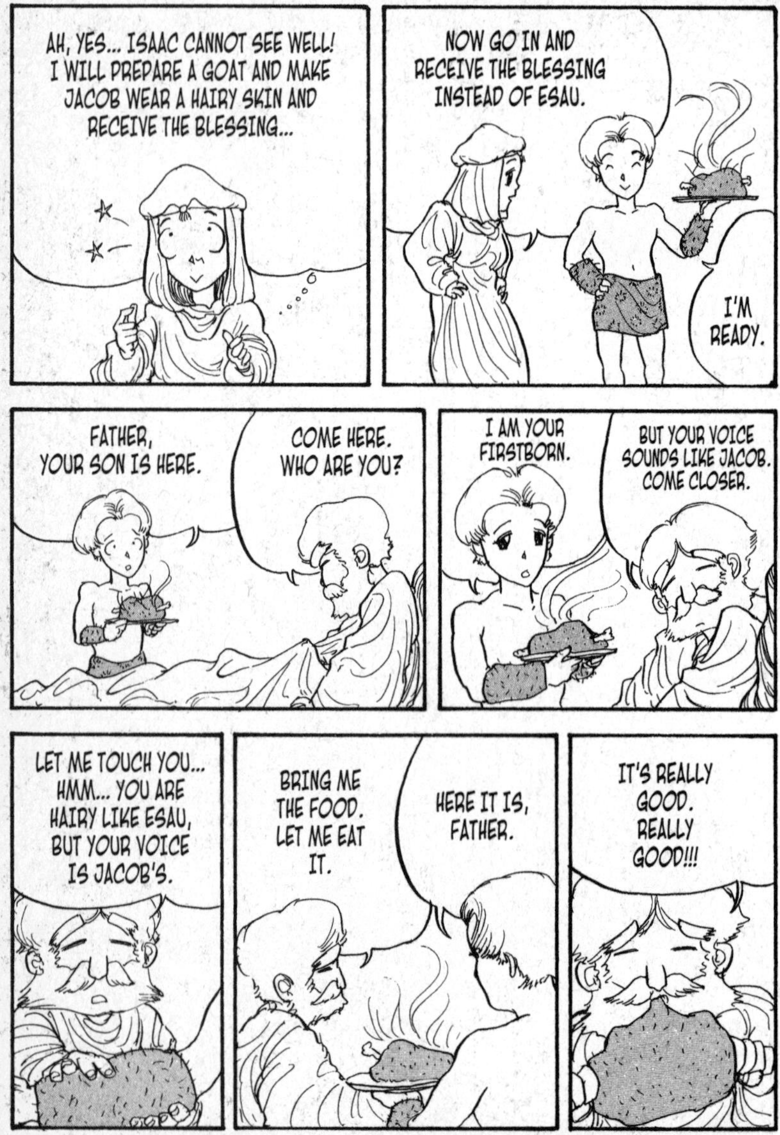
AH, YES... ISAAC CANNOT SEE WELL! I WILL PREPARE A GOAT AND MAKE JACOB WEAR A HAIRY SKIN AND RECEIVE THE BLESSING...
NOW GO IN AND RECEIVE THE BLESSING INSTEAD OF ESAU.
I'M READY.
FATHER, YOUR SON IS HERE.
COME HERE. WHO ARE YOU?
I AM YOUR FIRSTBORN.
BUT YOUR VOICE SOUNDS LIKE JACOB. COME CLOSER.
LET ME TOUCH YOU... HMM... YOU ARE HAIRY LIKE ESAU, BUT YOUR VOICE IS JACOB'S.
BRING ME THE FOOD. LET ME EAT IT.
HERE IT IS, FATHER.
IT'S REALLY GOOD. REALLY GOOD!!!

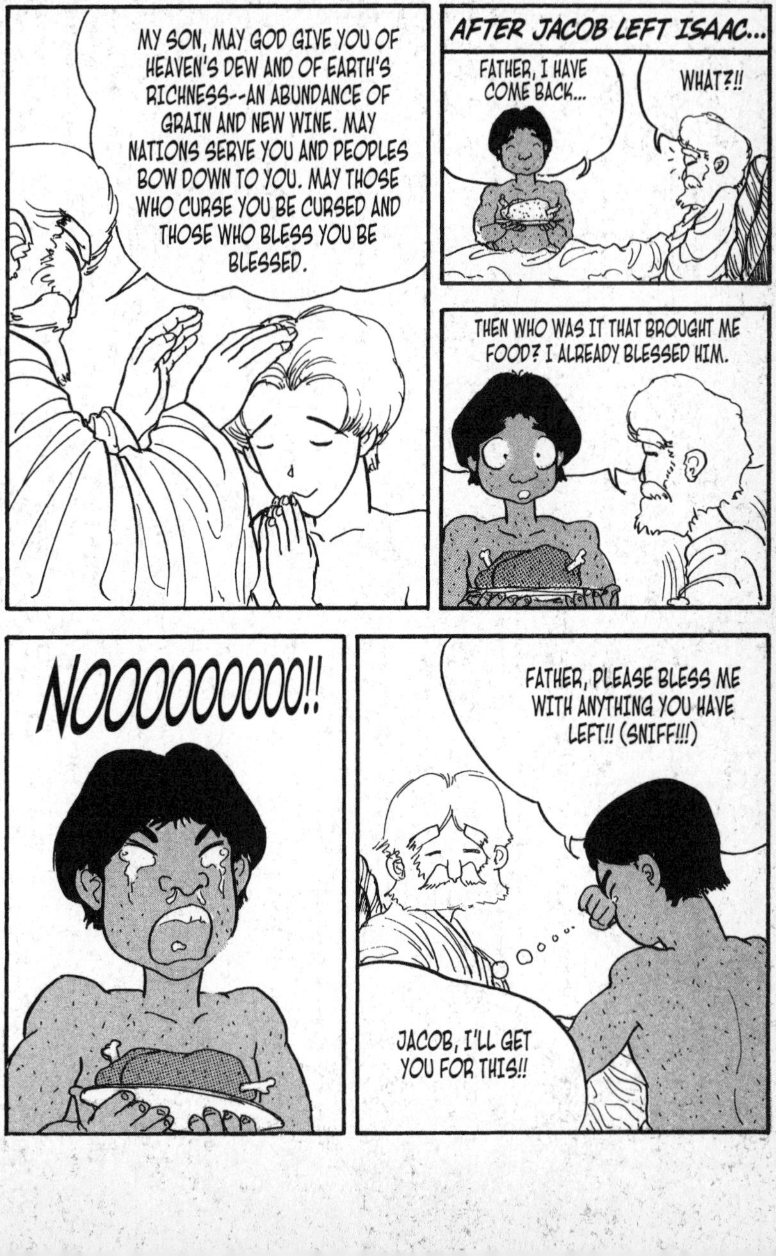
MY SON, MAY GOD GIVE YOU OF HEAVEN'S DEW AND OF EARTH'S RICHNESS--AN ABUNDANCE OF GRAIN AND NEW WINE. MAY NATIONS SERVE YOU AND PEOPLES BOW DOWN TO YOU. MAY THOSE WHO CURSE YOU BE CURSED AND THOSE WHO BLESS YOU BE BLESSED.
AFTER JACOB LEFT ISAAC...
FATHER, I HAVE COME BACK...
WHAT?!!
THEN WHO WAS IT THAT BROUGHT ME FOOD? I ALREADY BLESSED HIM.
NOOOOOOOOO!!
FATHER, PLEASE BLESS ME WITH ANYTHING YOU HAVE LEFT!! (SNIFF!!!)
JACOB, I'LL GET YOU FOR THIS!!

YOU WILL LIVE BY THE SWORD AND YOU WILL SERVE YOUR BROTHER.

WHAT KIND OF BLESSING IS THAT?

WHEN FATHER DIES I'LL KILL JACOB ONCE AND FOR ALL...

KRAKK!!

MY CHILD, YOUR BROTHER WILL HARM YOU IF YOU STAY HERE. GO TO YOUR UNCLE LABAN'S HOUSE AND COME BACK WHEN YOUR BROTHER'S ANGER HAS SUBSIDED.

DEAR, I AM NOT PLEASED THAT ESAU HAS MARRIED GENTILE WOMEN. I'M AFRAID JACOB WILL BE INFLUENCED TO DO THE SAME; LET'S SEND JACOB TO HIS UNCLE'S HOUSE.

TAKE CARE OF YOURSELF, MY SON. GOD WILL PROTECT YOU.

FATHER, MOTHER! GOOD-BYE...

JACOB LEFT FOR HIS UNCLE'S HOUSE IN PADDAN ARAM.

PADDAN ARAM - 2,000 STEPS AWAY -

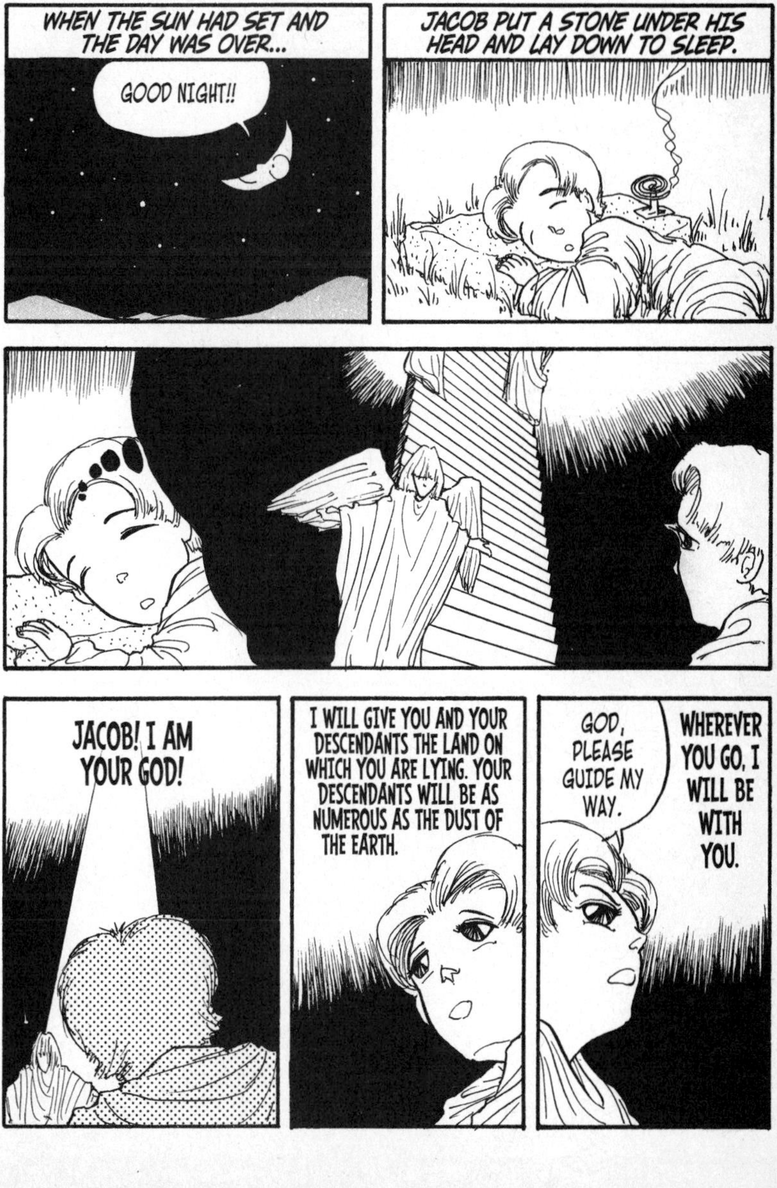
WHEN THE SUN HAD SET AND THE DAY WAS OVER...
GOOD NIGHT!!
JACOB PUT A STONE UNDER HIS HEAD AND LAY DOWN TO SLEEP.
JACOB! I AM YOUR GOD!
I WILL GIVE YOU AND YOUR DESCENDANTS THE LAND ON WHICH YOU ARE LYING. YOUR DESCENDANTS WILL BE AS NUMEROUS AS THE DUST OF THE EARTH.
GOD, PLEASE GUIDE MY WAY.
WHEREVER YOU GO, I WILL BE WITH YOU.

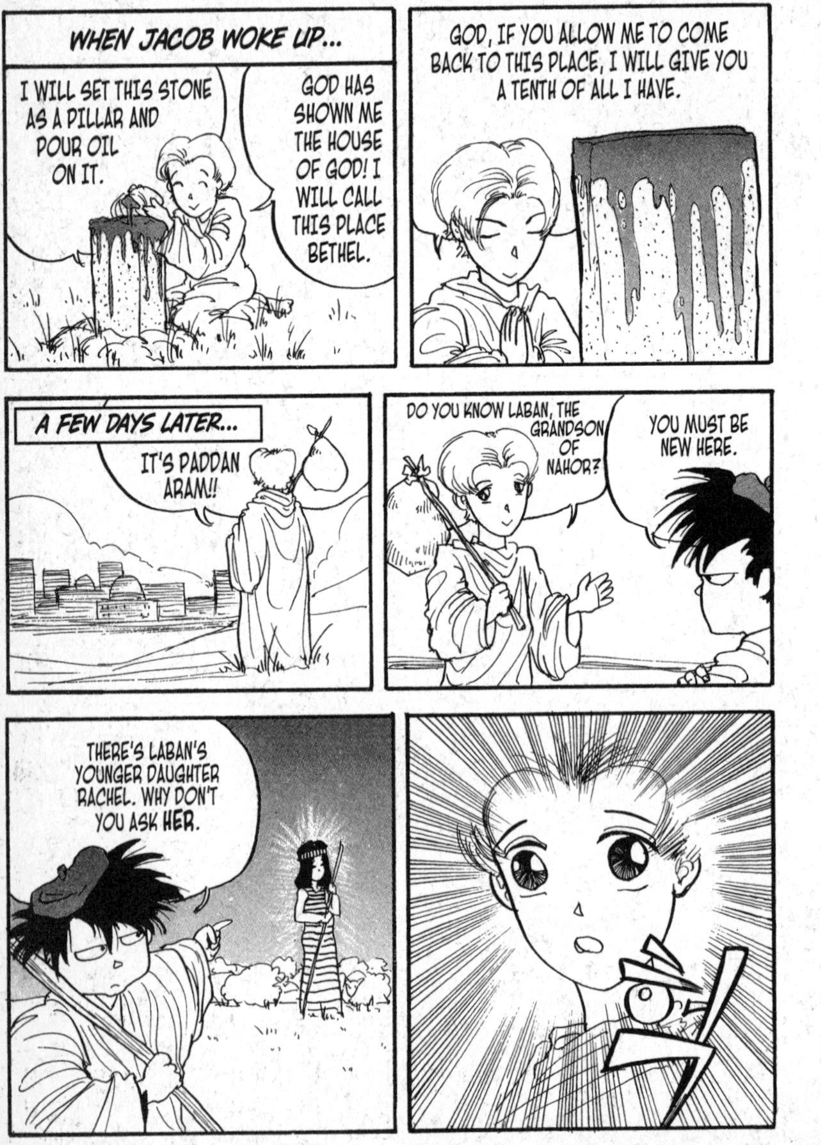
WHEN JACOB WOKE UP...
I WILL SET THIS STONE AS A PILLAR AND POUR OIL ON IT.
GOD HAS SHOWN ME THE HOUSE OF GOD! I WILL CALL THIS PLACE BETHEL.
GOD, IF YOU ALLOW ME TO COME BACK TO THIS PLACE, I WILL GIVE YOU A TENTH OF ALL I HAVE.
A FEW DAYS LATER...
IT'S PADDAN ARAM!!
DO YOU KNOW LABAN, THE GRANDSON OF NAHOR?
YOU MUST BE NEW HERE.
THERE'S LABAN'S YOUNGER DAUGHTER RACHEL. WHY DON'T YOU ASK HER.

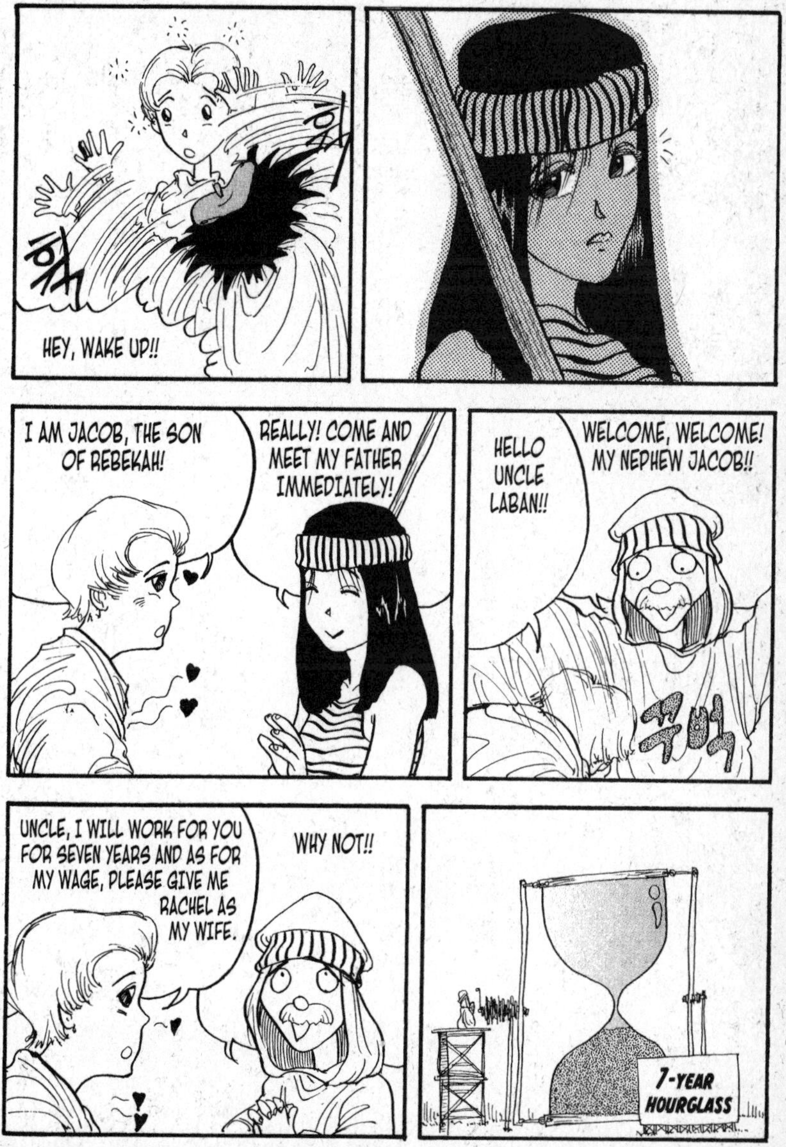
HEY, WAKE UP!!
I AM JACOB, THE SON OF REBEKAH!
REALLY! COME AND MEET MY FATHER IMMEDIATELY!
HELLO UNCLE LABAN!!
WELCOME, WELCOME! MY NEPHEW JACOB!!
UNCLE, I WILL WORK FOR YOU FOR SEVEN YEARS AND AS FOR MY WAGE, PLEASE GIVE ME RACHEL AS MY WIFE.
WHY NOT!!
7-YEAR HOURGLASS

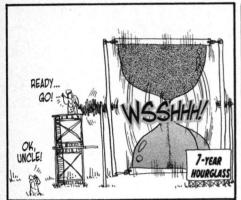

READY... GO!

OK, UNCLE!

WSSHHH!

7-YEAR HOURGLASS

SEVEN YEARS HAVE PASSED.

7-YEAR HOURGLASS

SEVEN YEARS HAVE PASSED, BUT I AM NOT GOING TO GIVE RACHEL TO JACOB... HE'S A HARD WORKER AND I WANT TO USE HIM SOME MORE... HEE HEE!!

HEY, JACOB! HERE IS YOUR BRIDE.

I AM LEAH, RACHEL'S OLDER SISTER... MY HUSBAND!

WHAT!! AW! NO WAY! I CAN'T BELIEVE IT!!

OH NO, UNCLE!! YOU BROKE YOUR PROMISE!!

IN OUR VILLAGE, THE FRONT CAR HAS TO MOVE BEFORE THE BACK CAR CAN GO--THE OLDER SISTER GETS MARRIED FIRST!

OK LOOK, I WILL GIVE YOU RACHEL. IN RETURN, YOU WILL WORK FOR SEVEN MORE YEARS.

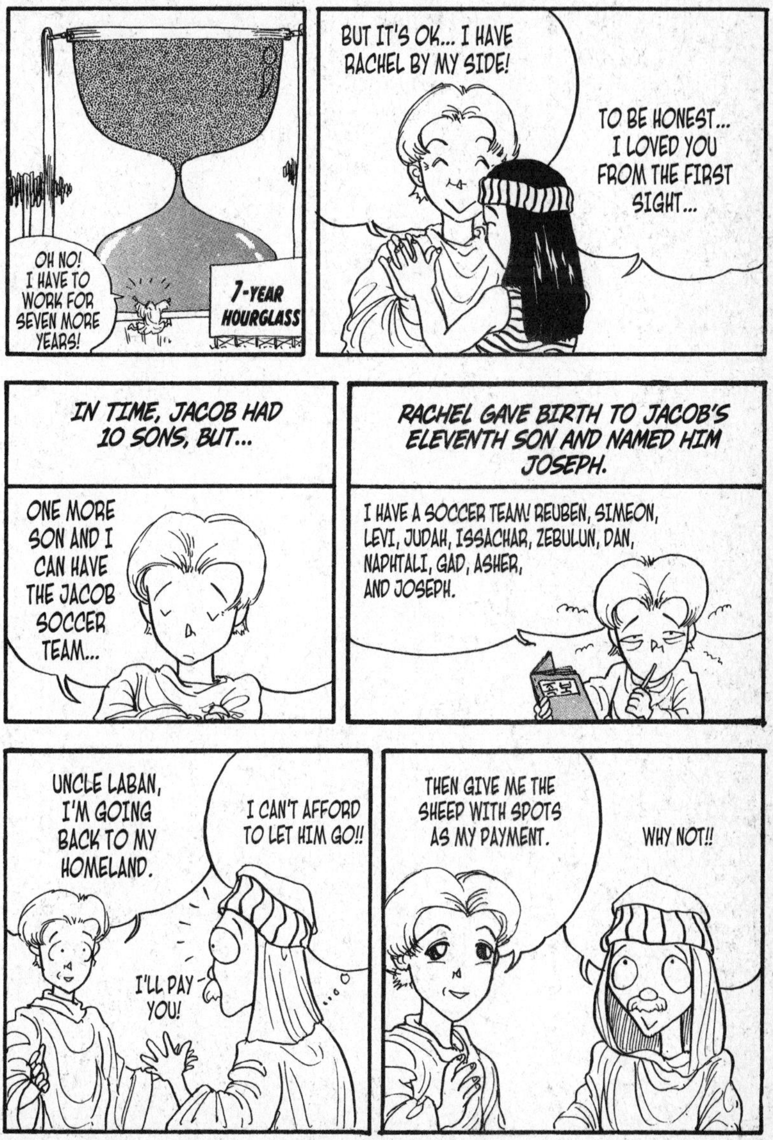
OH NO! I HAVE TO WORK FOR SEVEN MORE YEARS!
7-YEAR HOURGLASS
BUT IT'S OK... I HAVE RACHEL BY MY SIDE!
TO BE HONEST... I LOVED YOU FROM THE FIRST SIGHT...
IN TIME, JACOB HAD 10 SONS, BUT...
ONE MORE SON AND I CAN HAVE THE JACOB SOCCER TEAM...
RACHEL GAVE BIRTH TO JACOB'S ELEVENTH SON AND NAMED HIM JOSEPH.
I HAVE A SOCCER TEAM! REUBEN, SIMEON, LEVI, JUDAH, ISSACHAR, ZEBULUN, DAN, NAPHTALI, GAD, ASHER, AND JOSEPH.
족보
UNCLE LABAN, I'M GOING BACK TO MY HOMELAND.
I CAN'T AFFORD TO LET HIM GO!!
I'LL PAY YOU!
THEN GIVE ME THE SHEEP WITH SPOTS AS MY PAYMENT.
WHY NOT!!

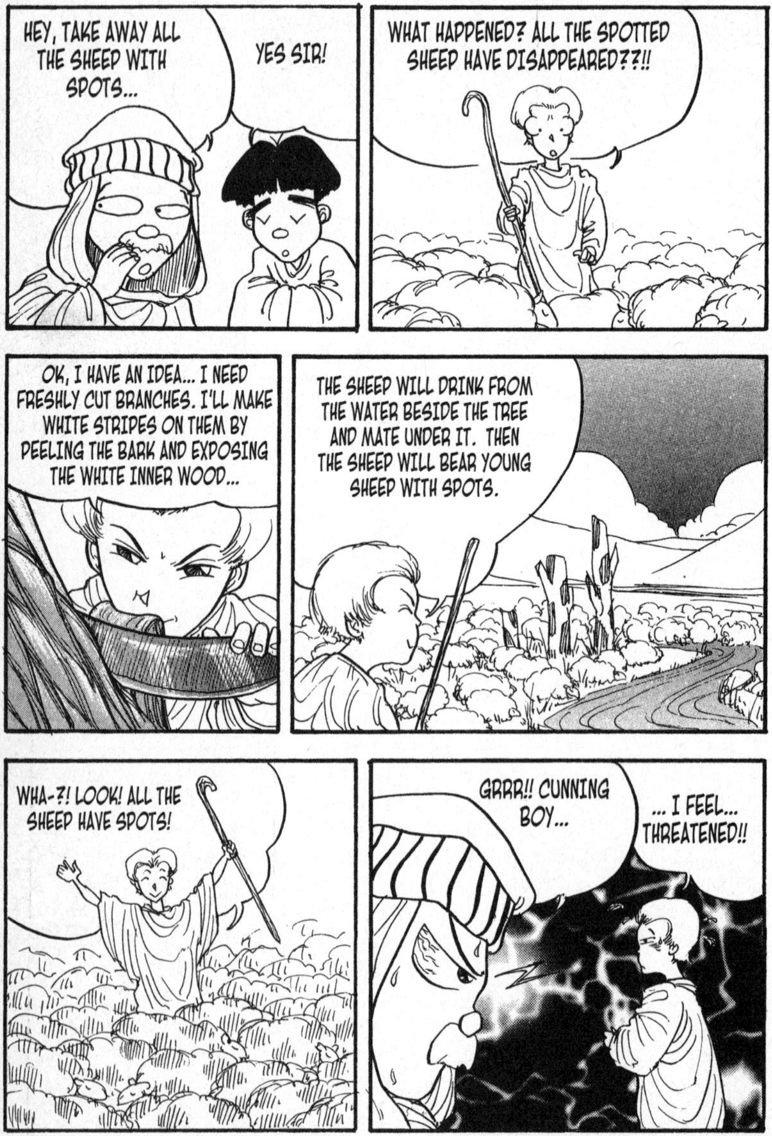
HEY, TAKE AWAY ALL THE SHEEP WITH SPOTS...
YES SIR!
WHAT HAPPENED? ALL THE SPOTTED SHEEP HAVE DISAPPEARED??!!
OK, I HAVE AN IDEA... I NEED FRESHLY CUT BRANCHES. I'LL MAKE WHITE STRIPES ON THEM BY PEELING THE BARK AND EXPOSING THE WHITE INNER WOOD...
THE SHEEP WILL DRINK FROM THE WATER BESIDE THE TREE AND MATE UNDER IT. THEN THE SHEEP WILL BEAR YOUNG SHEEP WITH SPOTS.
WHA-?! LOOK! ALL THE SHEEP HAVE SPOTS!
GRRR!! CUNNING BOY...
... I FEEL... THREATENED!!

HONEY, YOUR FATHER IS ACTING STRANGE. LET'S LEAVE THIS PLACE TONIGHT.
I'LL PACK IMMEDI-ATELY.
I'M TAKING FATHER'S SOLID GOLD IDOL!
LET'S REST OVER THERE BY THE MOUNTAINS OF GILEAD!
WHAT?! JACOB TOOK EVERYTHING AND RAN AWAY??
ATTACK! CHARGE!!!
IT'S ALREADY BEEN A WEEK... HOW FAR DID HE RUN AWAY?!

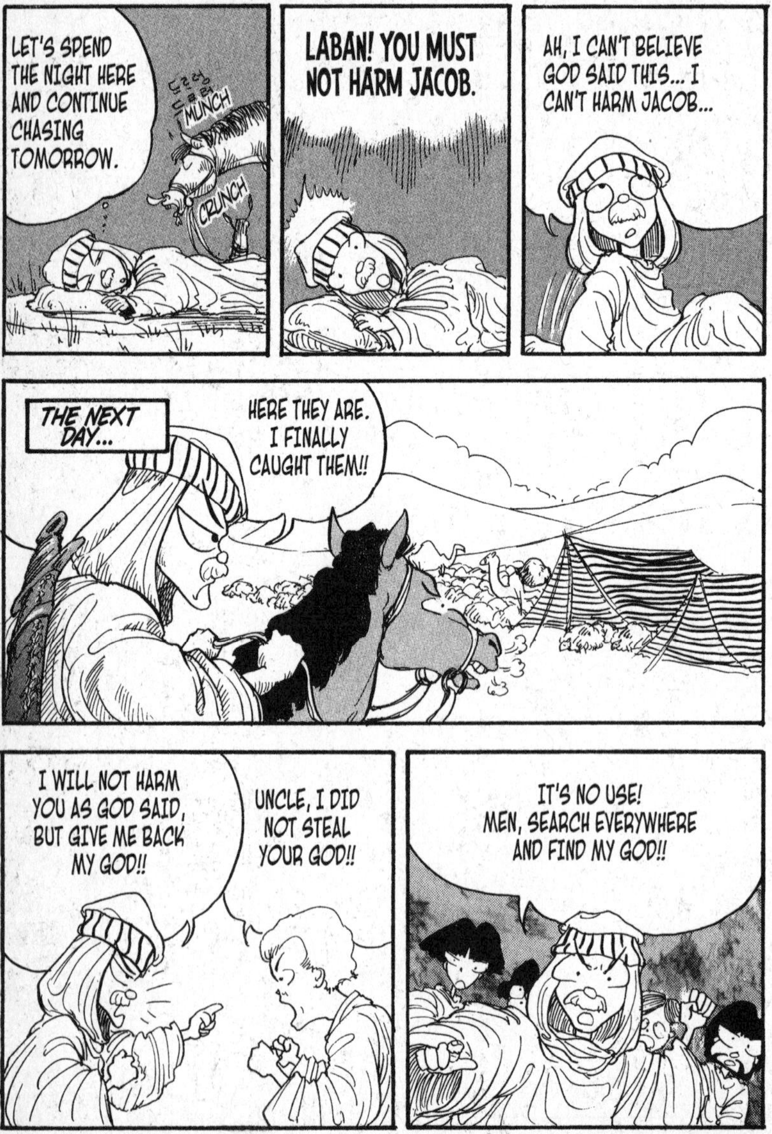
LET'S SPEND THE NIGHT HERE AND CONTINUE CHASING TOMORROW.
MUNCH
CRUNCH
LABAN! YOU MUST NOT HARM JACOB.
AH, I CAN'T BELIEVE GOD SAID THIS... I CAN'T HARM JACOB...
THE NEXT DAY...
HERE THEY ARE. I FINALLY CAUGHT THEM!!
I WILL NOT HARM YOU AS GOD SAID, BUT GIVE ME BACK MY GOD!!
UNCLE, I DID NOT STEAL YOUR GOD!!
IT'S NO USE! MEN, SEARCH EVERYWHERE AND FIND MY GOD!!

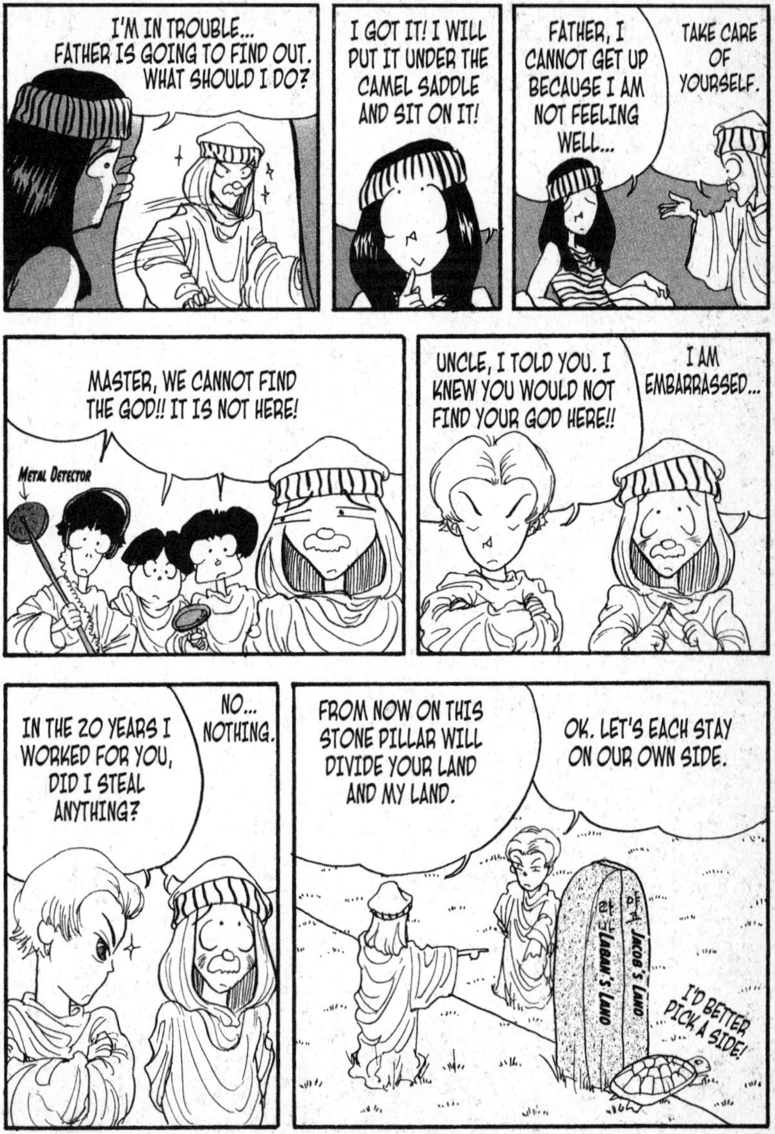
I'M IN TROUBLE... FATHER IS GOING TO FIND OUT. WHAT SHOULD I DO?
I GOT IT! I WILL PUT IT UNDER THE CAMEL SADDLE AND SIT ON IT!
FATHER, I CANNOT GET UP BECAUSE I AM NOT FEELING WELL...
TAKE CARE OF YOURSELF.
MASTER, WE CANNOT FIND THE GOD!! IT IS NOT HERE!
METAL DETECTOR
UNCLE, I TOLD YOU. I KNEW YOU WOULD NOT FIND YOUR GOD HERE!!
I AM EMBARRASSED...
IN THE 20 YEARS I WORKED FOR YOU, DID I STEAL ANYTHING?
NO... NOTHING.
FROM NOW ON THIS STONE PILLAR WILL DIVIDE YOUR LAND AND MY LAND.
OK. LET'S EACH STAY ON OUR OWN SIDE.
JACOB'S LAND
LABAN'S LAND
I'D BETTER PICK A SIDE!

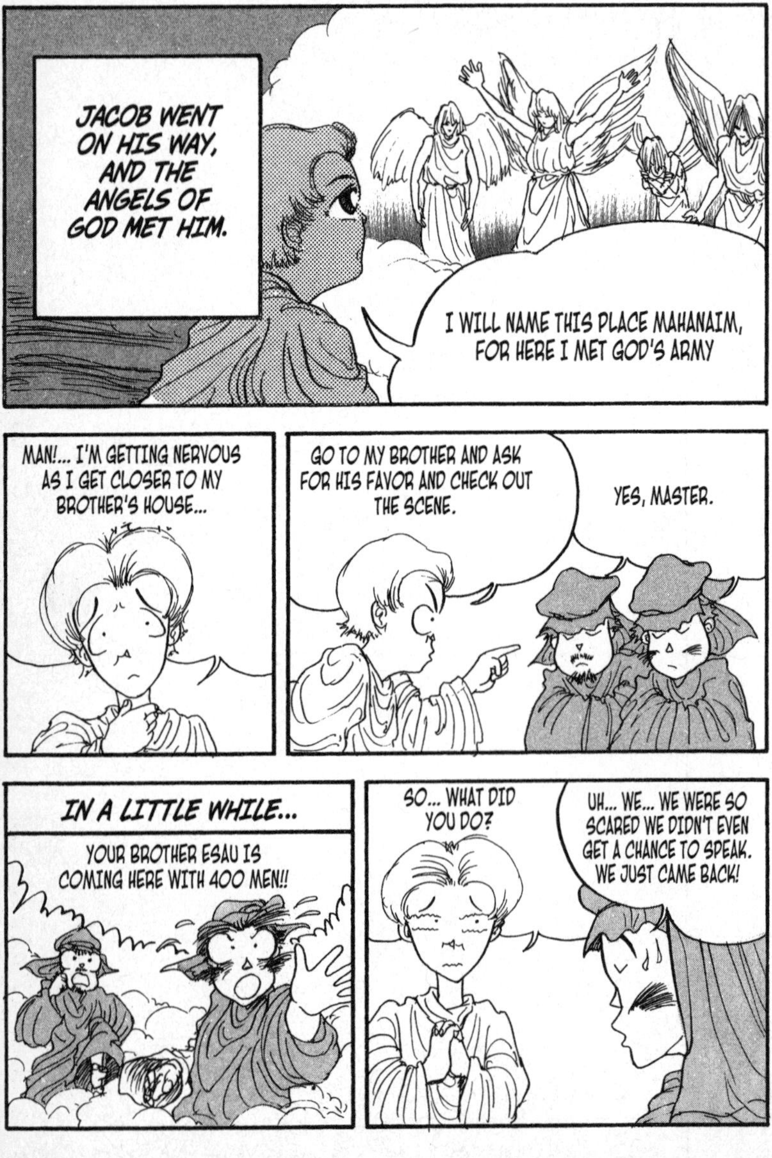
JACOB WENT ON HIS WAY, AND THE ANGELS OF GOD MET HIM.
I WILL NAME THIS PLACE MAHANAIM, FOR HERE I MET GOD'S ARMY
MAN!... I'M GETTING NERVOUS AS I GET CLOSER TO MY BROTHER'S HOUSE...
GO TO MY BROTHER AND ASK FOR HIS FAVOR AND CHECK OUT THE SCENE.
YES, MASTER.
IN A LITTLE WHILE...
YOUR BROTHER ESAU IS COMING HERE WITH 400 MEN!!
SO... WHAT DID YOU DO?
UH... WE... WE WERE SO SCARED WE DIDN'T EVEN GET A CHANCE TO SPEAK. WE JUST CAME BACK!

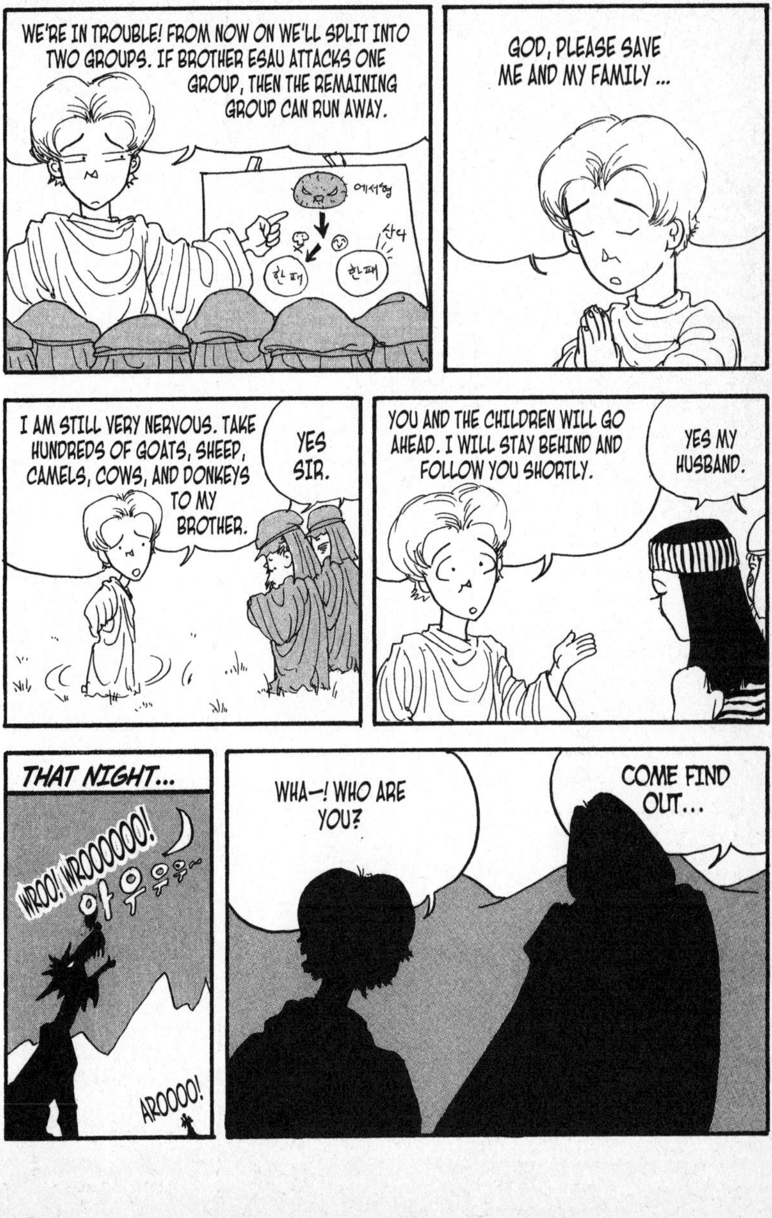
WE'RE IN TROUBLE! FROM NOW ON WE'LL SPLIT INTO TWO GROUPS. IF BROTHER ESAU ATTACKS ONE GROUP, THEN THE REMAINING GROUP CAN RUN AWAY.
에서형
한패
한패
GOD, PLEASE SAVE ME AND MY FAMILY ...
I AM STILL VERY NERVOUS. TAKE HUNDREDS OF GOATS, SHEEP, CAMELS, COWS, AND DONKEYS TO MY BROTHER.
YES SIR.
YOU AND THE CHILDREN WILL GO AHEAD. I WILL STAY BEHIND AND FOLLOW YOU SHORTLY.
YES MY HUSBAND.
THAT NIGHT...
WROO! WROOOOOOO!
AROOOO!
WHA—! WHO ARE YOU?
COME FIND OUT...

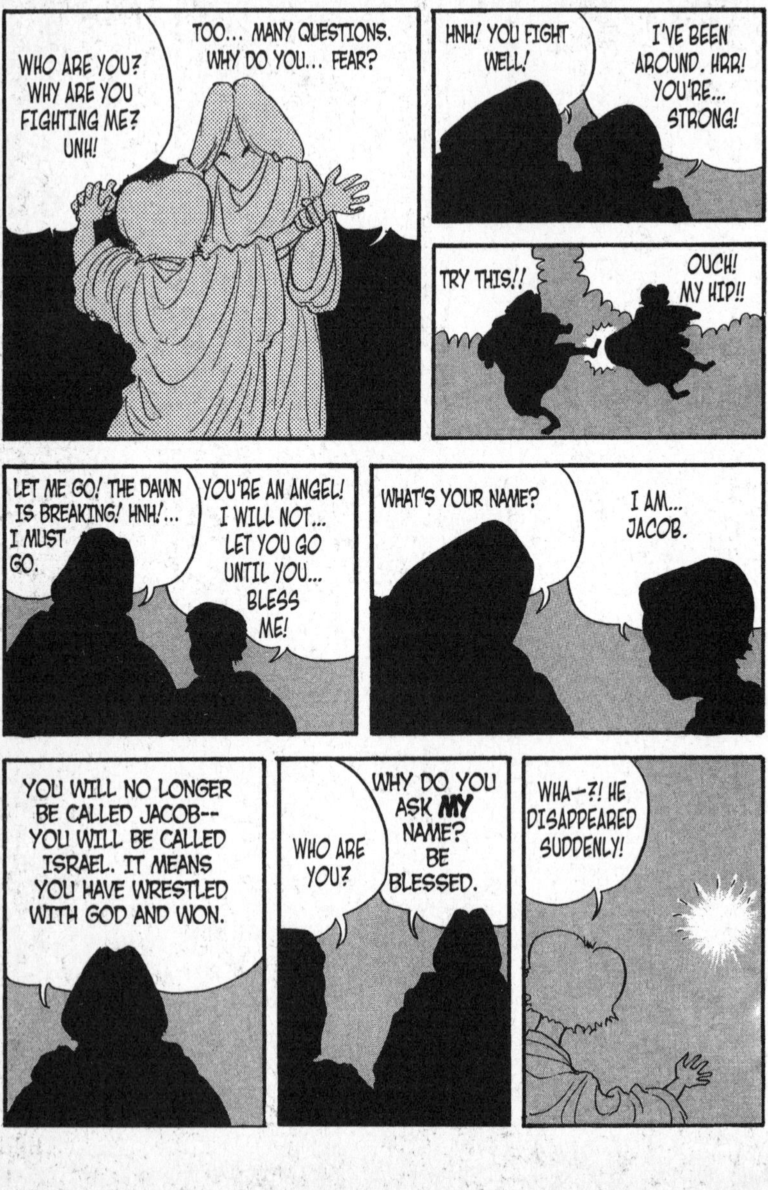
WHO ARE YOU? WHY ARE YOU FIGHTING ME? UNH!
TOO... MANY QUESTIONS. WHY DO YOU... FEAR?
HNH! YOU FIGHT WELL!
I'VE BEEN AROUND. HRR! YOU'RE... STRONG!
TRY THIS!!
OUCH! MY HIP!!
LET ME GO! THE DAWN IS BREAKING! HNH!... I MUST GO.
YOU'RE AN ANGEL! I WILL NOT... LET YOU GO UNTIL YOU... BLESS ME!
WHAT'S YOUR NAME?
I AM... JACOB.
YOU WILL NO LONGER BE CALLED JACOB-- YOU WILL BE CALLED ISRAEL. IT MEANS YOU HAVE WRESTLED WITH GOD AND WON.
WHO ARE YOU?
WHY DO YOU ASK MY NAME? BE BLESSED.
WHA--?! HE DISAPPEARED SUDDENLY!

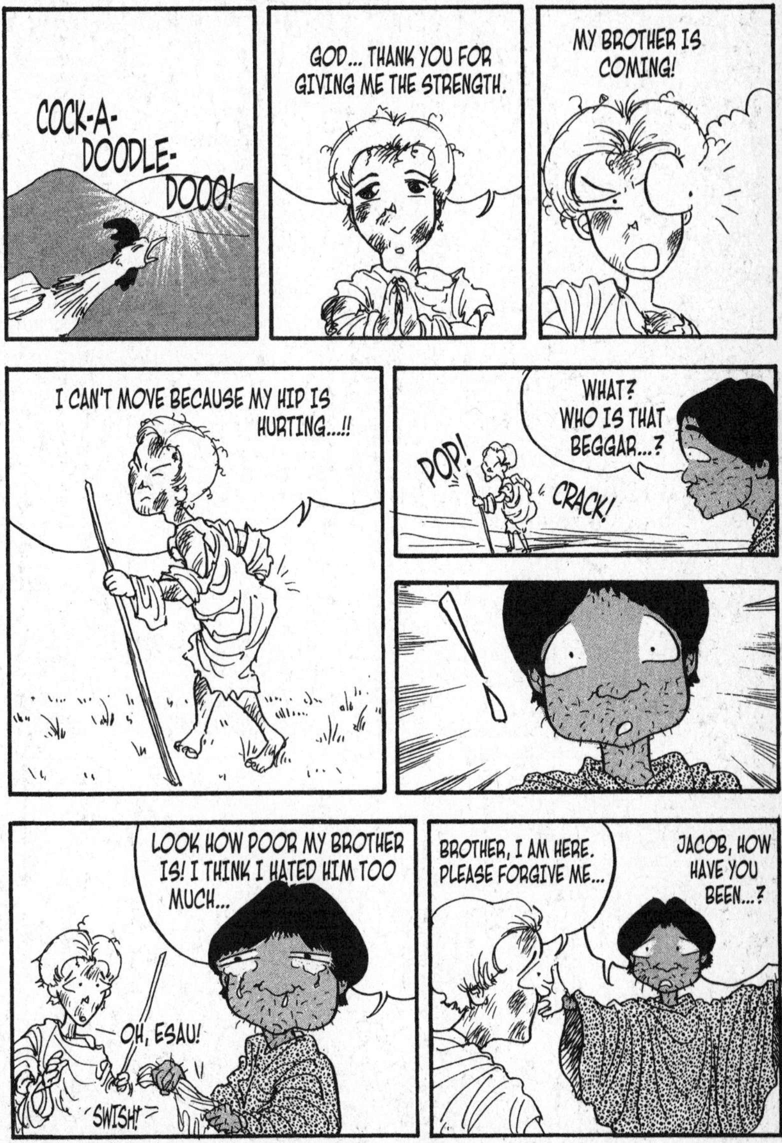
COCK-A-DOODLE-DOOO!
GOD... THANK YOU FOR GIVING ME THE STRENGTH.
MY BROTHER IS COMING!
I CAN'T MOVE BECAUSE MY HIP IS HURTING...!!
WHAT? WHO IS THAT BEGGAR...?
POP!
CRACK!
!
LOOK HOW POOR MY BROTHER IS! I THINK I HATED HIM TOO MUCH...
OH, ESAU!
SWISH!
BROTHER, I AM HERE. PLEASE FORGIVE ME...
JACOB, HOW HAVE YOU BEEN...?

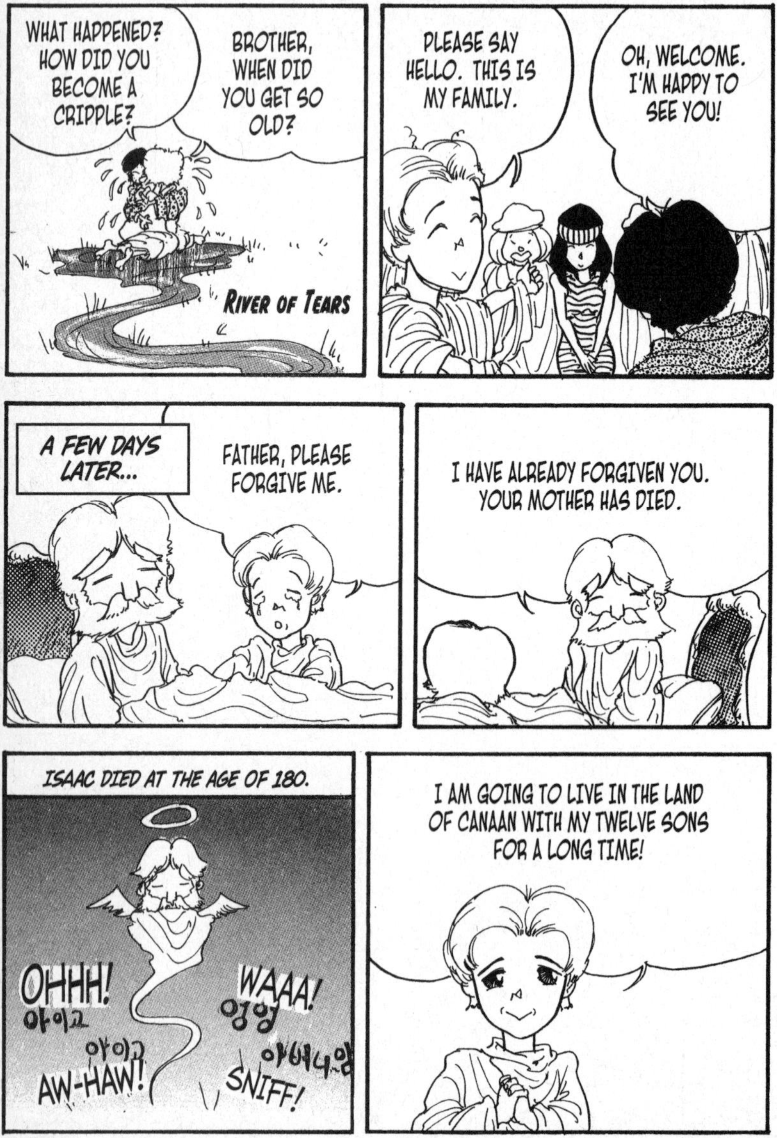
WHAT HAPPENED? HOW DID YOU BECOME A CRIPPLE?
BROTHER, WHEN DID YOU GET SO OLD?
RIVER OF TEARS
PLEASE SAY HELLO. THIS IS MY FAMILY.
OH, WELCOME. I'M HAPPY TO SEE YOU!
A FEW DAYS LATER...
FATHER, PLEASE FORGIVE ME.
I HAVE ALREADY FORGIVEN YOU. YOUR MOTHER HAS DIED.
ISAAC DIED AT THE AGE OF 180.
OHHH!
아이고
아이고
AW-HAW!
WAAA!
엉엉
아버니~임
SNIFF!
I AM GOING TO LIVE IN THE LAND OF CANAAN WITH MY TWELVE SONS FOR A LONG TIME!

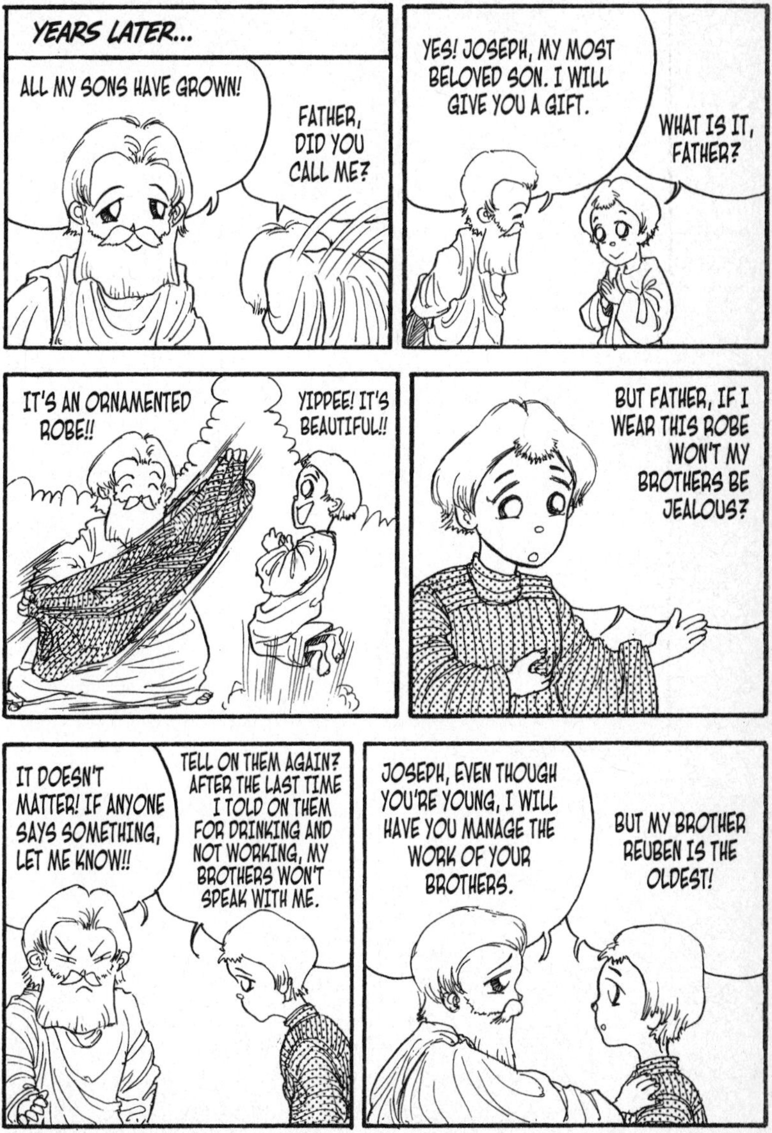
YEARS LATER...
ALL MY SONS HAVE GROWN!
FATHER, DID YOU CALL ME?
YES! JOSEPH, MY MOST BELOVED SON. I WILL GIVE YOU A GIFT.
WHAT IS IT, FATHER?
IT'S AN ORNAMENTED ROBE!!
YIPPEE! IT'S BEAUTIFUL!!
BUT FATHER, IF I WEAR THIS ROBE WON'T MY BROTHERS BE JEALOUS?
IT DOESN'T MATTER! IF ANYONE SAYS SOMETHING, LET ME KNOW!!
TELL ON THEM AGAIN? AFTER THE LAST TIME I TOLD ON THEM FOR DRINKING AND NOT WORKING, MY BROTHERS WON'T SPEAK WITH ME.
JOSEPH, EVEN THOUGH YOU'RE YOUNG, I WILL HAVE YOU MANAGE THE WORK OF YOUR BROTHERS.
BUT MY BROTHER REUBEN IS THE OLDEST!

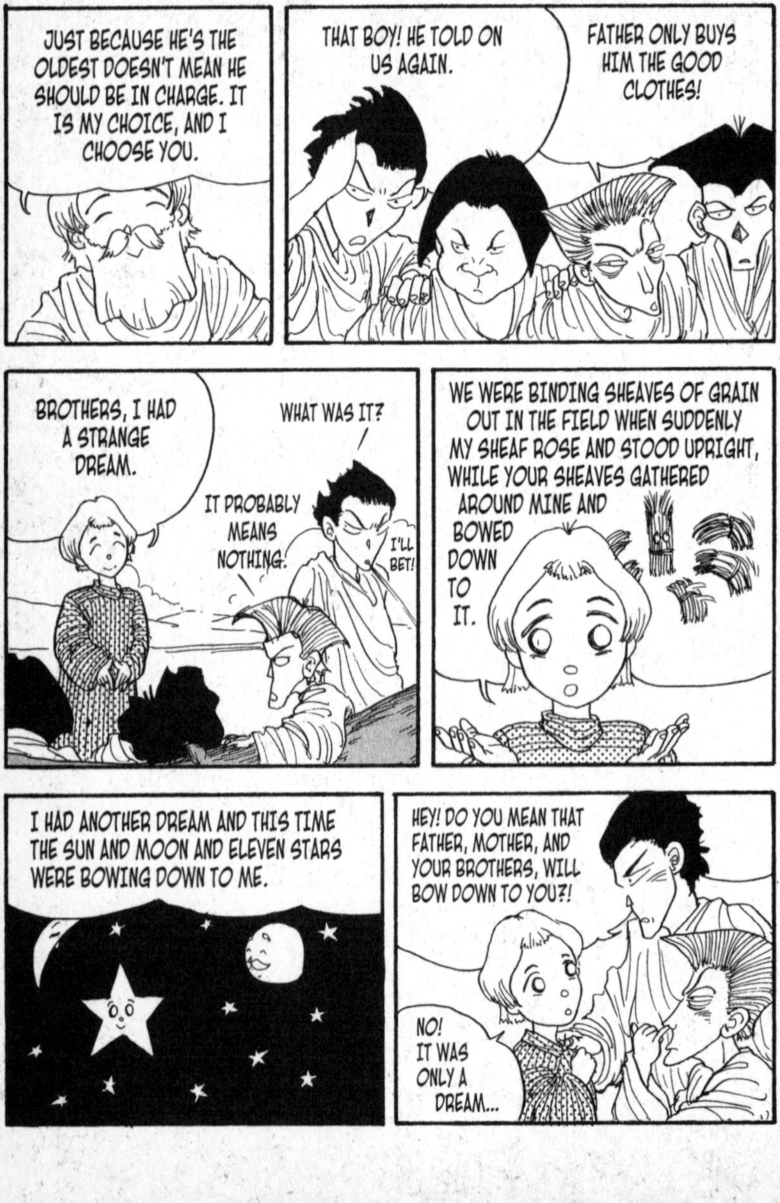
JUST BECAUSE HE'S THE OLDEST DOESN'T MEAN HE SHOULD BE IN CHARGE. IT IS MY CHOICE, AND I CHOOSE YOU.
THAT BOY! HE TOLD ON US AGAIN.
FATHER ONLY BUYS HIM THE GOOD CLOTHES!
BROTHERS, I HAD A STRANGE DREAM.
WHAT WAS IT?
IT PROBABLY MEANS NOTHING.
I'LL BET!
WE WERE BINDING SHEAVES OF GRAIN OUT IN THE FIELD WHEN SUDDENLY MY SHEAF ROSE AND STOOD UPRIGHT, WHILE YOUR SHEAVES GATHERED AROUND MINE AND BOWED DOWN TO IT.
I HAD ANOTHER DREAM AND THIS TIME THE SUN AND MOON AND ELEVEN STARS WERE BOWING DOWN TO ME.
HEY! DO YOU MEAN THAT FATHER, MOTHER, AND YOUR BROTHERS, WILL BOW DOWN TO YOU?!
NO! IT WAS ONLY A DREAM...

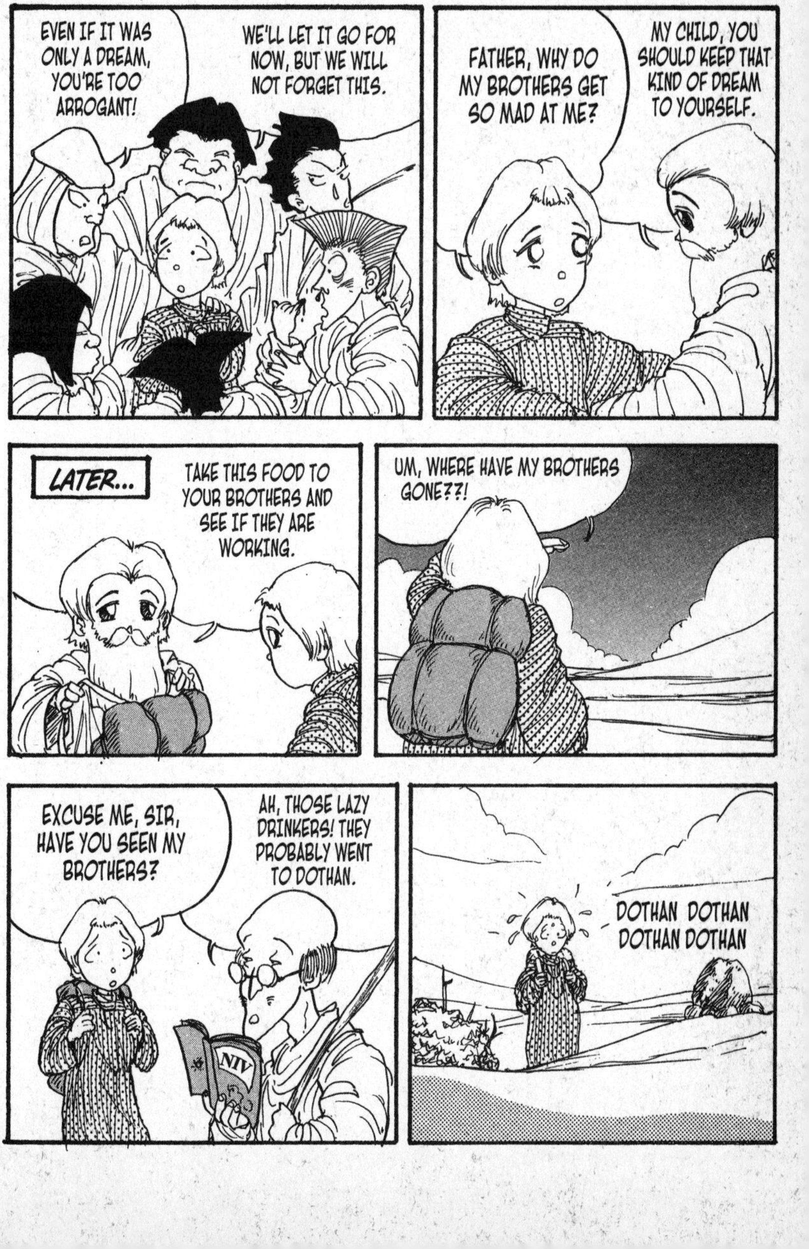
EVEN IF IT WAS ONLY A DREAM, YOU'RE TOO ARROGANT!
WE'LL LET IT GO FOR NOW, BUT WE WILL NOT FORGET THIS.
FATHER, WHY DO MY BROTHERS GET SO MAD AT ME?
MY CHILD, YOU SHOULD KEEP THAT KIND OF DREAM TO YOURSELF.
LATER...
TAKE THIS FOOD TO YOUR BROTHERS AND SEE IF THEY ARE WORKING.
UM, WHERE HAVE MY BROTHERS GONE??!
EXCUSE ME, SIR, HAVE YOU SEEN MY BROTHERS?
AH, THOSE LAZY DRINKERS! THEY PROBABLY WENT TO DOTHAN.
NIV
DOTHAN DOTHAN
DOTHAN DOTHAN

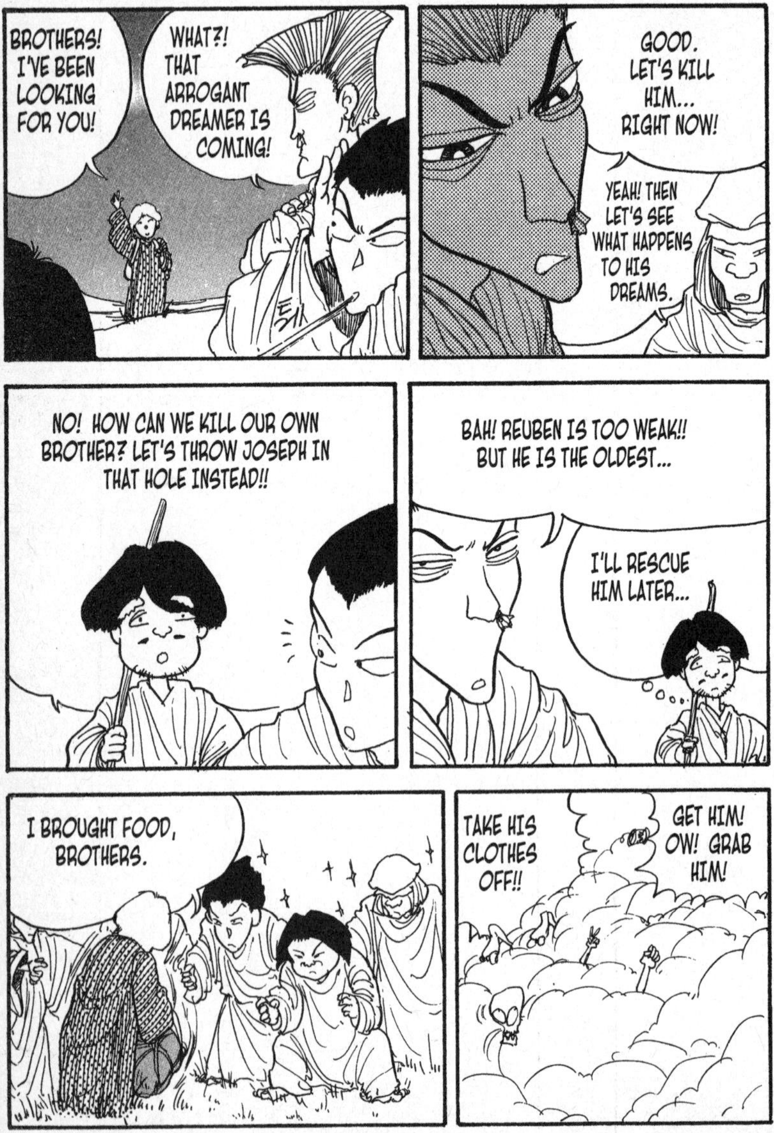
BROTHERS! I'VE BEEN LOOKING FOR YOU!
WHAT?! THAT ARROGANT DREAMER IS COMING!
GOOD. LET'S KILL HIM... RIGHT NOW!
YEAH! THEN LET'S SEE WHAT HAPPENS TO HIS DREAMS.
NO! HOW CAN WE KILL OUR OWN BROTHER? LET'S THROW JOSEPH IN THAT HOLE INSTEAD!!
BAH! REUBEN IS TOO WEAK!! BUT HE IS THE OLDEST...
I'LL RESCUE HIM LATER...
I BROUGHT FOOD, BROTHERS.
TAKE HIS CLOTHES OFF!!
GET HIM! OW! GRAB HIM!

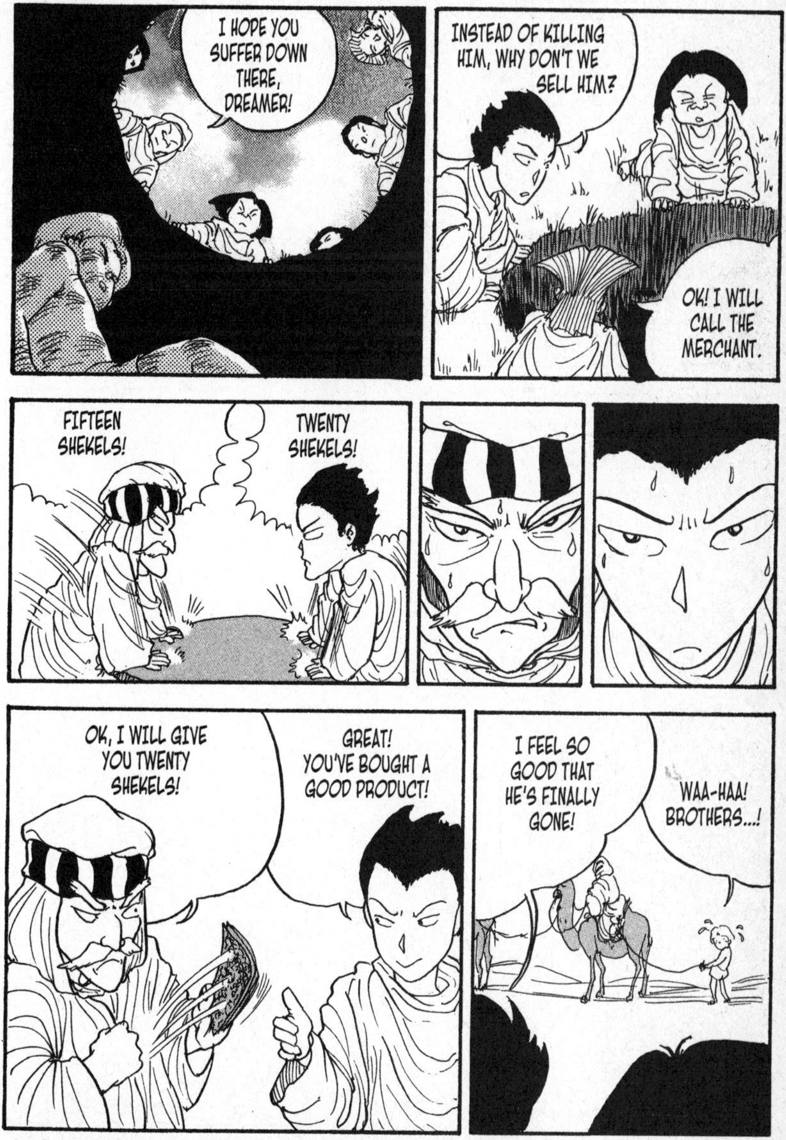
I HOPE YOU SUFFER DOWN THERE, DREAMER!
INSTEAD OF KILLING HIM, WHY DON'T WE SELL HIM?
OK! I WILL CALL THE MERCHANT.
FIFTEEN SHEKELS!
TWENTY SHEKELS!
OK, I WILL GIVE YOU TWENTY SHEKELS!
GREAT! YOU'VE BOUGHT A GOOD PRODUCT!
I FEEL SO GOOD THAT HE'S FINALLY GONE!
WAA-HAA! BROTHERS...!

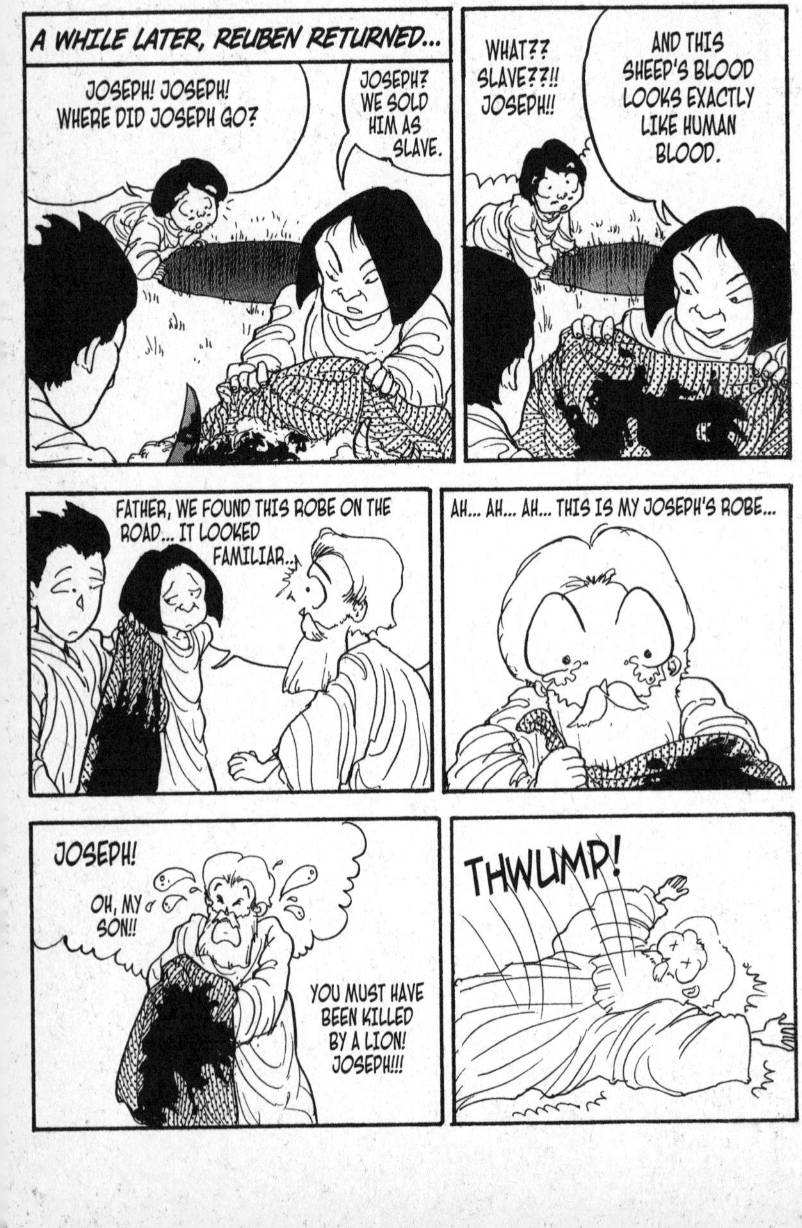
A WHILE LATER, REUBEN RETURNED...
JOSEPH! JOSEPH! WHERE DID JOSEPH GO?
JOSEPH? WE SOLD HIM AS SLAVE.
WHAT?? SLAVE??!! JOSEPH!!
AND THIS SHEEP'S BLOOD LOOKS EXACTLY LIKE HUMAN BLOOD.
FATHER, WE FOUND THIS ROBE ON THE ROAD... IT LOOKED FAMILIAR...
AH... AH... AH... THIS IS MY JOSEPH'S ROBE...
JOSEPH!
OH, MY SON!!
YOU MUST HAVE BEEN KILLED BY A LION! JOSEPH!!!
THWUMP!

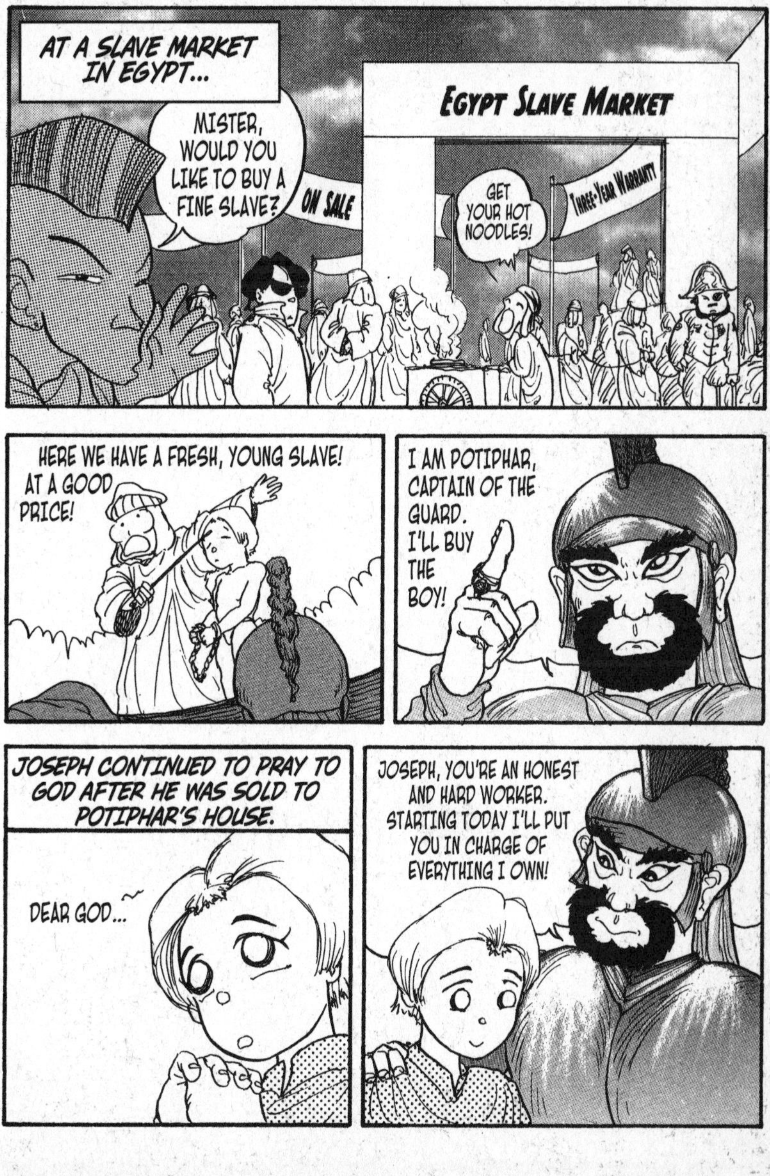
AT A SLAVE MARKET IN EGYPT...
EGYPT SLAVE MARKET
MISTER, WOULD YOU LIKE TO BUY A FINE SLAVE?
ON SALE
GET YOUR HOT NOODLES!
THREE-YEAR WARRANTY
HERE WE HAVE A FRESH, YOUNG SLAVE!
AT A GOOD PRICE!
I AM POTIPHAR, CAPTAIN OF THE GUARD. I'LL BUY THE BOY!
JOSEPH CONTINUED TO PRAY TO GOD AFTER HE WAS SOLD TO POTIPHAR'S HOUSE.
DEAR GOD...
JOSEPH, YOU'RE AN HONEST AND HARD WORKER. STARTING TODAY I'LL PUT YOU IN CHARGE OF EVERYTHING I OWN!

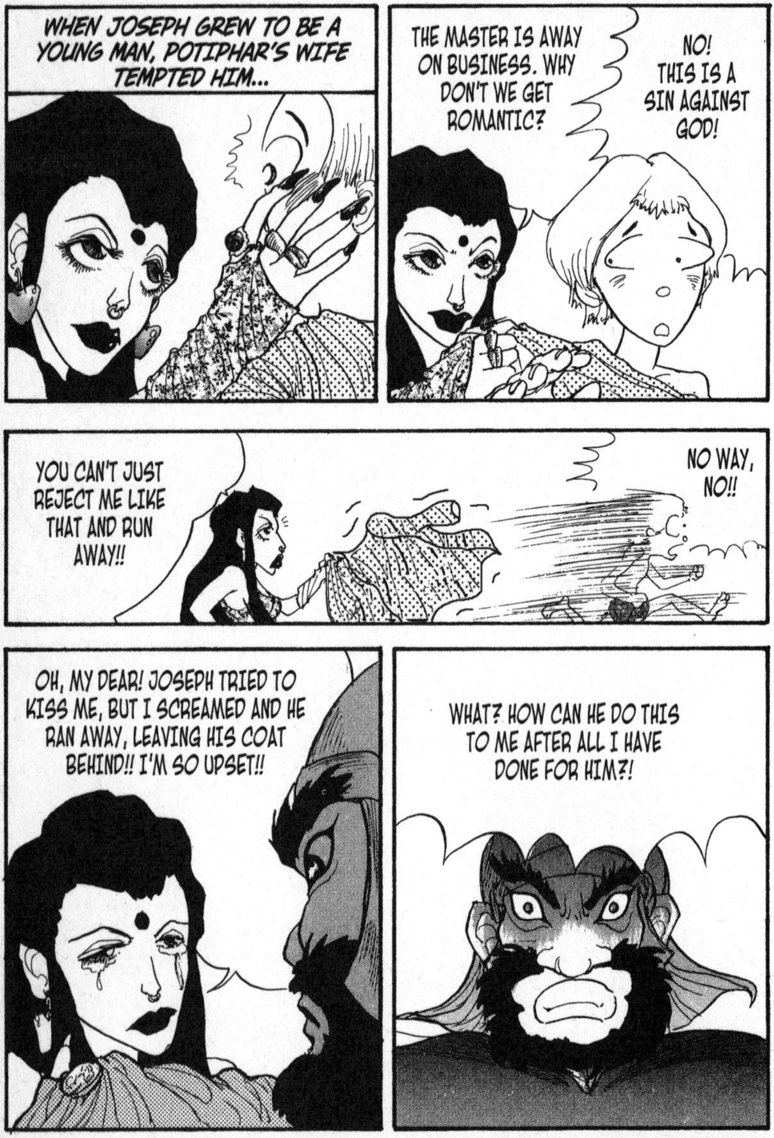
WHEN JOSEPH GREW TO BE A YOUNG MAN, POTIPHAR'S WIFE TEMPTED HIM...
THE MASTER IS AWAY ON BUSINESS. WHY DON'T WE GET ROMANTIC?
NO! THIS IS A SIN AGAINST GOD!
YOU CAN'T JUST REJECT ME LIKE THAT AND RUN AWAY!!
NO WAY, NO!!
OH, MY DEAR! JOSEPH TRIED TO KISS ME, BUT I SCREAMED AND HE RAN AWAY, LEAVING HIS COAT BEHIND!! I'M SO UPSET!!
WHAT? HOW CAN HE DO THIS TO ME AFTER ALL I HAVE DONE FOR HIM?!

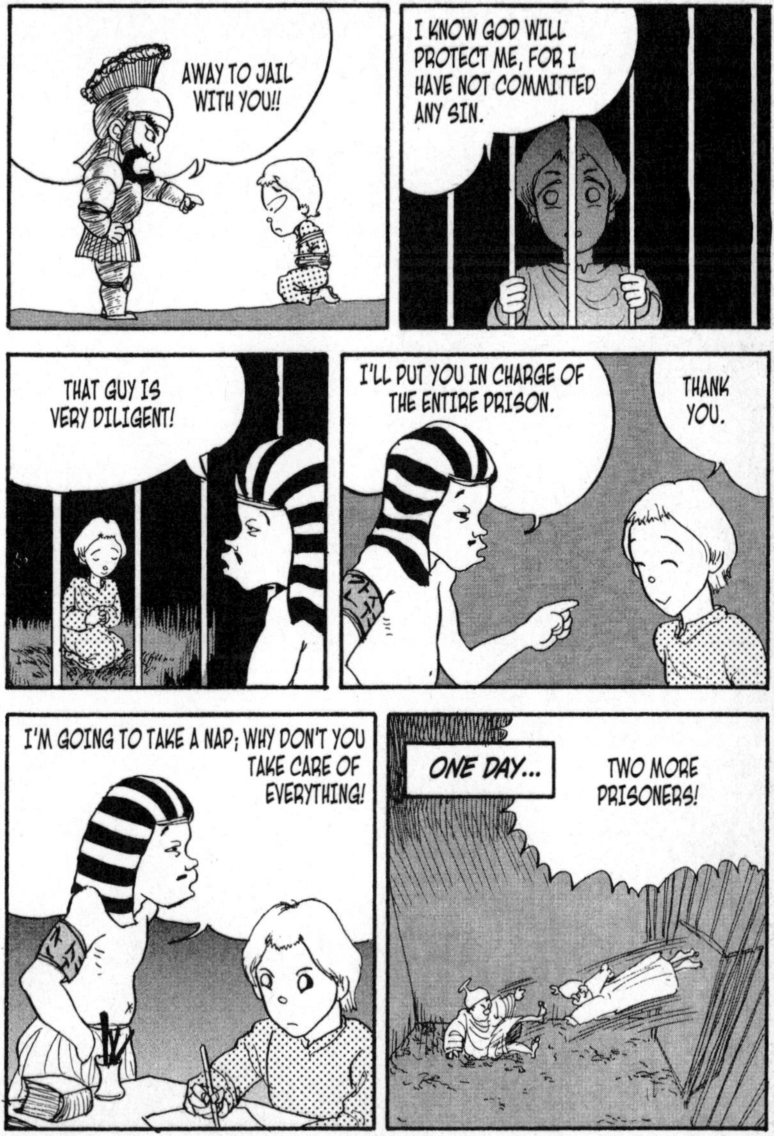
AWAY TO JAIL WITH YOU!!
I KNOW GOD WILL PROTECT ME, FOR I HAVE NOT COMMITTED ANY SIN.
THAT GUY IS VERY DILIGENT!
I'LL PUT YOU IN CHARGE OF THE ENTIRE PRISON.
THANK YOU.
I'M GOING TO TAKE A NAP; WHY DON'T YOU TAKE CARE OF EVERYTHING!
ONE DAY...
TWO MORE PRISONERS!

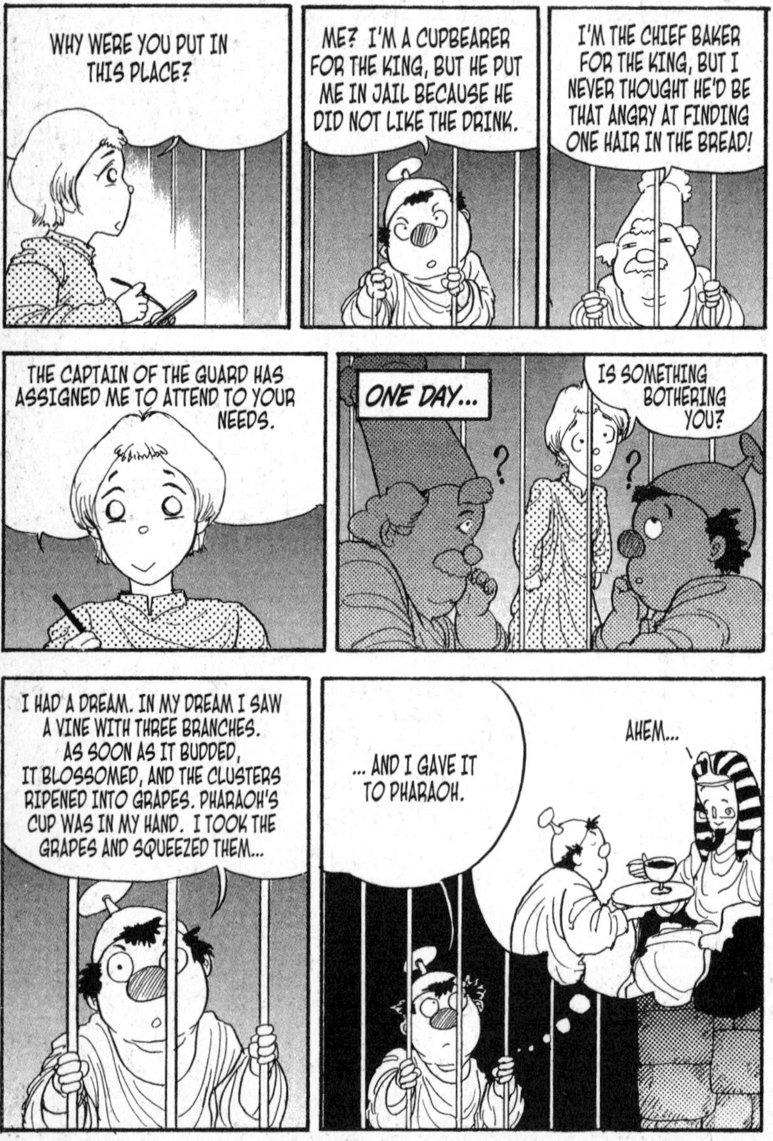
WHY WERE YOU PUT IN THIS PLACE?
ME? I'M A CUPBEARER FOR THE KING, BUT HE PUT ME IN JAIL BECAUSE HE DID NOT LIKE THE DRINK.
I'M THE CHIEF BAKER FOR THE KING, BUT I NEVER THOUGHT HE'D BE THAT ANGRY AT FINDING ONE HAIR IN THE BREAD!
THE CAPTAIN OF THE GUARD HAS ASSIGNED ME TO ATTEND TO YOUR NEEDS.
ONE DAY...
IS SOMETHING BOTHERING YOU?
?
?
I HAD A DREAM. IN MY DREAM I SAW A VINE WITH THREE BRANCHES. AS SOON AS IT BUDDED, IT BLOSSOMED, AND THE CLUSTERS RIPENED INTO GRAPES. PHARAOH'S CUP WAS IN MY HAND. I TOOK THE GRAPES AND SQUEEZED THEM...
... AND I GAVE IT TO PHARAOH.
AHEM...

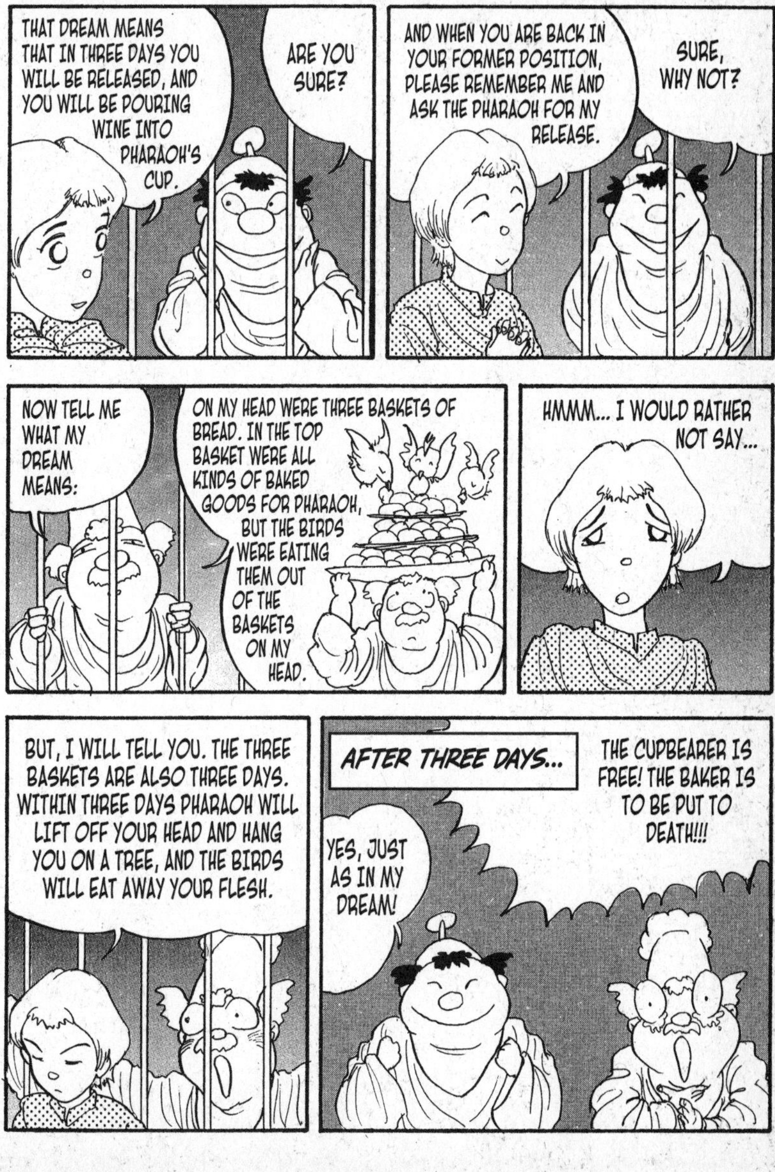
THAT DREAM MEANS THAT IN THREE DAYS YOU WILL BE RELEASED, AND YOU WILL BE POURING WINE INTO PHARAOH'S CUP.
ARE YOU SURE?
AND WHEN YOU ARE BACK IN YOUR FORMER POSITION, PLEASE REMEMBER ME AND ASK THE PHARAOH FOR MY RELEASE.
SURE, WHY NOT?
NOW TELL ME WHAT MY DREAM MEANS:
ON MY HEAD WERE THREE BASKETS OF BREAD. IN THE TOP BASKET WERE ALL KINDS OF BAKED GOODS FOR PHARAOH, BUT THE BIRDS WERE EATING THEM OUT OF THE BASKETS ON MY HEAD.
HMMM... I WOULD RATHER NOT SAY...
BUT, I WILL TELL YOU. THE THREE BASKETS ARE ALSO THREE DAYS. WITHIN THREE DAYS PHARAOH WILL LIFT OFF YOUR HEAD AND HANG YOU ON A TREE, AND THE BIRDS WILL EAT AWAY YOUR FLESH.
AFTER THREE DAYS...
THE CUPBEARER IS FREE! THE BAKER IS TO BE PUT TO DEATH!!!
YES, JUST AS IN MY DREAM!

CUPBEARER, PLEASE KEEP YOUR PROMISE!

OF COURSE I WILL!!

BUT, THE CUPBEARER FORGOT ALL ABOUT JOSEPH.

GOTTA TASTE IT... BEFORE I SERVE IT!

TWO YEARS HAD PASSED... AND THEN...

OH! I HAD A STRANGE DREAM LAST NIGHT. CALL THE MAGICIANS AND WISE MEN!!

TELL US! WE ARE WISE!

SCHOOL OF PROPHECY

FER SURE!

WE SEE ALL!

IN MY DREAM I SAW SEVEN FAT COWS COMING UP FROM THE RIVER.

WAIT!

SEVEN JUICY STEAKS...

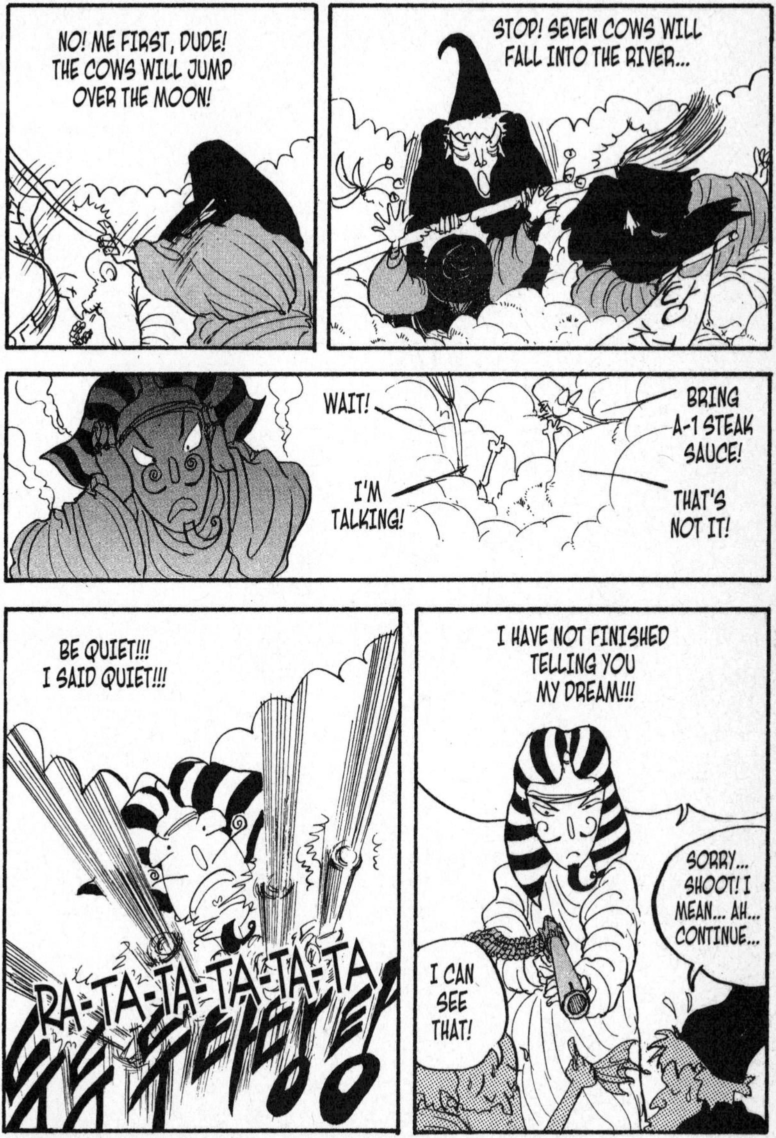
NO! ME FIRST, DUDE! THE COWS WILL JUMP OVER THE MOON!
STOP! SEVEN COWS WILL FALL INTO THE RIVER...
WAIT!
I'M TALKING!
BRING A-1 STEAK SAUCE!
THAT'S NOT IT!
BE QUIET!!! I SAID QUIET!!!
RA-TA-TA-TA-TA-TA
I HAVE NOT FINISHED TELLING YOU MY DREAM!!!
I CAN SEE THAT!
SORRY... SHOOT! I MEAN... AH... CONTINUE...

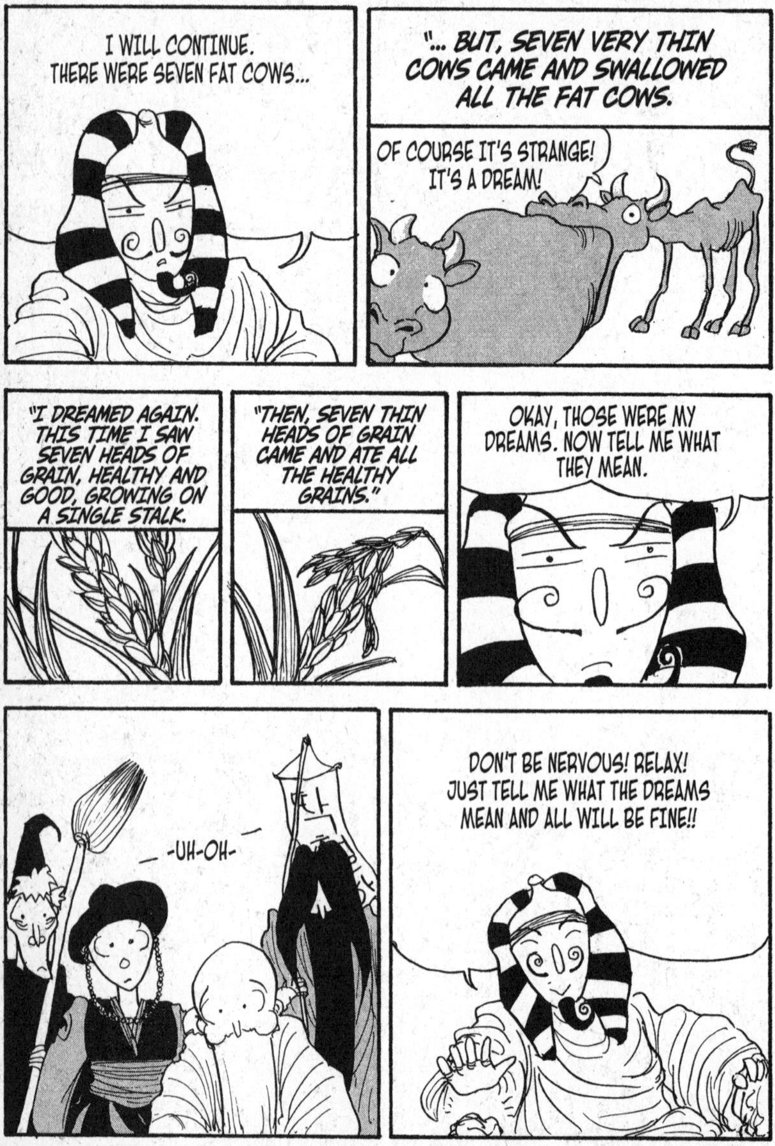
I WILL CONTINUE. THERE WERE SEVEN FAT COWS...
"... BUT, SEVEN VERY THIN COWS CAME AND SWALLOWED ALL THE FAT COWS.
OF COURSE IT'S STRANGE! IT'S A DREAM!
"I DREAMED AGAIN. THIS TIME I SAW SEVEN HEADS OF GRAIN, HEALTHY AND GOOD, GROWING ON A SINGLE STALK.
"THEN, SEVEN THIN HEADS OF GRAIN CAME AND ATE ALL THE HEALTHY GRAINS."
OKAY, THOSE WERE MY DREAMS. NOW TELL ME WHAT THEY MEAN.
-UH-OH-
DON'T BE NERVOUS! RELAX! JUST TELL ME WHAT THE DREAMS MEAN AND ALL WILL BE FINE!!

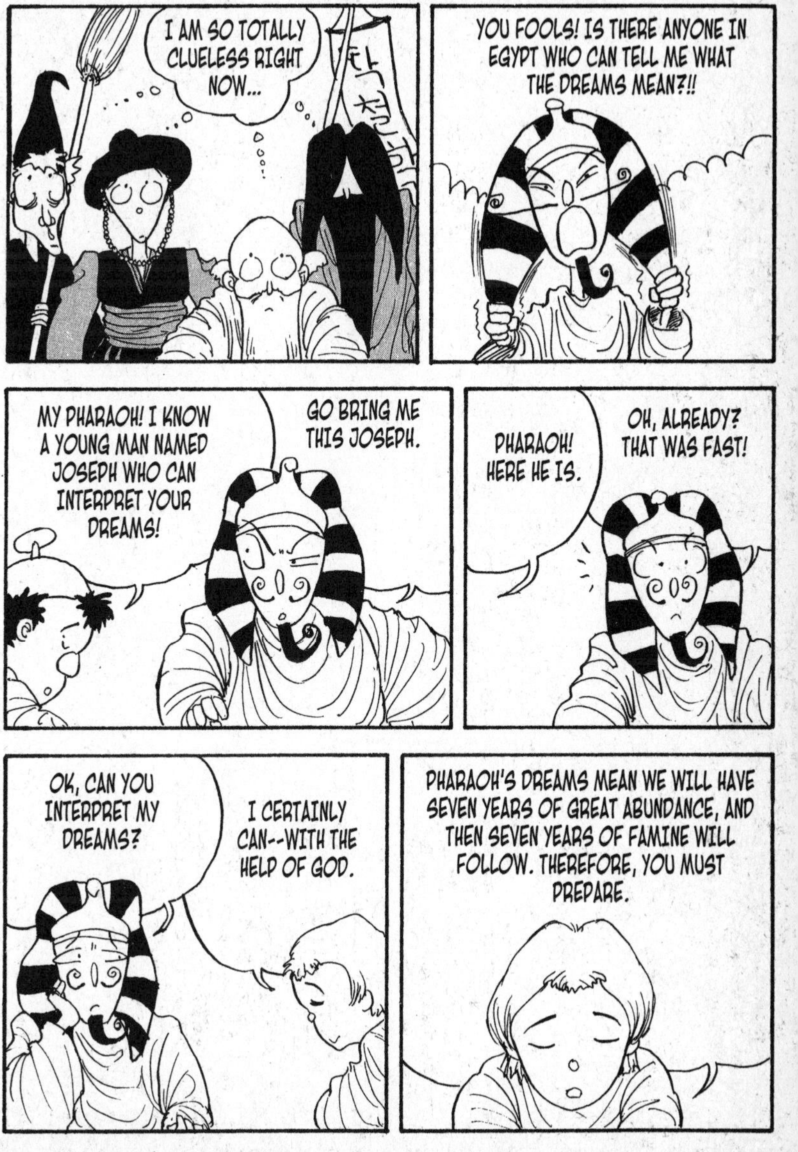
I AM SO TOTALLY CLUELESS RIGHT NOW...
YOU FOOLS! IS THERE ANYONE IN EGYPT WHO CAN TELL ME WHAT THE DREAMS MEAN?!!
MY PHARAOH! I KNOW A YOUNG MAN NAMED JOSEPH WHO CAN INTERPRET YOUR DREAMS!
GO BRING ME THIS JOSEPH.
PHARAOH! HERE HE IS.
OH, ALREADY? THAT WAS FAST!
OK, CAN YOU INTERPRET MY DREAMS?
I CERTAINLY CAN--WITH THE HELP OF GOD.
PHARAOH'S DREAMS MEAN WE WILL HAVE SEVEN YEARS OF GREAT ABUNDANCE, AND THEN SEVEN YEARS OF FAMINE WILL FOLLOW. THEREFORE, YOU MUST PREPARE.

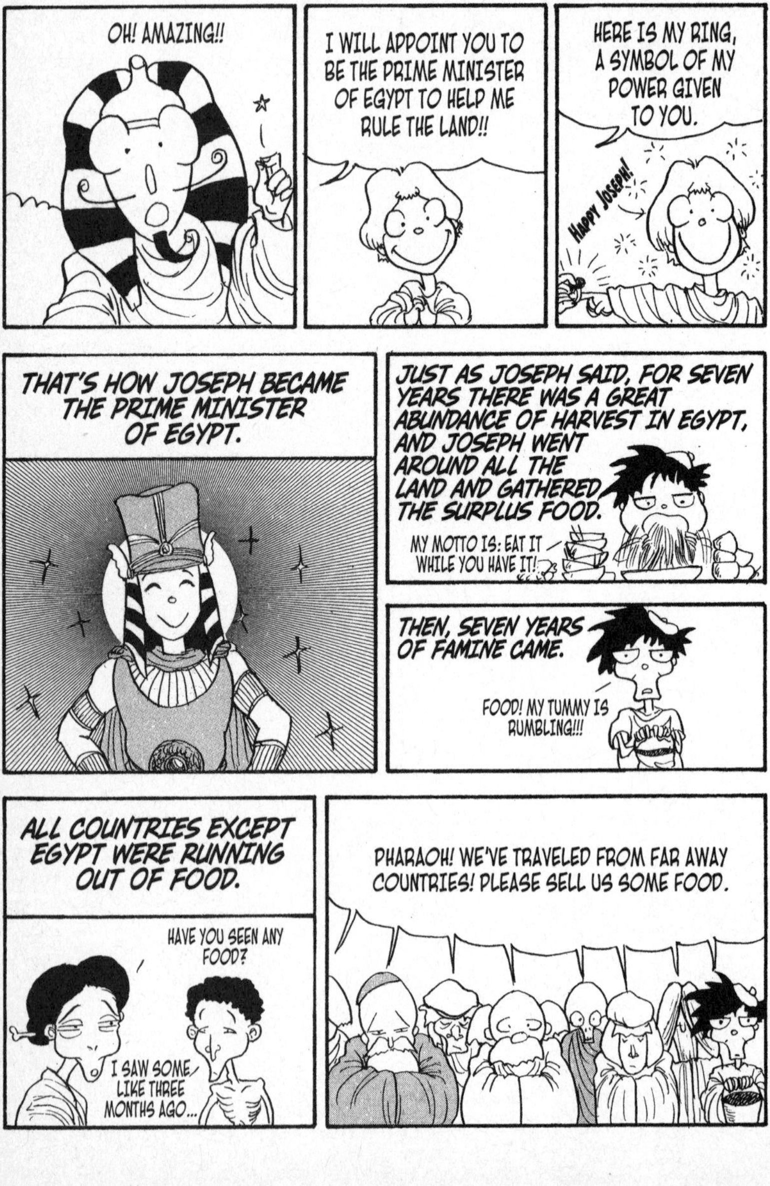
OH! AMAZING!!
I WILL APPOINT YOU TO BE THE PRIME MINISTER OF EGYPT TO HELP ME RULE THE LAND!!
HERE IS MY RING, A SYMBOL OF MY POWER GIVEN TO YOU.
HAPPY JOSEPH!
THAT'S HOW JOSEPH BECAME THE PRIME MINISTER OF EGYPT.
JUST AS JOSEPH SAID, FOR SEVEN YEARS THERE WAS A GREAT ABUNDANCE OF HARVEST IN EGYPT, AND JOSEPH WENT AROUND ALL THE LAND AND GATHERED THE SURPLUS FOOD.
MY MOTTO IS: EAT IT WHILE YOU HAVE IT!
THEN, SEVEN YEARS OF FAMINE CAME.
FOOD! MY TUMMY IS RUMBLING!!!
ALL COUNTRIES EXCEPT EGYPT WERE RUNNING OUT OF FOOD.
HAVE YOU SEEN ANY FOOD?
I SAW SOME LIKE THREE MONTHS AGO...
PHARAOH! WE'VE TRAVELED FROM FAR AWAY COUNTRIES! PLEASE SELL US SOME FOOD.

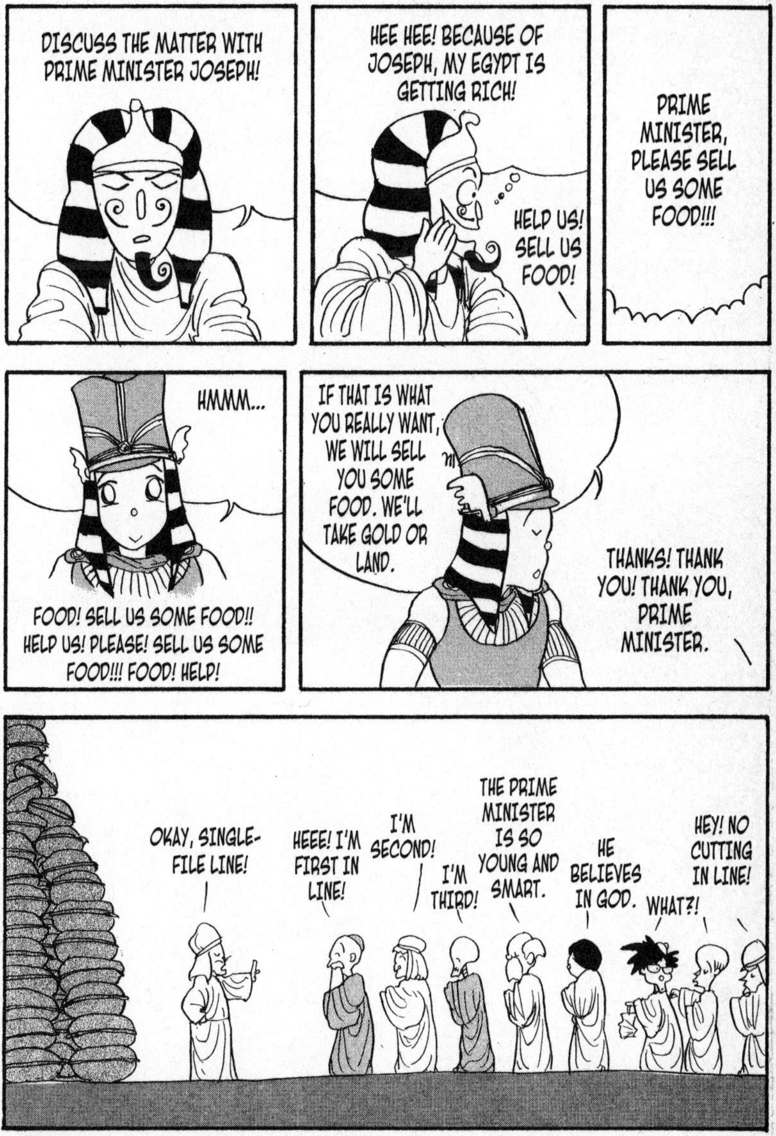
DISCUSS THE MATTER WITH PRIME MINISTER JOSEPH!
HEE HEE! BECAUSE OF JOSEPH, MY EGYPT IS GETTING RICH!
HELP US! SELL US FOOD!
PRIME MINISTER, PLEASE SELL US SOME FOOD!!!
HMMM...
FOOD! SELL US SOME FOOD!! HELP US! PLEASE! SELL US SOME FOOD!!! FOOD! HELP!
IF THAT IS WHAT YOU REALLY WANT, WE WILL SELL YOU SOME FOOD. WE'LL TAKE GOLD OR LAND.
THANKS! THANK YOU! THANK YOU, PRIME MINISTER.
OKAY, SINGLE-FILE LINE!
HEEE! I'M FIRST IN LINE!
I'M SECOND!
I'M THIRD!
THE PRIME MINISTER IS SO YOUNG AND SMART.
HE BELIEVES IN GOD.
WHAT?!
HEY! NO CUTTING IN LINE!

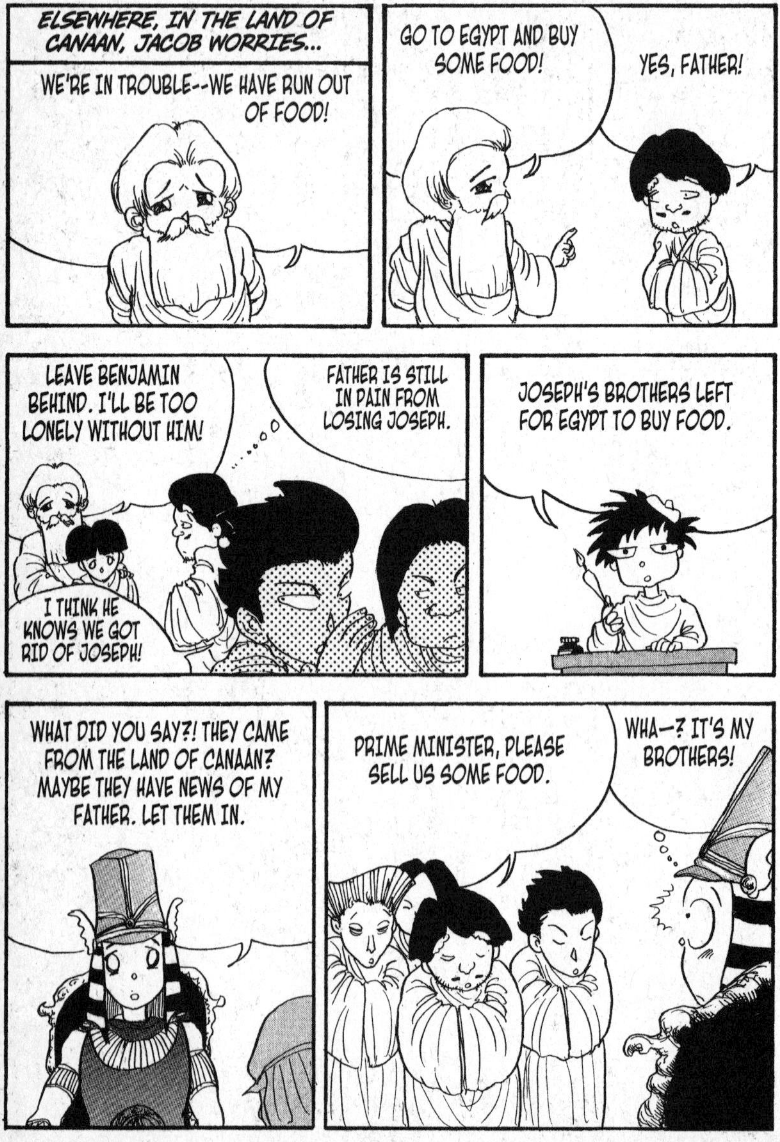
ELSEWHERE, IN THE LAND OF CANAAN, JACOB WORRIES...
WE'RE IN TROUBLE--WE HAVE RUN OUT OF FOOD!
GO TO EGYPT AND BUY SOME FOOD!
YES, FATHER!
LEAVE BENJAMIN BEHIND. I'LL BE TOO LONELY WITHOUT HIM!
FATHER IS STILL IN PAIN FROM LOSING JOSEPH.
I THINK HE KNOWS WE GOT RID OF JOSEPH!
JOSEPH'S BROTHERS LEFT FOR EGYPT TO BUY FOOD.
WHAT DID YOU SAY?! THEY CAME FROM THE LAND OF CANAAN? MAYBE THEY HAVE NEWS OF MY FATHER. LET THEM IN.
PRIME MINISTER, PLEASE SELL US SOME FOOD.
WHA—? IT'S MY BROTHERS!

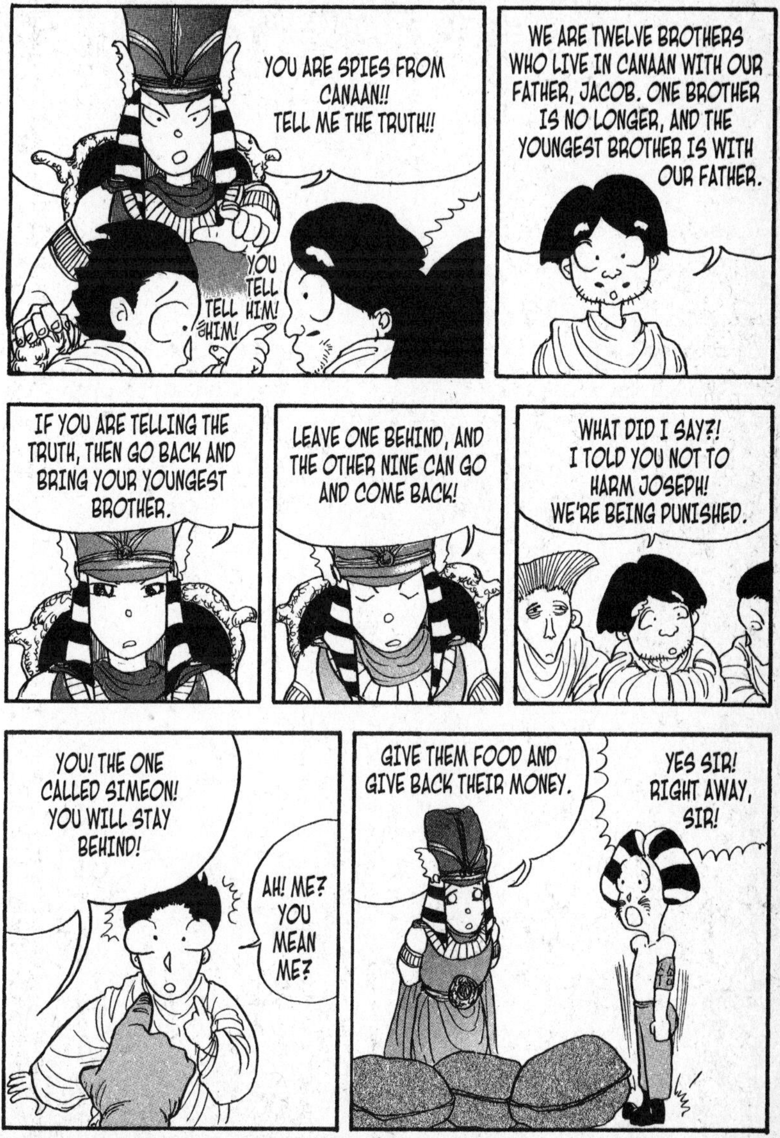

YOU ARE SPIES FROM CANAAN!! TELL ME THE TRUTH!!
YOU TELL HIM!
TELL HIM!
WE ARE TWELVE BROTHERS WHO LIVE IN CANAAN WITH OUR FATHER, JACOB. ONE BROTHER IS NO LONGER, AND THE YOUNGEST BROTHER IS WITH OUR FATHER.
IF YOU ARE TELLING THE TRUTH, THEN GO BACK AND BRING YOUR YOUNGEST BROTHER.
LEAVE ONE BEHIND, AND THE OTHER NINE CAN GO AND COME BACK!
WHAT DID I SAY?! I TOLD YOU NOT TO HARM JOSEPH! WE'RE BEING PUNISHED.
YOU! THE ONE CALLED SIMEON! YOU WILL STAY BEHIND!
AH! ME? YOU MEAN ME?
GIVE THEM FOOD AND GIVE BACK THEIR MONEY.
YES SIR! RIGHT AWAY, SIR!

WHEN THEY RETURNED TO CANAAN...

FATHER, THE PRIME MINISTER OF EGYPT TOLD US TO BRING BENJAMIN...

OH NO! I HAVE LOST JOSEPH... NOW BENJAMIN!! NO, NEVER!!

THEY GAVE US THE MONEY BACK.

I KNOW THEY ARE GOING TO SAY YOU ARE THIEVES AND SPIES.

NO!! NOT BENJAMIN!!

A FEW DAYS LATER...

WE'RE GONNA DIE FROM HUNGER! WE MUST LEAVE!

DEAR, ALL THE FOOD FROM EGYPT HAS RUN OUT.

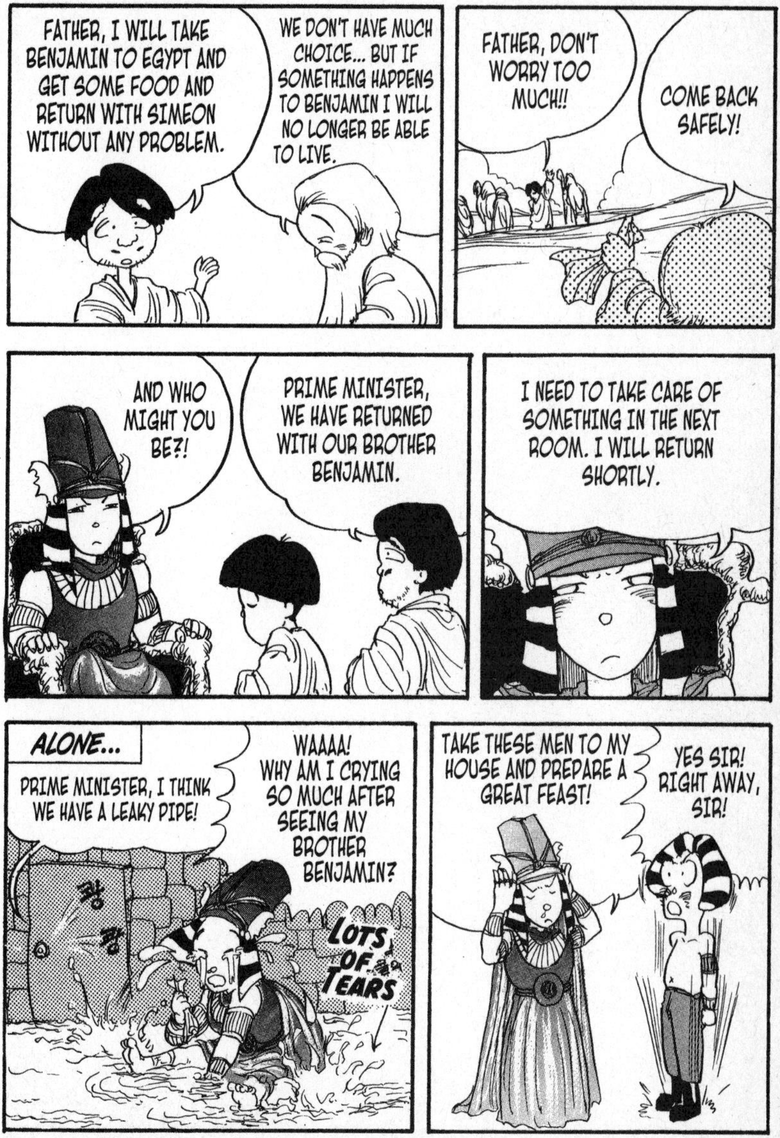
FATHER, I WILL TAKE BENJAMIN TO EGYPT AND GET SOME FOOD AND RETURN WITH SIMEON WITHOUT ANY PROBLEM.
WE DON'T HAVE MUCH CHOICE... BUT IF SOMETHING HAPPENS TO BENJAMIN I WILL NO LONGER BE ABLE TO LIVE.
FATHER, DON'T WORRY TOO MUCH!!
COME BACK SAFELY!
AND WHO MIGHT YOU BE?!
PRIME MINISTER, WE HAVE RETURNED WITH OUR BROTHER BENJAMIN.
I NEED TO TAKE CARE OF SOMETHING IN THE NEXT ROOM. I WILL RETURN SHORTLY.
ALONE...
PRIME MINISTER, I THINK WE HAVE A LEAKY PIPE!
WAAAA! WHY AM I CRYING SO MUCH AFTER SEEING MY BROTHER BENJAMIN?
쾅
쾅
LOTS OF TEARS
TAKE THESE MEN TO MY HOUSE AND PREPARE A GREAT FEAST!
YES SIR! RIGHT AWAY, SIR!

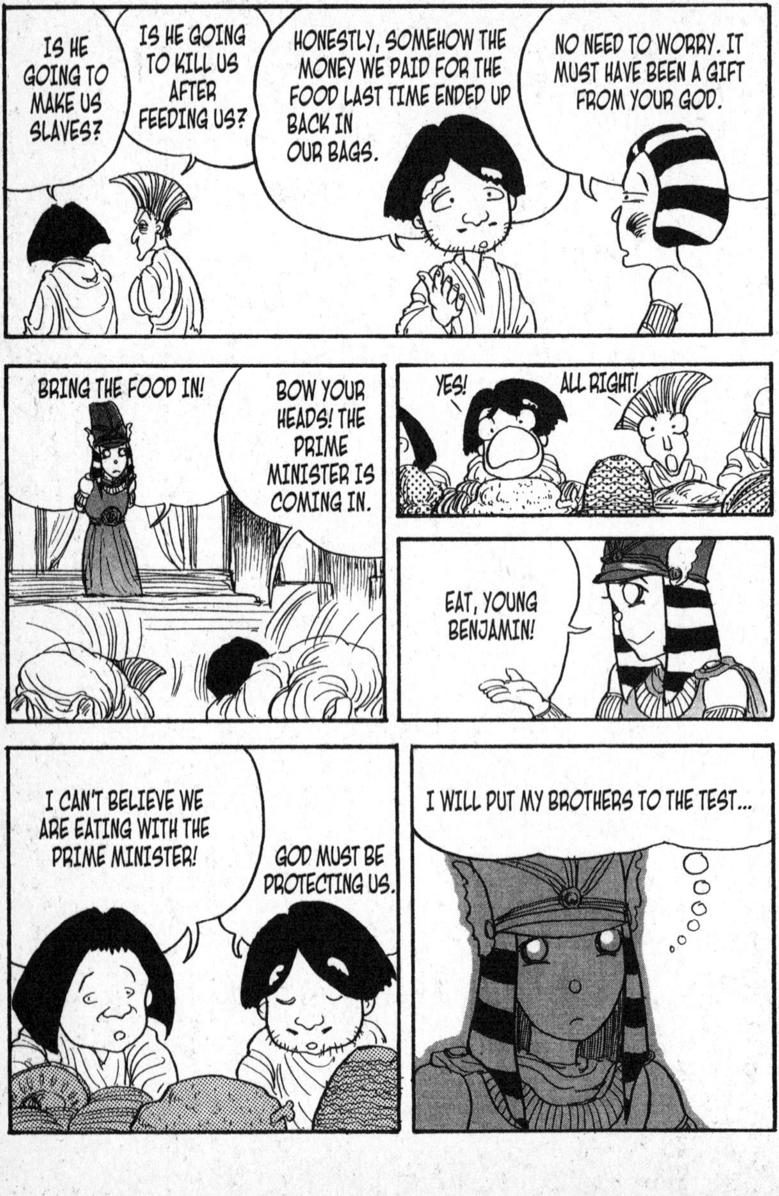

IS HE GOING TO MAKE US SLAVES?
IS HE GOING TO KILL US AFTER FEEDING US?
HONESTLY, SOMEHOW THE MONEY WE PAID FOR THE FOOD LAST TIME ENDED UP BACK IN OUR BAGS.
NO NEED TO WORRY. IT MUST HAVE BEEN A GIFT FROM YOUR GOD.
BRING THE FOOD IN!
BOW YOUR HEADS! THE PRIME MINISTER IS COMING IN.
YES!
ALL RIGHT!
EAT, YOUNG BENJAMIN!
I CAN'T BELIEVE WE ARE EATING WITH THE PRIME MINISTER!
GOD MUST BE PROTECTING US.
I WILL PUT MY BROTHERS TO THE TEST...

PUT THE SILVER CUP IN BENJAMIN'S FOOD BAG.

YES SIR! RIGHT AWAY, SIR!

THE NEXT MORNING...

I WILL PRACTICE HARD UNTIL I CAN CROW LIKE MY FATHER!

DEEP-A-PEEPLE-PEEP!

LOUDER!

HURRY, LET'S GO BACK HOME! FATHER IS WAITING!

STOP! STOP!

WHY DID YOU STEAL MY MASTER'S SILVER CUP!

IF YOU DON'T TRUST US, SEARCH US...

WHAT ARE YOU TALKING ABOUT?

HERE! LOOK! HERE IT IS!

THAT'S BENJAMIN'S BAG! HOW DID THAT SILVER CUP GET IN THERE?

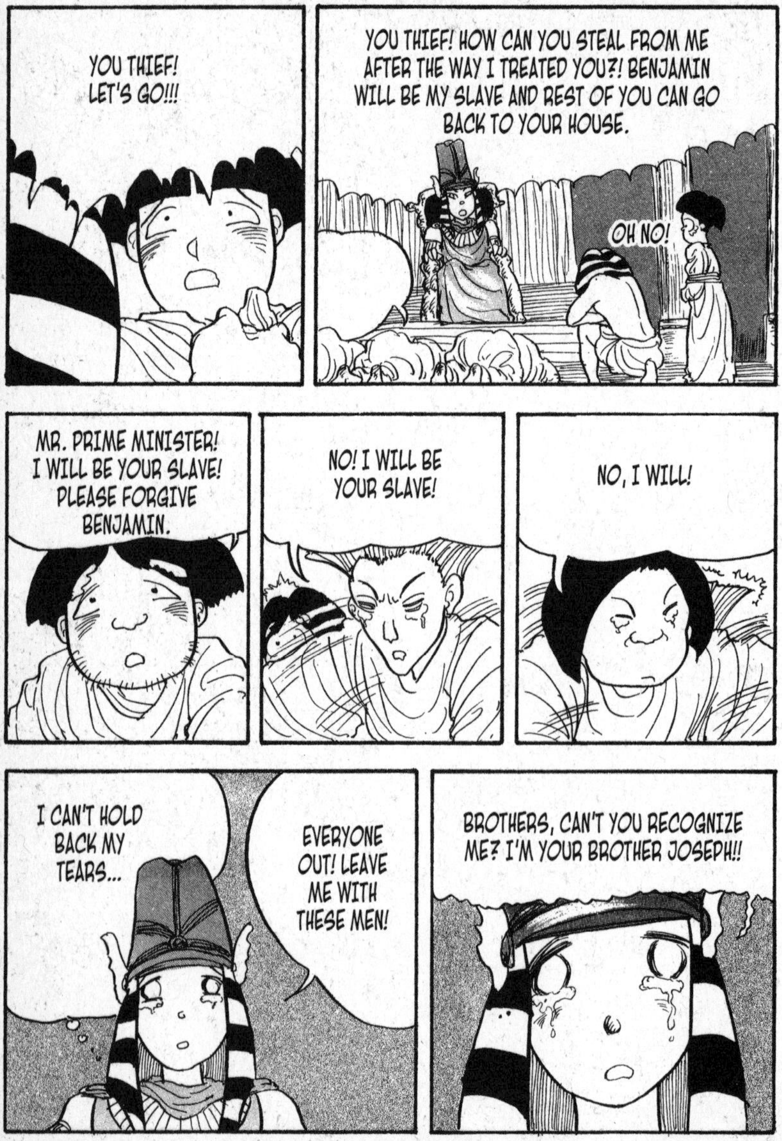
YOU THIEF! LET'S GO!!!
YOU THIEF! HOW CAN YOU STEAL FROM ME AFTER THE WAY I TREATED YOU?! BENJAMIN WILL BE MY SLAVE AND REST OF YOU CAN GO BACK TO YOUR HOUSE.
OH NO!
MR. PRIME MINISTER! I WILL BE YOUR SLAVE! PLEASE FORGIVE BENJAMIN.
NO! I WILL BE YOUR SLAVE!
NO, I WILL!
I CAN'T HOLD BACK MY TEARS...
EVERYONE OUT! LEAVE ME WITH THESE MEN!
BROTHERS, CAN'T YOU RECOGNIZE ME? I'M YOUR BROTHER JOSEPH!!

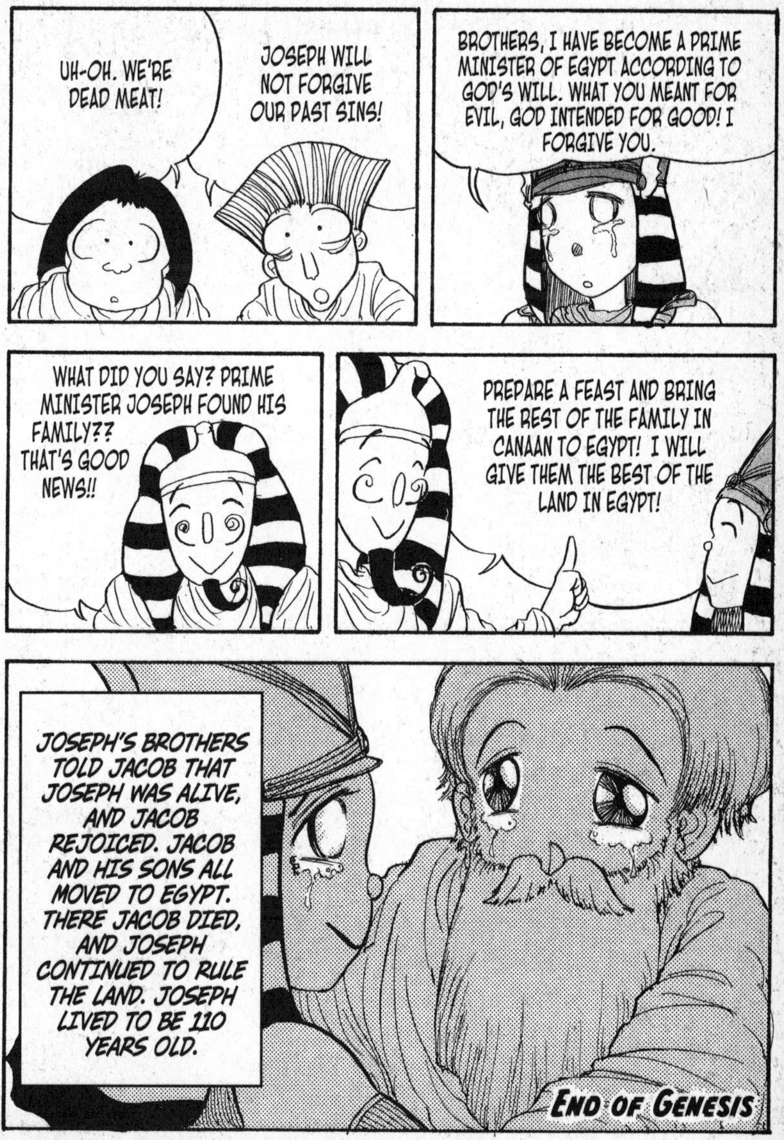
UH-OH. WE'RE DEAD MEAT!
JOSEPH WILL NOT FORGIVE OUR PAST SINS!
BROTHERS, I HAVE BECOME A PRIME MINISTER OF EGYPT ACCORDING TO GOD'S WILL. WHAT YOU MEANT FOR EVIL, GOD INTENDED FOR GOOD! I FORGIVE YOU.
WHAT DID YOU SAY? PRIME MINISTER JOSEPH FOUND HIS FAMILY?? THAT'S GOOD NEWS!!
PREPARE A FEAST AND BRING THE BEST OF THE FAMILY IN CANAAN TO EGYPT! I WILL GIVE THEM THE BEST OF THE LAND IN EGYPT!
JOSEPH'S BROTHERS TOLD JACOB THAT JOSEPH WAS ALIVE, AND JACOB REJOICED. JACOB AND HIS SONS ALL MOVED TO EGYPT. THERE JACOB DIED, AND JOSEPH CONTINUED TO RULE THE LAND. JOSEPH LIVED TO BE 110 YEARS OLD.
END OF GENESIS

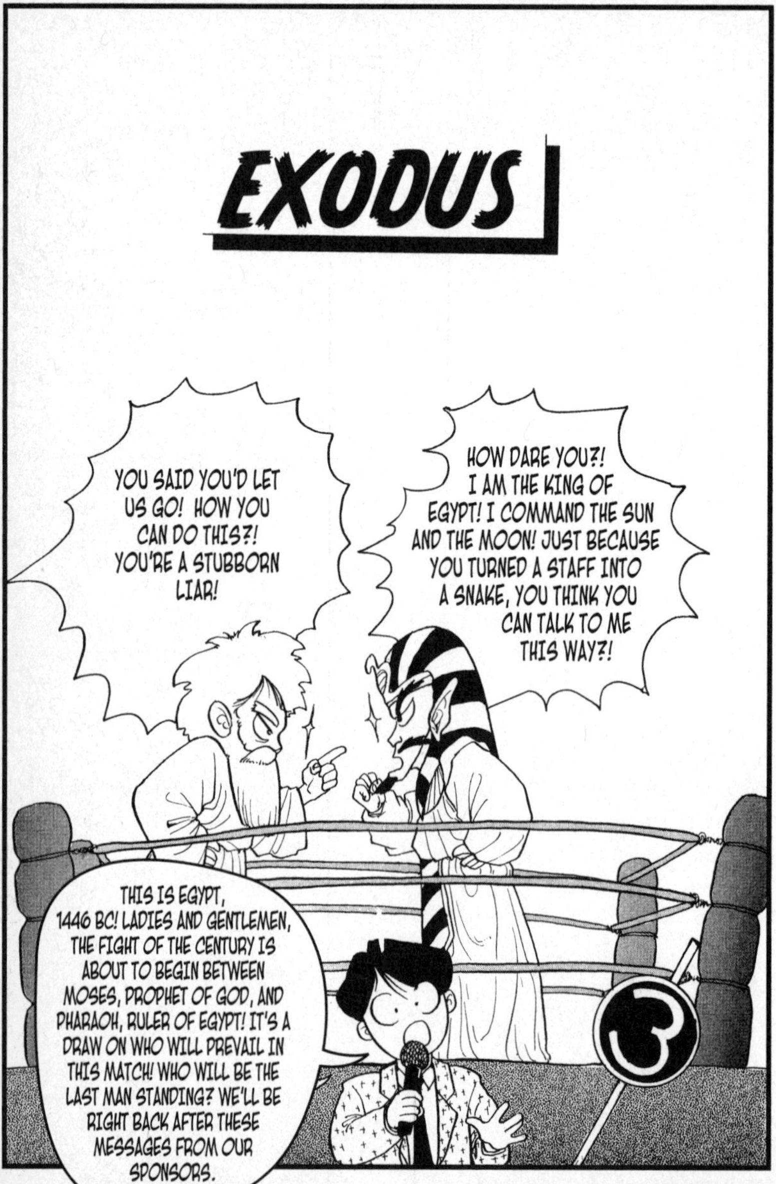
EXODUS
YOU SAID YOU'D LET US GO! HOW YOU CAN DO THIS?! YOU'RE A STUBBORN LIAR!
HOW DARE YOU?! I AM THE KING OF EGYPT! I COMMAND THE SUN AND THE MOON! JUST BECAUSE YOU TURNED A STAFF INTO A SNAKE, YOU THINK YOU CAN TALK TO ME THIS WAY?!
THIS IS EGYPT, 1446 BC! LADIES AND GENTLEMEN, THE FIGHT OF THE CENTURY IS ABOUT TO BEGIN BETWEEN MOSES, PROPHET OF GOD, AND PHARAOH, RULER OF EGYPT! IT'S A DRAW ON WHO WILL PREVAIL IN THIS MATCH! WHO WILL BE THE LAST MAN STANDING? WE'LL BE RIGHT BACK AFTER THESE MESSAGES FROM OUR SPONSORS.
3

THE PEOPLE OF ISRAEL WHO FOLLOWED JOSEPH INTO EGYPT GREW INTO TWO MILLION PEOPLE AND LIVED IN THE LAND OF GOSHEN.
ISRAEL
MOAB
GOSHEN
SINAI PENINSULA
EDOM
EGYPT
THE INTELLECTUAL CARTOONIST
THE PHARAOH THAT LIVED DURING JOSEPH'S TIME DIED...
IF YOU MAKE ME A MUMMY, I WILL LIVE FOREVER...
MANY PHARAOHS CAME AND WENT, AND A NEW PHARAOH WHO DID NOT KNOW JOSEPH'S WORK RULED EGYPT.
JOSEPH? IS HE A MOVIE STAR?
HMMM... THERE ARE MORE ISRAELITES THAN EGYPTIANS! WE HAVE TO DECREASE THEIR NUMBERS.
HA! I'LL TURN THEM INTO SLAVES AND WORK THEM HARD SO THAT THEY WILL HAVE NO POWER...

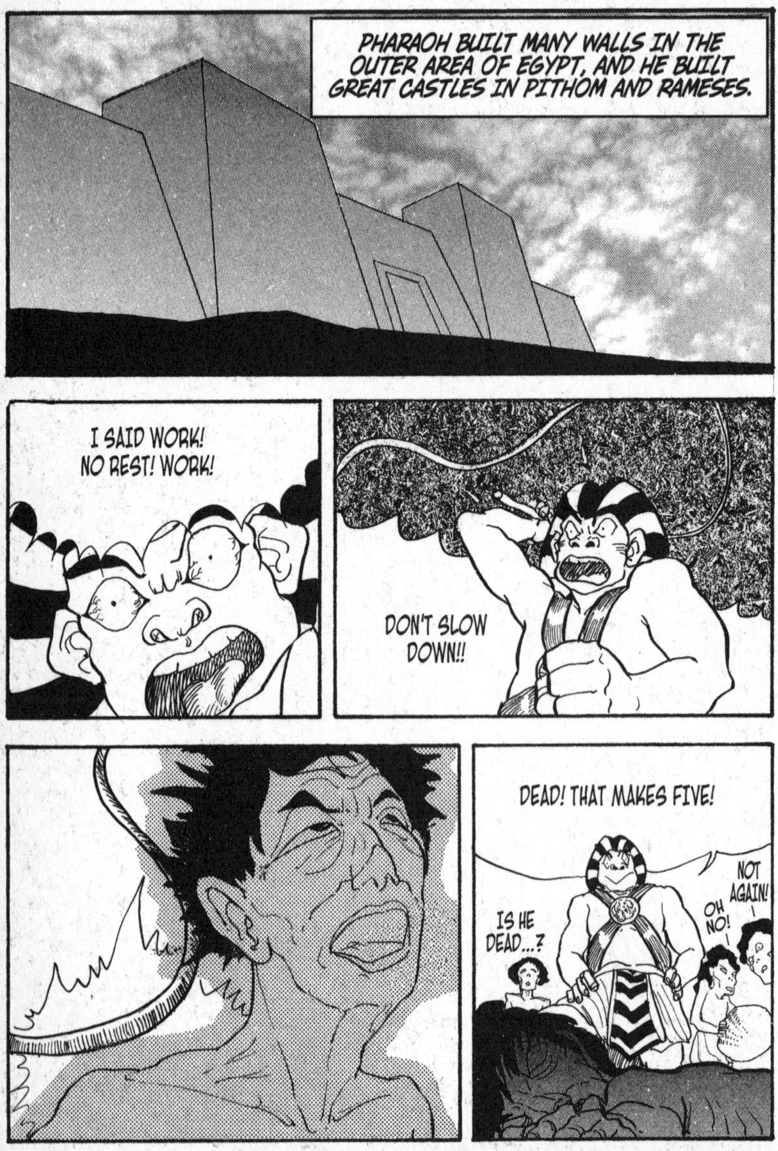
PHARAOH BUILT MANY WALLS IN THE OUTER AREA OF EGYPT, AND HE BUILT GREAT CASTLES IN PITHOM AND RAMESES.
I SAID WORK! NO REST! WORK!
DON'T SLOW DOWN!!
DEAD! THAT MAKES FIVE!
IS HE DEAD...?
OH NO!
NOT AGAIN!

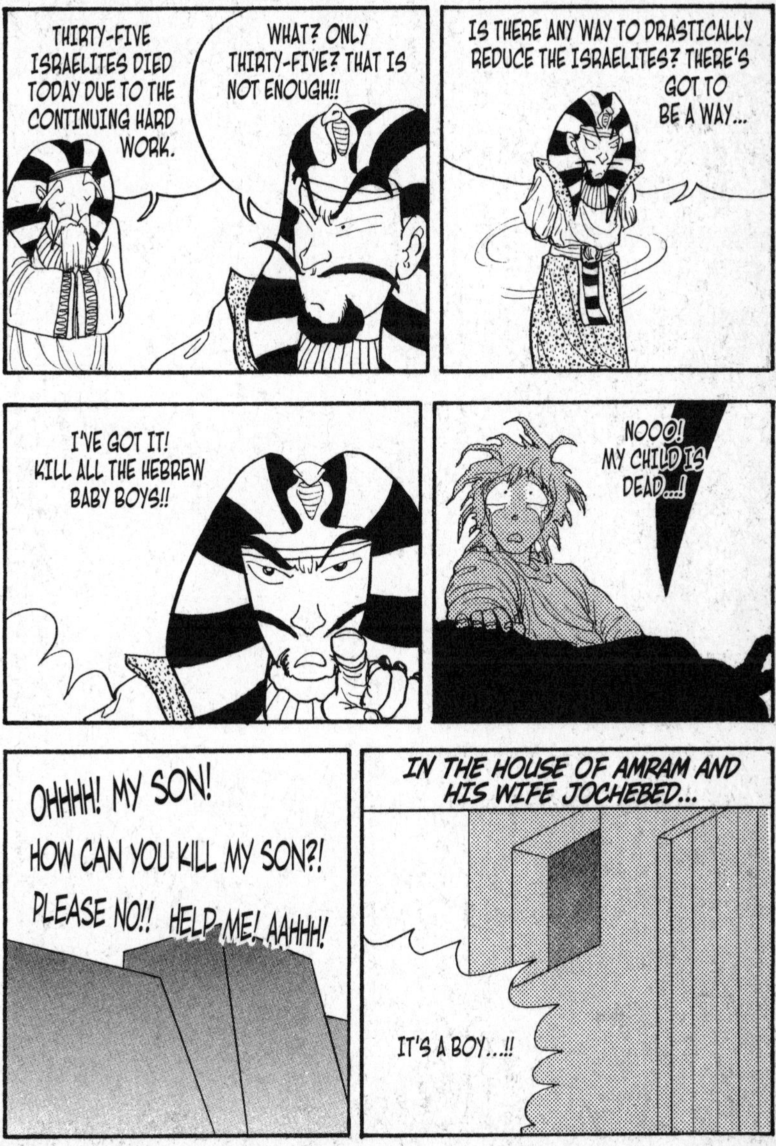
THIRTY-FIVE ISRAELITES DIED TODAY DUE TO THE CONTINUING HARD WORK.
WHAT? ONLY THIRTY-FIVE? THAT IS NOT ENOUGH!!
IS THERE ANY WAY TO DRASTICALLY REDUCE THE ISRAELITES? THERE'S GOT TO BE A WAY...
I'VE GOT IT! KILL ALL THE HEBREW BABY BOYS!!
NOOO! MY CHILD IS DEAD...!
OHHHH! MY SON!
HOW CAN YOU KILL MY SON?!
PLEASE NO!!
HELP ME! AAHHH!
IN THE HOUSE OF AMRAM AND HIS WIFE JOCHEBED...
IT'S A BOY...!!

I WOULD RATHER DIE THAN SEE THIS CHILD KILLED...

AARON AND MIRIAM, YOU MUST NOT TELL ANYONE WE ARE HIDING YOUR YOUNGER BROTHER! IF ANYONE FINDS OUT, WE WILL BE IN TROUBLE.

IT'S ALREADY BEEN THREE MONTHS...

WHOSE BABY IS CRYING?!

WAAH! WAAH!

WAAH!

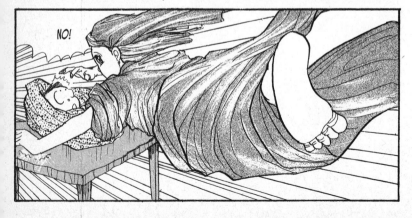

NO!

HEY, DID YOU HEAR A BABY CRYING?

MAYBE... I THOUGHT I HEARD IT TOO...

WE SHOULD CHECK THIS AREA TOMORROW!!

I CAN NO LONGER RAISE THIS CHILD IN HIDING...

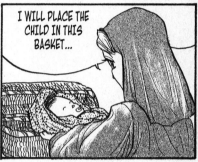

I WILL PLACE THE CHILD IN THIS BASKET...

DEAR CHILD... PLEASE LIVE...!

MOTHER, I'LL FOLLOW THE BABY AND COME BACK!

OH GOD! WHY ARE YOU ALLOWING SUCH TERRIBLE PERSECUTION TO OUR PEOPLE? PLEASE SAVE MY BABY'S LIFE!

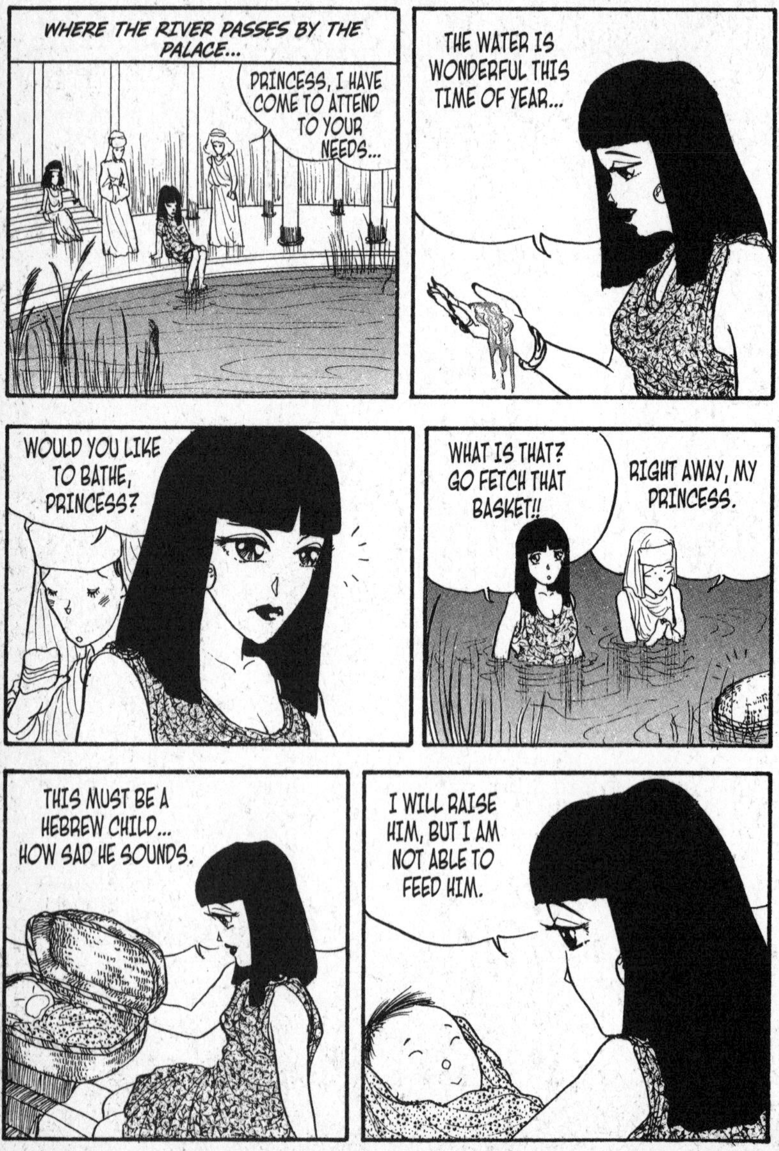
WHERE THE RIVER PASSES BY THE PALACE...
PRINCESS, I HAVE COME TO ATTEND TO YOUR NEEDS...
THE WATER IS WONDERFUL THIS TIME OF YEAR...
WOULD YOU LIKE TO BATHE, PRINCESS?
WHAT IS THAT? GO FETCH THAT BASKET!!
RIGHT AWAY, MY PRINCESS.
THIS MUST BE A HEBREW CHILD... HOW SAD HE SOUNDS.
I WILL RAISE HIM, BUT I AM NOT ABLE TO FEED HIM.

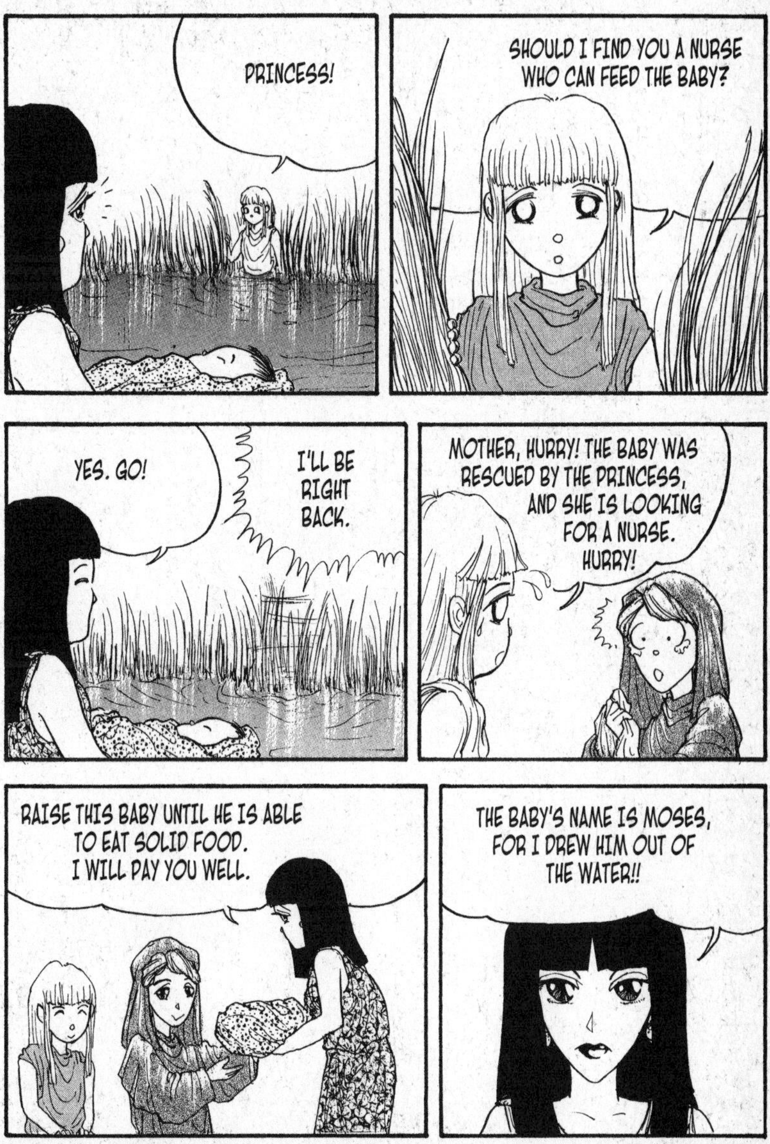
PRINCESS!
SHOULD I FIND YOU A NURSE WHO CAN FEED THE BABY?
YES. GO!
I'LL BE RIGHT BACK.
MOTHER, HURRY! THE BABY WAS RESCUED BY THE PRINCESS, AND SHE IS LOOKING FOR A NURSE. HURRY!
RAISE THIS BABY UNTIL HE IS ABLE TO EAT SOLID FOOD. I WILL PAY YOU WELL.
THE BABY'S NAME IS MOSES, FOR I DREW HIM OUT OF THE WATER!!

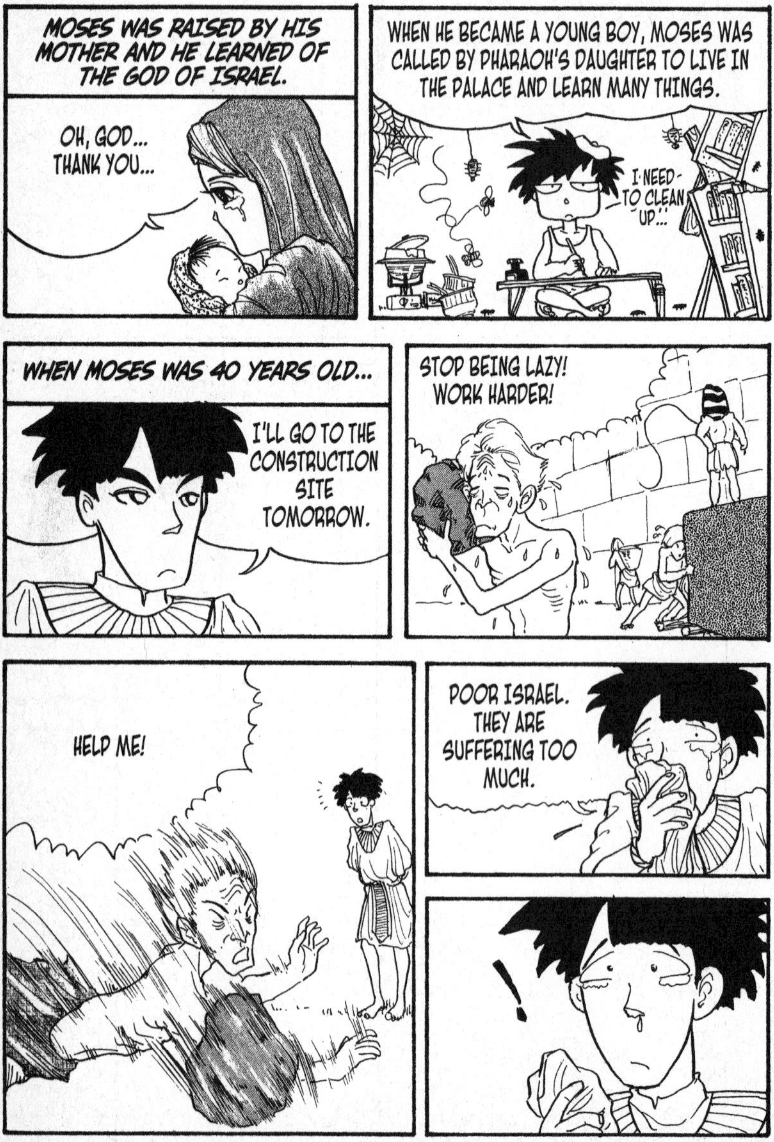
MOSES WAS RAISED BY HIS MOTHER AND HE LEARNED OF THE GOD OF ISRAEL.
OH, GOD... THANK YOU...
WHEN HE BECAME A YOUNG BOY, MOSES WAS CALLED BY PHARAOH'S DAUGHTER TO LIVE IN THE PALACE AND LEARN MANY THINGS.
I NEED TO CLEAN UP...
WHEN MOSES WAS 40 YEARS OLD...
I'LL GO TO THE CONSTRUCTION SITE TOMORROW.
STOP BEING LAZY! WORK HARDER!
HELP ME!
POOR ISRAEL. THEY ARE SUFFERING TOO MUCH.
!

YOU OLD FOOL!!

PLEASE... SAVE ME! I AM OLD AND I HAVE NO STRENGTH LEFT...

YOU USELESS OLD FOOL, I'LL KILL YOU!!

CHOKE!!

HOW CAN HE BE THAT MEAN? HOW CAN HE TREAT THAT OLD HEBREW MAN SO HARSHLY? I JUST CAN'T STAY OUT OF THIS!

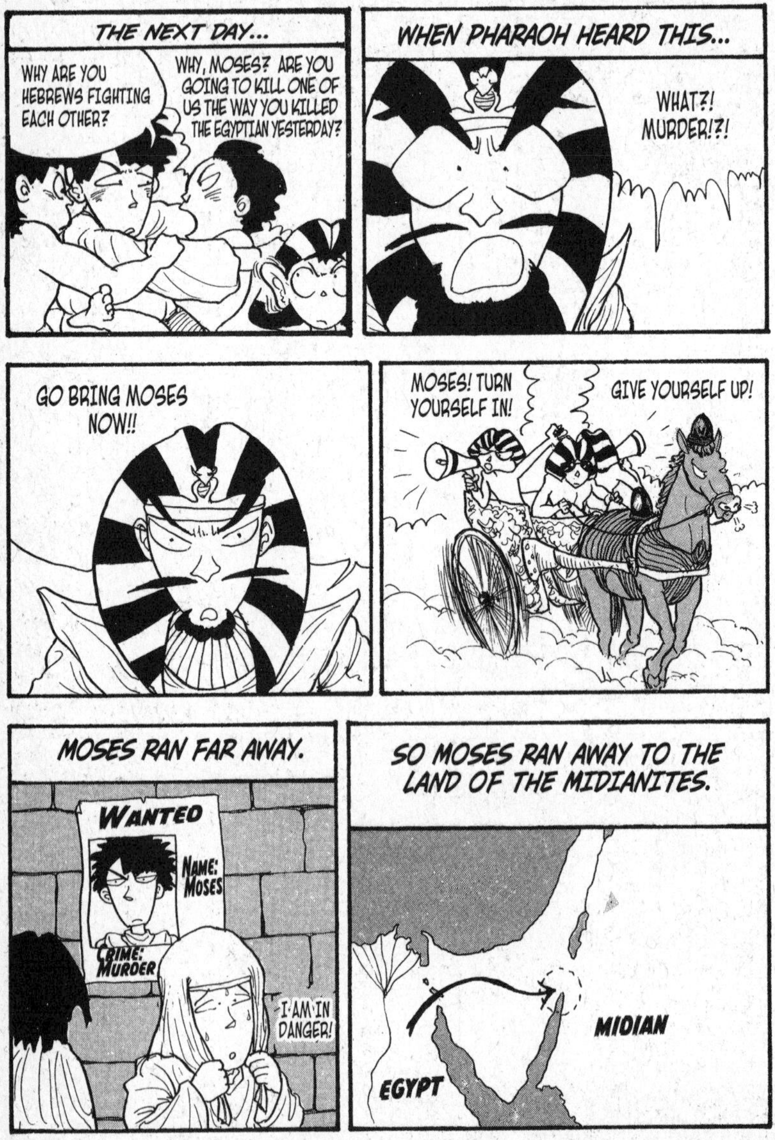
THE NEXT DAY...
WHY ARE YOU HEBREWS FIGHTING EACH OTHER?
WHY, MOSES? ARE YOU GOING TO KILL ONE OF US THE WAY YOU KILLED THE EGYPTIAN YESTERDAY?
WHEN PHARAOH HEARD THIS...
WHAT?! MURDER!?!
GO BRING MOSES NOW!!
MOSES! TURN YOURSELF IN!
GIVE YOURSELF UP!
MOSES RAN FAR AWAY.
WANTED
NAME: MOSES
CRIME: MURDER
I AM IN DANGER!
SO MOSES RAN AWAY TO THE LAND OF THE MIDIANITES.
MIDIAN
EGYPT

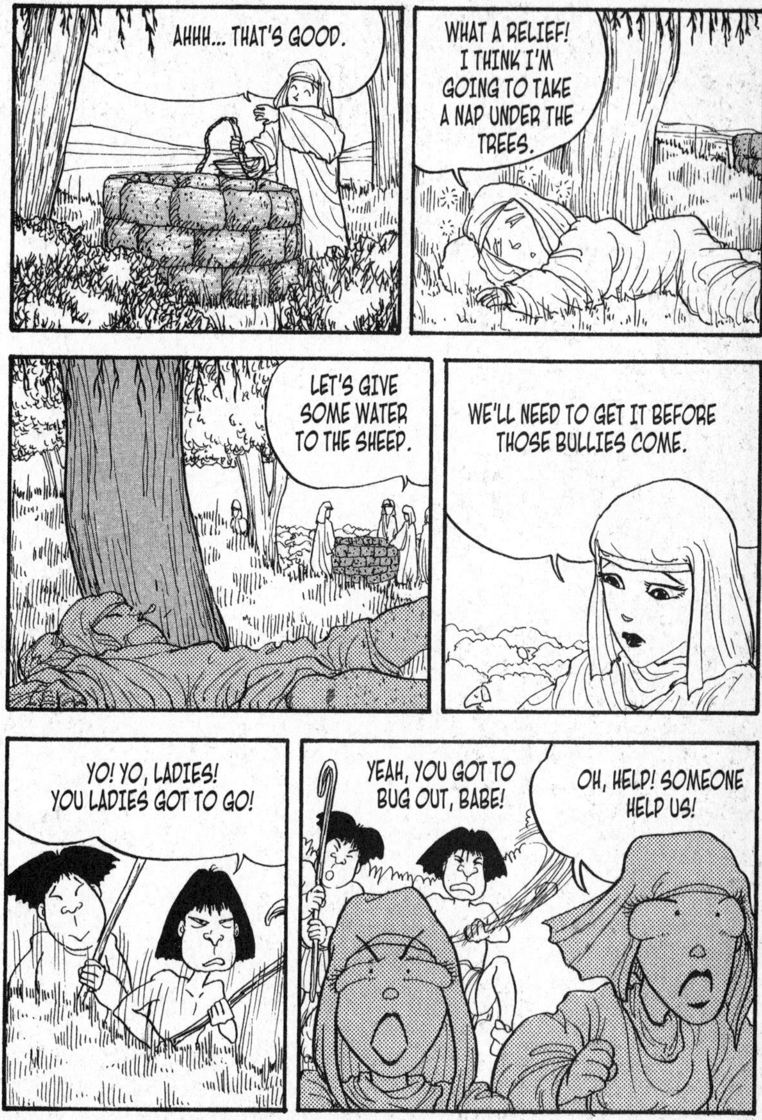
AHHH... THAT'S GOOD.
WHAT A RELIEF! I THINK I'M GOING TO TAKE A NAP UNDER THE TREES.
LET'S GIVE SOME WATER TO THE SHEEP.
WE'LL NEED TO GET IT BEFORE THOSE BULLIES COME.
YO! YO, LADIES! YOU LADIES GOT TO GO!
YEAH, YOU GOT TO BUG OUT, BABE!
OH, HELP! SOMEONE HELP US!

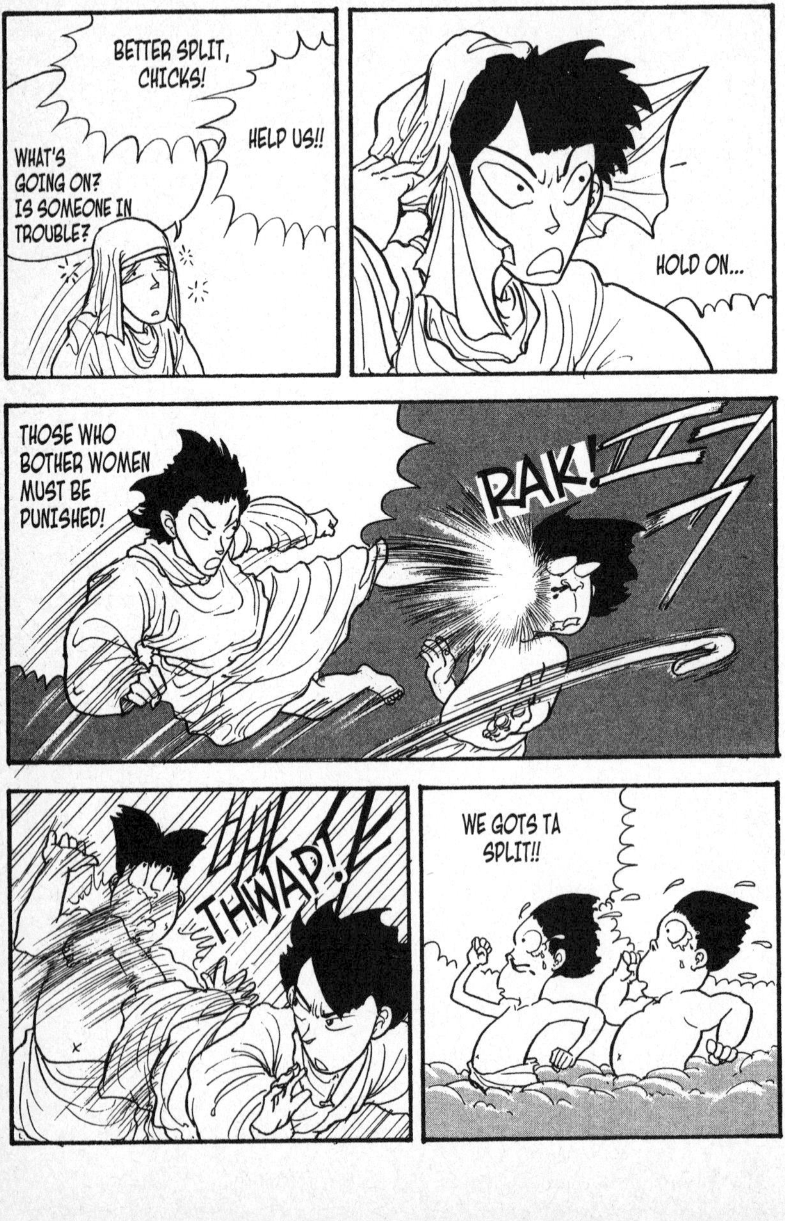
BETTER SPLIT, CHICKS!
HELP US!!
WHAT'S GOING ON? IS SOMEONE IN TROUBLE?
HOLD ON...
THOSE WHO BOTHER WOMEN MUST BE PUNISHED!
RAK!
THWAP!
WE GOTS TA SPLIT!!

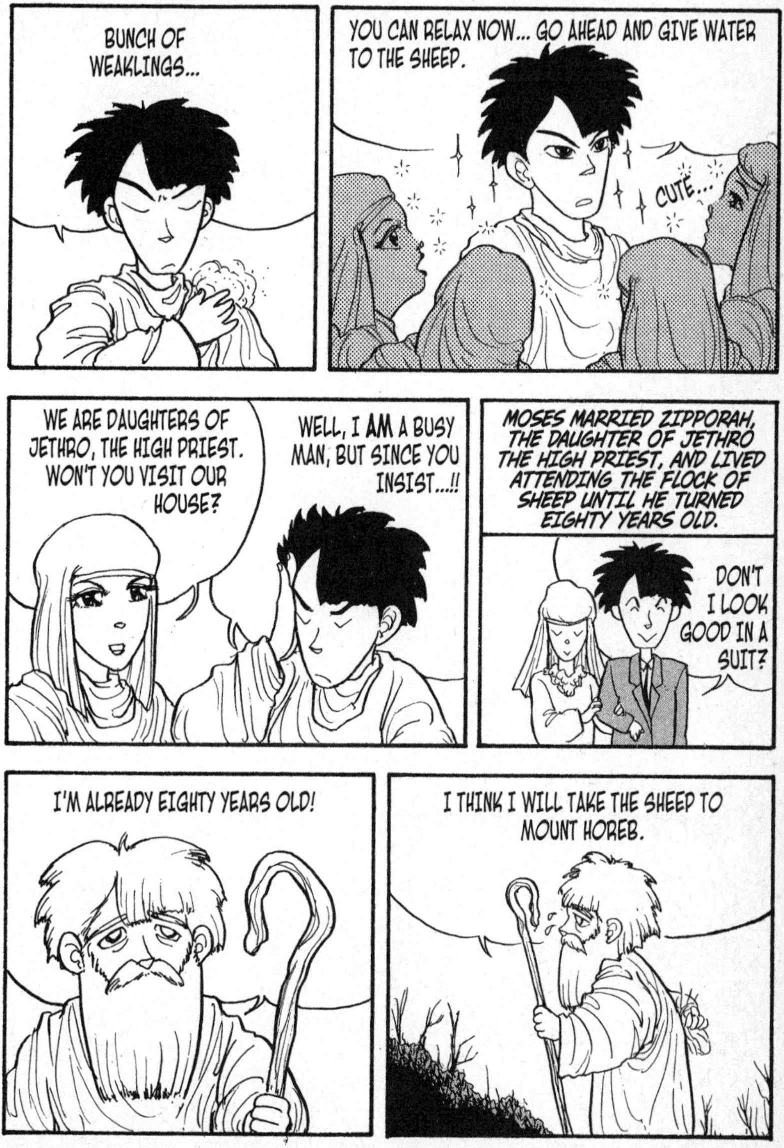
BUNCH OF WEAKLINGS...
YOU CAN RELAX NOW... GO AHEAD AND GIVE WATER TO THE SHEEP.
CUTE...
WE ARE DAUGHTERS OF JETHRO, THE HIGH PRIEST. WON'T YOU VISIT OUR HOUSE?
WELL, I AM A BUSY MAN, BUT SINCE YOU INSIST...!!
MOSES MARRIED ZIPPORAH, THE DAUGHTER OF JETHRO THE HIGH PRIEST, AND LIVED ATTENDING THE FLOCK OF SHEEP UNTIL HE TURNED EIGHTY YEARS OLD.
DON'T I LOOK GOOD IN A SUIT?
I'M ALREADY EIGHTY YEARS OLD!
I THINK I WILL TAKE THE SHEEP TO MOUNT HOREB.

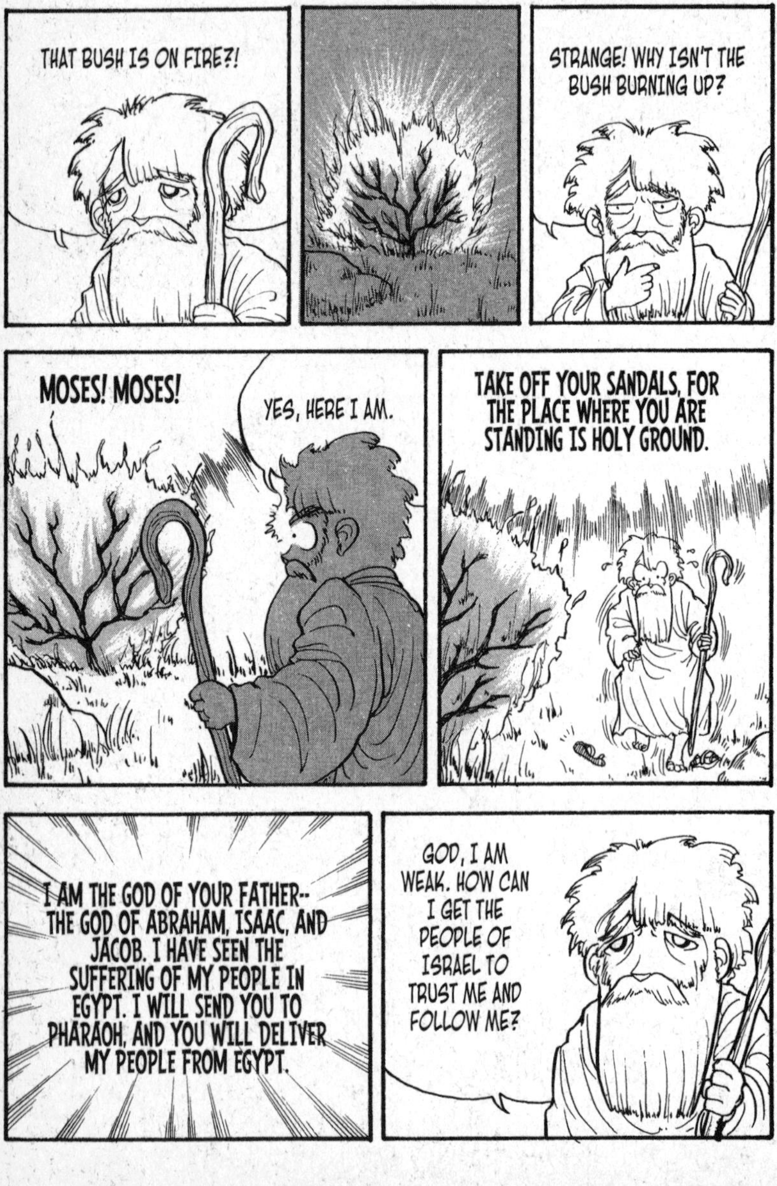
THAT BUSH IS ON FIRE?!
STRANGE! WHY ISN'T THE BUSH BURNING UP?
MOSES! MOSES!
YES, HERE I AM.
TAKE OFF YOUR SANDALS, FOR THE PLACE WHERE YOU ARE STANDING IS HOLY GROUND.
I AM THE GOD OF YOUR FATHER-- THE GOD OF ABRAHAM, ISAAC, AND JACOB. I HAVE SEEN THE SUFFERING OF MY PEOPLE IN EGYPT. I WILL SEND YOU TO PHARAOH, AND YOU WILL DELIVER MY PEOPLE FROM EGYPT.
GOD, I AM WEAK. HOW CAN I GET THE PEOPLE OF ISRAEL TO TRUST ME AND FOLLOW ME?

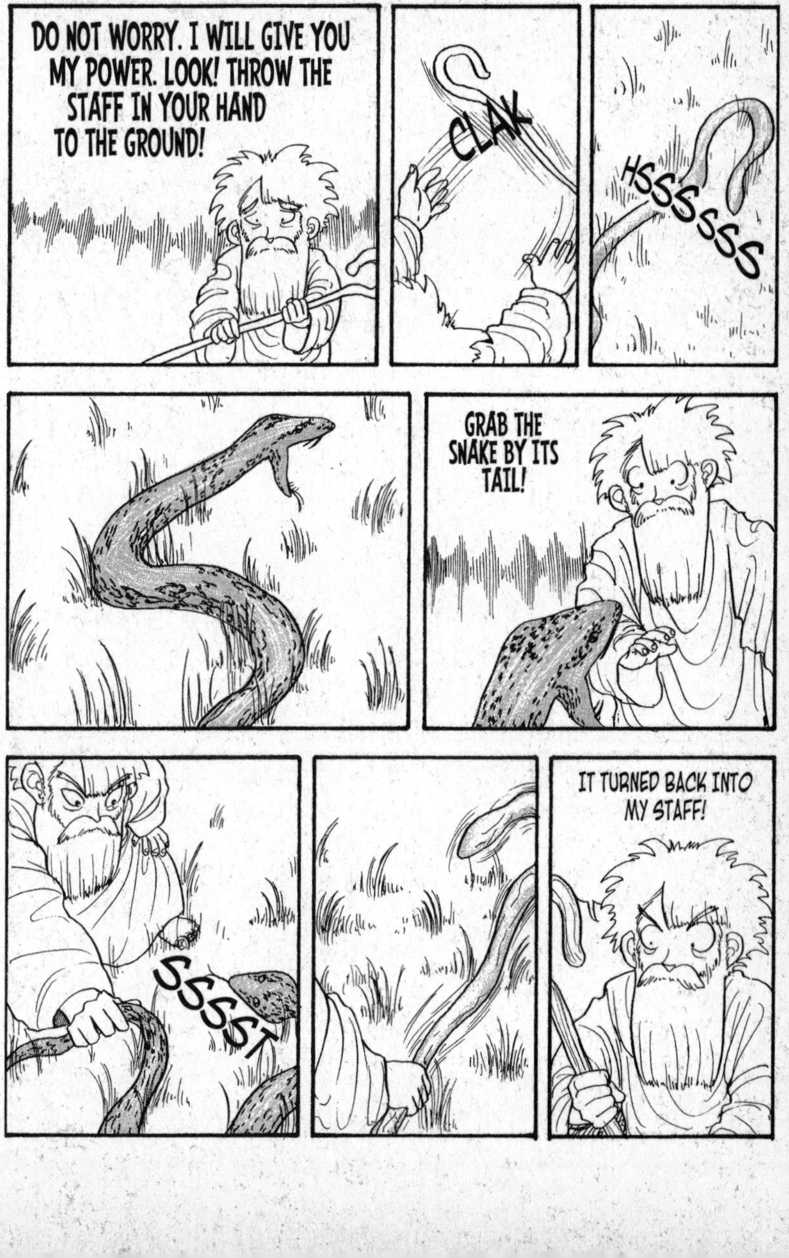
DO NOT WORRY. I WILL GIVE YOU MY POWER. LOOK! THROW THE STAFF IN YOUR HAND TO THE GROUND!
CLAK
HSSSSSSS
GRAB THE SNAKE BY ITS TAIL!
SSSST
IT TURNED BACK INTO MY STAFF!

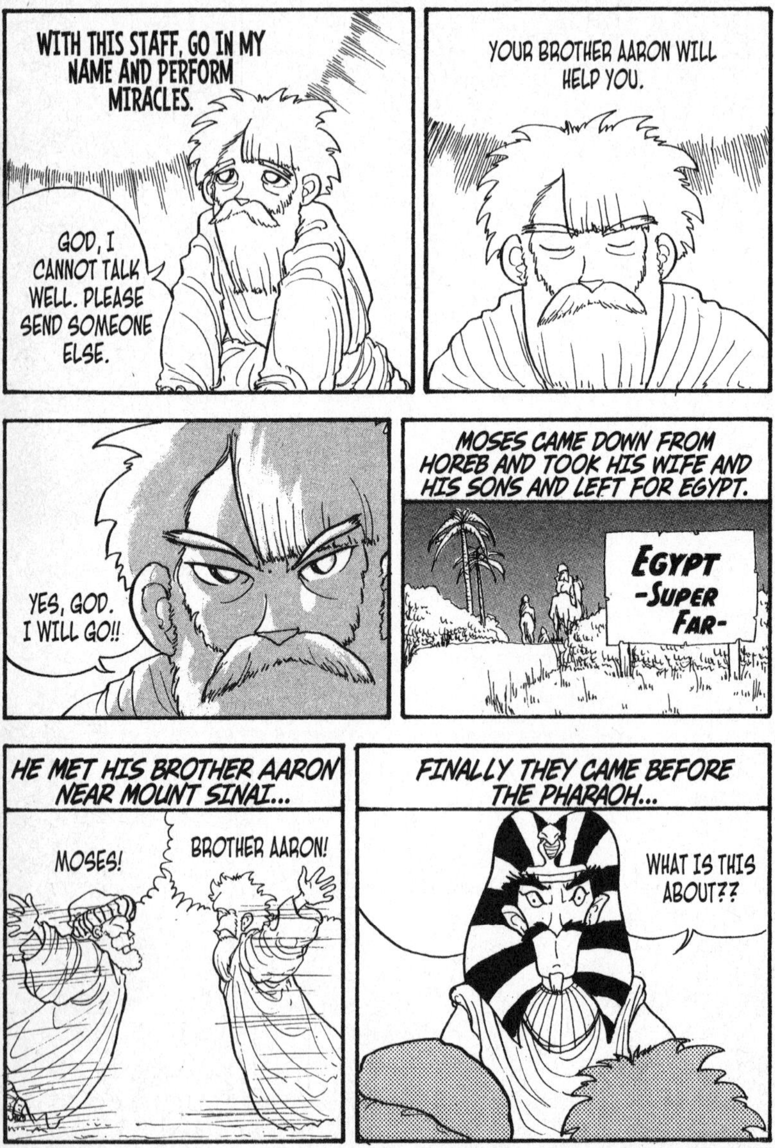
WITH THIS STAFF, GO IN MY NAME AND PERFORM MIRACLES.
GOD, I CANNOT TALK WELL. PLEASE SEND SOMEONE ELSE.
YOUR BROTHER AARON WILL HELP YOU.
YES, GOD. I WILL GO!!
MOSES CAME DOWN FROM HOREB AND TOOK HIS WIFE AND HIS SONS AND LEFT FOR EGYPT.
EGYPT -SUPER FAR-
HE MET HIS BROTHER AARON NEAR MOUNT SINAI...
MOSES!
BROTHER AARON!
FINALLY THEY CAME BEFORE THE PHARAOH...
WHAT IS THIS ABOUT??

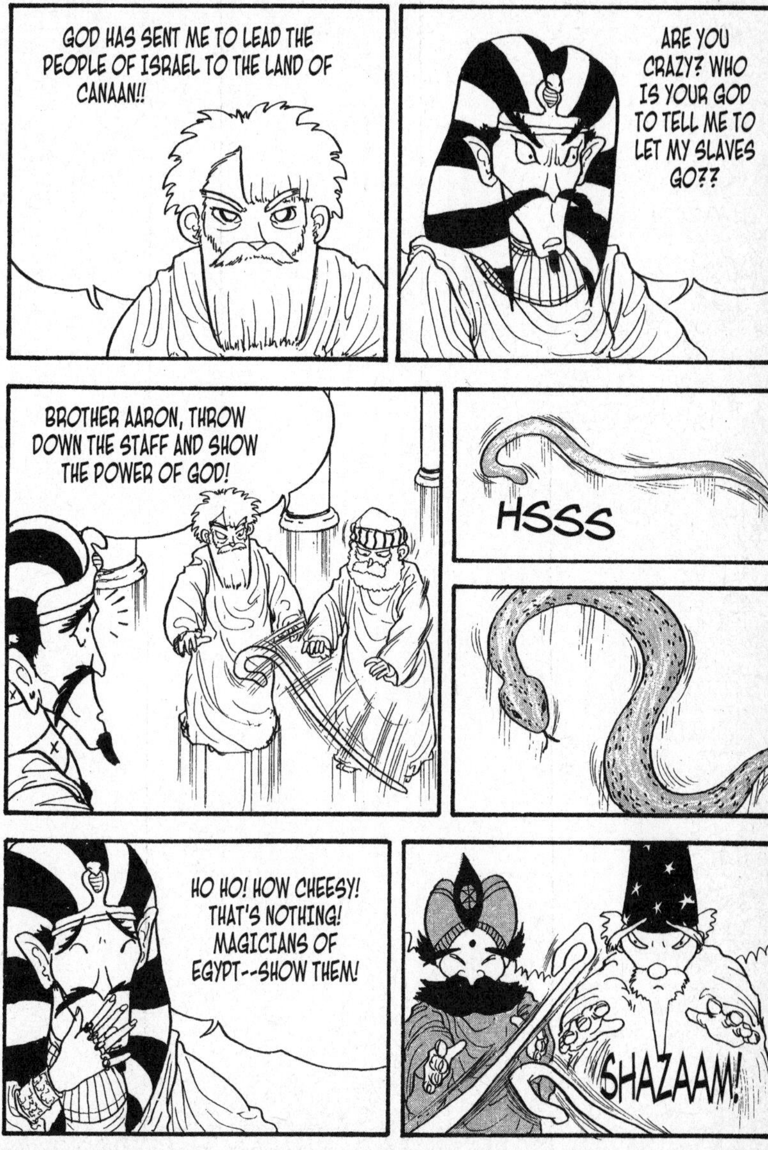
GOD HAS SENT ME TO LEAD THE PEOPLE OF ISRAEL TO THE LAND OF CANAAN!!
ARE YOU CRAZY? WHO IS YOUR GOD TO TELL ME TO LET MY SLAVES GO??
BROTHER AARON, THROW DOWN THE STAFF AND SHOW THE POWER OF GOD!
HSSS
HO HO! HOW CHEESY! THAT'S NOTHING! MAGICIANS OF EGYPT--SHOW THEM!
SHAZAAM!

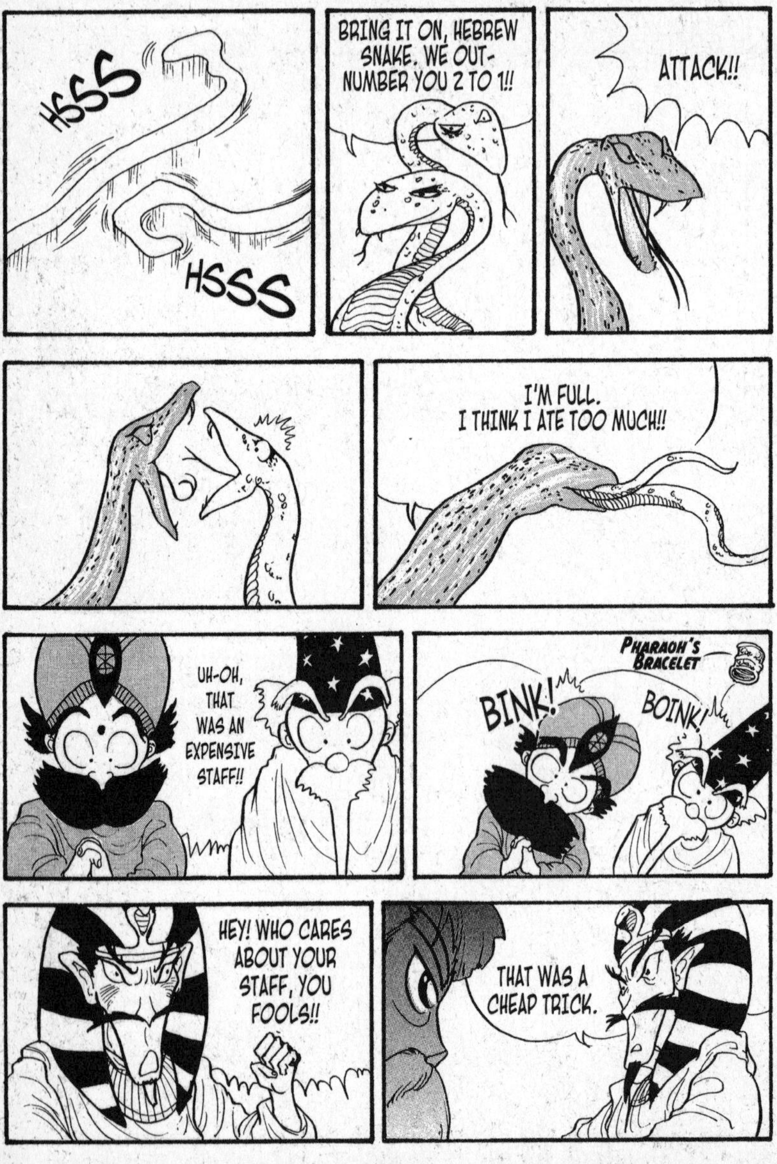
HSSS
HSSS
BRING IT ON, HEBREW SNAKE. WE OUT-NUMBER YOU 2 TO 1!!
ATTACK!!
I'M FULL. I THINK I ATE TOO MUCH!!
UH-OH, THAT WAS AN EXPENSIVE STAFF!!
PHARAOH'S BRACELET
BINK!
BOINK!
HEY! WHO CARES ABOUT YOUR STAFF, YOU FOOLS!!
THAT WAS A CHEAP TRICK.

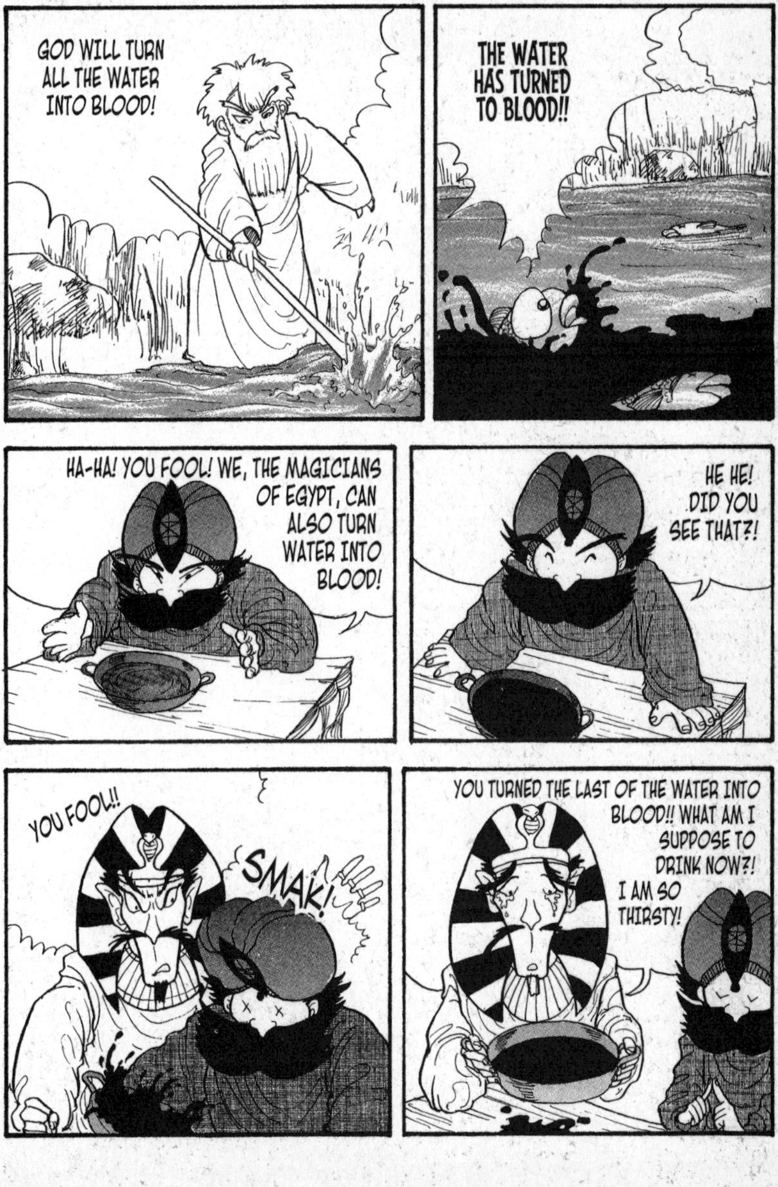
GOD WILL TURN ALL THE WATER INTO BLOOD!
THE WATER HAS TURNED TO BLOOD!!
HA-HA! YOU FOOL! WE, THE MAGICIANS OF EGYPT, CAN ALSO TURN WATER INTO BLOOD!
HE HE! DID YOU SEE THAT?!
YOU FOOL!!
SMAK!
YOU TURNED THE LAST OF THE WATER INTO BLOOD!! WHAT AM I SUPPOSE TO DRINK NOW?!
I AM SO THIRSTY!

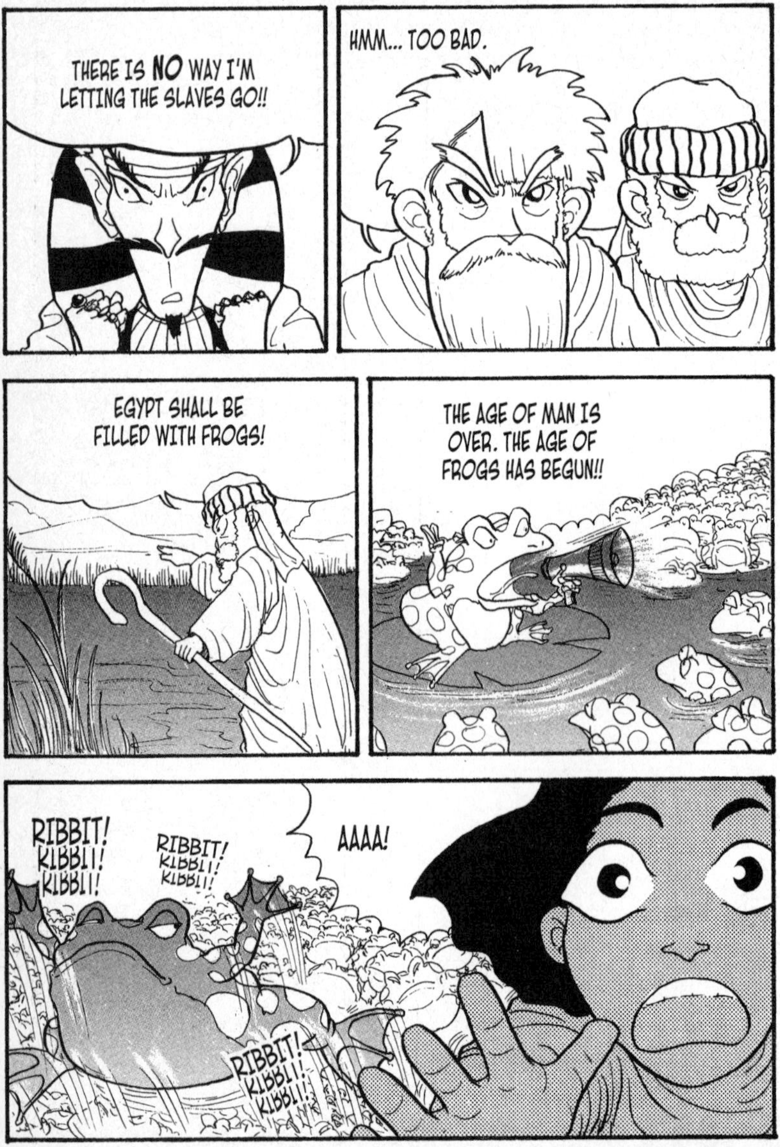
THERE IS NO WAY I'M LETTING THE SLAVES GO!!
HMM... TOO BAD.
EGYPT SHALL BE FILLED WITH FROGS!
THE AGE OF MAN IS OVER. THE AGE OF FROGS HAS BEGUN!!
RIBBIT! RIBBIT! RIBBIT!
RIBBIT! RIBBIT! RIBBIT!
AAAA!
RIBBIT! RIBBIT! RIBBIT!

I CAN DO THAT TOO!
SEE THAT?! FROGS!
RIBBIT! RIBBIT!! RIBBIT!!
YOU FOOL!
WHAT ARE YOU DOING? ARE YOU DOING THIS ON PURPOSE??!! WE ALREADY HAVE TOO MANY FROGS!!!
MOSES, I WILL GRANT YOUR WISH. JUST GET RID OF THESE FROGS!
GOD, PLEASE REMOVE ALL THE FROGS.

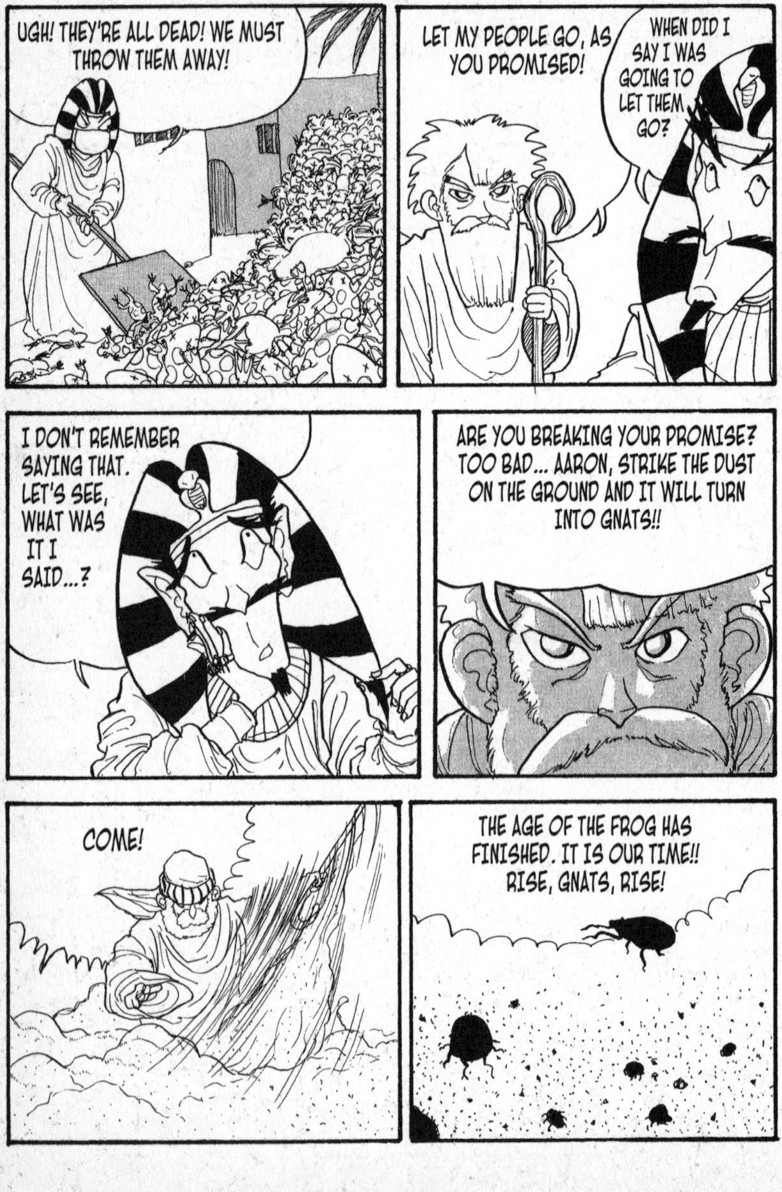
UGH! THEY'RE ALL DEAD! WE MUST THROW THEM AWAY!
LET MY PEOPLE GO, AS YOU PROMISED!
WHEN DID I SAY I WAS GOING TO LET THEM GO?
I DON'T REMEMBER SAYING THAT. LET'S SEE, WHAT WAS IT I SAID...?
ARE YOU BREAKING YOUR PROMISE? TOO BAD... AARON, STRIKE THE DUST ON THE GROUND AND IT WILL TURN INTO GNATS!!
COME!
THE AGE OF THE FROG HAS FINISHED. IT IS OUR TIME!! RISE, GNATS, RISE!

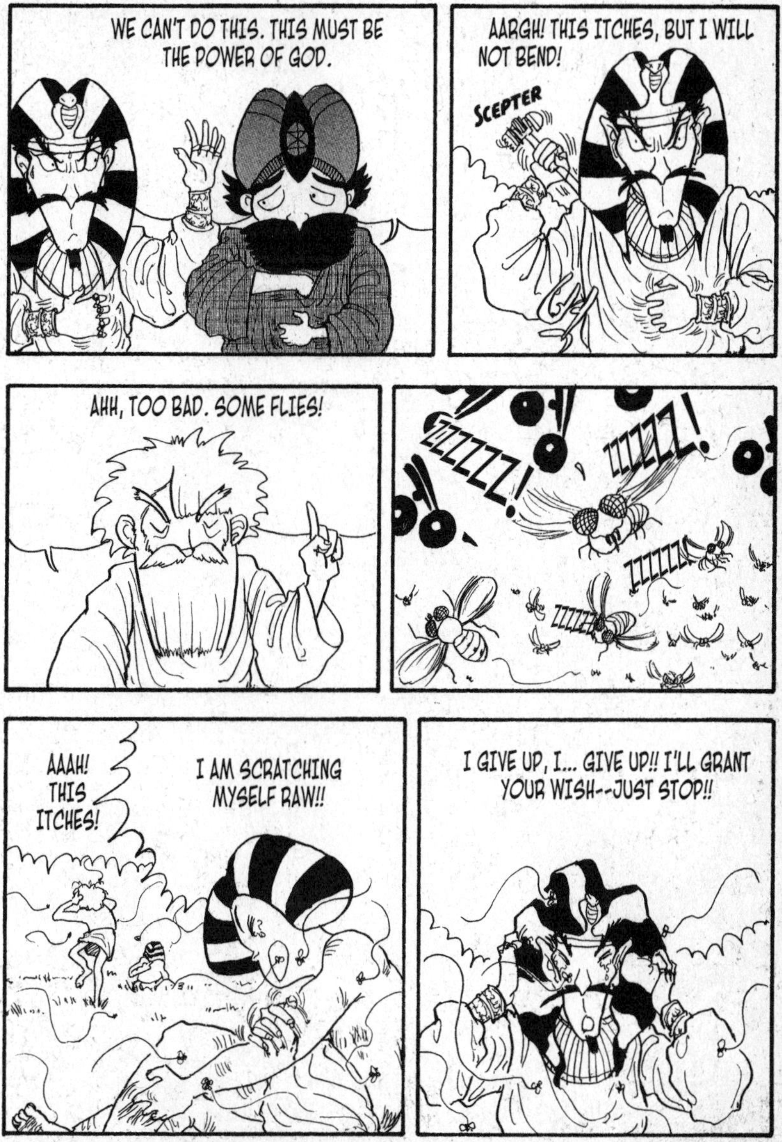
WE CAN'T DO THIS. THIS MUST BE THE POWER OF GOD.
AARGH! THIS ITCHES, BUT I WILL NOT BEND!
SCEPTER
AHH, TOO BAD. SOME FLIES!
ZZZZZZZ!
ZZZZZZ!
ZZZZZZ
ZZZZZ
AAAH! THIS ITCHES!
I AM SCRATCHING MYSELF RAW!!
I GIVE UP, I... GIVE UP!! I'LL GRANT YOUR WISH--JUST STOP!!

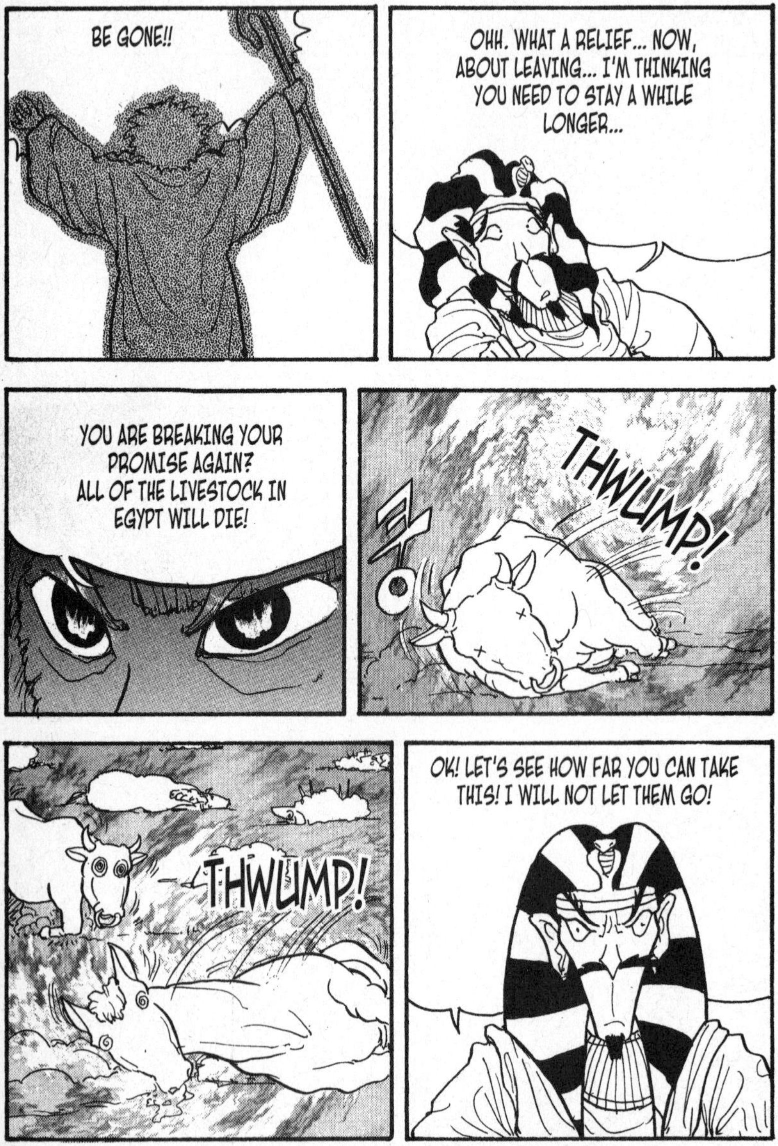
BE GONE!!
OHH. WHAT A RELIEF... NOW, ABOUT LEAVING... I'M THINKING YOU NEED TO STAY A WHILE LONGER...
YOU ARE BREAKING YOUR PROMISE AGAIN? ALL OF THE LIVESTOCK IN EGYPT WILL DIE!
THWUMP!
THWUMP!
OK! LET'S SEE HOW FAR YOU CAN TAKE THIS! I WILL NOT LET THEM GO!

ALL RIGHT. THEN AS I SPRAY THESE ASHES --WATCH AND SEE WHAT HAPPENS.

IS THERE ANYONE IN ALL OF EGYPT NOT COVERED HEAD TO FOOT WITH BOILS?! EVEN THE MAGICIANS ARE IN BED SICK!

I'M DYING.

NO! I STILL WON'T LET THEM GO!!!

THEN GOD SHALL SEND FIRE AND HAIL DOWN FROM THE SKY!!

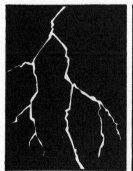

AHHH!

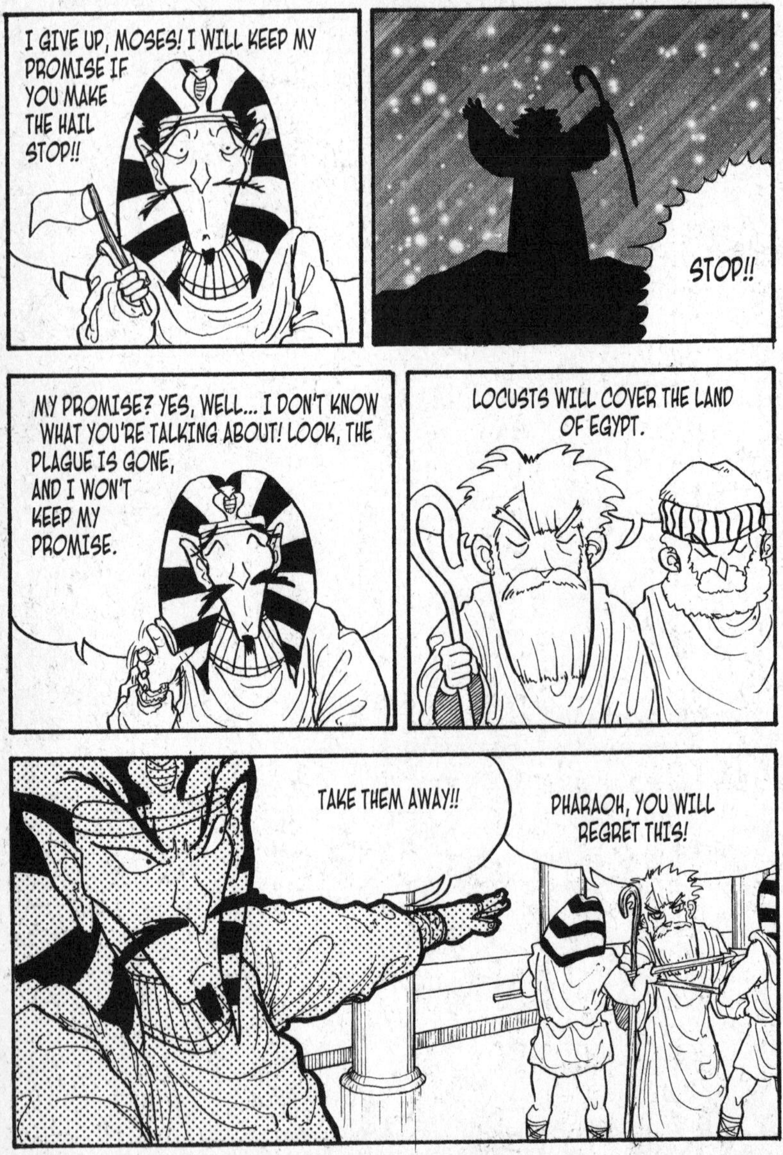
I GIVE UP, MOSES! I WILL KEEP MY PROMISE IF YOU MAKE THE HAIL STOP!!
STOP!!
MY PROMISE? YES, WELL... I DON'T KNOW WHAT YOU'RE TALKING ABOUT! LOOK, THE PLAGUE IS GONE, AND I WON'T KEEP MY PROMISE.
LOCUSTS WILL COVER THE LAND OF EGYPT.
TAKE THEM AWAY!!
PHARAOH, YOU WILL REGRET THIS!

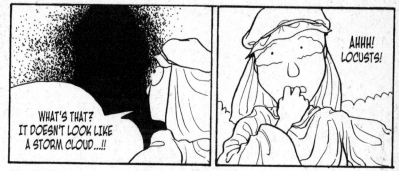

WHAT'S THAT? IT DOESN'T LOOK LIKE A STORM CLOUD...!!

AHHH! LOCUSTS!

THE AGE OF THE LOCUST IS HERE!! LET'S EAT!

EVERYTHING GREEN IN EGYPT HAS BEEN EATEN!!

I HAVE LOST. I WILL LET YOUR PEOPLE GO. PLEASE GET RID OF THE LOCUSTS.

IF THAT IS YOUR PROMISE, THEN I WILL PRAY TO GOD.

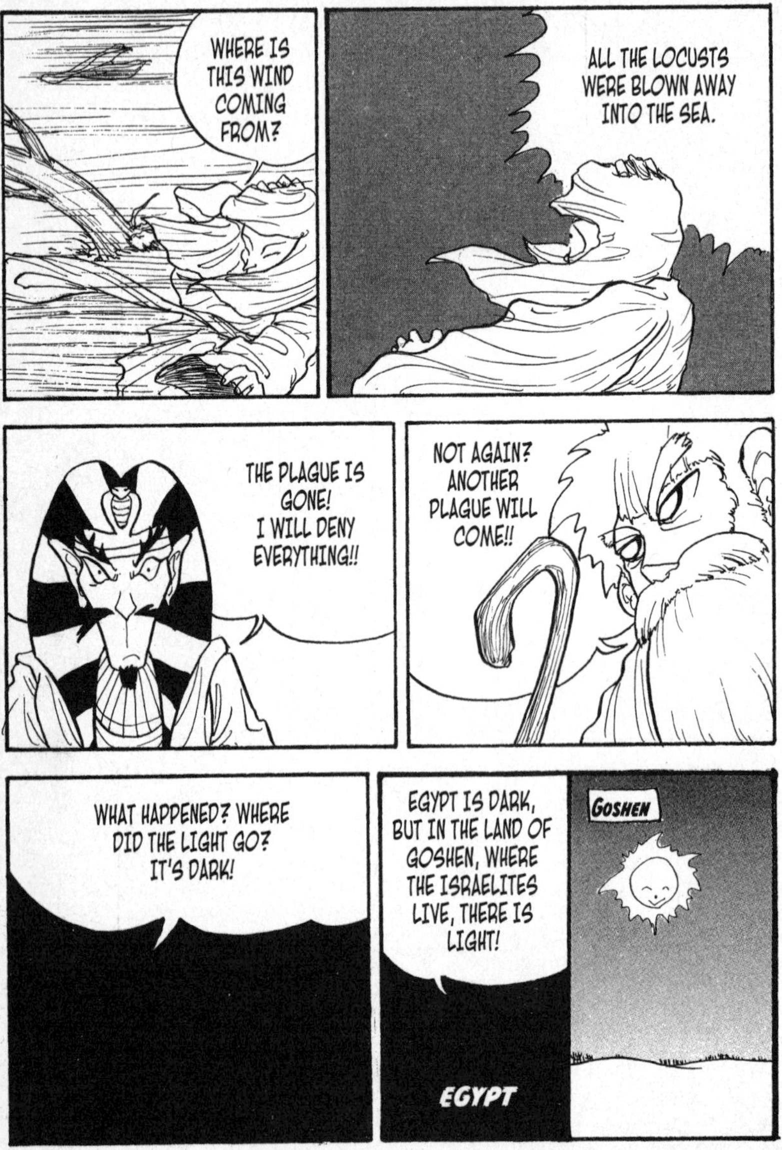
WHERE IS THIS WIND COMING FROM?
ALL THE LOCUSTS WERE BLOWN AWAY INTO THE SEA.
THE PLAGUE IS GONE! I WILL DENY EVERYTHING!!
NOT AGAIN? ANOTHER PLAGUE WILL COME!!
WHAT HAPPENED? WHERE DID THE LIGHT GO? IT'S DARK!
EGYPT IS DARK, BUT IN THE LAND OF GOSHEN, WHERE THE ISRAELITES LIVE, THERE IS LIGHT!
GOSHEN
EGYPT

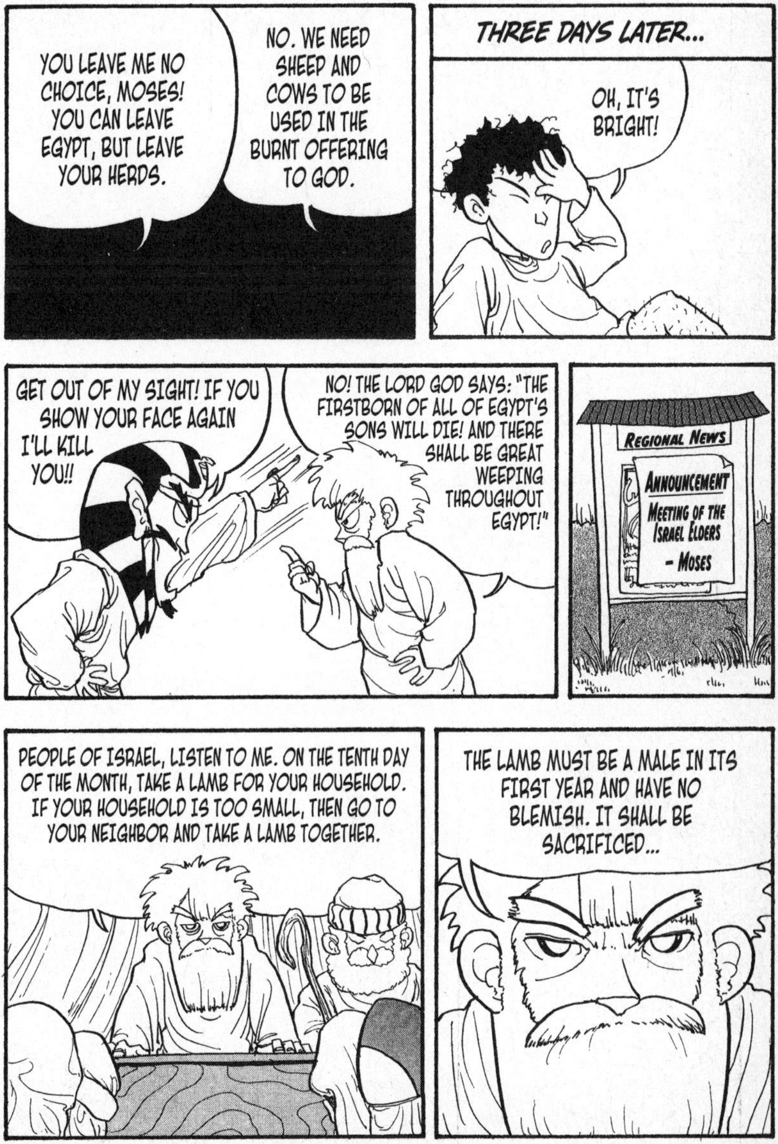
YOU LEAVE ME NO CHOICE, MOSES! YOU CAN LEAVE EGYPT, BUT LEAVE YOUR HERDS.
NO. WE NEED SHEEP AND COWS TO BE USED IN THE BURNT OFFERING TO GOD.
THREE DAYS LATER...
OH, IT'S BRIGHT!
GET OUT OF MY SIGHT! IF YOU SHOW YOUR FACE AGAIN I'LL KILL YOU!!
NO! THE LORD GOD SAYS: "THE FIRSTBORN OF ALL OF EGYPT'S SONS WILL DIE! AND THERE SHALL BE GREAT WEEPING THROUGHOUT EGYPT!"
REGIONAL NEWS
ANNOUNCEMENT
MEETING OF THE ISRAEL ELDERS
- MOSES
PEOPLE OF ISRAEL, LISTEN TO ME. ON THE TENTH DAY OF THE MONTH, TAKE A LAMB FOR YOUR HOUSEHOLD. IF YOUR HOUSEHOLD IS TOO SMALL, THEN GO TO YOUR NEIGHBOR AND TAKE A LAMB TOGETHER.
THE LAMB MUST BE A MALE IN ITS FIRST YEAR AND HAVE NO BLEMISH. IT SHALL BE SACRIFICED...

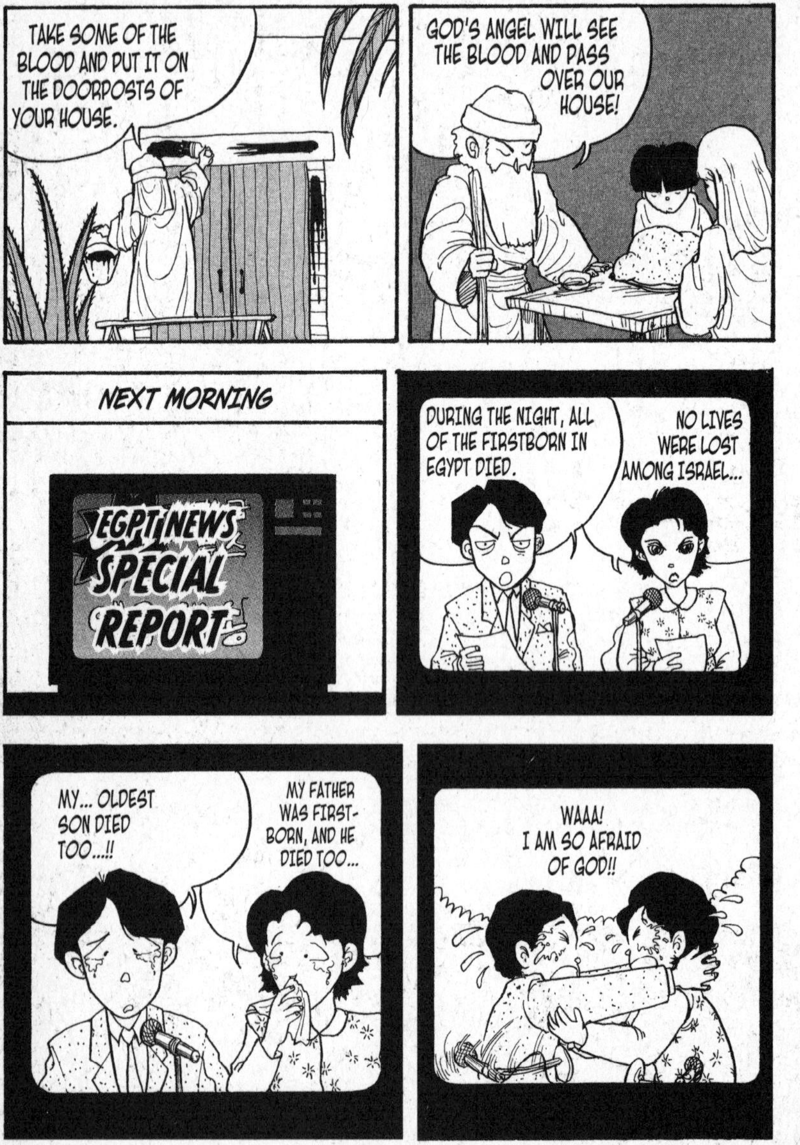
TAKE SOME OF THE BLOOD AND PUT IT ON THE DOORPOSTS OF YOUR HOUSE.
GOD'S ANGEL WILL SEE THE BLOOD AND PASS OVER OUR HOUSE!
NEXT MORNING
EGPT NEWS SPECIAL REPORT
DURING THE NIGHT, ALL OF THE FIRSTBORN IN EGYPT DIED.
NO LIVES WERE LOST AMONG ISRAEL...
MY... OLDEST SON DIED TOO...!!
MY FATHER WAS FIRST-BORN, AND HE DIED TOO...
WAAA! I AM SO AFRAID OF GOD!!

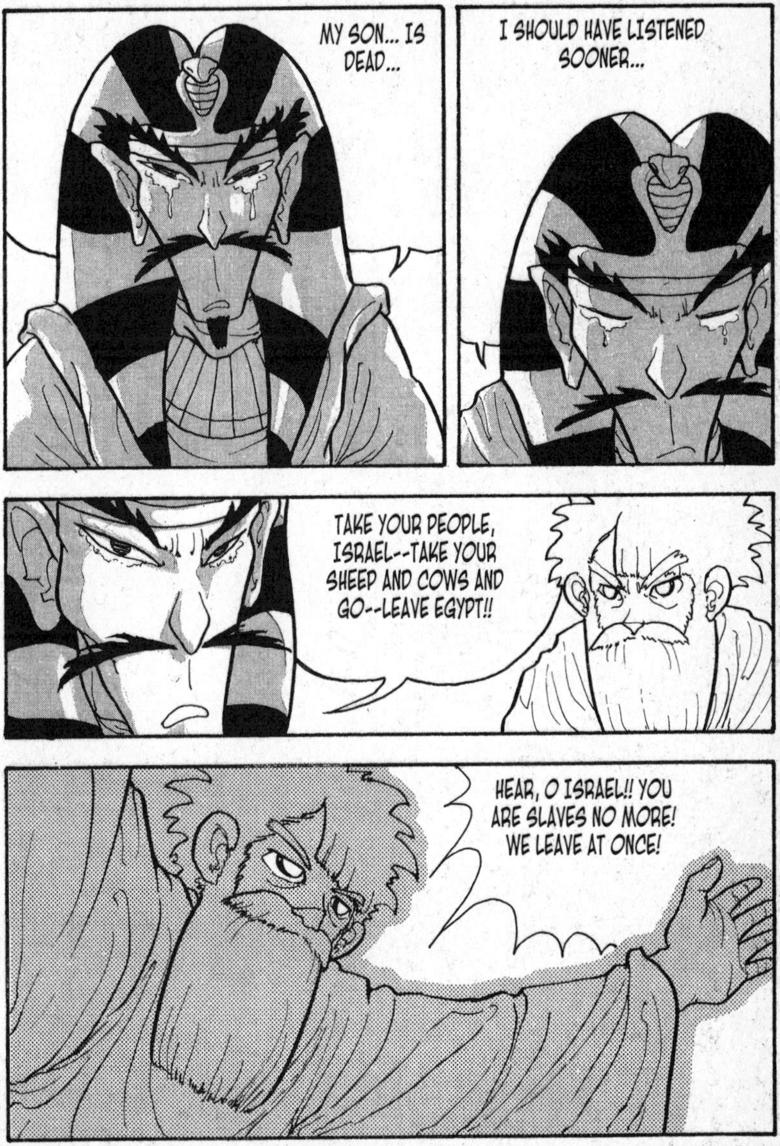
MY SON... IS DEAD...
I SHOULD HAVE LISTENED SOONER...
TAKE YOUR PEOPLE, ISRAEL--TAKE YOUR SHEEP AND COWS AND GO--LEAVE EGYPT!!
HEAR, O ISRAEL!! YOU ARE SLAVES NO MORE! WE LEAVE AT ONCE!

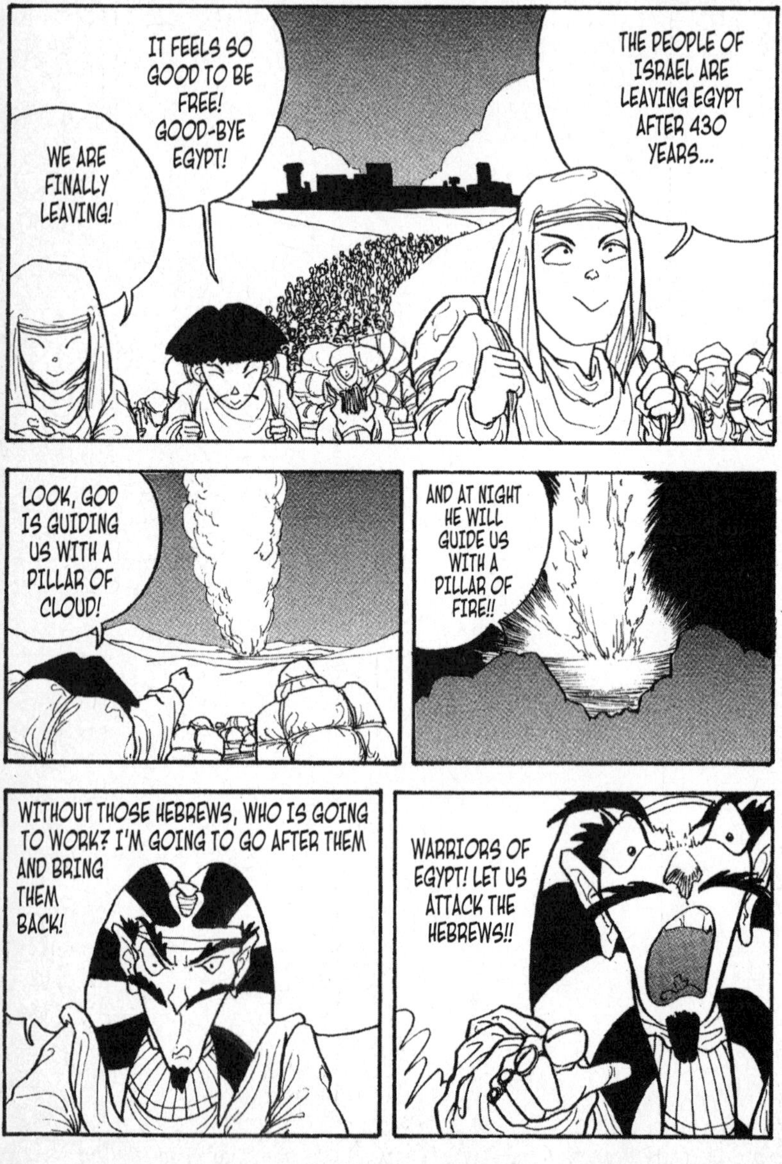
IT FEELS SO GOOD TO BE FREE! GOOD-BYE EGYPT!
WE ARE FINALLY LEAVING!
THE PEOPLE OF ISRAEL ARE LEAVING EGYPT AFTER 430 YEARS...
LOOK, GOD IS GUIDING US WITH A PILLAR OF CLOUD!
AND AT NIGHT HE WILL GUIDE US WITH A PILLAR OF FIRE!!
WITHOUT THOSE HEBREWS, WHO IS GOING TO WORK? I'M GOING TO GO AFTER THEM AND BRING THEM BACK!
WARRIORS OF EGYPT! LET US ATTACK THE HEBREWS!!

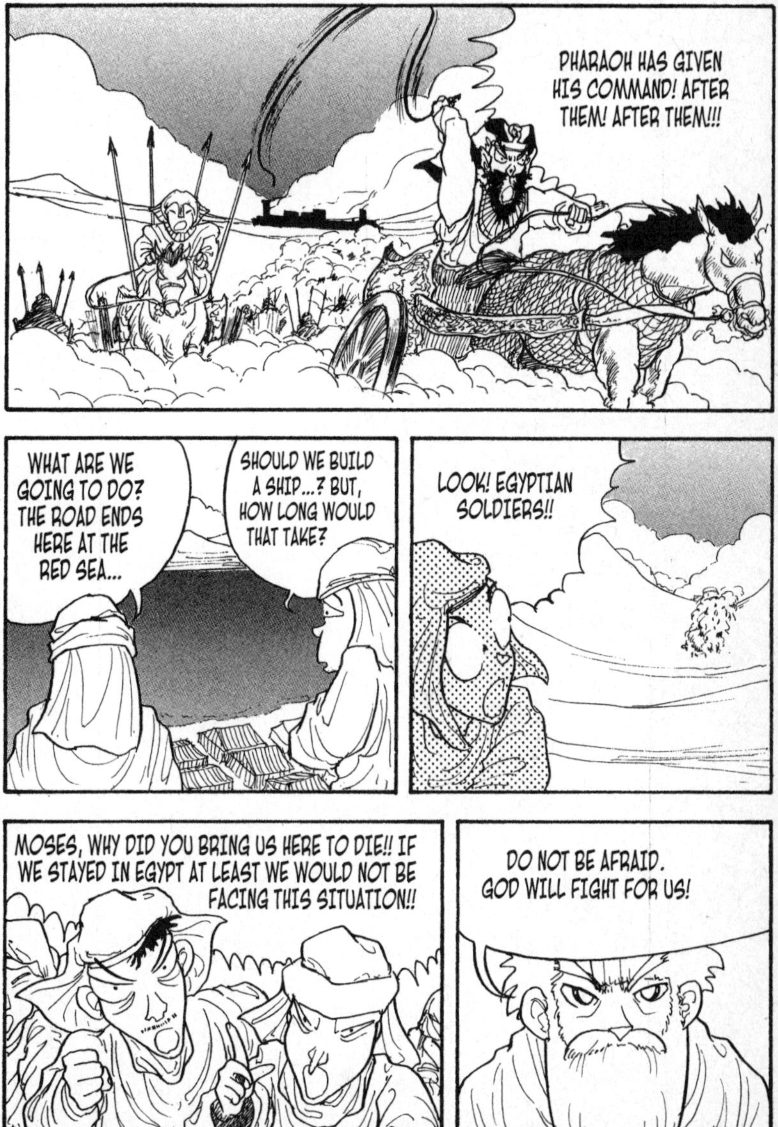
PHARAOH HAS GIVEN HIS COMMAND! AFTER THEM! AFTER THEM!!!
WHAT ARE WE GOING TO DO? THE ROAD ENDS HERE AT THE RED SEA...
SHOULD WE BUILD A SHIP...? BUT, HOW LONG WOULD THAT TAKE?
LOOK! EGYPTIAN SOLDIERS!!
MOSES, WHY DID YOU BRING US HERE TO DIE!! IF WE STAYED IN EGYPT AT LEAST WE WOULD NOT BE FACING THIS SITUATION!!
DO NOT BE AFRAID. GOD WILL FIGHT FOR US!

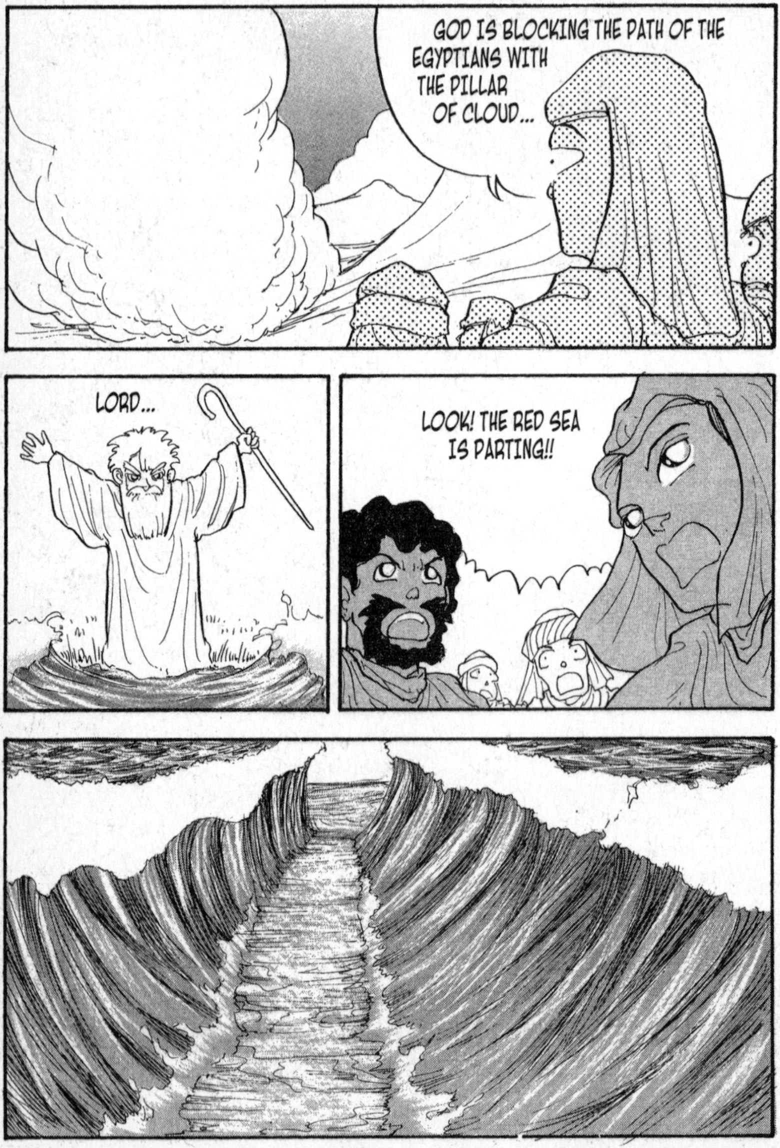
GOD IS BLOCKING THE PATH OF THE EGYPTIANS WITH THE PILLAR OF CLOUD...
LORD...
LOOK! THE RED SEA IS PARTING!!

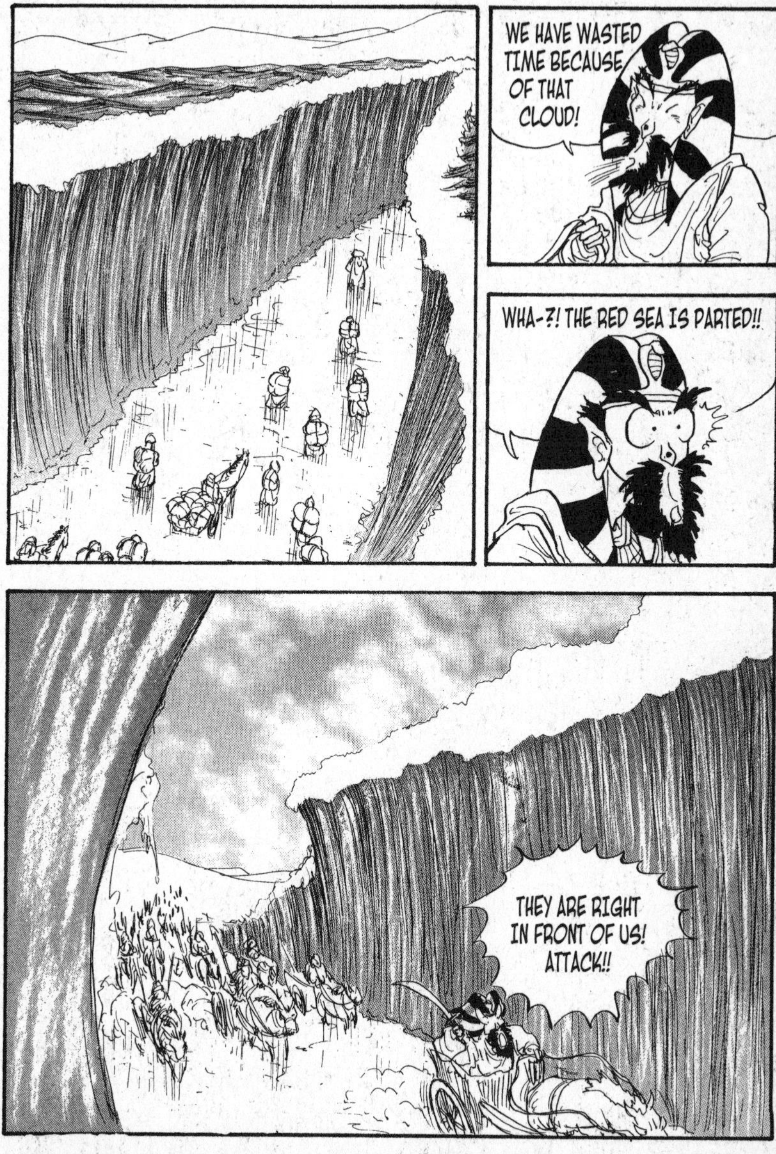
WE HAVE WASTED TIME BECAUSE OF THAT CLOUD!
WHA-?! THE RED SEA IS PARTED!!
THEY ARE RIGHT IN FRONT OF US! ATTACK!!

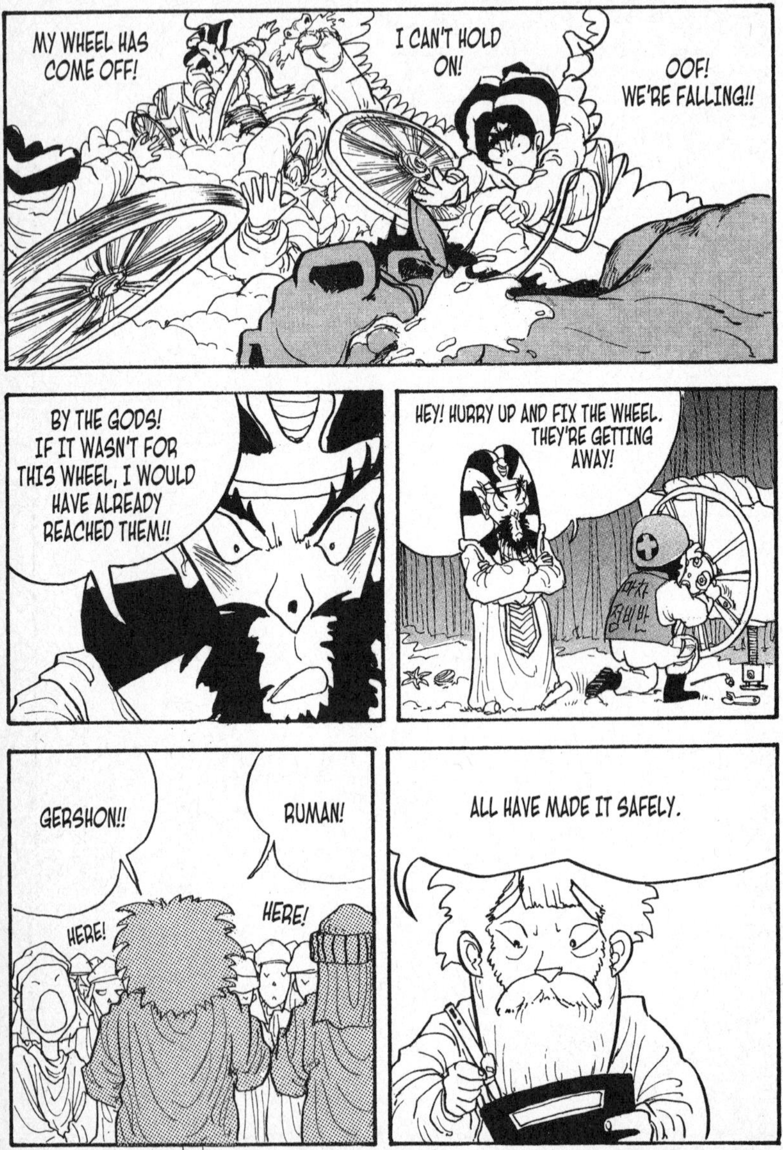
MY WHEEL HAS COME OFF!
I CAN'T HOLD ON!
OOF! WE'RE FALLING!!
BY THE GODS! IF IT WASN'T FOR THIS WHEEL, I WOULD HAVE ALREADY REACHED THEM!!
HEY! HURRY UP AND FIX THE WHEEL. THEY'RE GETTING AWAY!
마차 정비반
GERSHON!!
HERE!
RUMAN!
HERE!
ALL HAVE MADE IT SAFELY.

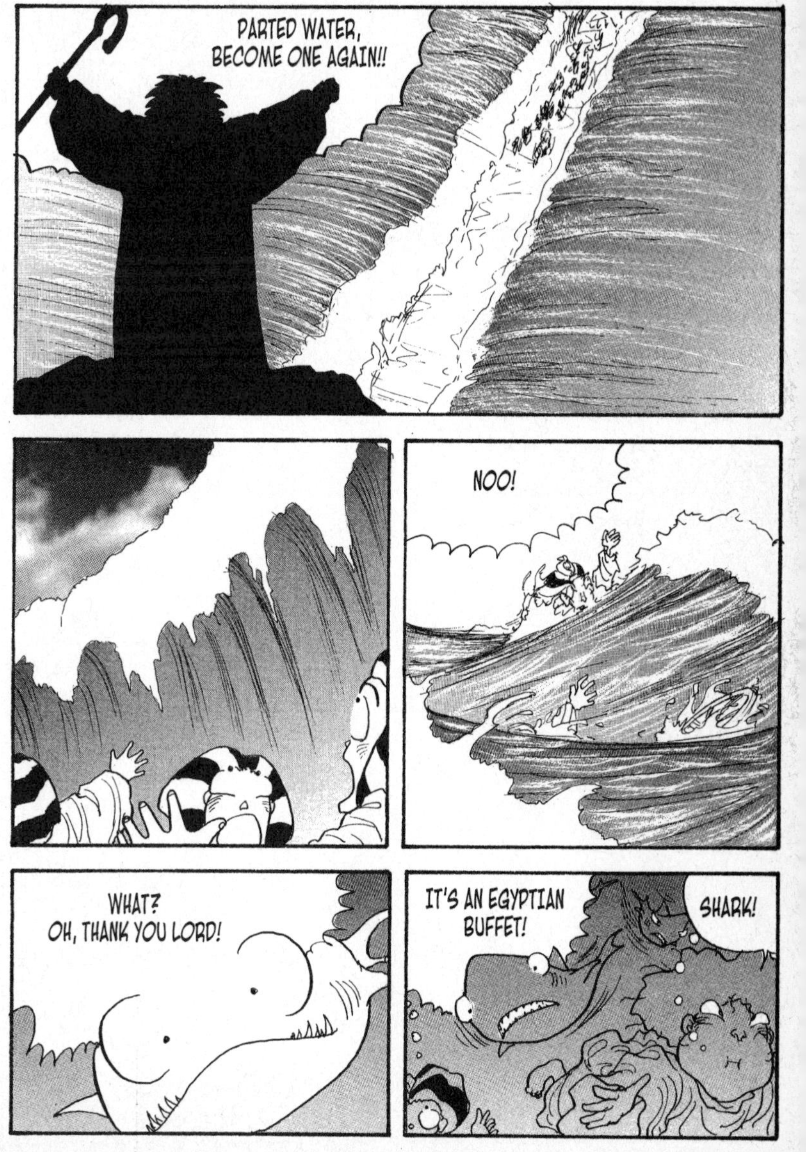
PARTED WATER,
BECOME ONE AGAIN!!
NOO!
WHAT?
OH, THANK YOU LORD!
IT'S AN EGYPTIAN
BUFFET!
SHARK!

HALLELUJAH! THANK YOU GOD!

HALLELUJAH!

THANK YOU, GOD!

HALLELUJAH! THANK YOU, GOD!

HALLELUJAH! HOORAY!

LET'S GO TO CANAAN!

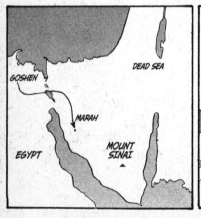

GOSHEN

EGYPT

MARAH

DEAD SEA

MOUNT SINAI

WE HAVEN'T HAD ANY WATER TO DRINK FOR THREE DAYS...!

WA-! --HUFF-- WA-WATER!

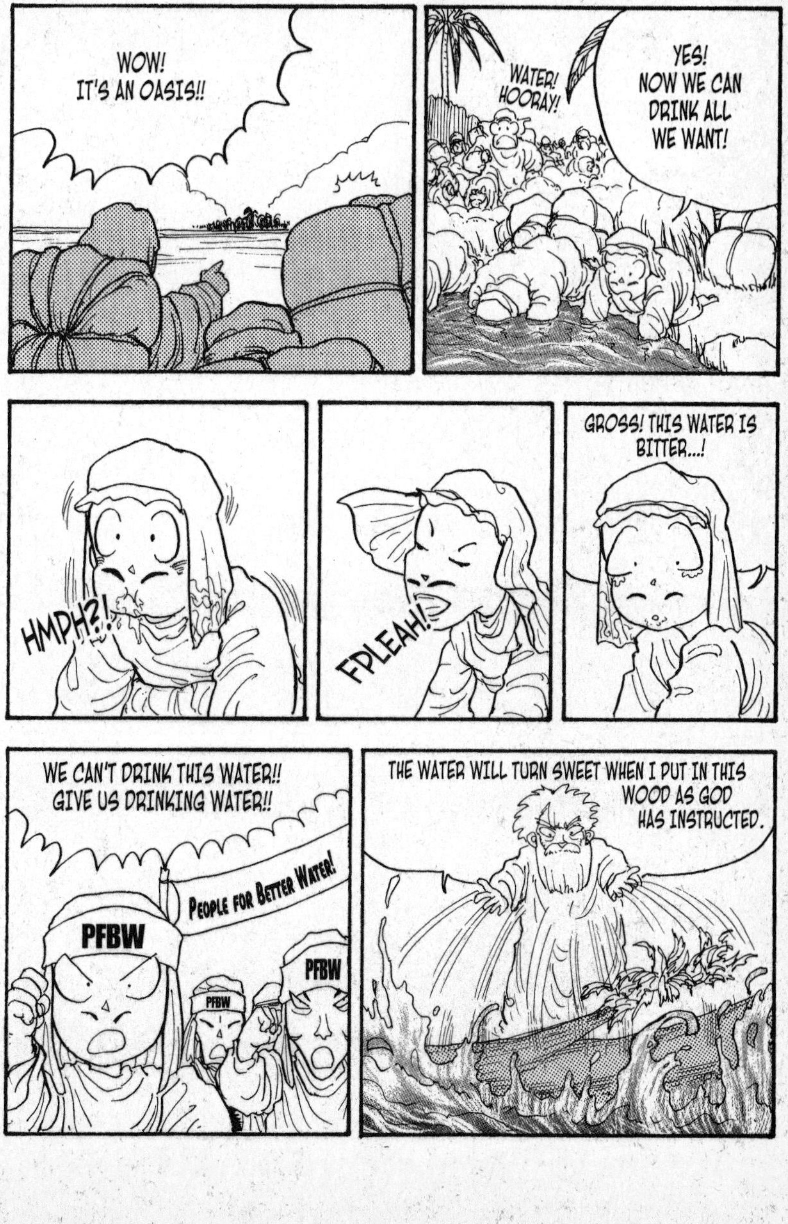
WOW!
IT'S AN OASIS!!
WATER! HOORAY!
YES! NOW WE CAN DRINK ALL WE WANT!
HMPH?!
FPLEAH!
GROSS! THIS WATER IS BITTER...!
WE CAN'T DRINK THIS WATER!! GIVE US DRINKING WATER!!
PEOPLE FOR BETTER WATER!
PFBW
PFBW
PFBW
THE WATER WILL TURN SWEET WHEN I PUT IN THIS WOOD AS GOD HAS INSTRUCTED.

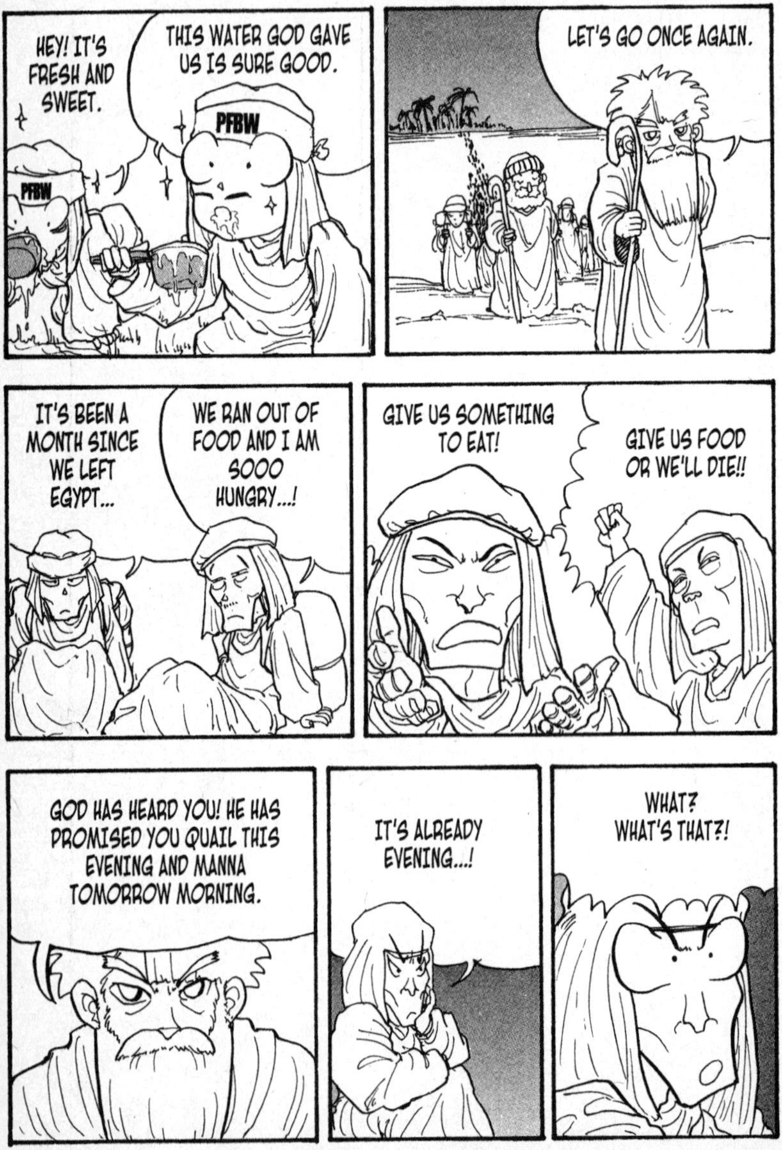
HEY! IT'S FRESH AND SWEET.
THIS WATER GOD GAVE US IS SURE GOOD.
PFBW
PFBW
LET'S GO ONCE AGAIN.
IT'S BEEN A MONTH SINCE WE LEFT EGYPT...
WE RAN OUT OF FOOD AND I AM SOOO HUNGRY...!
GIVE US SOMETHING TO EAT!
GIVE US FOOD OR WE'LL DIE!!
GOD HAS HEARD YOU! HE HAS PROMISED YOU QUAIL THIS EVENING AND MANNA TOMORROW MORNING.
IT'S ALREADY EVENING...!
WHAT? WHAT'S THAT?!

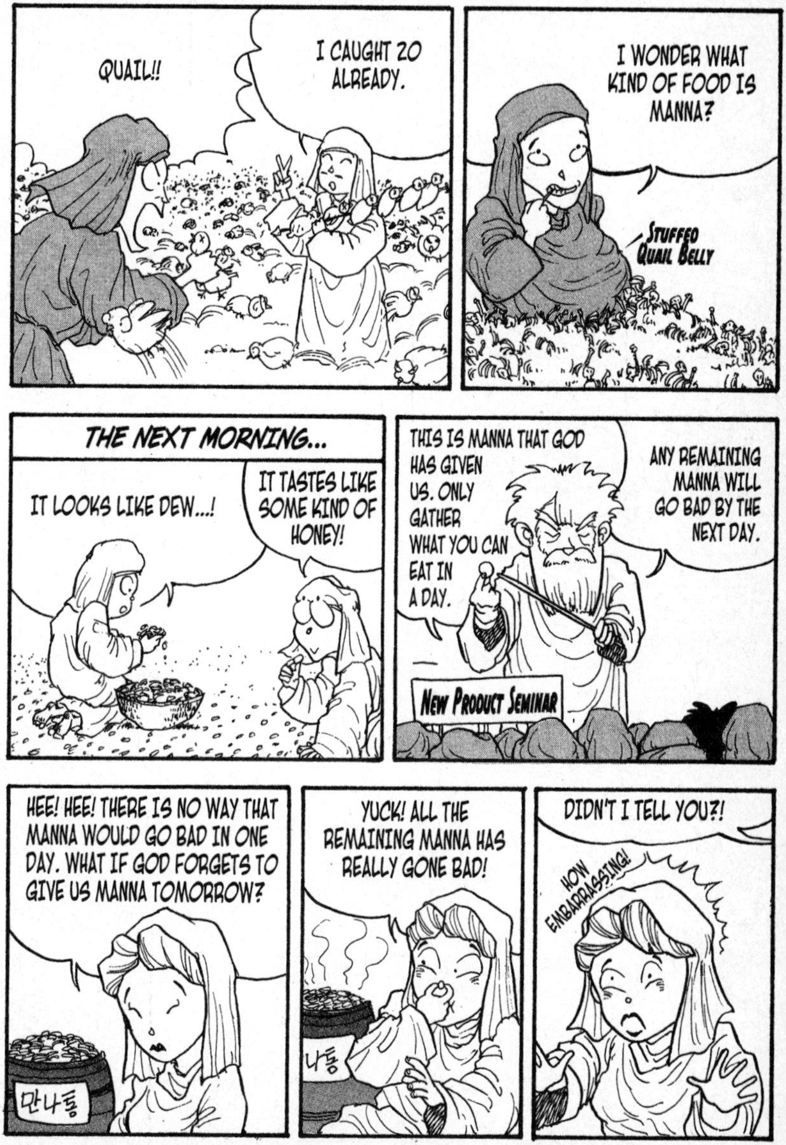
QUAIL!!
I CAUGHT 20 ALREADY.
I WONDER WHAT KIND OF FOOD IS MANNA?
STUFFED QUAIL BELLY
THE NEXT MORNING...
IT LOOKS LIKE DEW...!
IT TASTES LIKE SOME KIND OF HONEY!
THIS IS MANNA THAT GOD HAS GIVEN US. ONLY GATHER WHAT YOU CAN EAT IN A DAY.
ANY REMAINING MANNA WILL GO BAD BY THE NEXT DAY.
NEW PRODUCT SEMINAR
HEE! HEE! THERE IS NO WAY THAT MANNA WOULD GO BAD IN ONE DAY. WHAT IF GOD FORGETS TO GIVE US MANNA TOMORROW?
만나통
YUCK! ALL THE REMAINING MANNA HAS REALLY GONE BAD!
나통
DIDN'T I TELL YOU?!
HOW EMBARRASSING!

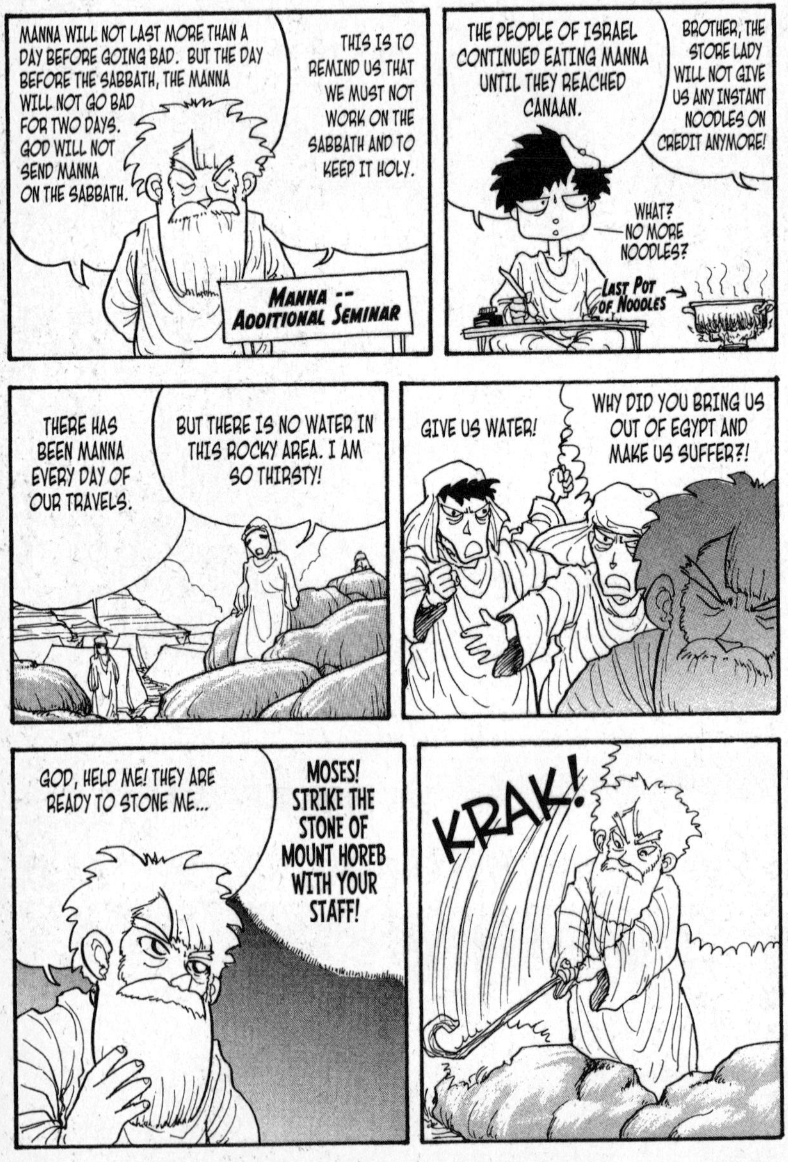

MANNA WILL NOT LAST MORE THAN A DAY BEFORE GOING BAD. BUT THE DAY BEFORE THE SABBATH, THE MANNA WILL NOT GO BAD FOR TWO DAYS. GOD WILL NOT SEND MANNA ON THE SABBATH.
THIS IS TO REMIND US THAT WE MUST NOT WORK ON THE SABBATH AND TO KEEP IT HOLY.
MANNA -- ADDITIONAL SEMINAR
THE PEOPLE OF ISRAEL CONTINUED EATING MANNA UNTIL THEY REACHED CANAAN.
BROTHER, THE STORE LADY WILL NOT GIVE US ANY INSTANT NOODLES ON CREDIT ANYMORE!
WHAT? NO MORE NOODLES?
LAST POT OF NOODLES
THERE HAS BEEN MANNA EVERY DAY OF OUR TRAVELS.
BUT THERE IS NO WATER IN THIS ROCKY AREA. I AM SO THIRSTY!
GIVE US WATER!
WHY DID YOU BRING US OUT OF EGYPT AND MAKE US SUFFER?!
GOD, HELP ME! THEY ARE READY TO STONE ME...
MOSES! STRIKE THE STONE OF MOUNT HOREB WITH YOUR STAFF!
KRAK!

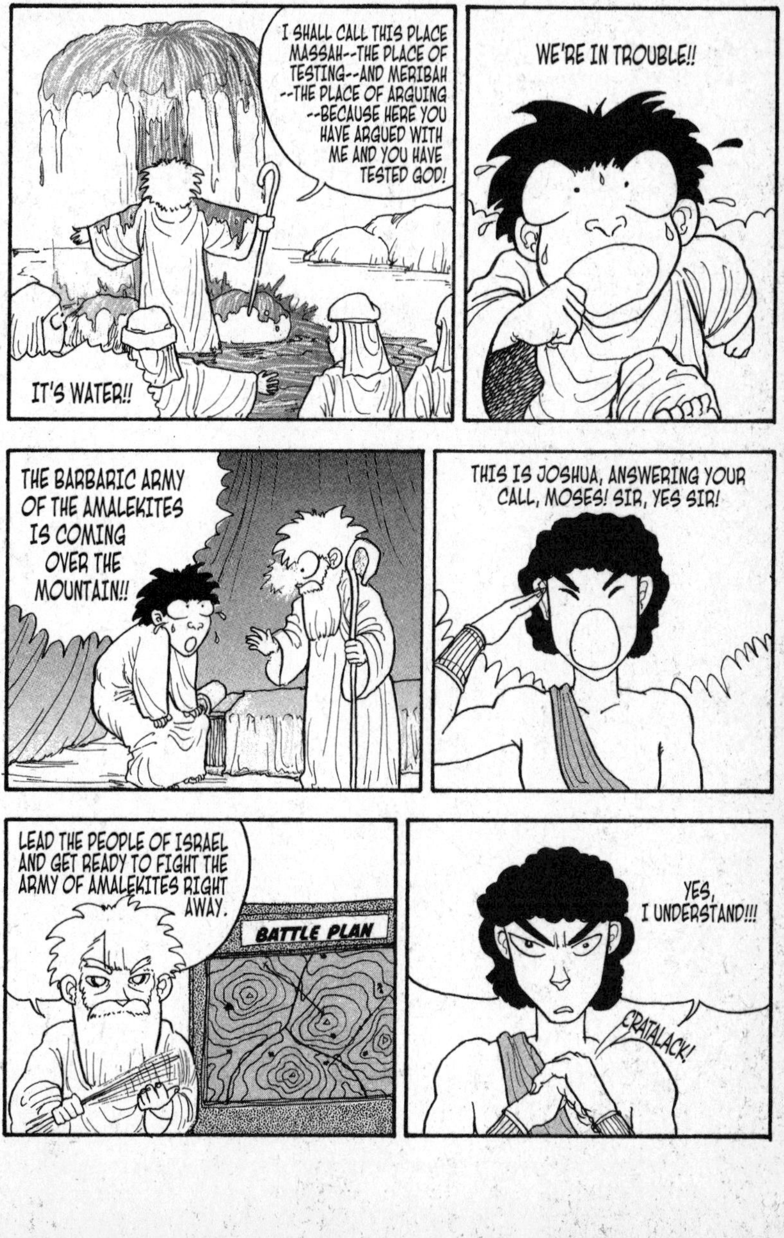
I SHALL CALL THIS PLACE MASSAH--THE PLACE OF TESTING--AND MERIBAH --THE PLACE OF ARGUING --BECAUSE HERE YOU HAVE ARGUED WITH ME AND YOU HAVE TESTED GOD!
IT'S WATER!!
WE'RE IN TROUBLE!!
THE BARBARIC ARMY OF THE AMALEKITES IS COMING OVER THE MOUNTAIN!!
THIS IS JOSHUA, ANSWERING YOUR CALL, MOSES! SIR, YES SIR!
LEAD THE PEOPLE OF ISRAEL AND GET READY TO FIGHT THE ARMY OF AMALEKITES RIGHT AWAY.
BATTLE PLAN
YES, I UNDERSTAND!!!
CRATALACK!

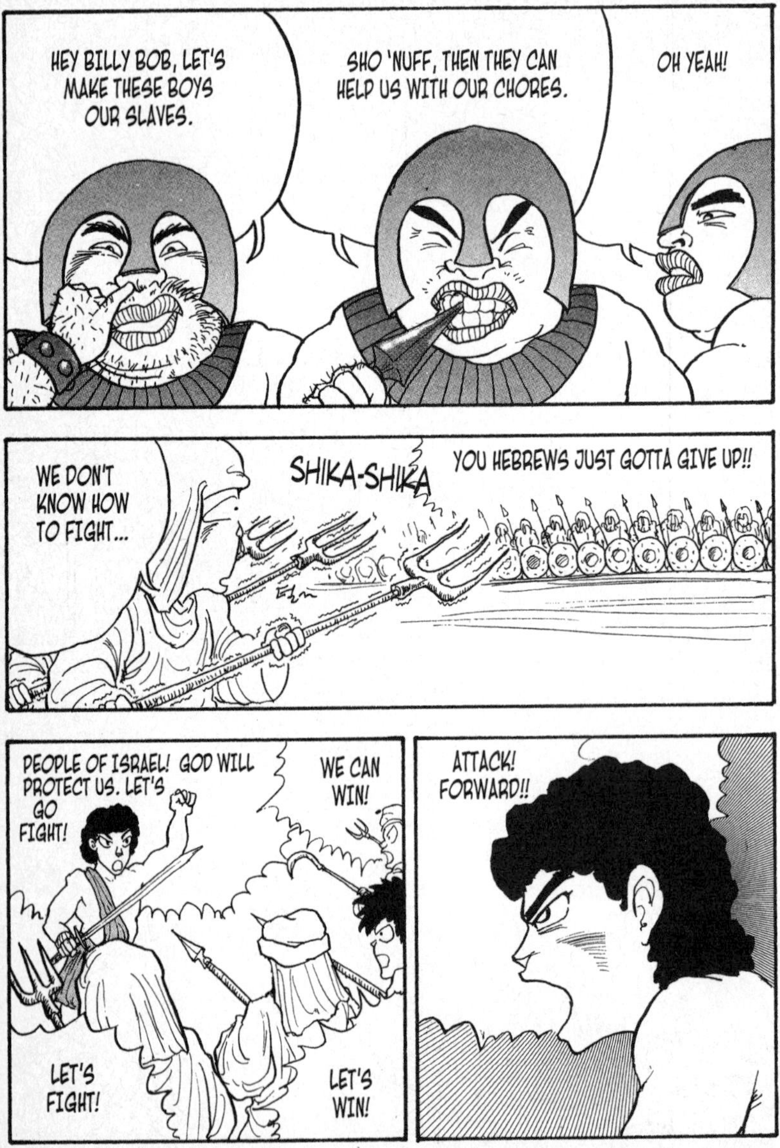
HEY BILLY BOB, LET'S MAKE THESE BOYS OUR SLAVES.
SHO 'NUFF, THEN THEY CAN HELP US WITH OUR CHORES.
OH YEAH!
WE DON'T KNOW HOW TO FIGHT...
SHIKA-SHIKA
YOU HEBREWS JUST GOTTA GIVE UP!!
PEOPLE OF ISRAEL! GOD WILL PROTECT US. LET'S GO FIGHT!
WE CAN WIN!
LET'S FIGHT!
LET'S WIN!
ATTACK! FORWARD!!

I WILL GO UP TO THE MOUNTAIN AND CHEER THEM ON!

DEAR LORD, PLEASE HELP YOUR PEOPLE WIN THE DAY!!

WIN ISRAEL!

GET THE AMALEKITES!!!

THE SOLDIERS OF ISRAEL ARE TOO STRONG!!

MY ARMS... LET ME PUT THEM DOWN FOR A MOMENT AND RELAX...

GET THE ISRAELITES!!

THE AMALEKITES ARE TOO STRONG!!

WHAT HAPPENED??!! WHEN MOSES HAS HIS ARMS UP WE WIN, BUT IF HE PUTS HIS ARMS DOWN WE LOSE!

LET'S SIT MOSES ON THE STONE AND HELP HIM KEEP HIS ARMS UP.

THANK YOU, BROTHER AARON.

I WILL KEEP YOUR ARMS UP.

BE STRONG, MOSES.

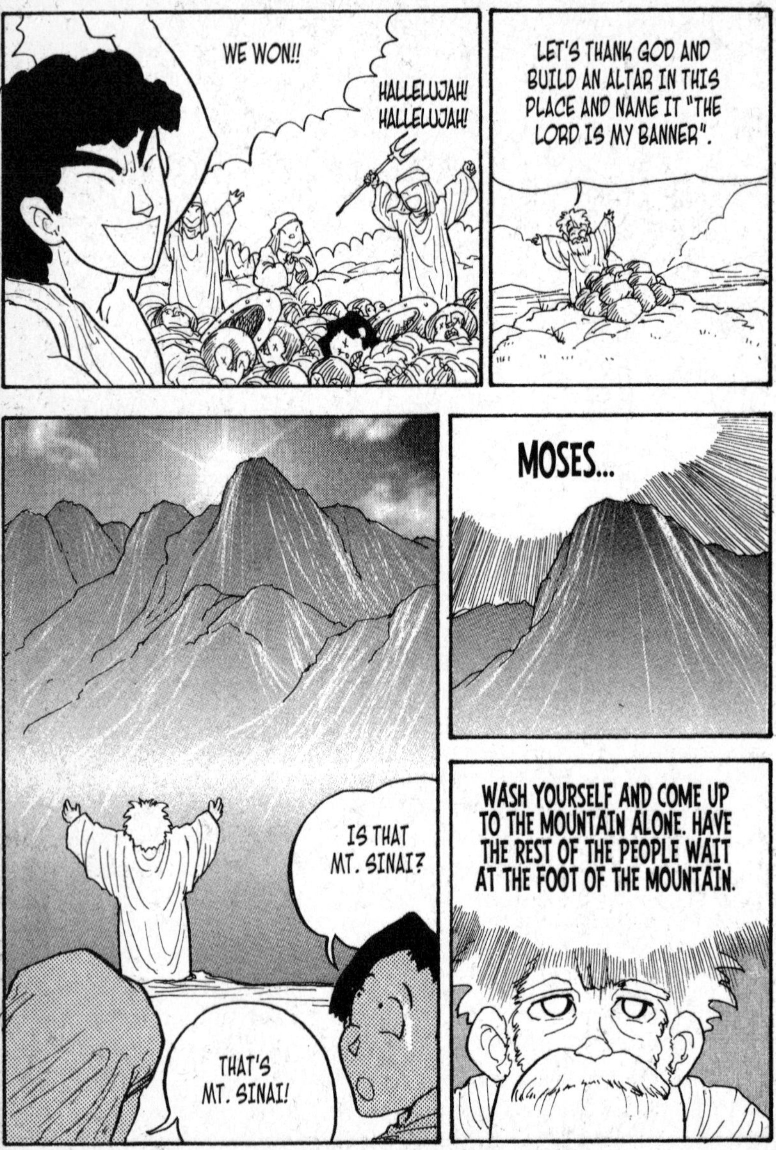
WE WON!!
HALLELUJAH! HALLELUJAH!
LET'S THANK GOD AND BUILD AN ALTAR IN THIS PLACE AND NAME IT "THE LORD IS MY BANNER".
IS THAT MT. SINAI?
THAT'S MT. SINAI!
MOSES...
WASH YOURSELF AND COME UP TO THE MOUNTAIN ALONE. HAVE THE REST OF THE PEOPLE WAIT AT THE FOOT OF THE MOUNTAIN.

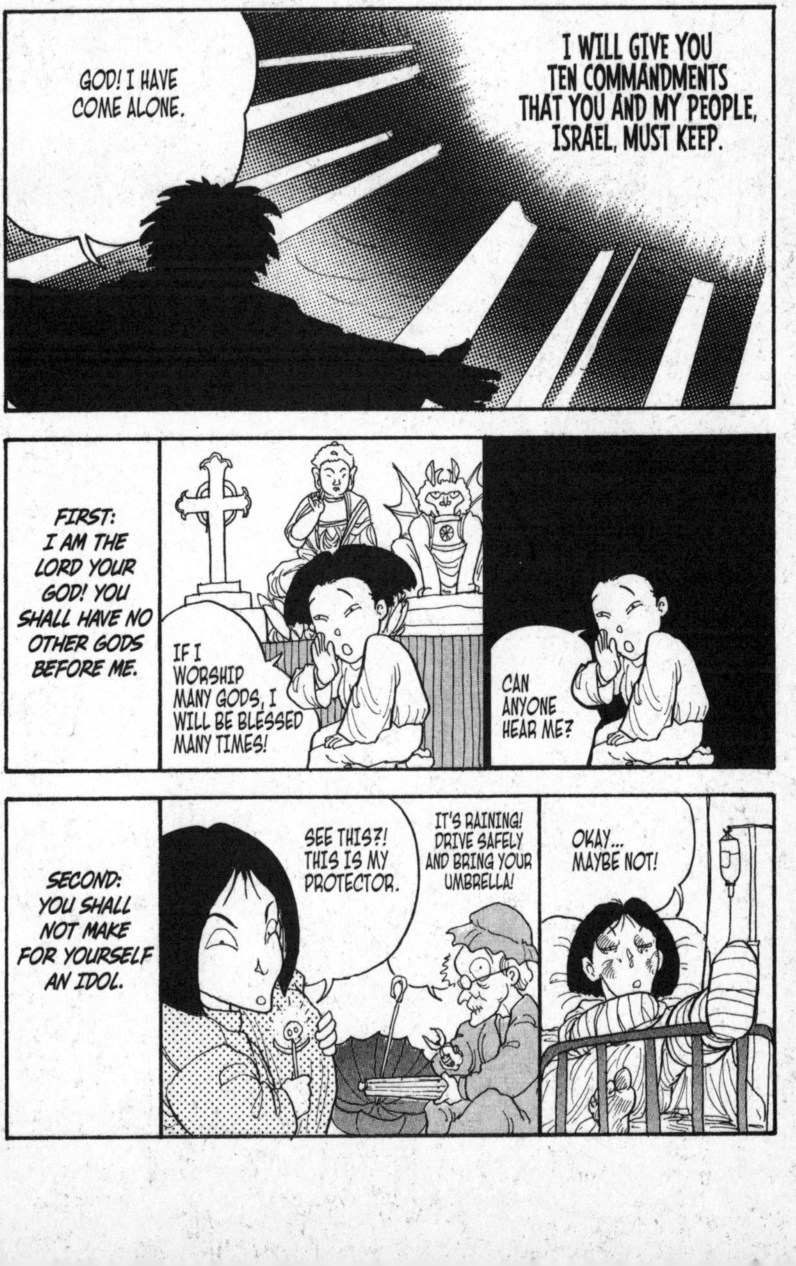
GOD! I HAVE COME ALONE.
I WILL GIVE YOU TEN COMMANDMENTS THAT YOU AND MY PEOPLE, ISRAEL, MUST KEEP.
FIRST: I AM THE LORD YOUR GOD! YOU SHALL HAVE NO OTHER GODS BEFORE ME.
IF I WORSHIP MANY GODS, I WILL BE BLESSED MANY TIMES!
CAN ANYONE HEAR ME?
SECOND: YOU SHALL NOT MAKE FOR YOURSELF AN IDOL.
SEE THIS?! THIS IS MY PROTECTOR.
IT'S RAINING! DRIVE SAFELY AND BRING YOUR UMBRELLA!
OKAY... MAYBE NOT!

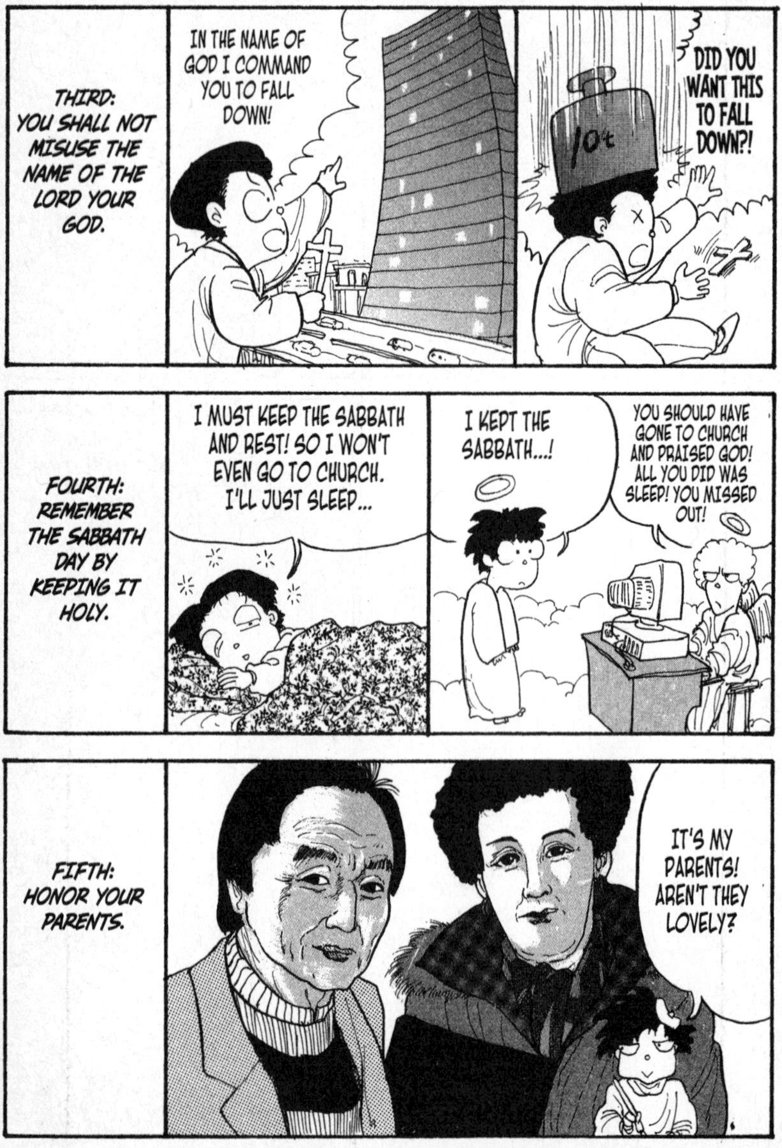
THIRD: YOU SHALL NOT MISUSE THE NAME OF THE LORD YOUR GOD.
IN THE NAME OF GOD I COMMAND YOU TO FALL DOWN!
10t
DID YOU WANT THIS TO FALL DOWN?!
FOURTH: REMEMBER THE SABBATH DAY BY KEEPING IT HOLY.
I MUST KEEP THE SABBATH AND REST! SO I WON'T EVEN GO TO CHURCH. I'LL JUST SLEEP...
I KEPT THE SABBATH...!
YOU SHOULD HAVE GONE TO CHURCH AND PRAISED GOD! ALL YOU DID WAS SLEEP! YOU MISSED OUT!
FIFTH: HONOR YOUR PARENTS.
IT'S MY PARENTS! AREN'T THEY LOVELY?

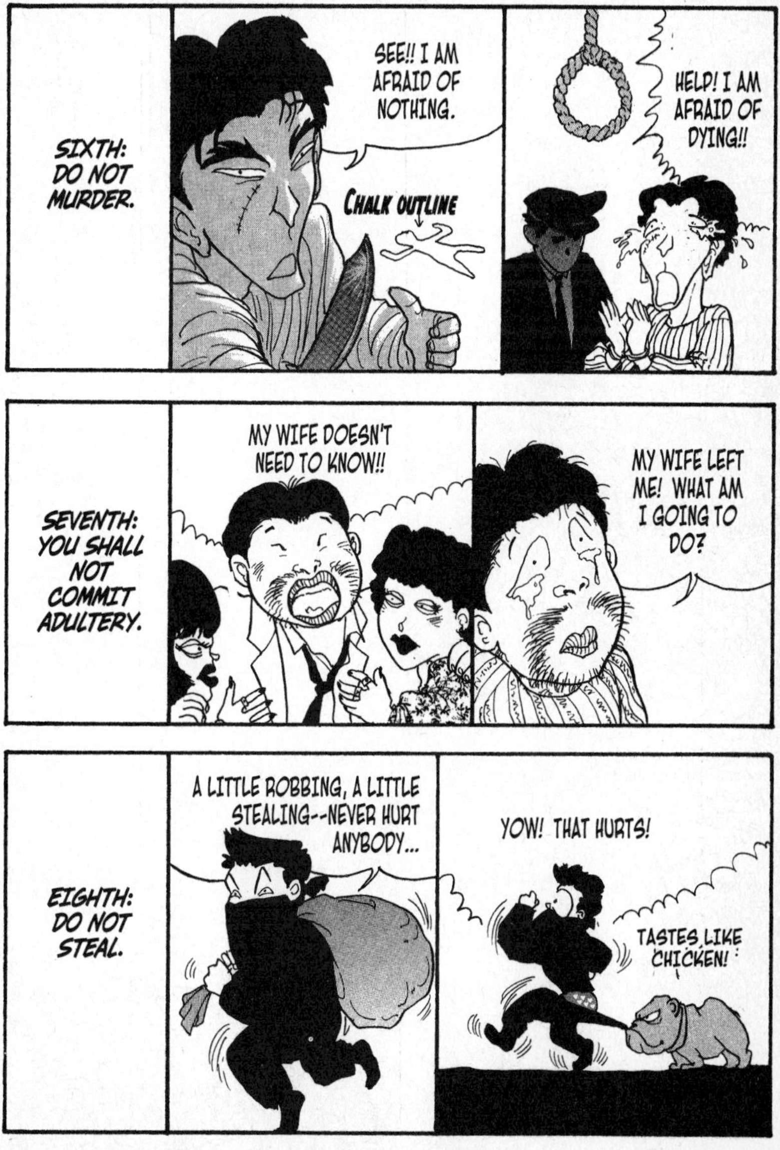
SIXTH: DO NOT MURDER.
SEE!! I AM AFRAID OF NOTHING.
CHALK OUTLINE
HELP! I AM AFRAID OF DYING!!
SEVENTH: YOU SHALL NOT COMMIT ADULTERY.
MY WIFE DOESN'T NEED TO KNOW!!
MY WIFE LEFT ME! WHAT AM I GOING TO DO?
EIGHTH: DO NOT STEAL.
A LITTLE ROBBING, A LITTLE STEALING--NEVER HURT ANYBODY...
YOW! THAT HURTS!
TASTES LIKE CHICKEN!

NINTH: YOU SHALL NOT GIVE FALSE TESTIMONY.

HE THINKS YOU'RE A WIMP! REALLY!

HE THINKS YOU'RE A LOSER! HONEST!

HE IS A LIAR! LET'S NOT PLAY WITH HIM ANY MORE.

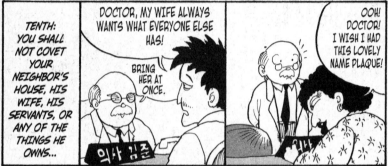

TENTH: YOU SHALL NOT COVET YOUR NEIGHBOR'S HOUSE, HIS WIFE, HIS SERVANTS, OR ANY OF THE THINGS HE OWNS...

DOCTOR, MY WIFE ALWAYS WANTS WHAT EVERYONE ELSE HAS!

BRING HER AT ONCE.

OOH! DOCTOR! I WISH I HAD THIS LOVELY NAME PLAQUE!

I WILL WRITE THESE TEN COMMANDMENTS ON STONE TABLETS.

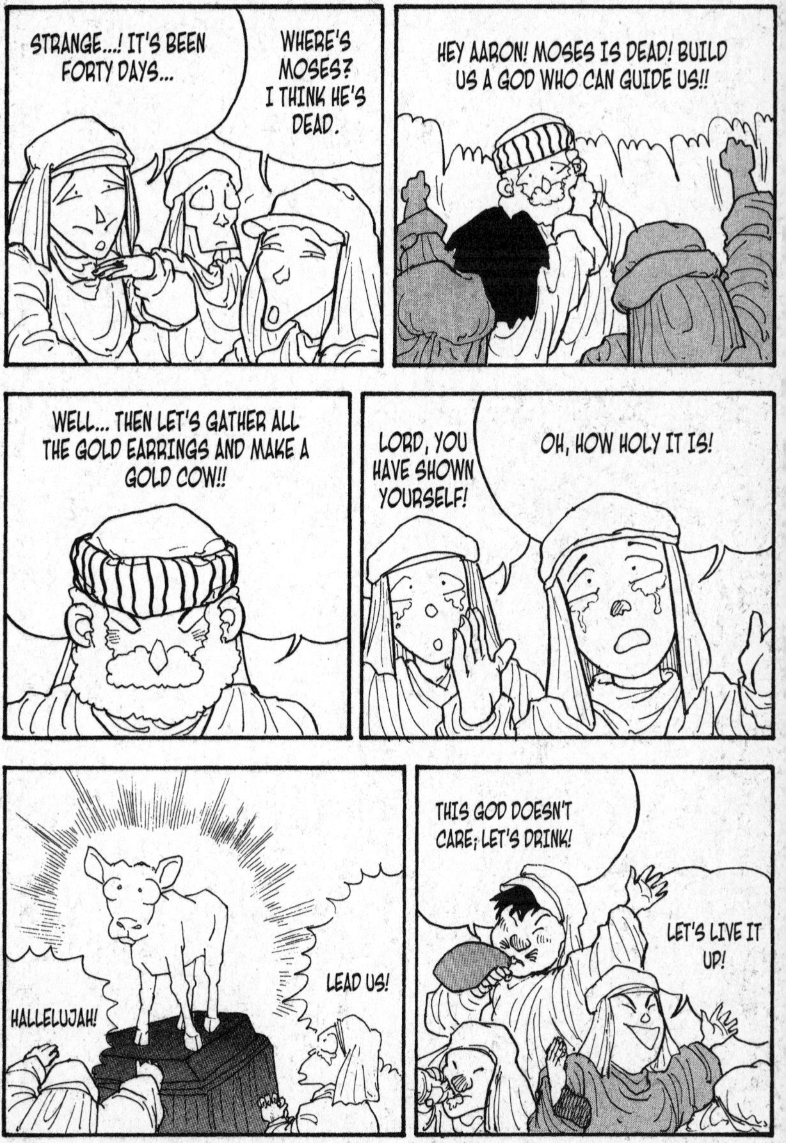
STRANGE...! IT'S BEEN FORTY DAYS...
WHERE'S MOSES? I THINK HE'S DEAD.
HEY AARON! MOSES IS DEAD! BUILD US A GOD WHO CAN GUIDE US!!
WELL... THEN LET'S GATHER ALL THE GOLD EARRINGS AND MAKE A GOLD COW!!
LORD, YOU HAVE SHOWN YOURSELF!
OH, HOW HOLY IT IS!
HALLELUJAH!
LEAD US!
THIS GOD DOESN'T CARE; LET'S DRINK!
LET'S LIVE IT UP!

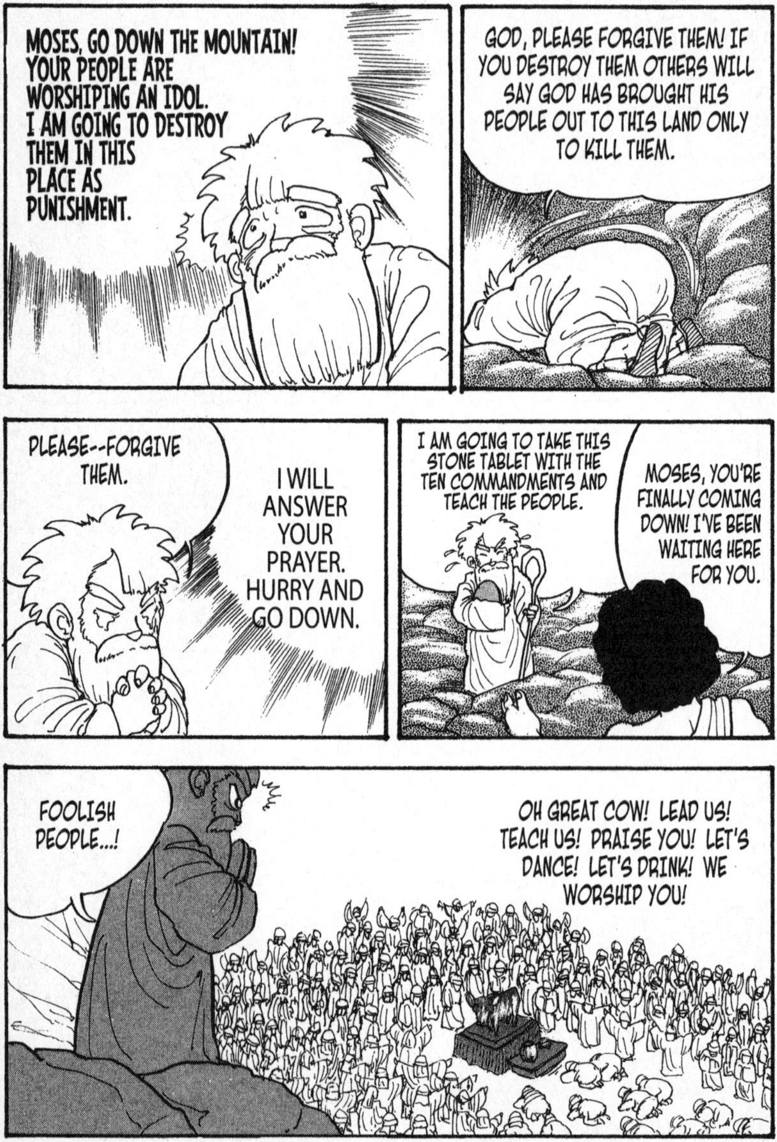
MOSES, GO DOWN THE MOUNTAIN! YOUR PEOPLE ARE WORSHIPING AN IDOL. I AM GOING TO DESTROY THEM IN THIS PLACE AS PUNISHMENT.
GOD, PLEASE FORGIVE THEM! IF YOU DESTROY THEM OTHERS WILL SAY GOD HAS BROUGHT HIS PEOPLE OUT TO THIS LAND ONLY TO KILL THEM.
PLEASE--FORGIVE THEM.
I WILL ANSWER YOUR PRAYER. HURRY AND GO DOWN.
I AM GOING TO TAKE THIS STONE TABLET WITH THE TEN COMMANDMENTS AND TEACH THE PEOPLE.
MOSES, YOU'RE FINALLY COMING DOWN! I'VE BEEN WAITING HERE FOR YOU.
FOOLISH PEOPLE...!
OH GREAT COW! LEAD US! TEACH US! PRAISE YOU! LET'S DANCE! LET'S DRINK! WE WORSHIP YOU!

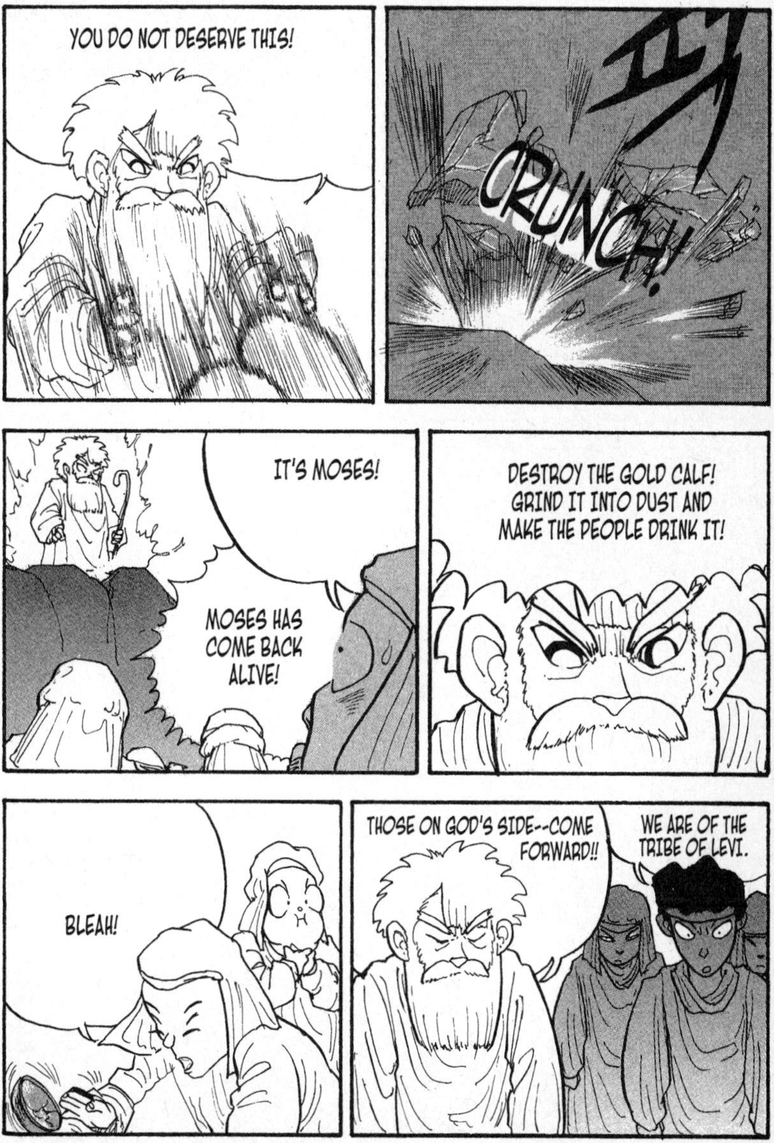
YOU DO NOT DESERVE THIS!
CRUNCH!
IT'S MOSES!
MOSES HAS COME BACK ALIVE!
DESTROY THE GOLD CALF! GRIND IT INTO DUST AND MAKE THE PEOPLE DRINK IT!
BLEAH!
THOSE ON GOD'S SIDE--COME FORWARD!!
WE ARE OF THE TRIBE OF LEVI.

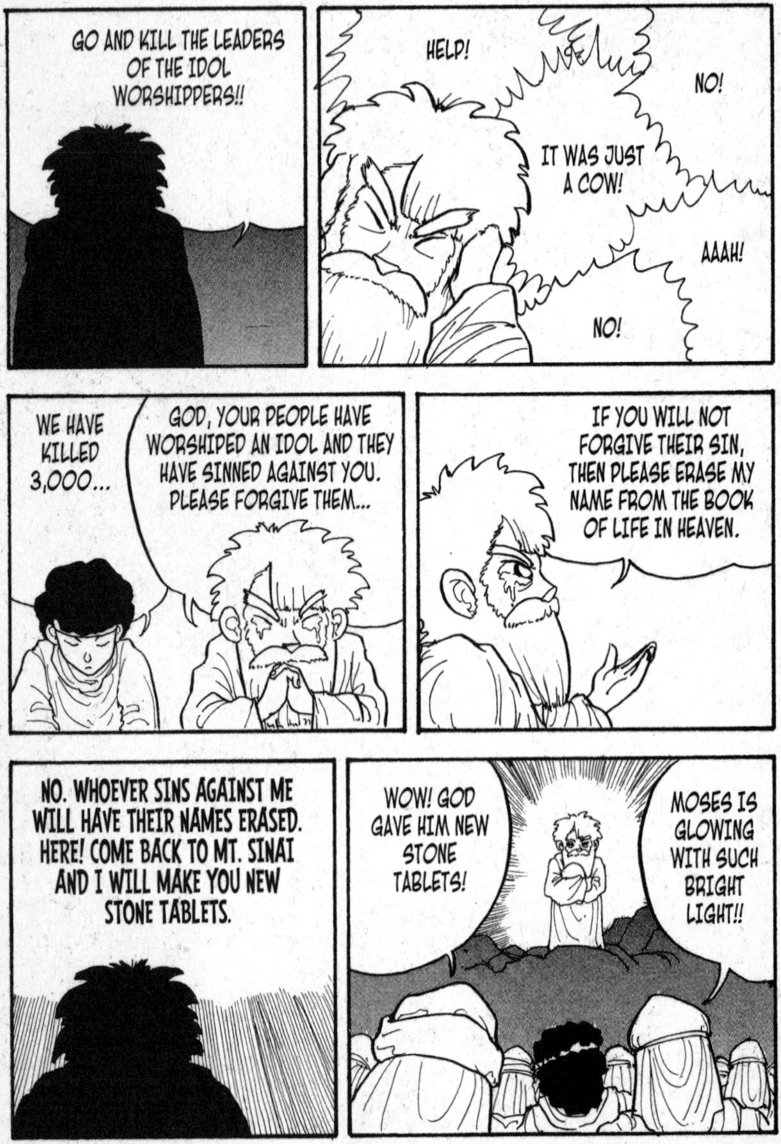
GO AND KILL THE LEADERS OF THE IDOL WORSHIPPERS!!
HELP!
NO!
IT WAS JUST A COW!
AAAH!
NO!
WE HAVE KILLED 3,000...
GOD, YOUR PEOPLE HAVE WORSHIPED AN IDOL AND THEY HAVE SINNED AGAINST YOU. PLEASE FORGIVE THEM...
IF YOU WILL NOT FORGIVE THEIR SIN, THEN PLEASE ERASE MY NAME FROM THE BOOK OF LIFE IN HEAVEN.
NO. WHOEVER SINS AGAINST ME WILL HAVE THEIR NAMES ERASED. HERE! COME BACK TO MT. SINAI AND I WILL MAKE YOU NEW STONE TABLETS.
WOW! GOD GAVE HIM NEW STONE TABLETS!
MOSES IS GLOWING WITH SUCH BRIGHT LIGHT!!

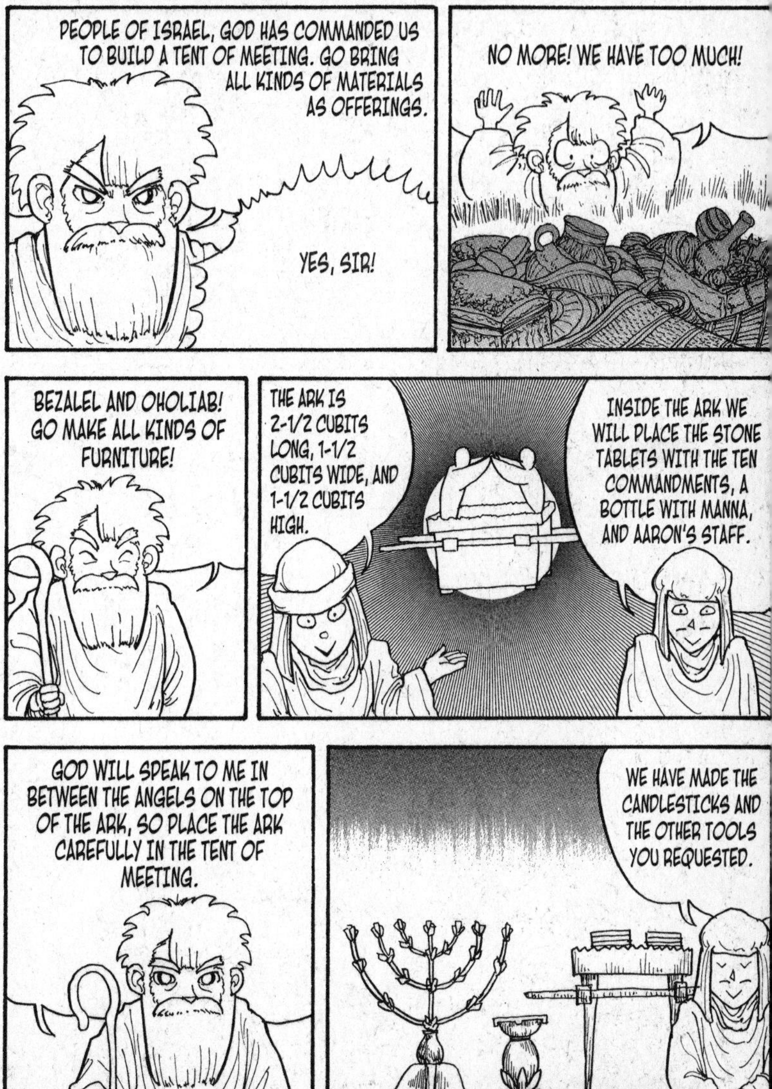
PEOPLE OF ISRAEL, GOD HAS COMMANDED US TO BUILD A TENT OF MEETING. GO BRING ALL KINDS OF MATERIALS AS OFFERINGS.
YES, SIR!
NO MORE! WE HAVE TOO MUCH!
BEZALEL AND OHOLIAB! GO MAKE ALL KINDS OF FURNITURE!
THE ARK IS 2-1/2 CUBITS LONG, 1-1/2 CUBITS WIDE, AND 1-1/2 CUBITS HIGH.
INSIDE THE ARK WE WILL PLACE THE STONE TABLETS WITH THE TEN COMMANDMENTS, A BOTTLE WITH MANNA, AND AARON'S STAFF.
GOD WILL SPEAK TO ME IN BETWEEN THE ANGELS ON THE TOP OF THE ARK, SO PLACE THE ARK CAREFULLY IN THE TENT OF MEETING.
WE HAVE MADE THE CANDLESTICKS AND THE OTHER TOOLS YOU REQUESTED.

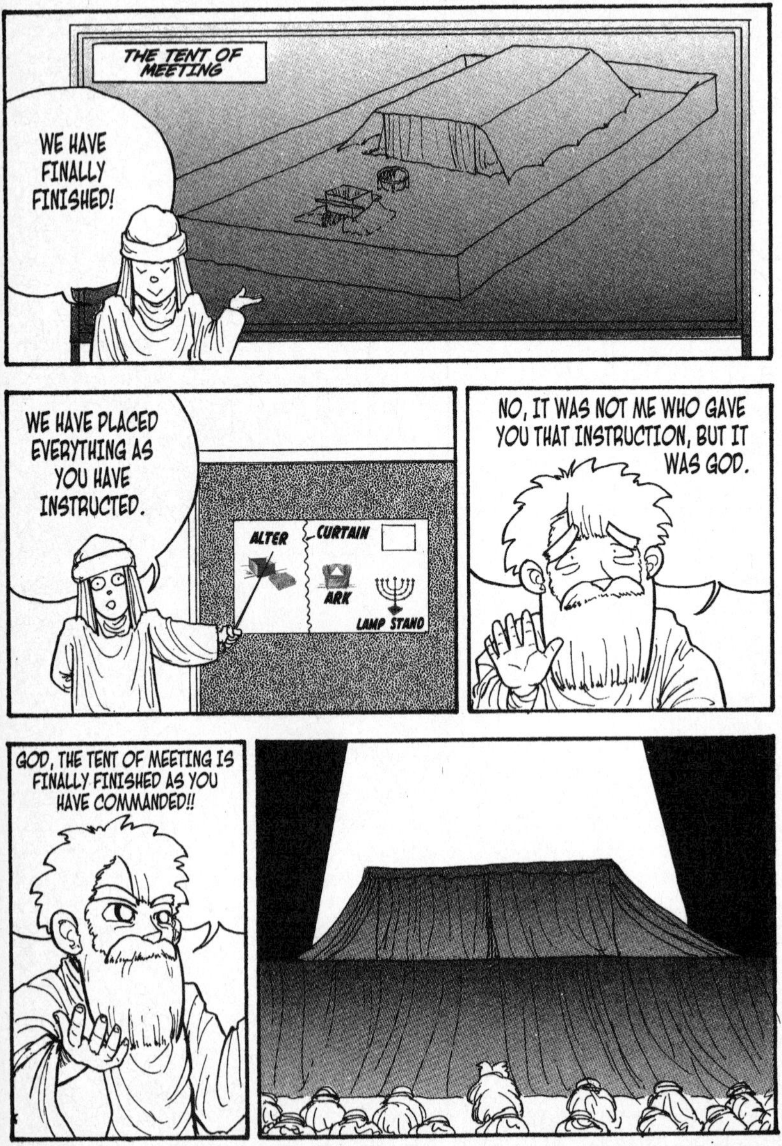
THE TENT OF MEETING
WE HAVE FINALLY FINISHED!
WE HAVE PLACED EVERYTHING AS YOU HAVE INSTRUCTED.
ALTER
CURTAIN
ARK
LAMP STAND
NO, IT WAS NOT ME WHO GAVE YOU THAT INSTRUCTION, BUT IT WAS GOD.
GOD, THE TENT OF MEETING IS FINALLY FINISHED AS YOU HAVE COMMANDED!!

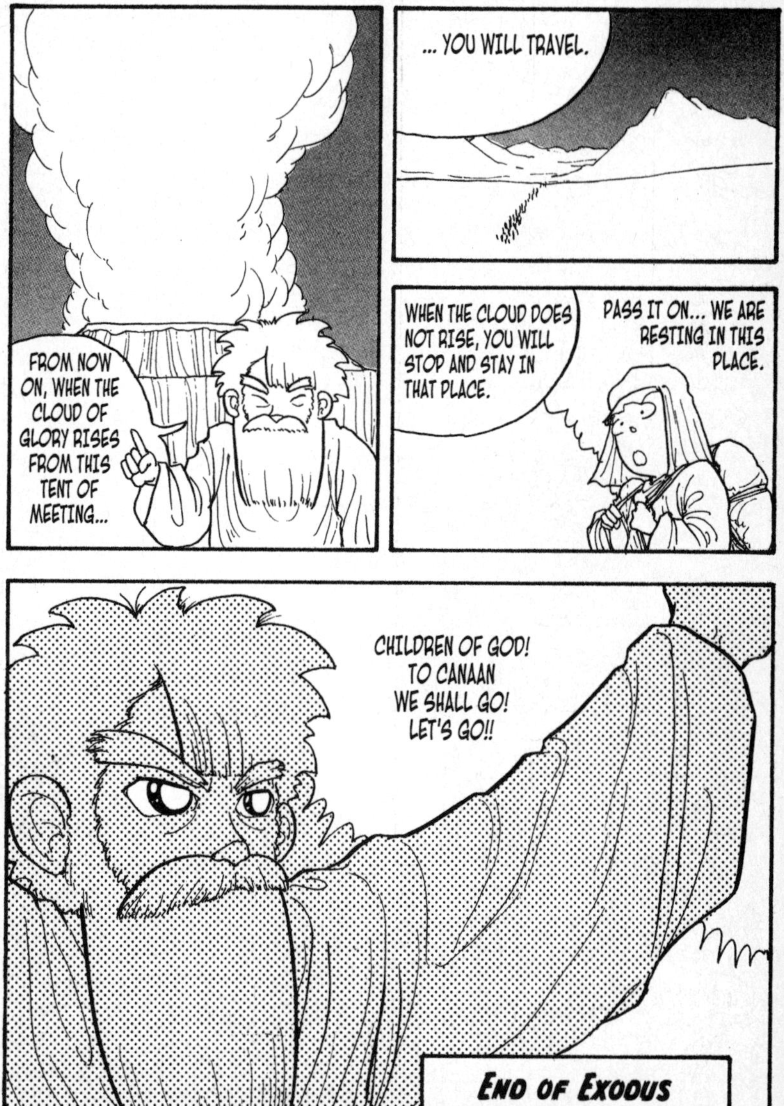
FROM NOW ON, WHEN THE CLOUD OF GLORY RISES FROM THIS TENT OF MEETING...
... YOU WILL TRAVEL.
WHEN THE CLOUD DOES NOT RISE, YOU WILL STOP AND STAY IN THAT PLACE.
PASS IT ON... WE ARE RESTING IN THIS PLACE.
CHILDREN OF GOD! TO CANAAN WE SHALL GO! LET'S GO!!
END OF EXODUS

CONTINUED IN BOOK TWO

ZONDERVAN®

We want to hear from you. Please send your comments
about this book to us in care of zreview@zondervan.com. Thank you.

Grand Rapids, MI 49530
www.zonderkidz.com

ZONDERVAN.com/
AUTHORTRACKER
follow your favorite authors